THE
WAY

THE WAY

A NOVEL

Kristen Wolf

Crown Publishers
New York

For the two miracles I live into—
my love and
my son, born on Christmas Day

This is a work of fiction. Names, characters, places, and incidents either are the product of the author's imagination or are used fictitiously. Any resemblance to actual persons, living or dead, events, or locales is entirely coincidental.

Published in the United States by Crown Publishers, an imprint of the Crown Publishing Group, a division of Random House, Inc., New York.

www.crownpublishing.com

CROWN and the Crown colophon are registered trademarks of Random House, Inc.

Library of Congress Cataloging-in-Publication Data
Wolf, Kristen.
The way: a novel / by Kristen Wolf. —1st ed.
p. cm.
I. Title.
PS3623.O547W39 2011
813'.6—dc22 2010041025

ISBN 978-0-307-71769-6
eISBN 978-0-307-71771-9

Printed in the United States of America

BOOK DESIGN BY ELINA D. NUDELMAN
JACKET DESIGN BY DAVID TRAN
JACKET PHOTOGRAPHY BY DREAMSTIME.COM

10 9 8 7 6 5 4 3 2 1

First Edition

I AM ANDROGYNOUS. I AM MOTHER (AND) I AM FATHER . . .
I AM THE WOMB THAT GIVES SHAPE TO THE ALL . . .
AND I AM INVITING YOU INTO THE EXALTED, PERFECT LIGHT.

—*The Gnostic Gospels*

PART ONE

ANNA

CHAPTER 1

A *village on the outskirts of ancient* Palestine*—7* A.D.

"Be a good girl and cover your face," her mother counseled.

Anna draped a shawl over her head and bound it halfway up her cheeks. She watched her mother arrange bowls of dates, cheese, and olives on a tray. She then placed a pitcher of milk among the bowls and capped it with a square of linen. As her mother did these things, her hands came to rest on her swollen belly then flew off, repeatedly, like frightened doves.

"Hurry to Grandfather and be home before morning meal," she said. She lowered the tray into her seven-year-old's waiting hands. She pulled back the camelskin hide that hung across the front door. Anna's head brushed the underside of her mother's belly as she slipped around her and stepped, blinking, into the light.

Early morning had bathed the village in its usual peach wash. Thirty or so dwellings huddled together as a liquid glow dripped down straw roofs and reddened clay walls.

Anna walked past the manger her father had built. Its thatched roof balanced sturdily on hand-carved wooden beams. Beneath, two cows and a small flock of goats sprawled about crunching mouthfuls of hay. When the smaller animals caught sight of the young girl, they nickered and trotted in pursuit. Anna clucked gently as they nibbled her elbows. Her father said goats were the most foolish creatures the Lord had created. But Anna found their antics and stubborn friendliness amusing. And she laughed at how their upper lips curled in pleasure whenever she scratched their chins.

In a few more steps, she came to her father's workshop. Its door was closed. The glow of an oil lamp shone through its crooked window. Anna heard the familiar *brush-brush* of the pumice stone used to polish wood. Whatever her father was making, he was close to finishing. For the past month, he had been rising earlier than usual to work on a special project. He had said it was a secret, and would not tell anyone what it was, but the mere mention of it brought a glimmer to his eye.

Curious to know what could be making her father so happy, Anna felt tempted to peek inside his shop. But she knew he would not welcome her visit and did not wish to anger him.

As she went along, the goats kept at her. A few guinea hens soon joined. Anna gripped the tray and kept her eyes on the shifting surface of milk. She did not need to watch where she was going. She could navigate by smell. When the scent of goats and hay gave way to the heavier odor of wood smoke, it meant she was near the farmers' houses where the women had stoked fires to bake bread. She heard the grunts of men loading their mules with supplies to take into the olive groves. The time of the harvest had come. Anna lowered her face deeper into her shawl and hurried past. Despite the familiarity of the routine, of lifting fabric to face, she hated the act of hiding herself. The tradition felt stifling—as though someone were standing on her chest.

Farther along, a light breeze cleared the scent of wood smoke and ushered in the spicier scent of olive leaves and earth. She had come to the clearing just before her grandfather's house. If she were to look to the west, she would see the olive groves stitched across the hills like embroidery. Beyond those, stark in its isolation, stood the great old sycamore.

Anna steadied the tray on her knee and knocked.

"Come in!" a voice croaked.

The door gave with a moan. Anna's sight faltered as it adjusted to the darkness. She smelled her grandfather. His scent was sharp and biting, like old metal.

"Where have you been?" he barked. He was seized by a torrent of wet coughs.

Anna knelt before the leathery man. She kept her gaze downward and arranged the bowls of food on the floor.

"Hurry up," he wheezed.

She poured milk from the pitcher. She handed him the cup and watched his brown-spotted hand curl around it.

"Is that goat cheese again?" he asked, pointing a knotty finger.

"Yes, Grandfather," she said, wincing at her mother's mistake.

He knocked the bowl with the back of his hand, spraying bits across the floor. "How many times must I tell you?" he roared. "Do not bring goat cheese. It upsets my stomach!" He popped olives into his toothless mouth. He gummed the oily fruits as he watched his granddaughter crawl about cleaning up the mess. When he had finished eating, Anna stacked the empty bowls on the tray. She bowed and left without looking back.

Outside, she yanked down her shawl and sucked in a breath of fresh air. She had barely begun to exhale when a clod of camel dung pelted the door beside her head. Startled, she looked up and saw a pack of boys. They scampered to duck behind an empty cart. She heard their giggles and knew the attack would escalate. Frightened, she lifted the shawl about her face, gripped the tray, and dashed for the village.

The boys leapt at their fleeing target. Ben, the stub-nosed ringleader, and Daniel, Anna's neighbor, hurled their usual insults. "Freak! Fool! Funny goat! Better keep running!"

Anna's grandfather rushed outside and began yelling about the dung on his door. Terrified of the old man, the boys scattered, abandoning their prey.

Anna's legs pumped with fury beneath her. She knew she could run faster than the boys, but there were more of them, and she did not want to risk being caught. When the roof of her house came into view, she slowed and let the shawl drop again from her face. She glanced over her shoulder but did not see her pursuers. She bent to catch her breath.

It was not the first time they had taunted her. Nor, she knew, would it be the last. Her mother told her the teasing arose from her unusual appearance.

"It is because you are a mixture," she had said. "Of boy and girl."

Anna had wondered at the strange classification. She did not *feel* like a mixture. She knew she was not a boy. Yet she did not feel entirely like a girl either. At least not like the ones in her village who kept silent and shadowed their mothers.

"Anna!" a voice cried from behind.

Anna spun and saw Zahra sitting in front of the well. She was leaning her humped back against the ring of stones and bracing her crooked leg along the ground. In truth, she looked more like a pile of plum-colored rags than an old woman.

When Anna drew near, Zahra's hand shot from between the folds of her robe. She grabbed the girl and pulled her close. "What would he not eat today?" she cackled, her voice dry and graveled, like the grit left in windowsills after a sandstorm.

"Goat cheese," Anna answered. She held up the bowl.

Zahra's eyes focused intently on the food.

"But it is unclean," Anna said. "It fell on the floor."

Zahra smiled. Her pale gray eyes gleamed with a wolfish light. "Given where goat cheese comes from, your grandfather's floor is the cleanest place it has been!" She chuckled and lifted the bowl to her lips.

Anna giggled at the old woman's foolishness.

A farmer approached, hurrying toward the groves. As he passed, he spat into the folds of Zahra's robe. She continued to eat, accustomed to the insult. Many of the villagers disliked the old woman. They said she was a heathen who spoke to animals and disparaged the Lord.

But if Zahra were so evil, Anna wondered, *why did everyone call on her whenever someone was ill?*

She remembered the day her neighbor, Daniel, had laid on his mat unable to breathe. When the priest who often visited their village could not restore the boy, Daniel's father had called for Zahra. The old woman had shown up immediately, as if she had smelled illness on the wind. With strong, wrinkled hands, she had spread a minty balm across the boy's chest and pressed her fingers into the narrow canals between his ribs. As she worked, she had spoken to him in a soft voice, asking questions and letting him speak.

Within hours Daniel was back outside playing with his friends.

Daniel's father had run through the streets shouting thanks to the Lord for the miracle. He later slaughtered a goat in gratitude. But to Zahra he offered no recompense, as if her efforts had played no role in the resuscitation of his son.

Unlike most of the other villagers, Anna was fond of the old woman. She especially admired the way Zahra could imitate birdsongs—so true were her calls that the creatures would flock around her! Whenever they could find a secret moment, away from the villagers' prying eyes, Zahra would help Anna learn to emulate the songs of wheatears, bee-eaters, tree creepers, ravens, and doves. Still, no matter how much she practiced, Anna could not lure the birds into responding as Zahra could.

The old woman swallowed the last of the cheese and lifted her face toward the sun. "Thank you, Great Mother," she whispered.

Anna often heard Zahra speaking to her mother, which she thought odd since her mother could certainly no longer be living. But when Anna asked her about it, the old woman would only shake her head and say, "Knowledge given too early can be more deadly than poison."

Fearing that she had been away too long, Anna looked back toward her house to see if her mother had come outside. When she turned, the sun's rays glinted across her face.

The old woman gasped, then marveled, as she always did, at how Anna's green eyes glimmered like rare jewels. How the masculine line of her jaw, set wide and solid, stood like bedrock beneath coppery cheeks. How the cascade of black curls spilled to her shoulders. How her lips swelled with the curves and fullness of fruit.

"Blessings be, you are a *handsome* child!" she said.

Anna's chest puffed at the compliment. "That is what Mother says."

"Your mother . . ." Zahra whispered, thoughtfully. "How is she?"

"She is weighed down like a camel with too big a load," Anna replied.

The old woman chuckled. "You are as clever as you are handsome." She gave Anna a gentle tap under her chin. Lowered her voice. "But we must pray that the child in your mother's belly is even more handsome than *you*," she said. "Otherwise, there will be much trouble in your house." She winced at the thought. Then waved her hand as if to shoo a goat. "Go home," she advised. "Your mother needs you."

Anna pecked a kiss on each of the old woman's cheeks and darted for home, kicking up a cloud behind her. Zahra remained still, thinking as the dust settled. She knew the child was special. She had read it across the stars at the hour of her birth. She had also foreseen that the girl's destiny would somehow entwine with that of The Way, though she could not yet perceive how.

Zahra had therefore not been surprised when Anna's mother had approached her, secretly, behind the great sycamore, to request that her daughter be taken to study the old ways.

"It is in her blood," Anna's mother had said. "Just as it was in my sister's." She gazed into the distant fields. Her eyes reddening. "But if you do not take her, Anna's life will unfold without purpose or honor. And she will wind up as miserable as—" She choked on her last words, unable to say more.

Having known Anna's mother since she was a child, Zahra had understood and agreed to fulfill the request—but only after Anna had matured enough to endure the hazardous journey. The delay, she had said, would enable her to arrange for the girl's transport, which, given the tragic losses they had recently suffered, required extraordinary care.

Until then, Zahra promised she would watch over the child and do all she could to protect her. Just as she had once promised to safeguard the child's mother.

As she remembered these things, the old woman closed her eyes. Knowing that her efforts would involve great risk, she asked for strength to fulfill her duty and, even more urgently, for time.

Anna peered around the hide hanging in the doorway of her house. Finding the front room empty, she snuck inside and busied herself tending the fire. Moments later, her mother slipped through the partition of goatskins that walled off her private living area. She had changed into a fresh blue robe.

Anna kept her eyes low, staring at the hem of her garment.

"Where have you been?" her mother asked.

"At Grandfather's," Anna said. "He threw cheese at me."

Her mother tossed her a skeptical look. "And did you let the cheese go to waste?"

Anna shook her head. "Zahra ate it."

Before she could hide it, a smile of approval swept across her mother's face. Then, just as quickly, it disappeared. "Your father will be here soon," she said. "See if the bread is ready."

Anna went to the flat rock nestled in the coals. A thin disk of bread was baking, curling brown at the edges. She lifted it from the heat and set it on a linen cloth.

Her mother knelt slowly, negotiating her considerable weight.

Anna marveled at how big her belly had grown. "Mother," she asked, "how will the baby get out?"

"He will find a secret passageway. Just like you did, my little dove."

Anna nestled close to her mother, bending until she could lay her head in her lap. Gazing up, she relished her beauty—her dark eyes flecked with hints of olive, her long onyx curls framing cinnamon-dusted cheeks, her neck curving gently as a wheat stalk, her lean limbs rippling with the strength of sycamore branches.

Anna's father called her Mari, though the women who gathered at the well once a week to wash sleeping mats had said that was not her real name. Hiding in the bushes behind the gossiping women, as she often did, Anna had also heard them whisper that her mother came from a distant land, far to the south. Which explained, they said, why her face bore the fuller features of the desert dwellers and why her words sometimes rose on a musical curl.

Mari began to hum as she smoothed her daughter's hair. Anna loved to listen to her mother's songs. The melodies were simple yet uplifting. And though Mari was careful not to enunciate the words, sometimes a phrase or two would slip from her lips and Anna would hear, "Queen of Heaven around us," or "Bless the earth that is to be blessed." She noticed, too, that her mother would never hum such songs when her father was near. Since she had never heard anyone else singing the particular melodies, Anna came to believe that the songs were special, and something her mother shared only with her.

"Hurry, both of you!" her father shouted from the doorway.

"What is it, Yoseph?" Mari asked.

"A surprise. Come look!" he answered.

"Can it not wait until after our meal?"

"No, no! Come now! I want to show you."

Anna helped her mother to her feet.

"In here," Yoseph told them, running ahead.

Inside her father's workshop, Anna smelled the familiar scents of cedar and lamp oil. A soft layer of woodchips cushioned their steps.

"Can you guess?" he asked, placing his hand on top of a large object covered with goatskins.

Mari smiled broadly. "What is it, Yoseph? Show us!" she begged.

"Behold!" he shouted, lifting the skins with a flourish. He revealed a small but ornate cradle. It hovered above two curved runners. On its sides, elaborate designs had been inlaid with different colored woods. Her father touched the cradle lightly and it began to rock. "For our son," he said. "Our future blessing from God."

Anna's mouth fell open. Awash in disbelief, her eyes traveled back and forth from her father to the cradle.

What was this? she wondered. *Her father had never made a special gift for* her. *And her brother was not even born yet!*

"It is beautiful, Yoseph," Mari said.

Yoseph turned. Studied her swollen belly. "Not nearly as beautiful as you," he said. He took his wife into his arms. Leaned to kiss her on the mouth.

Smiling, Mari turned so that his lips found her soft cheek instead.

Yoseph sat cross-legged on the mat to prepare for his meal. He seemed taller than Mari remembered, as she watched him out of the corner of her eye. His face was beaming and even the gray in his beard and the stoop in his shoulders seemed suddenly youthful. She felt relief for the joy she would soon bring him. After long years of waiting, finally, he would have a son.

Anna knelt to remove her father's sandals. When his feet were bare, she poured a bowl of water and held it before him. Yoseph scooped his hands into the bowl then held them aloft, allowing the water to run to his elbows. He dunked a second time, keeping his hands down, sending the water to drip off his fingertips. Anna lifted a towel from her forearm. He took it and dried his hands. He then tossed the damp and crumpled cloth into her lap.

Mari came and sat.

Glancing over at her parents, Anna thought the two made a strange pair. Her mother stood tall, lean, and exotic, a lush sweep cupping her dark eyelashes. Her father, by contrast, was light-skinned, short, and broad. Her mother, Anna thought, rose toward the sky like a vine, while her father clung to the earth like a shrub. The women at the well said that her father had married with luck on his side because, though older, and not altogether handsome, he had taken a striking young woman as his wife. As for her mother, Anna did not know if she had married with luck on her side or not.

Leaning forward, Yoseph began to chant. His voice took on a mournful hue as he recited his morning prayers. "Blessed are you, O Lord our God, King of All, who rules over us with a mighty hand," he intoned, his voice torn with ache. "May we, your sinful children, learn to serve your glory. Amen."

Anna and her mother kept their heads bowed until Yoseph was finished. They then waited patiently for him to take the first bite before helping themselves.

Yoseph lifted a disk of flatbread and tore off a ragged piece.

No one spoke.

After several minutes, Yoseph's eyes cut to his daughter. He noticed that she was not eating. "Daughter," he said, "what do you think of the cradle I have made for your brother?"

Both Anna and her mother started at his words. It was rare for Yoseph to speak to his daughter. Thrilled by his unexpected attentions, Anna wriggled with excitement. "You are the best carpenter in the village, Father!" she spouted. "No one could make a more beautiful cradle than you!" She glanced up, hoping her bold statement had pleased him. Her heart swelled when he chuckled lightly.

"But, Father?" she said, emboldened by his response. "Now that you have finished the cradle, what will you make for *me*?"

Mari froze at her daughter's insolence.

Yoseph reached over and patted Anna on the head. Three rough taps. "I have made a brother for you," he said. "For what more could you possibly wish?"

Anna's eyebrows crinkled.

She did not want a brother. What good would that do her? He would just be another person she would have to share her parents with. And her meals!

"But—" she tried.

Yoseph tossed a hand into the air. "Be patient, daughter," he said. "And someday soon, God willing, you will be a wife. Then your husband can make cradles for your sons."

Mari smiled at Yoseph's words but threw a sideways glance at her daughter. Seeing her about to ask another question, Mari snapped, "Anna! Go to the fire and bake more flatbread. Your father's joy has clearly increased his appetite."

Though Anna always obeyed her mother's orders, this time she delayed. Feeling reluctant to step away from her father's notice.

Seeing Anna hesitate, Mari swatted her knee. "Go *now*," she urged.

A few minutes passed before Yoseph spoke again. His words were suddenly serious in tone. "Have you thought about what I said last night?" he asked.

"About what, dear husband?"

"About the choice of midwife."

Mari sat back and put a hand on her belly. "Yes," she said, "I have."

"And what have you thought?" He dipped his bread into the salted oil.

Mari drew a deep breath as if knowing her words would not be welcome. "I want Zahra to deliver our son," she said.

Yoseph interlaced his fingers beneath his chin. "I see."

Mari said nothing further, reasoning that silence would be more acceptable than words.

Yoseph drew a hand down his beard. Tugging at its length. "You say this knowing that she is a pagan who curses the Lord."

Mari nodded. "She is most knowledgeable in the ways of childbirth. That is all that concerns me."

Anna returned and set down the flatbread. She could tell by the way her parents were leaning back that they were going to have a difficult conversation. Retaking her seat, she used the opportunity to pour herself an extra cup of milk.

Yoseph's eyes narrowed. Several months ago, he had spoken in private with the priest who visited their village. The youthful holy man thought it unwise for Zahra to play a role in the birth of Yoseph's child. He had said he suspected, though could not prove, that Zahra was involved in a wicked and dangerous sect. One that adhered to the old ways—the ancient and barbaric practices followed by those who did not embrace the one true God.

"Unholy and vulgar factions such as these continue to sprout up across the land," the priest had told Yoseph. "Some are led by women. Some by madmen. Some worship false gods, while others refuse to accept the Lord's existence entirely! Thus refuting Him and distorting His plan for us, they stand among His enemies." He then added with a whisper, "I shudder to think of such evil hands upon your child."

Recalling the priest's warning, Yoseph glared toward the ceiling. "Women such as Zahra wish only to desecrate the Lord and pervert

His plan! If she could, she would teach our son to slander the name of God and bow before his wife!" he said, stabbing a finger skyward, his cheeks reddening.

Yoseph's resistance to Zahra and her wisdom infuriated Mari. But she could not show this. Instead, in a desperate attempt to calm him, she leaned forward and rested a hand on his arm. "But it is *we* who will raise our child, not the midwife," she said. She then took his hands into her own, knowing how that pleased him. "And I should think you would want the most experienced one to attend the birth of our son. Just as she successfully attended the birth of our daughter."

Yoseph's shoulders shuddered with emotion. He took several breaths. Then, with effort, surrendered to his wife's touch. He did not think it wise to upset her with the hour of birth drawing near.

"You trusted Zahra when she told you that the child I carry is a son," Mari continued. "So why will you not trust her with—?"

Yoseph waved his hand. "So be it," he said. He no longer wished to speak of the matter. It was true that he had deferred to the old woman in this one respect. Though despising her beliefs and her ways, he and the other villagers relied on Zahra's expertise in childbirth—and her uncanny ability to predict the sex of their children—just as they relied on her healing abilities.

But their dependence on the healer—and the heresy of it—only made Yoseph's hatred burn hotter.

He lifted the milk pitcher and found it empty. Mari spotted the white mustache above Anna's lip and motioned to her. Anna turned from her father and brushed a sleeve across her face.

"I will bring more," Mari told her husband, taking the pitcher from his hands. "But know that you have pleased me." She allowed a radiant smile that no man could refuse to blossom across her face.

When she returned, Yoseph held his wife's gaze and felt the pounding in his chest. "Have Anna put the milk in a goatskin," he told her. "I will travel to Sepphoris today."

Anna sat up at the mention of her favorite village. Sepphoris lay an hour's walk to the north and was a place of spice traders, musicians, and exotic foods.

"May I come with you, Father? May I?" she blurted.

Yoseph frowned. "Daughter, do not disappoint me," he said, standing.

"Please!" Anna begged. "I will carry your tools for you. Both ways!"

Mari cringed. Over the years, she had come to dread her daughter's yearning for her father's attention, knowing how battered it would become.

All the more reason, Mari thought, for Anna to leave home.

Yoseph scowled down at his daughter. "Your place is to stay and help your mother," he said, an edge coming into his voice. "Do not make me tell you again."

CHAPTER 2

A village on the outskirts of ancient Palestine—7 A.D.

Anna sat in the shade outside her house grinding barley into meal for the evening's bread. Between her knees sat a long, boatlike vessel. Inside its hollow, she dragged a stone back and forth over the grain. Though she performed this task almost every day, it was her least favorite. Sometimes, when she grew bored of the repetition, she felt the urge to roam, to see what she might discover.

Fortunately, a thunderous rain the night before had brought out clouds of orange and blue butterflies. Hurrying about, they painted crooked and colorful trails in the sky. Watching them with delight, Anna soon found her morning chore less wearisome.

With steady hands, she poured the ground meal into a clay bowl. She had just tossed another fistful of grain into the grinding vessel when the sound of shouting made her freeze. Out of nowhere, a pack of boys appeared. They were stomping and swatting at the butterflies with long sticks.

"I got it!" one of them said, laughing while a broken creature beat frantic circles on the ground.

When they came closer, Anna grabbed a goatskin pouch and leapt to her feet. She dashed about collecting as many of the stunning creatures as she could, hoping to spare them from attack.

Before she knew it, the boys were upon her.

"Hey, funny goat! What do you have in that pouch?" Ben called out.

Anna took a step back. "Nothing," she said.

"Oh no? Then show me," he demanded.

The rest of the boys trotted over to their ringleader.

"No," Anna said, clutching the pouch. "It is not for you." She glanced behind her. Knowing she would have to run.

Anticipating her flight, a few boys broke from the group and circled behind her.

Ben waved his stick threateningly. Daniel glared with menace.

"Give me that," Ben said. "Or I will swat you like an insect."

Anna's eyes darted around the circle. But she could find no opening. Her mouth went dry.

Ben raised the stick above his head. "I said—"

"Greetings, children!" a voice rang out.

Anna turned around to see Zahra hobbling toward them.

Lifting her walking stick, the old woman parted the boys' circle.

"What have you got there?" she asked.

Anna lifted her pouch.

The boys snickered but drew back. Though they had little respect for the old woman, they feared her ability to cast spells, as some villagers insisted she could.

Zahra stepped forward and glanced inside the pouch. "Ah, the shape shifters!" she cried.

Anna kept still as the sound of fluttering rose from the goatskin.

The old woman turned to the boys. "Tell me, have any of you learned yet how to grow wings?" she asked, referring to the butterflies' recent transformation.

Not wanting to engage the strange woman, the boys kept silent. One swept the dust with his sandals.

"Of course not!" Zahra said. "But these little creatures *have*. That is what makes them so magical." She leaned toward the children. "Such miracles as these must be worthy of our respect, would you not agree?"

The boys mumbled.

Zahra smiled. "Perhaps, then, you would like to help us find them some food?" she asked.

The boys shook their heads and drifted back, uncertain where to go.

Thinking quickly, Ben rallied his comrades. "Come! My mother will make us stuffed dates!" he told them.

Cheered by this idea, the boys trotted off, their sticks waving limply at their sides.

When they were gone, Anna sagged with relief. Zahra sighed and laid a hand on her shoulder. "I was coming to look in on your mother. How is she this morning?"

Anna shrugged. "She seems well."

Zahra frowned. "We shall see," she said, as though she had expected a different answer.

Flutters sounded again from within the goatskin.

Zahra glanced down. "You can release your little friends now," she said. "They will be safe."

Anna smiled and opened the mouth of her pouch, releasing a spray of color.

At that same moment, having heard the commotion, Yoseph stepped out of his workshop. He spotted the old woman standing next to his daughter.

"Anna! This is no time for idle chatter. Go help your mother with the milking!" As his daughter departed, Yoseph cast an angry glare upon Zahra.

Anna held the cow's head steady. Below, her mother balanced awkwardly on a stool, bending over her swollen belly to knead the animal's teats. Mari worked in silence and Anna could sense her mind wandering. Hoping to capture her attention, she asked, "Mother? Who puts milk in the cow?"

Mari's fists pumped up and down in absent rhythm. "God does," she droned.

Anna eyed her mother. She then stroked the cow's side and searched under its belly. "But where does He put it in?" she asked.

Mari leaned back and wiped her brow with the back of a hand. She swooned slightly to one side as if dizzied. "Only the Mother knows," she said.

Anna's eyes widened. "Whose mother?" she asked.

Mari flinched. "What?"

"Do you mean *your* mother? Like Zahra sometimes thanks her—?"

"No," Mari said, interrupting. Her lips tightened. "I did not mean to say *Mother*," she said quickly.

"But you—"

"I made a *mistake*," she insisted, startled at having made such a potentially perilous slip. She glanced over her shoulder.

Anna kicked a toe into the ground, thinking.

"Mother?" she asked. "Why does Father not like Zahra?"

"Anna!" her mother gasped, exasperated. "Will you never run out of questions?"

Anna flinched. Her mother was never cross with her.

Mari sat back, wobbling slightly atop the stool. "Hand me the rag," she said.

Anna handed her a small cloth. Mari wiped each of the cow's teats. "That is enough for today," she said, a strange tremble coming into her forearms. She covered the mouth of the milk jar with a swatch of linen.

Anna noticed beads of sweat forming above her lip. "You are melting."

"I need air," Mari mumbled. She stepped outside and fell against a beam, squinting as if her vision had blurred.

"Greetings," a voice called out. "Blessings on your house."

A youthful shepherd approached from behind. Anna smelled the sharp stink of goat urine.

Mari steadied herself. "Greetings," she said.

Anna had never seen so young a shepherd. He was not much older than she, maybe nine or ten years of age. And he looked remarkably like her. They both shared long, curly dark hair, high coppery cheeks, and succulent green eyes shaped like almonds. She noticed too that his teeth were so white they shimmered even when he was not smiling.

Mari looked back and forth between the shepherd and her daughter thinking they could easily have been mistaken for brother and sister.

"Do you have any spare milk for a poor band of shepherds?" he asked.

"We do," Mari said. "Anna, bring a small jar from the house."

Anna hesitated. She did not want to leave her mother alone with the bad-smelling shepherd.

"Anna!" her mother urged.

Anna ran to the house. When she returned with the jar, her mother filled it with milk.

"Double blessings on your house," the shepherd said.

"And on yours," her mother replied.

Anna was relieved when the boy finally left. His smell had made her eyes sting.

With a noticeable wobble, Mari lifted the jar and headed back to the house. Anna tripped behind and was preparing to ask if she could have a sling like the one the shepherd boy carried when her mother yelped in pain. Mari staggered back and dropped the jar. A tongue of milk licked across the dirt. She groaned and clutched her belly as a flood of water splashed down between her legs.

"Anna," Mari said, bracing herself in the doorway. "Get Zahra." A dark stain bloomed across the front of her robe.

Anna tried to move, but her legs were frozen. She thought her mother was dying.

"Go!" her mother yelled, staggering through the puddle of milk and water.

Yoseph threw a cedar branch onto the fire. It spit sparks into the night. His father sat across the flames, reciting an endless prayer. Yoseph looked nervously toward his house and wrung his hands.

Mari's cries split the air.

Anna tried to gauge her father's concern by counting the lines denting his forehead. Her neighbor, Daniel, approached the fire with his father, Ishmael. They hardly reacted when Mari screamed again.

"The happy day has come," Ishmael said.

"Yes, thanks to the Lord," Yoseph replied. The men embraced.

Mari's cries came again, quick and urgent. Anna could not understand what was happy about her mother's agony.

Daniel turned to Anna and stuck out his tongue. She ignored him.

"Is Mother going to die?" she asked her father.

Yoseph held up a hand. "Hush," he told her.

Frustrated, Anna gazed back into the fire. While they waited, a breeze lifted from the west, carrying the scent of the olive trees. As if riding the breeze, a group of three men walked out of the darkness. One of them led a camel. A light dressing of sand salted their coffee cheeks. They were, Anna knew, desert dwellers.

"Blessings on your house," the man with the camel said to Yoseph. "May we sit by your fire?"

"Blessings to you. Please join us," Yoseph answered. The men laid down their staffs and circled the flames. Yoseph's father ignored them.

Mari screamed again. Anna flinched.

"Who is the fortunate man?" one of the dwellers asked.

"I am," Yoseph said. He looked to Anna. "Pour these men some tea. No one will go thirsty at the birth of my first son."

"Yes, Father."

The man with the camel pointed to Anna. "Is that not your first son?" he asked, mistaking her for a boy.

"Do not joke with me on this happiest of nights," Yoseph replied. He turned to see that his daughter's shawl had fallen, leaving her face fully exposed. "Anna, cover yourself!" he commanded. "And hurry with their tea!"

The three men traded looks of bewilderment.

Inside the house, Mari squatted on a short, three-legged stool. Zahra knelt before her, rubbing her belly with oil and wiping blood from her legs. Mari buckled under a new wave of pain that cramped her sides and pulled at her teeth. "Something is wrong," Mari hissed. "Something is *wrong*!"

"Shh, Yadira!" Zahra whispered, accidentally calling Mari by her childhood name. The two women locked eyes.

Startled by her slip, Zahra quickly gathered herself and wiped the sweaty hair from Mari's forehead. "He is more stubborn than your daughter, that is all," she said. "Keep pushing."

Mari held her breath and bore down with all her strength. When nothing moved inside her, she bellowed into the night.

Yoseph laid his hands on his father's shoulders. "Tonight you will have your grandson," he said.

Retreating to the shadows, Anna pouted, irritated by her father's joy.

"And what will you name him?" the man with the camel asked, peering through the steam rising from his tea.

Yoseph stood tall. He took considerable pride in his son's name. He had even carved the letters into the cradle. "He will be named after my father," he said. "And he will be called Jesus."

The three men nodded. It was, they thought, a good name.

One of the men then gazed into the starry, indigo sky. He squinted as if he could read something within it. "It is a holy night," he said, pointing to a star that hovered above.

Mari's final cry pierced the air. Her scream rose until it stopped, abruptly, as if cut with a blade. No one moved. The crackling of the fire grew louder. Yoseph's father looked up. The silence remained.

"Why does my son not cry?" Yoseph whispered.

A bloody hand lifted back the camel hide. Zahra stepped into the night, dragging her crooked leg. Behind her, Mari began to wail.

Yoseph faced Zahra. "Is it a boy?"

Zahra nodded. She looked him straight in the eye. "But he does not live."

Yoseph went still as stone. Only his eyelids twitched.

The others kept silent, afraid to move.

"What did you say?" he asked, but did not wait for an answer. He shoved the old woman aside and strode through the door. Once inside, he froze. His wife lay weeping on her mat, shrunken and bloodstained. In her arms, she clutched a waxy, blue body. The glistening, vine-like cord of their connection twisted around his neck like a snake.

Yoseph's knees gave way and he crumpled to the ground.

"My God, my God!" he wailed. "Why have you forsaken me?!"

Three days later, Mari was still too weak to rise. Lying on her mat, her eyes stared wide and empty at the ceiling. Anna busied herself at the fire. Earlier that morning, Zahra had met her behind the sycamore and given her a handful of roots and leaves. She then outlined specific instructions for steeping a special tea.

"But you must be certain to prepare this only when your father is away," the old woman had cautioned.

Anna poured the dark, foul-smelling liquid into a cup through a linen swatch, as Zahra had instructed. She then lifted the cup to her mother's lips but Mari would not drink.

Outside, Anna could hear the bells ringing on the necks of the donkeys. The people of the village had gathered.

It was time to bury her brother.

"Go be with your father," Mari mumbled.

"But, Mother, I want—"

"Go!"

Not wanting to upset her, Anna wrapped her mother in blankets and ran outside.

She found her father leading his donkey at the front of the caravan. Lashed to the animal's back was her brother's body. Barely the size of a bread loaf, it lay wrapped in cloth strips dusted with spices.

Anna watched the faceless bundle roll from side to side with the donkey's lurching steps. For the first time, she was glad for the cover of her shawl. Glad that no one could see her glowering. Unlike the others, she felt no grief. She was too furious at her brother for having caused her mother so much pain. And she could not help but wonder if death was the price he had paid for hurting her.

After a short journey, the caravan arrived at the chosen cave. Anna and the others remained outside as her father and a group of men passed the body inside. It was not long before the hollow of the cave reverberated with the sound of wailing.

There was, she had heard Ishmael say, no pain greater than that of a father who must bury his only son.

One day stretched into the next like sluggish strands of molasses. Mari still did not rise. Anna pressed a piece of damp flatbread against her mother's lips. She did not respond.

"Eat, Mother, please," Anna begged.

"Where is Yoseph?"

"I do not know. The men came to get him," Anna said.

Upon hearing this, Mari's eyes flew open. Wide. She braced her elbows and struggled to stand up. "Find him! *Now!*" she gasped. "I need him here. Tell him I need him *here*!"

Anna struggled to hold her mother down. "Lie back, Mother! I will find him. I will bring him," she said, alarmed by her mother's look of terror.

When she had gotten Mari resettled, Anna threw a log on the fire and dashed into the night.

The village street was empty. Everyone had gone inside. Thin edges of firelight seeped around doorways and windowsills.

Trotting toward the well, Anna spotted the silhouette of a lone, dark figure. The person was rocking back and forth, eyes glued to the sky.

"Zahra?"

"Oh!" the old woman cried, losing her balance and tumbling against the stones. Her breath came ragged and quick. Her pale gray eyes were wide with fear.

"What is wrong?" Anna asked, helping her up.

"Daughter, you must go from here. I am done." She tore open the top of her robe and lifted a chain that hung around her neck. A solid copper medallion slipped along its links. Zahra turned to Anna and threw the chain over her head. She quickly tucked the medallion under Anna's robe and pressed her hands along the girl's shoulders. "Tell no one," she urged. "Tell *no one* you have this."

"What is it?" Anna asked, lifting the medallion.

"No! Keep it hidden!" Zahra hissed.

"But what is it?"

Zahra grew angry. "Go away! You must not be here! Go away and do not look back!"

Anna reached for the old woman, but Zahra slapped away her hand. "Leave me! Leave *now*!"

Anna cradled her hand. It stung from the old woman's slap. Not wanting Zahra to see her tears, she turned and fled into the night.

After an hour of searching for her father, Anna prepared to give up. It had been a long day and she was tired. On her way home, she passed by a dwelling on the outskirts of the village. She heard men grumbling inside. Curious if her father might be among them, she hopped on a rock alongside the dwelling and peered through a crack in its wall. Through the narrow gap she saw her father, her grandfather, her neighbors Daniel and Ishmael, and many other men seated around a fire.

"She has great power over our women!" Anna heard her grandfather say. He was angry and the spit from his lips hissed in the flames.

"She is a keeper of the old ways and speaks against the Lord!" another man shouted.

The men mumbled among themselves.

Ishmael rose to his feet. "What say you, Yoseph?" he asked.

Yoseph wiped tears from his cheeks.

Anna gasped. She had never seen her father cry.

"I have asked . . . why *me*?" Yoseph said with difficulty, his voice weak with grief. "I am a good man. I have remained clean. I have kept myself in the eyes of God."

The men nodded.

"Why then have I been left childless? Without the honor of a son?"

Anna started at his words. Baffled.

Father! You are not childless. You have me*!* she wanted to yell. But something inside her told her to keep silent.

Yoseph continued to speak. "Tonight, my brothers, during prayers, I was given the answer. God, in His infinite mercy, has shown me the error of my ways. Through His grace, I now understand why He is angry and has punished me."

Astonished, the men lifted their faces into the flickering light and held their breath.

"I was *weak*!" Yoseph blurted in confession. "I allowed a heathen to influence my wife and touch my newborn son." He pointed in the direction of the well. "The old woman tricked my mind. It was *she* who lowered my eyes from God and brought His wrath upon me!"

The men mumbled in assent.

"That woman is a demon," Yoseph spat, his rage spinning around itself, tensing into a tight coil. "She practices the ways of those who think they are gods. Who deny the Lord. And hold themselves above His laws." His head fell in remorse. He pressed a palm along his eyes. "But it is I who am to blame. For our priest gave me warning."

The men gasped.

"Yes. He did. Many months ago," he confessed. "But I did not heed his words. Much to my sorrow."

Yoseph fell silent. No one dared move. After a moment, he spoke again.

"Today she broke my family. Tomorrow she will break yours," he whispered, his voice cracking. "I tell you, my brothers, she must not be allowed to work her evil on our village again."

The men nodded like a single beast, their eyes shining with tears.

When it seemed as if Yoseph was done speaking, Ishmael raised his voice. "But what is to be done?" he asked.

Anna's grandfather looked up from the flames. He then rose to his feet. His face cleared of expression. "Kill her," he said.

Anna's bladder went cold as ice.

The men turned to one another, nodding. Their whispers grew louder and more animated. The solution of death, of ridding their community of the unwanted evil, spread among them quick as a plague until they were on their feet shouting. Anna cringed as they charged out the door. They moved en masse, dragging a single shadow behind them as they grunted and picked up stones. Other villagers, alerted by the shouting, leaked from their houses to join the mob, oblivious of its cause. Anna ran behind, keeping herself hidden.

She watched Daniel's mother, Rebecca, and three other women Anna often saw at the well rush out and push through the crowd. Finding Yoseph, they clung to his tunic and begged him to stop. To come to his senses.

"She is the only one who possesses the healing knowledge! What will we do when our children are sick?" they pleaded.

But they could see Yoseph was not in his right mind. That he stared without seeing. Grief and rage having taken his sight. Unable to keep their grip on his tunic, the women fell away, the crowd trampling around them.

Zahra heard the men approaching. She turned to face them, lowering her shawl so they could see her face. The mob stopped before it was upon her. The men writhed, unsure how to proceed, until someone, deep within the crowd, shouted, "Old woman, you are accused of slandering the name of God and practicing evil on our women and children. How plead you?"

Zahra looked up. Her eyes were calm. "You have come to kill me," she said. No one answered. She leveled her stare. "You have come to kill an old woman. Where is the hope in that?"

A charge ran through the crowd. "Do not let her speak!" someone shouted.

"Stone her!" another cried.

Anna kept hidden behind a bush. Her mouth dry as dust.

Zahra thrust a trembling hand into the sky. The men recoiled. She lifted her voice. "I have done nothing to harm you, yet you wish to destroy me. Have you lost all respect for life?" She challenged them, "Let he who is without human blood cast the first stone!"

The crowd stood silent, muted by doubt and shame. Anna felt something drip down her chin. She wiped her mouth and drew away blood. She had bitten her lip.

The middle of the crowd began to shudder. A single man pushed his way to the front. Anna recognized her father. Yoseph strode out of the crowd and stood before the old woman. His eyes blind with rage. A large stone weighting his hand. "You have spurned the Lord," he said, "and brought evil into our homes. You are in no position to counsel *us*, old woman. For you have snuffed out new life with your own hands!"

"Yes! That is so!" the crowd shouted, its vigor renewed.

"With this," Yoseph said, "I avenge the death of my only son."

The stone struck its target, smashing into Zahra's face, crushing her nose to a bloody pulp. Zahra did not cry out, but swayed, disoriented and broken.

"Stone her! Kill her!" the others shouted, unleashing an angry flock of stones into the air.

Anna felt urine curling around her legs.

A stone hit Zahra in the neck, cracking her windpipe. The sound of her wheezing infuriated the crowd. "Silence her!" they shouted. The more the old woman bled, the more bloodthirsty the crowd became. Stone by stone her cheeks were sliced, her eye sockets shattered, her jaw splintered, the ears torn from her head, her organs pounded. Slowly, she folded, boneless, to the ground.

Anna watched in horror as the man she called Father kicked through Zahra's battered remains until satisfied she was dead.

Anna arrived home before Yoseph. She peeked around the goatskin curtain that walled off her mother's private living space. She found her asleep. Thankfully, the yelling had not wakened her. Hurrying, Anna slipped back into the main room and dropped onto her mat. When she heard her father approaching, she feigned sleep, keeping one eye slit open, to watch him.

Yoseph swept into the house like an intruder. He smelled of sweat and anger. He bent to remove his sandals and headed for his mat.

Mari stirred. "Yoseph?" she whimpered.

"Yes, I am here," he grunted. Without another word, he disappeared behind the partition.

Anna heard him lie down on the mat next to Mari.

Mother! she wanted to cry out. *He has killed Zahra!*

But her mother did not know. And let him lie next to her. Let his bloodstained hands touch her, and his lips press on hers. Anna's stomach rolled. She grabbed at her throat as if she might choke. It was then she felt the chain around her neck. And recalled Zahra's last words.

Tell no one!

Anna buried the medallion deep within her robe, fearful that her father might see it and kill her, too.

CHAPTER 3

A village on the outskirts of ancient Palestine*—10* A.D.

It was the sound of scratching that woke Anna. An insistent digging at the floor next to her head. She opened her eyes and saw their scrawny guinea hen, a dull patchwork of missing feathers, raking the ground with its claws. Across the room, dusty spots of light poured through holes in the camel hide, the day's heat burning the dank animal odor. Anna's eyes focused and found her father tending a fire that starved along with their animals.

Yoseph held his hands above the stunted flames. The bit of warmth brought relief to his joints. His once-limber fingers had grown bulbous and knotted, like gnarled tree branches. It had been three years since he had been able to hold his carpentry tools. Discarded and rusting, they lay askew in a wooden box outside the door.

"Anna," Mari called from behind the partition, "go to the well."

Leaping to her feet, Anna wrapped the tattered remains of her shawl around her face and pushed through the camel hide.

Outside, the village was quiet. Only the breeze moved. Everyone had gone about their day.

She walked past the manger. The roof had caved in like a saddle, and the stones above the door tumbled into a pile at the entrance. The family's remaining cow, guinea hen, and goat were now kept, shamefully, inside the main house.

Beyond the fallen manger, Yoseph's workshop lay dark and sealed, still as a tomb. He had stopped going inside three years ago, following the death of his son.

Anna arrived at the well but found no one there. She filled the jar and water began to seep from a crack in its side. She hurried back to the house, pressing her finger over the leak. Mari took the jar and set it in the coals. Just the smell of warming water urged a gnawing in Anna's stomach. She tried to turn her mind against it, knowing her hunger would grow throughout the day.

Mari hovered above the flames, Anna thought, like a skeleton. The skin around her cheeks was ashen and taut. Her once olive and chocolate eyes were a lightless gray. When Yoseph had stopped working, Mari had stopped talking, and it scared Anna the way they avoided each other.

During one of his visits, the priest had proclaimed that Mari was barren. Daniel told Anna the word meant "empty." But Anna found that confusing.

How could her mother be empty?

After all, it was her mother's hands that pulled milk from the cow and patched holes in her tunic. It was her mother's words that dried Anna's tears and her wisdom that lit her days.

Later, Anna overheard the women at the well discussing the matter. One insisted that the priest was wrong. That he could not possibly know of such things. And that it was not the jar, but the *spigot*, that was empty.

But what did it matter? another whispered, beating stone against cloth. Either way, the jar was always to blame!

After Anna helped her father wash his hands, Mari came and sat for morning prayers.

Yoseph's incantations began slowly, pushing their way through his persistent cough. Anna listened to the familiar phrases. "Our blessed Father who protects us." "He who rules with a just and mighty hand." "We, your chosen children." "Born into this land of milk and honey."

Glancing sideways at her mother's fallen features, Anna could find no place for her father's words in her life.

How wise and mighty could God's hand be if her mother was to starve—despite her father's ardent prayers?

When he was finished, Yoseph tucked his ruined hands into his sleeves. "Is my father's meal ready?" he asked, avoiding Mari's eyes.

Anna felt trapped in the tension between them. "Are you going to Sepphoris today?" she asked her father, hoping to distract him.

"Do I not always go to Sepphoris on this day?" he growled, hurling a bitter look at his wife's back.

Mari handed over the tray. Anna stared at the four wrinkled olives, the half a cup of watery milk, and the stale flatbread. She felt her mouth flood.

"And the blessing for our *son*?" Yoseph asked his wife, hitting the last word with extra breath. Mari handed him a small bundle tied in cloth. Without a word, she disappeared behind the partition. Yoseph stared after her. Lifting his voice so she would be sure to hear, he said, "Since the Lord will not bless my house, may He bless my journey." With that, he pushed through the camel hide.

Anna followed him with the tray, feeling the tug of her mother's sorrow at her back.

As Anna and her father passed the well, a single desert dweller, washing sand from his face, called to them.

"Greetings," he said. "Would you and your son have milk to spare for a faithful traveler?"

Anna saw her father's eyes glance angrily off her exposed face. "Satan is in your eyes!" he spat. "I do not have a son."

The man looked again at Anna's chiseled cheeks and was bewildered.

Yoseph stormed off. Anna scurried close behind.

Yoseph's father did not greet them when they arrived. Instead, he scowled at the meager offerings. Yoseph bowed and shuffled across the floor on his knees. Arriving at the fire, he poured a cup of tea. "How does the day greet my father?"

His father reduced his eyes to slits and stared at Anna. He shook his head, noting how tight and short her robe. "She grows like a weed," he muttered.

Yoseph said nothing.

After another moment, his father spoke again. "How much longer must I wait, Yoseph? Eh? Tell me. How long?"

Yoseph's head fell. Anna held her breath.

"I am not to blame," she heard her father mutter, quietly, without conviction.

Looming over them, Anna's grandfather pressed, "How old is she?"

"She is ten now, Father."

Her grandfather sucked an olive pit between toothless gums. "Ten years," he said, shaking his head. "For *ten years* I have waited."

Yoseph's spine bent under the weight of his father's judgment. "Father," he said, "you know how I have suffered."

"You?" his father shrieked. "How *you* have suffered?" He spit a wet olive pit onto the floor. Anna scuttled to retrieve it. "It is *I* who have suffered! It is I who raised my son from the dust only to have him watch me grow old and die without a grandson on my knee. It is *I* who must bear the shame!"

Yoseph squirmed in the dust. "I beg your forgiveness, Father," he said. "But I must go. I have an hour's journey." He lifted his sack and pushed through the door.

Outside, Anna and her father could hear the old man hurling insults. "An hour's journey! To beg for coins! To live in a manger!"

Trembling, Yoseph leaned back against his father's door and stared into the horizon. "Bring the blessing to your brother," he commanded and thrust the small pouch into Anna's hands. He then turned and wiped a large knuckle across his eyes.

As Anna took hold of the pouch, the shawl dropped once more from her cheeks.

Yoseph glanced down. He stared at her face as if he had not seen her in years. He noticed how much older she had become. How her features had matured. He also noticed the increasingly masculine cast that tainted her appearance. She was not unattractive, that he could see, but she clearly lacked the delicate grace of other girls. His heart sank as a new realization struck him.

How would he ever be able to marry her off? Who would want such a hard young woman for their son?

Was he therefore to be burdened with her for the rest of his life?

But he barely possessed the means to feed and clothe her now*!*

Agitated by these thoughts, he dropped his gaze further. To his daughter's sprouting frame. And the budding strength in her build. His eyes narrowed. Something about the breadth in her shoulders, and the confident way she carried herself aloft, struck him as a challenge. As a threat to his own sense of worth and manhood.

Must everything he created be somehow deformed? Was he not even man enough to produce a gentle daughter?

Still reeling from his father's condemnation, Yoseph grabbed his daughter and dragged her to him. Handling her roughly, he squashed her body against his.

"Father, please! That hurts!" a surprised Anna cried out.

With all his strength, he yanked up her shawl and wound it tight about her face until she could barely breathe.

Gasping for air, Anna turned and ran.

"Speak to no one!" he shouted after her.

Anna arrived at her brother's grave shaky and troubled. She could not understand what she had done to bring on her father's wrath. She dropped to a rock to catch her breath.

Thinking back, she could not pretend that she had not noticed a change in the way he looked at her. Whereas before her father's gaze had almost seemed to pass through her, now when he watched her removing his sandals or fetching his tea, his eyes were laced with disappointment. As though she had failed him. Terribly. And this look of despondency brought more pain to her heart than his anger ever could.

Yet she had no idea what she had done! Nor what she could do to make things right.

A sudden flapping interrupted Anna's thoughts. She looked up to see the gray blur of a mourning dove landing on a nearby rock. Remembering that Zahra had said doves traveled in pairs, she scanned the sky for the bird's mate. But none appeared. The bird was alone.

Anna drew her lips into an O and mimicked its mournful coo. Hearing the sound, the dove cocked its head and held Anna in the gaze of a single, focused eye. It did not, however, return the call.

Anna shook her head. She still could not speak to the creatures as well as Zahra once had. She would have to keep practicing.

Recalling the old woman made Anna's heart feel heavy. She pressed her fingers to her chest until they found the outline of the medallion resting on her breastbone. She glanced quickly about then lifted the chain from her tunic. In the morning light, she could see the raised silhouette of a giant sycamore fig tree, hundreds of years old, its branches spreading voluptuously to the edges of the disk. On the other side, the copper was smooth, the metal worn to a sheen from years of contact with human skin.

At one point, Anna had been tempted to show the medallion to her mother. To ask if she knew where the disk had come from or why Zahra had given it to her. But, with the horrific memory of Zahra's murder still before her eyes, and her final warning—"Tell no one!"—Anna did not dare. She was too afraid of the harm that might come.

The dove burst from the rock with a furious flap, startling Anna from her reverie. She glanced up at the sun and felt its heat beating down. Felt the dry air drawing the last of her strength. Wanting to complete her errand so that she could leave the desolate area, she stood and approached the cave. The grave's entrance appeared less frightening than she remembered. At the time of her brother's burial, it had seemed as deep and ragged as a camel's mouth. Now it looked unremarkable, like a crack in dry leather. Kneeling, she untied the small pouch. Inside, she found a bit of cheese, two olives, and a dried date. Her stomach rolled on a swollen wave of hunger.

Shaking off the pain in her belly, she laid the food down before the grave.

When her brother had died, Anna had thought that he deserved it. After all, he had caused her mother terrible pain and had nearly killed her! But this morning, she could feel her anger transforming. In the face of her family's ruin, she felt a fresh fury rising within her—this time the anger rose not because her brother had died, but because he had not possessed the courage to *live.* If he had, she found herself thinking, her grandfather would finally be satisfied and Zahra would not have been stoned. If he had lived, her mother would not be starving in her stomach and heart, and her father would still be a carpenter rather than a withered, discontented man.

Resisting the urge to keep the offering for herself, Anna turned her back to the cave. She nudged her cheeks into the folds of her tattered shawl and forced herself to depart. Peering into the sky as she went, she contemplated the one question that, more than any other, would not stop pestering her heart: *Why was a dead son worth more than a living daughter?*

The branches of the great sycamore tree wove themselves into the stitch of the sky like crooked threads. Lying on her back and gazing up at the maze, Anna could not tell where tree ended and sky began.

Zahra, she recalled, had also loved the sycamore. Anna had often seen her tucked between its rippling roots, asleep. When she was killed, some of the men in the village had suggested cutting down the tree. Anna did not know why. She wondered if it had to do with Zahra having worn its image around her neck. But, after a long debate, it came down to the fact that, whatever their beliefs against the tree, no one was willing to sacrifice its supply of sweet figs.

But had they not once tolerated Zahra in the same way? Because of her ability to heal? Yet on the night of her murder, her value as a healer was forgotten.

Perhaps, one day, it would be the same with the tree?

Anna shuddered to think of it.

Sitting up, she glanced about to make sure no one was watching. She then stood to climb. The tree's trunk divided early, splitting into a bouquet of branches that scooped low to the ground, making it easy to find a foothold. She lifted herself along a familiar lattice and dropped into her favorite seat, high and hidden, among the heart-shaped leaves.

From her vantage point, she could see the olive groves and the road to Sepphoris. She could also see out to where the mountains gave way to desert. Within the heat waves shivering above the sand, she spotted a wavy band of shepherds. They moved so slowly that they seemed almost not to be moving at all. She wrinkled her nose at the thought of their bad smell and wandering ways.

When the sun slipped from behind a cloud, Anna found herself inside a sphere of illuminated green. The leaves glowed with loud, confident color. Staring into the brilliance, she wondered, briefly, what it would be like to be all green. Imagining this, the leaves began to swirl around her.

Then the insults began.

"Look in the tree. Anna the monkey!"

The boys loomed beneath her, circling the trunk like wolves. "Tell the truth, Anna! Are you a girl monkey or a boy monkey?" They broke into laughter, one of them striking another to the ground in merriment.

Anna felt a burning lump rise in her throat. Ever since watching

Zahra fold into ruin, she no longer fled from the rampant energy of milling boys. Instead, she fought.

"Go home, all of you!" she shouted. "You are too ugly for my eyes!"

The boys snickered. "Why do you not come down here and say that to our faces?"

"I do not want to get too close. You all smell like goats!" she retorted.

Daniel grabbed up a stone. "Come down here, you freak!" he shouted. He launched the stone. It cut an arc above Anna's head, ripping through the leaves with a violent staccato. Anna gripped the branches.

"My father says you will never have breasts!" Ben shrieked while the other boys searched frantically for ammunition to hurl at their target.

Anna ducked and dodged their flying rocks. "Even monkeys throw better than that!" she said, laughing, her anger fanning her courage. She climbed higher, beyond their reach. "Is not that your mother calling you?" she shouted to Daniel.

Her mockery infuriated the boys and they scrounged the ground for stones like crazed guinea hens pecking meal. Luckily, the earth on the western ridge did not have many stones and the boys quickly tired.

"Let us untie the old man's donkey!" one said, dashing toward the village. The others cheered the idea and followed.

Anna hurled insults after them. "Cowards!" she shouted.

When the danger had gone, she lowered herself from limb to limb on shaky legs. Pausing only to wipe away tears.

"Where have you been?" her mother asked when Anna arrived home, trembling. Mari was balanced on all fours rolling up the carpet in the main room. "Never mind," she said when Anna did not answer. "See to the hen."

Eager to be of help, Anna peered into the nesting box but found it empty. "No eggs today," she said.

Her mother groaned. She dropped the carpet outside, picked up a broom, and began to sweep up the dung.

Anna lifted a pan and scooped up the piles her mother had made.

After the confrontation with the boys, she felt better just for being near her, as if her mother's very breath was medicine and comfort.

When the floor was swept, Mari stepped outside to retrieve the carpet.

"Milk the goat," she told her daughter.

Anna rustled the animal from its bed. She set a pail beneath its belly and dropped to sit cross-legged beside it on the floor. The goat whinnied as Anna alternately knocked her fist into its udder and tugged rhythmically on its teats.

Across the way, Mari knelt to patch a hole in the carpet. She went about her chore in silence, but Anna wanted desperately to reach her.

"Mother? Why do hens lay eggs instead of little hens?" she asked.

"I do not know," Mari said. Her flat tone indicated that she did not want to talk. But Anna needed to talk. *Needed* to connect with her mother. She looked about, wondering if it might be safe to ask questions about Zahra. But when a shadow passed along the doorsill, she decided against it.

"Then tell me this," she said. "Why do hens not make milk like cows and goats do? Is it because they make eggs?"

Mari sighed and pulled a thread between the carpet's weave. "Not now," she said.

Anna looked down into the pail. It contained only a shallow disk of milk. The goat, it seemed, had very little to give. But Anna refused to burden her mother with more bad news.

She tugged again at the animal's teats. "I am going to get milk enough for you to make a great ball of cheese!" she bragged, trying to put a good face on their predicament. She then gave the goat a scratch under its chin, hoping to encourage it.

When Mari did not respond, Anna sought again to reach her. This time asking a question from deeper in her heart.

"Mother? Do you think God loves all of us equally? Or does He like boys more than girls?"

Anna heard her mother groan. Puzzled by this response, she glanced over. When she did, Mari bolted upright, her spine snapping straight. "Oh!" she cried. She dropped the carpet and plastered her palms along her abdomen.

"Mother!" Anna cried.

Mari groaned louder and with greater urgency. She folded onto herself, her arms wrapping around her middle as if to keep her insides from spilling.

"Mother, you must lie down," Anna said, pressing her fingers into Mari's shoulders. She remembered the first time her mother had experienced the pain. Almost a year ago. It had come suddenly, as it did now. When it had first struck, Anna thought her mother was going to have another baby. Even Yoseph had believed it, and had gone so far as to slaughter a chicken.

But as time rolled on, periods of hope gave way to lingering doubt when Mari failed to produce another child.

Yet the bouts of pain continued. Growing worse each time they came.

"Mother, please. Let me help you."

With her daughter's support, Mari lifted herself from the floor and scrambled toward her mat. On the way, the color fled her face and beads of sweat broke out along her brow.

"Help me, Great Mother," she whispered through lips the color of death.

Yoseph sat cross-legged in the dust. The vibrant sounds and colors of Sepphoris surrounded him. Whenever someone walked by, he called out, "Alms? Alms for the poor?" When he tired of begging, he would squint directly into the sun, waiting until he could no longer stand the stab of light. After a time, he came to welcome the accompanying pain. It was something he could control.

His eyes were still closed when a man approached wearing a richly colored silk robe.

"What are you doing here?" the man asked.

Keeping his eyes closed, Yoseph pleaded, "Alms? Alms for the poor and . . . his family?" he added, the last with some reluctance.

The man ignored the beggar's request. "Are you not Yoseph?" he asked.

Yoseph opened his eyes. He looked up but did not recognize the man's face. "How do you know me?"

"I am Zebediah. I used to visit your village. Do you not remember me?"

Yoseph stared, but his eyesight was dim. "No, my friend, I do not.

But clearly this is my misfortune." But Yoseph lied. He *did* remember Zebediah. He was a renowned silk trader who occasionally traveled through their village. Despite his great success, however, tragedy had marred the man's life. One day, while he and his son were out of the house, a band of men had broken into his home and taken the lives of his wife and young daughter.

Rumors later surfaced that the women were pagans and were planning to run away and join one of the clans waging war against God. Given this gossip, some came to hail the men who killed them not as murderers, but as heroes.

But Yoseph did not care to think of Zebediah's troubles. The silk trader, at least, had a *son*.

Zebediah considered Yoseph's threadbare tunic and gnarled hands. "Have you had additions to your family?" he asked.

"No," Yoseph said, looking down. "But thank you for including me in your prayers."

Zebediah cocked his head. "And your wife is well?"

Yoseph felt the heat of embarrassment rising up his face.

Was Zebediah mocking him?

When Yoseph did not answer, the silk trader said, "I have only three shekels with me. They are yours."

"A most generous gift!" Yoseph said, groveling in the dust. "Many blessings on your house." Inside, he wanted to scream.

When Zebediah left, Yoseph stuffed the coins into his tunic and headed for home. He could not bear the humiliation any longer.

As he walked alone on the road, he thought of disappearing. He then imagined hanging himself from the nearest tree. That particular thought terrified him and, with great effort, he kept his feet moving toward home. Leaving his family would bring unbearable shame. And retribution from God. He was a man, he told himself over and over. There was no escape from the grave responsibilities of his life.

But how much more could the Lord make him suffer?

He shuddered at the thought.

Anna poured hot water into a goatskin and tied off the top. Behind the goatskin partition, her mother writhed on her mat, her fists tight and yellowed from clenching against the pain. Anna pried her mother's hands from her stomach and replaced them with the warm goatskin. Mari curled around the warmth, gritting her teeth.

While she rested, Anna stepped outside and sifted through her father's rusted tools. Perhaps one day he would allow her to use them. Then she could repair the fallen manger and the workshop. And her mother could rest.

"Anna?" Mari called from inside.

Anna returned and lay next to her. "Yes, Mother, I am here."

Mari rolled to face her daughter. Brushed the curls from her forehead. Despite the dull pain inside her, she marveled at the color and allure of Anna's eyes.

"You," she whispered. "What will become of you?"

"I will become a carpenter like Father!" Anna said.

Mari gave a doubtful smile. Her eyes filled with tears. She cupped Anna's face in her hands. She drew her close and whispered, "I had so hoped that you would be taken from here—" she began, then stopped herself. There was no point in clinging to impossible dreams. Mari knew that all hope for her daughter's escape had died with Zahra.

Submerging into fresh despair, she gripped Anna's eyes with her own. "Being a woman in this world is a curse," she sobbed. "Do you hear me?" Mari shook her head against the tears. "My poor daughter," she wailed. "I wish you had never been born!"

Anna's heart pounded in her ears.

Mari read the hurt and confusion in her daughter's face and regretted that she had not held her tongue. "Never mind," she said, wiping her eyes with the backs of her wrists. "Your mother is tired. I am speaking foolishness. Go collect wood. Your father will be home soon and he will be angry if the fire is out."

When Yoseph returned, he found Mari kneeling over the flames, boiling water for his tea. He said nothing as Anna scurried to remove his sandals. He tried to be grateful for the end of his journey, but found himself disgusted by the stink of their animals. His father's words banged inside his head: "A son who lives in a manger! Who *begs* for his bread!"

Mari set a cup in front of her husband. She could feel the anger lurking within him and knew to be silent. She poured his tea and waited patiently as he took his first sip. As soon as the liquid touched his lips, he spat it violently across the room. "What is this?!"

"Forgive me," Mari whispered. "It is a remedy for your hands. I thought—"

"You need not *think*," Yoseph hissed. "Make me a fresh cup."

Mari bent to gather the few remaining coals. She could feel Yoseph's eyes riveted to her back. Daring her to look up. Seeking a reason to attack.

Yoseph watched his wife grovel before the fire. His barren wife. The cause of his shame. Looking her over, he was struck by how quickly her beauty had faded. Like everything else, she had become a burden. Her brewing of the strange tea made him suspect that she was returning to the ways of her family. To their evil and godless rituals.

Had he not heard her, just the other day, humming one of their peculiar melodies?

When he had taken her as his wife, he had made her forswear the beliefs of her childhood and embrace the Lord as her only God.

Had she now relapsed and betrayed him?

The thought made him furious.

His mind returned to the day she and her family had arrived in his village. They had come up from the southern lands, carrying bags of salt for trade. He knew then that they were pagans. But the daughters possessed such infinite beauty that he could not resist! It was Mari's sister who caught Yoseph's eye and stirred his passions. *She* was the one he wanted. But the family would not allow him to take their eldest, saying that she was already promised. Hearing this, the younger daughter, being a fiery spirit, stepped forward and announced that she wished to become his wife. Though her request was unexpected, and caused her family much anguish, Yoseph was lulled by the beautiful girl's desires, and agreed to take her.

How different his life would have been had he been given his first choice!

Tangled in these thoughts, he glared into the fire. The flames wavered for lack of fuel. Soon, he thought, they would die.

Anna pushed blindly through the camel skin, her eyes barely visible above the load of firewood she carried. Her face beamed with pride. It was the most wood she had brought back in months. She saw her father's back and her mother kneeling at the fire. The silence between them made Anna nervous. She hoped that her prize would please them. But when she stepped past her father, the logs slid out of her grip and crashed to the floor, spraying hot coals and ash across the room.

Yoseph rose to his feet and grabbed his daughter. His eyes bore into hers. "What have you done?" he roared. His hand followed quickly behind his words and struck her face.

Anna staggered back, dizzied by the blow.

Yoseph turned to the sky. His anger began to feed on itself. "Have you no mercy, my Lord?" he bellowed. He pointed to Anna. "Night and day I have begged for your forgiveness. Yet you taunt me with false treasure! With a child who only *looks* like a son!" He fell to his knees sobbing. "I am cursed, I am cursed, I am cursed . . ."

Anna watched in horror as her father crumbled. She then felt her mother's hand reaching for her. "Come to me, Anna," Mari whispered.

Yoseph looked up to see his daughter cowering in her mother's arms. "Let her go."

"She is only a child," Mari begged.

Yoseph lunged toward them, grabbed Anna by the arm, and yanked her to him. "I will not be disobeyed in my own house!" he shouted.

Mari held tight to her daughter.

His wife's resistance infuriated Yoseph and he grabbed Mari by the neck. "You are my ruin!" he wailed, shaking her. "Would that I had never cast eyes upon you!"

"Father, no!" Anna shouted. Trapped between their anguished bodies she felt a surge of panic ignite her limbs. She pushed against her father, struggling to pry him loose. When he would not relent, she kicked the edge of her sandal into his shin.

Enraged, Yoseph threw Mari to the floor. Seeing blood dripping down his leg, he spun to face his daughter.

"Father . . ." she pleaded.

Yoseph leaned into a new attack when a commotion arose at the door. He turned to see someone pull back the camel hide. Behind it stood a group of children, watching.

"Go away, all of you!" he cried. The children scattered but, like a shifting cloud of locusts, returned quickly to cling at the house's windows and cracks. Yoseph made several attempts to scare them off, but each time they rushed back.

Startled by their tenacity, and ashamed at having anyone witness the failure of his authority, he growled and stormed from the house.

Relieved by his departure, Anna bent to help her mother. Mari recoiled and pushed her away. "Do not touch me!" she hissed.

"Mother, it is *me*," Anna said.

Wheezing, Mari crawled behind the partition. Anna wept as her mother disappeared. She lifted a hand to dry her tears but came away with blood. A split ran along her cheekbone.

Later that night, her father not yet returned, Anna listened to her mother weeping. Her cries tugged on the skin of Anna's heart. The pain was so great she feared it would tear.

One day, she thought as she lay on her mat, *I will take my mother away. And build her a big house. And give her beautiful clothes. And protect her. And praise her. Yes. One day, I will save her.*

And in the darkness of that night, Anna promised, on her life, that these things would come to pass.

Yoseph huddled in a bank of rocks near his son's grave. He had sat still for hours, his heart fighting the urges of hunger and despair. He had wanted to pray, but felt hindered by bitterness. By his anger at the Lord for having abandoned him. For having denied him a life more befitting his faithfulness.

At some hour his thoughts turned toward home. And he struggled to think how he might escape. How he might free himself from the trap.

"Ah, there you are! Your father said I might find you here," a voice called out.

In a daze, Yoseph turned and saw a young man approaching. When he drew closer, Yoseph recognized the priest. The same one who had warned him about Zahra, and who had proclaimed Mari barren.

Yoseph sat up and wiped a sleeve across his face, not wanting the priest to see his misery. "My father sent you?" he mumbled.

"Yes! I have just spoken with him," he replied. "He said you might be in need of counsel." The priest looked over the man beneath him.

Noted his disrepair. The wild roll about his eyes. Unafraid, he sat beside him. He let a moment pass and then said, "The truth is, your father has serious concerns about you. He seems to believe that the godless influences that once preyed on your community have now come to roost, shall we say, closer to *home*." He let his words sink in before continuing. "And he further believes, as do I, that these influences are bringing an undue amount of suffering upon your head."

Yoseph listened intently, his mouth agape.

"But do not think that in your time of need the Lord has abandoned you. Oh no! Rather, you must believe that through your trials He has been testing you. Calling you to a higher purpose. One for which your past actions have shown you to be amply prepared."

When the priest paused, Yoseph felt a lump expanding in his throat. Feeling the weight of his burdens suddenly lifted, and having little strength with which to contain his relief, he broke down and wept.

The priest laid a hand on Yoseph's back. "There, there, my brother. Have courage! And let us, together, consider how you might best serve the Lord. How you might help rid yourself, and your fellow men, of those who would spread their evil among us."

Long before the sun rose, even before the roosters crowed, Anna woke, her head heavy from a sleepless night. She went to check on her mother but a voice stopped her.

"Your mother will rest today," her father said. He was kneeling by the fire.

Anna wanted to disobey, but the dull ache on the side of her face made her fear crossing him a second time.

Yoseph pulled the pot from the fire and poured two cups of tea. He watched his daughter step a wide arc around him. Her bright, emerald eyes hung dark and dazed. A swollen knob rose from her cheek.

"I thought you could come with me today to Sepphoris," he said, offering a smile.

Anna's eyes hugged the floor. She felt the pull of the marketplace. The spices, the musicians, the colors, the adventure. Anyplace would be better than home. But the temptation did not outweigh the concern for her mother. She shook her head.

"No?" Yoseph asked, his smile fading. Her disobedience fortified his convictions. It was clear the girl had already been tainted. First by the old woman. And now, no doubt, by her mother.

Behind them, the cow urinated with a loud fizz.

Yoseph grunted. Then chuckled. A strange eerie cackle that made the hairs on the back of Anna's neck tingle.

She held still, her nerves on alert.

Without warning, Yoseph sprang to his feet.

Anna toppled back.

"Bring my father's tray," he commanded. Then disappeared through the camel hide.

Relieved, Anna dropped to her knees and gathered their last remaining morsels. Three leathery olives and a hard crust of bread. She set these on a tray and followed quickly behind her father.

When they came to the well, a shepherd approached Yoseph. He was a wall of a man with a reddish beard and eyes the color of doves. In his hand he wielded a shepherd's staff. "Greetings of the day," he said.

"And to you," Yoseph muttered.

The shepherd's gaze fixed on Anna. As if he were studying her.

Anna lowered her cheeks deeper into her shawl, though the press of the fabric made her jaw ache.

The man turned to Yoseph. "I am in need of more hands to tend my flock," he said. "Would you know of any family who might be willing to offer their son?"

Yoseph's eyebrows rose.

"I pay well," the shepherd added.

Yoseph opened his mouth as if to say something, then shook his head. "No, I do not," he said. "The sons here are much wanted," he added and continued on his way.

Anna strained to look back at the man, thinking something seemed familiar about him, but Yoseph hissed at her hesitation and dragged her behind him.

When they arrived at her grandfather's house, Yoseph pushed Anna through the door alone. Through a small window, she saw him tighten his sandals and trudge toward Sepphoris. Watching him depart, she thought it odd that he had not greeted his father and offered him blessings for the day.

While her mother slept, Anna went to the olive groves. She wove between the shaggy trunks of the trees, scanning the ground. She lifted the belly of her robe in front of her like a bowl and collected fruits overlooked by the farmers.

As she neared her house, Anna felt that something was wrong. Something in the air was taut, like an overstretched goatskin. It made her bones hum. Fearful of entering the door, she stood outside the camel hide and listened. She heard the voice of a woman, but it was not her mother. Then she heard her father's voice.

What was he doing home?

The voices rose, reaching a hysterical shrill.

"What has happened? What has happened, Yoseph?" the woman shrieked. Anna heard her father trying to calm the woman. Fearing for her mother's safety, Anna yanked back the camel hide and ran straight into Daniel's mother, Rebecca. The collision sent Anna's olives flying through the air like sluggish confetti. Rebecca grabbed Anna and dragged her from the house. But not before Anna caught a glimpse of her mother. Mari lay on her mat. Still. Her mouth open. Her face blue. Her eyes unseeing.

Off to the side Anna spotted her father, his face hidden in shadow.

Rebecca screamed for help and tried to pull the girl with her, but Anna would not move. She felt as if the ground beneath her were unfastening, yawning wide to swallow her whole. Her heart began to leak and she sank to her knees. Through tears, she begged with all her might for someone to restore her mother's life.

The entire village stood beneath the setting sun, watching the tragedy unfold. Off to one side huddled the women from the well, their morning activity interrupted. From this group rose an occasional wail, spawning one echo after another, as if the women were milking grief from their souls.

Rebecca held Anna tight against her and would not let her back inside the house. Anna shivered in her neighbor's embrace, her teeth chattering despite the heat.

Daniel and the other boys sat in an oxcart, spitting seeds at one another. But even they grew silent when Yoseph stumbled out of his house. His face was pale and empty of expression. His gaze focused on something in the distance. Ishmael stepped forward to embrace him. He then ushered Yoseph through the crowd and took him to his father's house.

Later, Rebecca brought Anna home and bedded her next to Daniel. Despite the circumstance, her son did not miss the opportunity to torment the family's guest. From his mat, he stuck out his tongue and hurled lewd gestures. But Anna did not notice. She kept listening for her mother's voice.

When Daniel finally fell asleep, Anna wandered alone into the night. The air chilled the glaze of tears on her face. The bright smear of a falling star stretched across the dark, vanishing as quickly as it came. She wished she were that sudden disappearance.

On the western horizon, she could make out the great sycamore's silhouette, silvered in the light of a half moon. She headed for its shelter.

In the early dawn, Anna was jolted awake by a sudden tug on her shawl. With her face exposed to the chilly morning air, she flailed against her unseen attacker. "No!" she shouted.

"Be silent!" a voice warned. A voice she recognized. Her father.

He yanked her to her feet. Confused and still half asleep, Anna thought he was angry at her for leaving her face uncovered. When he grabbed at her, she braced, expecting him to coil the shawl tightly about her face.

Instead, he tore off her robe.

Stunned, Anna stood shivering in her thin tunic.

Yoseph then gripped the fabric at her shoulders in both hands and split the tunic down her back. Terrified, Anna fought to get away, but he held her fast. In her nakedness, she felt Zahra's medallion on her chest. She clasped her hands around the copper disk, afraid of what her father would do if he saw it. But Yoseph kept his eyes turned from the shame of his daughter's naked body and did not see it.

"Put this on," he growled, hurling a thicker tunic at her feet.

Anna scrambled to dress quickly. The new tunic was made of a coarser material than her own. And shorter. Yoseph looped a leather sash around her waist and tied it tight. She felt an uncomfortable pressure on her ribs. She had never worn a sash before. It was then that she realized her father had dressed her in a boy's tunic. She smelled sweat and the scent of Daniel in the fabric. It had been *his* tunic.

Before she could protest, Yoseph pushed her down to her knees. He grabbed a fistful of her black curls and wound it between his crooked knuckles. Anna felt her scalp pop as strands of hair were uprooted. She bit down on her tongue. She dared not scream.

Yoseph slipped his carving knife from its sheath and brought it alongside her ear. "Hold still," he hissed.

Anna's head bobbed as Yoseph sawed through her hair. Wheezing from the effort, he threw black tails onto the ground in a semicircle around her knees. When he was done, he yanked her up. He slipped two worn leather sandals onto her feet. One had a broken strap. He stood and looked straight at her, but to Anna, it felt as though his gaze passed through her. "Follow me," he hissed.

Anna walked behind her father, dragging the unfamiliar sandals that chafed her feet. She did not know where he was taking her until she smelled the faint odor of goats. The scent grew sharper until it stung her eyes. They were approaching the shepherds.

But why?

Soon she could see the outline of men, standing in a circle, murmuring around the smoky remains of a fire.

"Stay here," her father commanded.

Anna watched as he walked toward the men. She saw him greet one, only to be directed to another. The second shepherd he approached was leaning, half seated, on the back of a sheep.

"Blessings on you," Yoseph said, bowing before the red-bearded shepherd.

While her father spoke, he gestured back toward Anna. The shepherd looked over Yoseph's shoulder to where she stood. Anna expected her father to yell at her for having her face exposed, especially before a man. But, strangely, Yoseph was not angered.

The shepherd returned his eyes to Yoseph and shook his head. Yoseph spread his arms wide in supplication. The shepherd shook his head again. Yoseph fell to his knees. He peppered the shepherd's feet with kisses. Throwing a second look at Anna, the shepherd stood and lifted her father to his feet. He reached into a leather pouch at his waist and dropped a few coins into Yoseph's hands. Behind, the other shepherds rolled their eyes. Yoseph bowed before the man. Then, without looking back, he fled.

Anna stared after him in disbelief. Too frightened to cry out. To call him back.

"Your heart is too soft!" one of the shepherds jeered at the red-bearded one. "Of what use to us is an untrained village boy?"

The red-bearded shepherd shrugged. "Peter needs help with his duties," he said. "And I have a good feeling about this one."

The others snorted and tossed up their hands in mock exasperation. Despite Solomon's rationale, they suspected he had purchased the boy out of pity. Still, they did not question his actions. No shepherd worth his salt would ever be foolish enough to challenge the decisions of his leader.

Shaken by their banter, Anna scanned the horizon looking for her father. But he was gone.

She then noticed the red-bearded shepherd walking toward her. He came to within a few feet and stopped. His gaze rose from her sandaled feet to her chopped hair and settled on her bruised face.

"I am sorry about your mother," he said.

Anna kept silent.

Was he taunting her?

"I, too, lost my mother in this village," the man said. He looked off quickly, blinking.

Anna's head jerked up.

Zahra! she thought, seeing an echo of the old woman's gaze in the gray eyes of her son.

The shepherd drew a forearm across his eyes. "Yours is a difficult path," he said. "But, sometimes," he added, his eyes drifting toward the horizon, "we are called upon before we are ready."

Anna's eyebrows wrinkled.

"You do not agree?"

She kept silent.

Did he know it had been her father who had taken Zahra's life? Would he kill her to avenge his mother's death?

The shepherd stepped closer and patted Anna on the back. "My name is Solomon," he said. "Come join your brothers."

Anna refused to follow and stood her ground. She wanted to run. To hide.

But where?

Her resistance made Solomon grin. He came back and led her by the shoulder. "Do not be afraid," he said.

As they came closer to the other shepherds, Anna could smell their filth. Their deep, gruff voices scraped her ears. The pungent odor of goat urine stung her throat. She needed to escape. She looked in the direction that her father had run but could not find him on the horizon. When she felt Solomon's hand drop from her shoulder, she bolted. Her legs splayed like scissors. Before she could take five steps, a strong arm hooked around her waist. "Where do you think you are going?" a rough voice asked. "We paid six shekels for you!"

Anna smelled old sweat and dirty leather. She fought her captor like a wildcat. The shepherd kept his grip firm. He knew well how to restrain animals that did not wish to be caught. He turned to Solomon. "Let us leave this forsaken village," he said.

"You speak with wisdom, Judas," Solomon said with a nod. His heart ached, having learned from the village women of his mother's violent death. But he knew that Zahra had accepted the risks of her path. Just as he knew she would expect him to carry on. Strengthened by this knowledge, he lifted his chest and faced the others. "Gather yourselves!" he shouted. "We are off!"

Anna felt Judas's arm tighten and lift her into the air. She came down hard on a donkey's back. Judas wrapped the lead rope around his wrist, tapped the animal's head, and stepped forward. He swung a crooked staff ahead of each step and stared out with vacant eyes.

Whistles, like extravagant birdcalls, looped through the air, followed by the nickers and whinnies of sheep. Like a single entity, the shepherds and their flocks lumbered toward the rising sun.

CHAPTER 4

Desert region outside of ancient Palestine—10 A.D.

Anna swayed headless atop the donkey. She had sunk her face into the collar of her tunic to deflect the sun. And to hide from the surrounding danger. She hoped that if she could not see the dirty shepherds, they might somehow disappear. Might leave her unharmed.

Her hands had gone numb hours ago. She could no longer feel, the coin-sized blisters rising along the sides of her fingers where she gripped the blanket. Beneath her, the donkey's sweat soaked into her legs and buttocks, staining the lower half of her tunic with hair and froth.

The sun shimmered overhead, pressing light and heat into the ground. To Anna, the journey seemed monotonous. Heat was the only constant. She could not appreciate the litany of subtle hand signals and whistles through which Solomon steered his band across the mountains and down into the arid valley below. She also did not notice the frequent changes in the group's pace as it slowed or sped with the rise and fall of the day's temperature.

Every few hours, a young boy, who appeared not much older than Anna, scurried through the flocks hauling a goatskin of water and a wooden ladle. He carried the skin to Judas and walked alongside him as he drank. The elder shepherd relished several gulps, smacked his lips, and returned the ladle. When the boy turned to go, Judas snatched him by the collar and yanked him back. He motioned behind them. "You have forgotten one."

The boy shook his head. "He refuses to drink."

"Try again," Judas insisted.

The boy shrugged and trotted back. When he approached Anna's feet, she wrapped the tunic tighter about her face, despite the stifling discomfort.

The boy stumbled alongside the donkey and lifted the skin. Anna ignored him.

"How can you not drink? Are you part camel?" he joked, hoping to cajole a response.

Startled by his words, Anna dared to look down for the first time. The boy's feet wove deftly between the donkey's hooves. He did not smile but his teeth flashed with the whiteness of eggshells. The flash sent Anna into a tailspin of memories.

He was the young shepherd! With green eyes. From three years ago. The one who had asked her mother for milk moments before water poured from between her legs. Hours before the birth and death of her only brother . . .

The image of her mother rose quickly behind the remembrance. Her night-colored skin, her powerful arms, her spicy scent. Anna began to drown in a pool of thick, warm grief.

The boy nodded toward the ladle. "You have not had water all day," he said. "You will die if you do not—"

A large hand, seemingly from the sky, dropped on Anna's leg. She braced, ready to fight. Her eyes latched on to the owner of the hand. It was Solomon. His eyebrows knelt together above his gray eyes. He was frowning. In a swift motion, he unraveled the tunic from her face. He lifted the ladle to her lips. "Drink," he said.

Anna clenched her jaw. If she were to refuse water, she might die of thirst. But the smell of wetness, of damp wood, enticed her. She trembled with need. With mortal craving. Until instinct overcame reason. Her hands leapt out and clutched the ladle. She pushed the tunic beneath her chin and sucked the liquid between greedy lips. The first gulp stung her throat. The second loosened her tongue. The third rinsed her spine.

The young boy watched the newest shepherd with curiosity. Able to see Anna's face for the first time, he was surprised to find that they looked much alike. Solomon noticed the boy's stare and hurried him on. "The others are waiting," he told him. Solomon gave his newest shepherd a firm pat on the back then stepped forward, strong in his stride, to retake his position at the helm.

Later in the day, Anna peered into the vast land before them. Nowhere along the horizon could she find the interruption of a village. Or trees. Or shelter of any kind.

Where were they going? What would they do to her?

If only she could go home!

Her eyes squeezed shut against the sting of new tears. As if reading Anna's mind, the donkey stopped and rooted its legs into the earth. Without thinking, she slid from her seat and dropped like a sack of olives to the ground. Feeling its load lightened, the donkey resumed its pace, leaving Anna behind.

"What are you doing?" Judas yelled at her over the flock's bobbing backs. He kept his forward stride. "Get up or the animals will crush you!"

Anna tried to stand but toppled over. Lines of noisy sheep and goats streamed by on either side. She fought to stand amidst the trampling, but her legs folded like soft leather, her ankles buckling. The hours of riding had numbed her joints. The stream of animals continued. Anna moaned. She heard a shepherd's piercing whistle. She struggled to rise, fighting gravity and exhaustion. Pushing herself onto her knees, she tore the blisters from her hands. Her movements became increasingly frantic until two arms slipped beneath her own.

"Push with your knees," the boy whispered as he lifted her from behind. Anna strained to her feet. "Hold on to my shoulder," he said. Anna held on, but bent as a painful wave of tingles rolled down her legs. "Shake them out," he urged. She did as he said and, after a few minutes, the tingles began to subside. "Let us walk."

The first steps were tenuous but then her legs grew in strength. Slowly the two look-alike shepherds caught up with the rest. When she was walking on her own, Anna noticed Solomon, perched high on a crag. He was watching. Everything.

"My name is Peter," the boy said.

Anna felt the air on her cheeks. A wave of fear rolled through her as she stared him openly in the face. His youthful maleness reminded her of the boys in the village who had chased her. Who had thrown stones and raised sticks.

"Can you not speak?" Peter asked, wondering if the new boy was a half-wit.

Anna lifted her tunic and wrapped her face, tight.

"Do not do that," he said, tugging at the material. "You will die of the heat. Keep it loose. Understand?"

Anna fought against him.

"Listen to me!" Peter cried.

She pulled away and hid her face in the folds.

"What kind of an idiot are you, brother?" He spat at the ground.

A whistle pierced the air. Peter looked up. "Coming, Solomon!" he shouted and dashed off.

Anna held still, watching him leave.

Had he not called her brother*? But he had looked her right in the face!*

You are a mixture, she heard her mother say. Her mind raced as she realized the depth of her disguise. She let the tunic drop from her face. The air felt cool against her cheeks. And inviting.

Being a woman in this life is a curse.

On the horizon, a new set of hills, pinkish in color, became visible just beyond the shimmer. As the flocks sauntered forward, and the outline of the hills grew more distinct, Anna considered her mother's words and began to know their truth.

When the sun dipped just below the horizon, balancing on the edge like a yellowed half-moon, Solomon lifted his staff and released an ear-splitting whistle. At the signal, every shepherd began gathering the sheep toward the center of an imaginary circle. The day's travel had ended. Within minutes, a fire was started, the donkeys unloaded, water drawn from a hidden spring, and goatskins billowed into tents.

Simon, a middle-aged shepherd with a red patch over one eye, was chosen to take first watch. He climbed to the top of a rocky escarpment. From there, he could gaze over the entire flock, watching for strays and predators.

Back in their camp, Peter bent over the fire, boiling pots of water and heating rocks on which to bake bread.

Anna stood outside the men's activity. A chill slithered through the air as the sunlight faded. For the first time since beginning the journey, she felt the sudden urge to urinate. Her urge grew worse when two younger shepherds pulled open their tunics and relieved themselves in the thorny bushes.

"Where is our tea?" Judas demanded.

Anna flinched, thinking he had spoken to her. She prepared to answer when Peter said, "Coming, brother." He shifted the pot but the flames were dwindling and the water refused to boil. He looked up at Anna. "Get more wood," he said.

Just outside of camp, Anna found a series of caves cut into the rock. She approached the opening of one and felt its icy breath surround her. Intent on her duty, she stepped into the nearby scrub and broke off several large, dead branches. She was breaking these into logs when she noticed a shepherd within the brush. It was Judas. He had lifted his tunic and was urinating against a boulder. When he finished, he slipped a dagger from his waist and drew its blade back and forth over a stone to sharpen it. Anna watched in fear, noticing the strange sickle shape of the dagger's handle.

When finished, Judas whipped the blade over his head and eyed its edge against the sky. Thrusting the weapon toward the clouds, he cried out as if to empty himself of an unbearable agony. "Ahhh!" he wailed again and again, anger scraping his throat.

Fearing for her life, Anna turned and ran. As soon as she was out of sight, she knelt within her tunic and relieved herself between shaky knees. She leapt up suddenly when she heard someone grumbling in the brush nearby.

But when she went to look, no one was there.

Anna returned to camp carrying a full armload of wood. The stacked branches hid her eyes as she walked cautiously toward the fire. On her way, she failed to notice the rock that Peter had laid out and her toe caught its edge. She fell forward with a lurch. The branches flew from her arms and scattered noisily across the ground. Anna saw Solomon jump at the racket and her ears began to ring.

Now they know. They know I am a useless girl and they will kill me.

Solomon rushed upon her like a wave. She lifted her hands in front of her face. Ready for the blow. But it never came. She peered between her fingers and saw Solomon smiling down at her, his gray eyes twinkling.

"You are brave to carry more than you can manage," he said, patting her on the back. "Today was a long journey. I am proud of how well you did."

The ringing in Anna's ears diminished. Her face flushed.

He was proud? Of me*?* Her mind swam in circles.

The fire's warmth attracted the men. They sat cross-legged around the flames awaiting their evening meal. Some of them mended sandals. Some mumbled prayers. Others passed a long-spouted samovar. It was the first time Anna had gotten a good look at them. Akbar, with his long, frizzled beard and brown, worn-down teeth, was by far the oldest. Then there was his son, Rahim, quiet, his eyes always on the horizon. The fair-skinned Simon, with his faded red eye patch, who appeared only briefly to retrieve his meal before returning to his watch. Mathias with his crooked nose and gold earrings. And Judas, lithe and strong, but seeming ever distant and preoccupied.

Some of the men, like Akbar, wore turbans. Others wore keffiyehs. But no one was bareheaded.

Peter laid two large platters on either side of the fire. Each was dotted with small heaps of figs, grapes, goat's cheese, and an oily spread of mashed olives and lentils. Tongues of flatbread lay on top. It was, Anna would later learn, a generous meal.

The men scooped their fingers into the delights and fed their hungry mouths. Emboldened by her disguise, Anna tore off a piece of bread for herself. While they ate, the men conversed in several languages, some of which she did not recognize. Judas, Solomon, and Peter spoke in her own rough, guttural tongue, while Akbar and Rahim spoke with creamier tones that rolled, edgeless, across their lips. Simon and Mathias communicated in whispers using a hurried language that sounded urgent, even when they smiled. Despite the differences, Anna noticed that they could all speak or understand enough of one another's languages to communicate.

After the meal, the men leaned back and passed a curved pipe, slender as a bird's bill. Anna was relieved by the heavy, sweet-smelling smoke as it covered the less pleasant odors of sweat and breath.

Mathias leaned toward her. His gold earrings glittered in the firelight. "So, little goat, what is your name?" he asked as a ghostly haze of smoke twisted around his head.

The question startled her.

What was her name?

She looked Mathias in the face, knowing that to maintain her disguise she would have to act as bold as a boy.

But what could she reveal that would not give her away?

Fearing discovery, she said nothing.

"Can you not speak?" he asked. He turned to Solomon. "Have you wasted six shekels on a mute?"

Solomon pointed upward. "I wasted nothing. He came to us from above."

The men snorted.

"Is he an angel, then?" Akbar questioned.

"Perhaps," Solomon said, straight-faced. Akbar sucked air through the gaps in his teeth.

"And I suppose his mother was a virgin, too?" Mathias scoffed. The men laughed.

"He will steal the women with those eyes," someone said.

"No. He is too shy," said another. "And besides, shepherds are the last to get the women." The men let out a collective moan.

Judas, who had gone to sit farther off, sucked at a pipe clamped between his teeth. At his side rested a stack of blankets in need of mending. Saying nothing, he bent to his labors, weaving leather cords through holes and split seams. He seemed disinterested in the men's talk. But every so often, his gaze traveled to the new shepherd.

The banter continued long into the night. Until the last pipe was smoked. And the question of the young shepherd's name forgotten. One by one, the men stood and disappeared into the dark.

"Come with me," Solomon said when he saw Anna's head dipping into her lap.

They climbed to the top of the ridge where Simon sat, smoking his pipe. "Greetings of the night," Simon said and unwrapped the sheepskin from his shoulders. He smiled at Anna, his one eye carrying the mirth of two. "Solomon sees a shepherd in you, I think," he said, giving her a firm pat on the back. He then knocked the ash from his pipe and headed back to camp.

Solomon lowered himself into the spot from which Simon had risen. He set down his staff and invited Anna to sit next to him. The night had grown cold and the rocks beneath them remembered only a little of the day's heat. He wrapped the sheepskin over their shoulders.

Anna waited for Solomon to give her a task or a command. But, as she found out, watching the flock was a still and silent duty. She observed the elder shepherd's eyes as they flitted back and forth across the animals, looking for what, she did not know.

A small breeze rose and caressed their faces. Anna pushed her vision deep into the stars. They seemed to sit wider apart than she remembered, appearing less tethered. Despite the remnants of her grief, she wanted to ask Solomon a question about the sky.

Did she dare? What if he grew angry and reminded her that girls should not ask questions, as her father always had?

But if Solomon thought she was a boy, could not boys ask questions?

Anna weighed the urgency of her curiosity against the heft of fear. She decided that she needed to know. "Why does the wind not blow away the stars?" she asked.

Solomon raised his eyebrows and drew on his pipe. He chuckled and exhaled a mouthful of smoke. His mother had been right. The child was brave. Gentle. And open to miracles.

He thought about how Zahra might have answered the question. After a moment, he cleared his throat. "It is the stars themselves that make the wind," he said. "Can the one who makes the wind be blown by it?"

Anna frowned.

"Do you make your own breath?" Solomon asked. Anna nodded. "Then try it," he said. "Try to blow yourself down."

Anna puckered her lips and blew, hard as she could, against her chest. Solomon laughed at the innocence and admired the child's pluck. "See there?" he said.

Anna smiled. And for just a moment, forgot her pain.

Solomon sucked heavily on his pipe. Soon they were entwined in a shawl of sweet smoke. He looked deep into the sky's belly. "Brother," he said, addressing Anna. She noted that he did not demand to know her name. "There are different ways of looking at things," he continued. She followed his gaze, trying to intuit his meaning. "For example, some people see patterns, or constellations, as outlined by the stars. There is a hunter. There is a bear," he said, pointing. "But there are other people, other believers, who see patterns, or spirits, outlined by the spaces *between* the stars. Dark shapes. Like ravens, and trees, melting through the black."

Anna was jolted by the idea. She had never thought to look *between* the stars. She squinted, trying to make out the figures, her vision freed by this new perspective.

"It is important to remember that there are other ways," Solomon said, returning his gaze to the flock.

At some hour of the early morning, Anna had a dream. In the dream, a wreath of fingers slipped around her neck and tugged on the medallion at her throat. She struggled to stand and fend off her attacker. But when she woke, there was only stillness. And the moon overhead.

She sat up and in the silvery light saw Judas standing farther down the ridge. In his hands he held the goatskin pouch that he carried, always, on his back. She could just make out the figure of Solomon, fallen on his knees, beside him. The gray-eyed shepherd cradled his face while his back rose and fell on waves. Anna watched the great sobs rack his body.

Was he grieving the loss of his mother?

With this thought, Anna's hands flew to her neck. She found the medallion resting safely against her chest. She then heard a rustle and looked up just in time to see Judas helping Solomon to his feet. Together they turned and began to walk toward her. Fearful of how they might react if they saw the medallion, she pushed it deeper inside her tunic and feigned sleep.

The men came and stood above her. For a while, both were silent. Finally, Solomon spoke.

"Do you sense that the others suspect? Peter perhaps?" he asked.

"No," Judas grunted. "Peter is too eager to please. And the others have not the imagination."

Following a prolonged silence, Solomon spoke again.

"The journey will be long," he said. "And the risks great."

Judas swallowed hard. "Yes."

Anna then sensed him kneeling beside her. She froze, afraid of what he might do.

Judas lowered his voice. "Even so, brother, we must not fail," he said, his voice girded with determination. But when he spoke again, his words wobbled. "Enough blood—most precious blood—has already been shed. And to lose another . . ." he choked, unable to continue. Anna felt him press a hand along her back.

"I know," Solomon whispered.

Anna sensed Judas bending closer. She smelled his sharp sweat. She tensed at a feeling of sudden warmth. Then relaxed when she realized its cause—the shepherd had covered her with a sheepskin.

Solomon took a deep breath, as if not wanting to disturb his friend's thoughts. "The hour grows late," he said. "Let us retire."

After a moment, Anna heard the churn of footsteps.

She wanted to watch them, to make sure they would not return, but did not dare open her eyes.

In the darkness, her thoughts returned again to Judas's words.

What journey were they planning to take? she wondered.

And, more important, whose blood had already been shed?

Anna ran her tongue across her lips. They were dry and cracked from the heat. The merest hint of saliva made them sting. They had traveled for days, stopping to rest only at night. Solomon drove the flocks hard, assuring the men that a timely arrival at Dara would bring a worthwhile reward. When the nights grew colder, the shepherds built long tents with goatskins suspended on ropes and branches.

Anna crawled quietly from her sleeping spot between Akbar and Rahim. Most of the men were still snoring. Only Peter, Judas, and Solomon had woken and gone. Not wanting to wake the others, she slipped underneath the bottom of the tent and into the blush of early morning.

The land, it seemed to her, had changed overnight. Wherever she looked grew thick green trees. Some had broad leaves like flatbreads; others had bare trunks that curved high into the sky where their heads exploded in bursts of blade-like foliage. Between the trees wriggled vines and bushes of every kind. Even the air felt alive and moist. Anna had never seen so many different types of plants. The lush and elaborate display of life astonished her.

Peter arrived with a basket of freshly picked fruit. "Finally! You are awake," he said. "I thought you might sleep your life away." He handed her a small golden orb. "Try one," he said. Anna bit into the skin and a syrupy juice flowed from its pink center. Her tongue stung with flavor. Peter jostled from leg to leg. "Here," he said, handing her three broad-faced leaves. "They are good for cleaning yourself."

Anna took the leaves. She marveled at their size. "Where are we?" she asked, her voice croaky from lack of use.

Peter's eyes grew wide. "So you *can* talk!" A bright smile slashed across his face. "We are in the oasis, outside of Dara," he answered. "Have you never been here?" Anna shook her head. Peter's legs squeezed shut. "I cannot wait," he said.

Anna followed him into the bushes. Hidden from the others, they lowered themselves and lifted the bottoms of their tunics. Whenever she had to relieve herself, Anna took care to keep folds of material bunched around her middle so as not to expose her sex.

While they waited for their sleepy bowels to move, Anna looked over at her fellow shepherd and noted again their shared features and coloring. They truly looked like siblings. And though Peter stood several inches taller, he was considerably thinner, his arms and legs nowhere near as thick as hers. His slighter build made Anna feel stronger. More sure of herself. More comfortable in the pelt of her disguise.

"So, brother," Peter said, "now that you have found your voice, why do you not tell me something about yourself?"

The question knocked her fledgling confidence.

Peter waited, then shook his head at her silence. "Maybe you really *did* fall from the sky," he said, punching her arm. He stood to readjust his tunic. "Do not be long," he cautioned. "The others will expect their tea." He gave her a second glance, as if he had seen something, then disappeared behind a streak of white.

After breakfast, Solomon announced that they would rest for an additional hour since the city was no more than half a day's journey. Several of the men sat in the shade and began to pray.

Peter turned to Anna. "Come say prayers with me." When they sat, he said, "You may lead us."

Anna froze. Though she remembered some of her father's words, she had never said prayers aloud *herself.*

Feeling sweat break out along her hairline, she struggled to think back. "Oh Great Father," she began. "We . . . your most humble servitudes—"

Peter screwed up his face. "Who taught you to pray like that? A guinea hen?" Before he could say more, a voice called out.

"Peter!" It was Judas. "Since you are so good at leading prayers, remember to keep me in yours," the shepherd slurred. "And pray that this day brings the hour in which I avenge my family!" He approached them at a rapid pace.

"Judas!" Solomon shouted from the sheepfold. "Come here *now*!"

Startled, the shepherd froze mid-step. He stared at the new boy. His gaze sobered, then softened. After another moment, his head fell. Saying nothing more, he stumbled off.

Peter looked to his friend and saw concern crossing his face. He leaned over and whispered, "Do not be afraid," he said. "Some years ago, a group of men killed his mother and sister. He was the first to find them. They say he has never been the same. And that sometimes he loads his pipe with herbs that make him crazy. You will get used to it, but it is best to keep your distance."

They watched Judas weave away on uncertain feet. His goatskin pouch sagging against his back.

Peter shook his head with disdain. "I do not understand why he grieves so deeply over the death of two women. It was not like they killed his *father* and *brother*," he said, tenting his eyebrows to indicate how much worse that scenario would have been. "As my father always said, women are like weeds and from time to time need to be hacked down."

Anna was shocked by his words.

She wanted to scream that he was wrong, that she knew the worth of women, that she had seen firsthand the horror of a woman being murdered! But she bit her tongue and kept silent.

Solomon's whistle broke the tension. "Gather yourselves!" he shouted. The men came and circled him. "Today we will enter Dara," he said, leaning on the woolly back of a sheep. "We should arrive before the sun folds." Saying this, he assigned each man a duty for the day. Akbar and Rahim were to lead the flocks, while Judas would flank the eastern side. "Peter, watch the rear. And take our new brother with you."

Peter smiled and threw his arm around Anna's shoulders. "I hope you will be better at shepherding than you are at leading prayers!" he said with a laugh.

The two young shepherds walked side by side, trailing the ragged ends of sheep. When an animal fell behind, Peter showed Anna how to snap the air with an olive branch to frighten it back into formation. He then showed her how to throw a pebble just in front of a sheep's head to keep it out of a particular area. And if the animals ventured farther than throwing distance, he showed her how to load stones into a sling and fire them off. Anna's jaw dropped at his accuracy.

"And what else?" she asked over and over, eager to understand the special tactics and signals.

Peter's heart swelled at his new friend's interest. He had never been made to feel so important. The regard fed an insatiable hunger inside him. For the rest of the afternoon, he regaled his apprentice with the finer points of his trade: the varieties of whistled signals and their meanings, the behavioral differences between sheep and goats, how to use the sun to maintain a straight path, and how to flush cobras from the rocks. He put a wooden staff and an olive switch into Anna's hands. "You will be of no use without these," he said.

Anna nodded. For the first time since leaving home, she felt a future spreading before her. It was as if the secret knowledge of shepherding had been given to her as a replacement for all she had lost. After she had mingled among the sheep, trying to memorize each one, the animals seemed to inherently trust her. Those she was sent to wrangle often returned to the fold before she arrived. And when she strove to steer the flock, it shifted with little effort on her behalf.

Peter was amazed by the phenomenon. "I have never seen anything like it," he said. "The animals seem to read your mind. Even the goats!"

Anna smiled. The success helped soothe the ache in her heart.

After they guided the flock down a long slope, Peter suggested they stop for tea. They found a cool spot in the shade beneath a craggy overhang. They sipped in silence, watching the flock open slowly, like a shaggy flower.

Peter felt thankful for the arrival of his new friend. It was the first time he had ever felt at ease around another boy his age.

"I used to hate shepherding," he confessed, surrendering to the sudden urge to speak. "My father was an instructor of letters. He sent me to school when I was five. For years I studied, sometimes through the night, but could never learn. The other boys used to tease me and call me foolish. One day my father told me to stand up. He told them I was a disappointment. That I was not smart enough to be among them, and that I would never become a teacher."

Peter took a shallow breath. It seemed to Anna that his throat had tightened.

"My mother worried that if I did not learn a trade, I would turn to thievery. So my father sent me away with the shepherds," he said. He then thought about continuing. About telling the *real* reason he had been sent from home. But even contemplating the confession made his body tense. And his lungs stiffen.

Anna studied him as he spoke. Saw the invisible weight loaded on his lean shoulders. He, too, had been cast out. It was their bond.

"Your father was wrong," she told him. "You *are* a good teacher."

Solomon whistled from up ahead. The flock was scattering.

"We must go," Peter said, though he did not want to leave. He wanted, instead, to stay and soak in the feeling of his friend's approval.

When Anna leapt up, her tunic caught on a rock and tore to her waist. She fell over the split, grappling to keep the ends of the garment together.

Peter knelt for a closer look. "I can repair this," he said, running the torn fabric through his hands.

Anna was panic-stricken.

Had he seen?

She pulled away. "No," she said. "I can do it." She tried to slow her breath.

Peter shrugged. "You should get a new tunic in Dara. Yours is old and frayed. It hardly protects you. You need one like mine," he said, lifting the thick linen from his shoulders.

Solomon sounded a second whistle.

Without another word, Peter dashed off. When he was gone, Anna stepped behind the rocks to urinate. Her heart was pounding from fear of discovery. While she squatted, she unlaced a cord from her sandal and bound the split in her tunic. When satisfied it would hold, she lifted her staff and ran to join the others.

By the time the sun had climbed overhead, Anna and Peter had established a rhythm between them. In their minds, there existed an invisible divide. Peter was responsible for herding the right side, and Anna, the left. The work was so lightened by their cooperation that Peter found time to frolic. When Anna was not looking, he snuck up behind her and flicked the back of her legs with his olive switch. A chase ensued. She cornered him against a stand of boulders. Laughing, they raced back to the flock. It was a thrill for Anna to find friendship with a boy rather than hostility.

Perhaps all was not lost?

"Look," Peter said, turning toward the eastern horizon. Anna followed his gaze and gasped at the sight. Before them rose the bright silhouette of Dara. Its army of reddish spires jutted proudly into the sky. "Come on!" Peter urged, and they ran toward the city.

Just outside the gates, Solomon gathered the shepherds. They were to watch the flock while he negotiated with the townsmen. He returned later with good news. They had sold a band of sheep and half as many goats. He held a pouch full of coins. "Cull the herd and you will be paid," he told them.

The shepherds worked quickly to separate the purchased animals. Akbar mixed a bowl of yellowish dye while the others led the sheep, single file, into a sheepfold. As the animals paraded by, Rahim dipped the end of his staff into the dye and tapped the back of every tenth sheep, thus ensuring an accurate count. When they were done, Anna helped to usher the animals through the gates.

The shepherds then gathered to receive their due from Solomon's pouch. When he came to Anna, Solomon said, "Open your hand." She did. And into her palm he placed three gold coins. When he moved on, she lifted the money to her eyes.

Was it truly hers?

It was unimaginable.

"Are you going to spend that or eat it?" Peter mocked. "Come on, I want to show you something!"

Anna locked her fingers tight around the coins and followed. As they prepared to enter the gates, an old woman accosted them. "Alms for the poor! Alms for a leper!" she wheezed. Anna leapt back at the sight of her. Her skin was mottled with pus-filled sores that emitted a foul odor. A young man, similarly afflicted, lingered behind her. Saddened by the woman's misfortune, Anna opened the hand that held her coins. But before she could offer them, Peter grabbed her arm and pulled her through the gates. "Save your coins," he whispered. "God has cursed her kind."

Anna had turned to rebuke him when the city's frenzy struck her senses. Her eyes widened at the festival of sights and sounds. In one corner, a group of men dressed in long blue djellabahs stood arguing among themselves. In another, a woman and her daughter spun wool onto a twirling wooden ball. In every open space, vendors under thatched roofs sold vegetables, fruits, grains, and charms. Beyond these, fortune-tellers and thieves loitered in shady alleyways.

Anna felt the coins growing hot in her palm. Before she had time to choose a direction, Peter gave one of his coins to a vendor selling sugary dates stuffed with sweet cheese. He took a handful and offered one to Anna. Her teeth bit into the treat and hummed at its sweetness.

The sound of a lyre, plucked and melodic, floated through the air. Anna turned to search out the sound's source and spotted a craftsman demonstrating the instrument. She soon found herself at the man's feet, listening.

The lyre maker looked down. "See?" he said to his customer. "Even this boy knows expert work when he sees it!"

Anna took a step back, afraid he had seen through her disguise. To her relief, he merely grunted and resumed his playing.

She then turned to rejoin Peter. But he was gone. She ran from vendor to vendor, but could not find him. Her searching led her back to the stall where the mother and daughter were spinning yarn. All about them rose tall stacks of folded fabrics. Some of the material was coarse and pale, some glistened with a fine sheen and rich color. A crowd of women filled the stall. They shouted prices and insults.

Anna slipped inside and ran her hand over a bolt of thick fabric.

"That would make a fine shepherd's tunic," a woman's voice said. It was the mother. She lifted the fabric to Anna's shoulders and began sizing her up. Twists of wool, like fluffy bracelets, rolled up the woman's forearms. A wooden spool, on which she was winding the fluff into yarn, dangled at her wrist.

"How old are you? Ten or eleven?" she guessed. Without waiting for an answer, she said, "You are about my son's size. Wait here." She disappeared between the stacks. Anna looked at the other women. They averted their gaze, out of respect, and continued browsing in silence. Anna noticed their reaction and felt a sense of power rush through her.

The mother returned with a rugged tunic folded over her arm. The material was tough but pleasing to the touch. It had never been worn. "Put this on," she said.

"Oh no," Anna said, stepping away, the rush of her disguise suddenly deflating. "I could not."

The mother looked the boy up and down. "Bashful, are you?" She put the tunic in Anna's arms and motioned toward the fabric wall. "You can go behind there. Though I doubt you have anything we have not seen!"

Blushing, Anna stepped behind the wall. She could hear her heart pounding in her ears.

Everyone thinks I am a boy. Even the women*!*

It was one thing not to have the shepherds notice, but entirely another to have her own kind equally deceived.

Even more surprising than the potency of her disguise was how good it was beginning to feel. And how natural.

With haste she removed her clothes and slipped the tunic over her head. The weight of the material rooted her body. When she re-emerged, the other women struggled to avert their gazes, but could not.

"Great Moses!" the mother said. "How handsome you are!"

Anna's cheeks grew warm. Her green eyes sparkled.

Peter burst into the stall waving a hand-carved flute. "Look what I bought!" he cheered. He then froze, captivated by his friend's transformation.

"Wait," the mother insisted and went to retrieve a square of polished tin that she used as a mirror. Anna held the reflective metal at arm's length and angled it up and down.

"Is it not a handsome tunic?" the mother asked Peter.

Anna held her own gaze in the shiny metal surface. She marveled at the new person she had become. The ghost, no doubt, of her brother. She imagined returning to her mother. And the pride that would melt across her face.

The mother watched Anna with a sharp eye. "Young man, if you would tell me please, what is your name?"

Anna's eyes bore into her own image, memorizing her appearance, absorbing it, knowing it. She felt a rush enter her blood and a sense of destiny galvanize her bones. Staring straight into her own eyes, she answered, "My name is Jesus."

Peter's mouth dropped. "Of course! Of *course*!" he cried, shaking the flute at his friend. "You will tell your name to a complete stranger, but not to *me*!"

The mother held still. Her eyes narrowed. "Where are you from, Jesus?" she asked.

Jesus said nothing. He was matching his chosen name to the face before him. He was being born, a father's only son, right before their eyes.

"He is from Nazareth. A carpenter's son," Peter said, recalling the morning the strange boy had been sold to them. He slapped Jesus on the back. "Look at him," he teased. "He is falling in love with himself!"

"Jesus of Nazareth," the mother whispered. She frowned and held out her palm. "That will be three shekels," she said.

PART TWO

SHEPHERD

CHAPTER 5

Somewhere in the Middle East—12 A.D.

Jesus stood quietly on a hill, balancing on one leg. Time had added length to his body. The hem of his tunic, once at his shins, hung just above his knees. In the two years since joining the shepherds, he had outgrown Peter by several inches, despite his lesser years. Along with the increase in height had come a new adolescent vigor that showed itself in the swelling knots of muscle at his calves and biceps.

When a broad-winged hawk flew overhead, Jesus lifted a hand alongside his mouth and called out in the bird's throaty cry. Hearing the sound, the creature tipped a wing mid-flight. Jesus cheered at its response. Though it had not been entirely fooled, it had hesitated. And, given that the long solitary hours of shepherding provided ample time for him to practice, Jesus felt certain that the fidelity of his mimicry would soon convince the birds themselves.

Below him, the animals appeared calm and healthy. But Jesus knew that was not so. One of his sheep was sick. Following behind the animals, he had studied the piles of pellets in the tall grass. A few were runny, indicating illness. From Solomon he had learned to observe the sheep's excrement as a way of gauging the flock's health. "You can look a sheep in the eyes all day long and never know if it is sick," he had said. "But what it leaves behind always reveals the truth."

Unable to locate the sickly sheep, Jesus let his eyes drift toward the west where the sun was folding her vermilion robes along the horizon. Having traveled slowly to track the unhealthy animal, he was far behind the main flock. He paused to slip open his tunic and relieve himself. He did so standing. It had taken him many months to perfect the technique but, out of desperation, he had mastered it. From behind, he looked like any other young boy urinating in the desert.

Without warning, he saw the lead sheep make an unexpected turn to the south, luring the flock astray. Jesus dropped his tunic and drew his sling. To an outsider, his weapon would have seemed unremarkable. Nothing more than a flap of leather held at either end by cords of rope. But with careful and constant practice, he had become an expert in its use and could hit a target no bigger than a fist from a hundred yards away.

Crack! A stone ricocheted off his shinbone. Jesus yelped in confusion.

Had he shot himself?

"Gotcha!" Peter cried, laughing from a distance.

Jesus scowled at his trickery. With animal speed, he loaded his sling and took up pursuit. Light and swift on his feet, it did not take him long to corner Peter against a bank of cypress trees. Finding themselves in a standoff, the two took cover and fired stones at each other with speed enough to sting, but not pierce, the skin.

"Ow!" cried Peter when a stone ricocheted off his elbow.

Jesus rolled on the ground in mock agony. "I am hit! I am done!" he cried.

The two fell into laughing at their antics.

Then Peter slipped free of the trees and sunk to his heels. His breathing came tight and fast.

"You have overdone it," Jesus said, alarmed at his friend's shallow inhalations. For the first time in a long while he thought of Zahra and wished he had learned the cure she had applied to Daniel when he had experienced difficulty breathing.

Peter held up a hand. "It will be better soon," he said. Eventually his breath returned. He drew a generous mouthful of air and asked, "Why have you moved so slowly today? I have composed a dozen new songs in the time it has taken you," he said, running his fingers along the flute at his waist.

"One of my sheep is sick," Jesus said. He then asked, "How is the pregnant ewe in your flock?"

"She, too, is slow," Peter said. "But her teats have not fallen, so there is time. Maybe I shall compose another dozen songs," he added, wryly.

Jesus frowned. The ewe's impending labor made him anxious. "Let me see her," he said.

Peter shook his head. "It is getting dark. We have to hurry if we are to make camp. And Solomon will be angered if I am late preparing our meal."

Jesus closed his eyes. He returned to the day his own mother was to give birth. Her bending in agony. Clutching at the doorway. The sudden splash between her legs. It had been a long time since he had let himself remember.

"Please," he urged. "I want to see her."

Peter rolled his eyes. He knew his friend to be stubborn when he set his mind to something. "All right then, come along," he said. "But let us hurry!"

They found the ewe lying on her side, heaving. Thick ringlets of wool rose and fell with her labored breathing. Her long ears drooped from her head in opposite directions. Her back hooves scraped at the air. Her eyes were wide with expectation.

Peter stared in shock at the sudden change in her condition.

"It is tonight," Jesus said.

Peter moaned. Knowing the time for games was over, he set about gathering sticks to build a fire. Together the two boys sat to drink tea and wait.

While the steam billowed from their cups, Peter's gaze shifted frequently to Jesus. He noticed how the light was dusting his copper skin with gold.

"How did you know she would be giving birth?" he asked, impressed by his friend's judgment.

Jesus shrugged. "I am not sure. Just an intuition, I guess." He considered telling Peter about watching his mother. Then decided against it. Instead, he said, "My family kept goats. Maybe I learned something from watching them."

Peter nodded. Jesus rarely spoke of his family or his childhood. But, since Peter did not wish to speak further of his, he never prodded.

After a moment, Peter let out a snort. "You know, if I did not like you so much, I would probably be jealous!" he confessed.

"Jealous? Of what?" Jesus asked, bewildered.

Peter tossed a stone. "Because in just two years you have already become a better shepherd than I will ever be," he said. Wagging his head, he added, "It took me *at least* two years to learn the signals and calls. Not to mention gaining the animals' trust. But, for whatever reason, you seem to come about such things naturally. Even crusty old Akbar has admitted to your skill!"

Jesus sipped his tea and shrugged. He knew his friend's words were true, though he was unsure from where his gift arose. Still, he did not wish to rub salt in Peter's wound. Besides, in observing Solomon and the other shepherds at work he realized there was a great deal left for him to learn.

The ewe thrashed and kicked the air.

Watching the delivery unfold, the boys drifted into separate thoughts. Soon the sun had sunk halfway below the horizon, frosting the landscape with magical light.

When the birth did not advance, Peter grew agitated. "I knew I should have hurried the flock along," he said.

"For what purpose?" Jesus asked.

"So that we would have made camp before she started with . . . *this*."

Jesus nodded toward the ewe. "You do not like watching it, do you?" he asked.

Peter screwed up his face. "It turns my stomach," he said. He poked a stick into the fire. The truth was, the mess and intimacy of birth aroused visceral memories of the things in his past he wished to forget. "I find everything about the female animal repulsive," he confessed. "The stench, the stickiness . . ." He shivered at the thought.

Jesus looked up in surprise. He was about to dispute his friend's attitude when Peter swatted the fire violently with his stick. Flames skittered across the ground until they were extinguished. "We have waited long enough. The others must be at least an hour ahead by now," he grumbled. "Let us join our flocks and drive them to camp."

"But what about the ewe?"

Peter shook his head. "Leave her. She cannot be helped," he said. "Soon it will be dark," he added, a slight wheeze clipping his words.

Jesus rose to his feet. "I cannot leave her," he said.

"What?"

"She will die without our help."

A wolf howled in the distance.

Peter gestured toward the sound. "No matter what we do, she will not survive. Nor will *we*!"

Jesus held his ground. "That is a chance I am willing to take."

"Do not be an idiot!" Peter blurted, angered by his friend's tenacity. "Let us move on!"

When Jesus shook his head, Peter reached out and grabbed him by the collar.

Jesus recoiled. Being larger and stronger, he easily freed himself.

Peter lunged again and, in a flash, Jesus drew back and loaded his sling. He cocked his arm and took aim at his friend. "I am not going," he said, his voice steady. His heart pounding.

Peter froze in shock. "This is insane," he cried. "Solomon will be furious!"

"Lend me your water," Jesus said.

Peter made again to protest but the ewe bawled between them. He looked down at the sweating animal, then up at the loaded sling. He groaned in frustration and tossed Jesus his skin of water. He then spun and snapped his olive branch at the sheep. As he drove them down the slope, he glared over his shoulder. "Get it done quickly!" he shouted.

Hearing the clop-clop of departing hooves, the ewe struggled to retake her feet. Jesus laid his staff between her legs to immobilize her. "Easy now," he whispered. "I am here."

The sheep, like Peter, relented.

Darkness came. Stars glittered with ancient colors overhead. Cypress trees transformed into shadowy creatures. Crickets trilled at the moon, pausing only at the crunch of paws on dry grass. A wolf howled in the distance, beckoning others to join her.

Jesus opened his ears. In his time among the shepherds, he had learned how to listen large. How to thresh the sounds that forebode danger from the night's ceaseless symphony. Beneath him, the ewe struggled to unburden herself. But something was wrong. She had strained against the new life inside her for several hours without success. Her eyes stared wide, her tongue draped along the dirt.

The wolf howled again. Closer this time. Frightened by the sound, the ewe kicked at the air and bleated repeatedly. As Jesus restrained her, he noticed a shiny black hoof, a rear one, protruding from her opening. A pearly sack sheathed its hock. Jesus took in a quick breath.

The lamb was coming out backwards!

He would have to act quickly if he was to save both lives.

But what should he do first?

On two separate occasions, Solomon had asked Jesus to assist him while he righted a crooked birth.

But he had only watched, not participated!

The young shepherd knelt slowly, swallowing down his rising panic.

Solomon and his men sat about the fire, their bellies rumbling. Their patience dwindling.

Having heard Peter's report, they broke into quarreling. The men had grown more short-tempered than usual due to the fact that their food was running low. It having been over two weeks since they had visited a village to replenish their supplies.

Gazing into the dark, Akbar said wistfully, "The boy is too stubborn for his own good."

The others nodded.

Just beyond the circle of the firelight, Judas sat alone smoking a pungent and debilitating herb, his head wobbling after each tug on the pipe.

Leaving the men to their arguments, Solomon rose from the fire and went to his friend. When he approached, the inebriated shepherd hissed, "He should have arrived by now."

Solomon nodded and wrung his hands.

Judas threw down his pipe with a growl. "I will go find him," he said.

"No," Solomon commanded, pressing his staff down on the shepherd's shoulder. "That would only make the situation more dangerous," he whispered. He looked behind them to make sure the others had not overheard.

Judas frowned. "Then send Rahim. Or Mathias. Send *someone*!"

Solomon raised a hand. "I cannot ask another shepherd to risk his life," he said. "If I did, it would raise suspicions." He glared at Judas. "I would have sent *you*. But you are in no condition to help anyone."

Judas's eyes flew open. Solomon's words had struck him like a fist. Ashamed, he snatched up his pipe and staggered into the dark.

Solomon's head fell at his departure. He wished he had held his tongue. He knew Judas to be loyal and trustworthy beyond question. His past actions had repeatedly proven his valor. Which was why, when the time was right for Jesus to undertake the final segment of his journey, Solomon had decided it should be Judas who escorted him through its perils.

If only Judas could keep himself together until then . . .

At that moment, a fearsome wailing leapt from the darkness beyond. Solomon rushed back to the group. The men remained still as stone, listening as the howling came again.

Akbar raised his head, reading the tonal cries. "They are circling their prey," he said.

Peter looked up and caught a flash of fear crossing Solomon's eyes. He was shocked. He had never known Solomon to be afraid of anyone, or anything.

How he now wished he had not abandoned his friend!

The wolves' howling rose again, its intensity quickening.

Some of the shepherds bowed their heads. Others scanned the horizon in silence.

Working quickly, Jesus threw himself to the ground behind the ewe. He fluted his fingers and scooped a hand into the sheep's birth canal, as he had seen Solomon do. He then shimmied his arm deep inside her. He closed his eyes, trying to see the unborn body with his fingers. The ewe's muscles contracted around his forearm, numbing it. He followed down along the damp, familiar shape of the lamb's rear leg. He grabbed hold of its rump. He waited until the ewe relaxed between contractions. When he felt the pressure subside, he pushed the newborn back into the mother. The ewe panted with exertion.

Jesus closed his eyes. He thought of his own mother. "Please help me," he whispered. Bit by bit he began to realign the unborn lamb, fighting membrane and muscle, turning it slowly inside the womb. The ewe's side caved and bulged with his manipulations. When he had rotated the lamb fully around, he sat up, braced his legs on the mother's backside, and pulled with all his strength.

The ewe's mouth opened wide and soundless as a wet knob started to emerge from behind her. A pair of shiny black hooves broke first through the sack of blood and water. Then the forelegs. Elbows. A head. And, finally, an entire body, slick and trembling, slipped into the night. It was female.

Jesus cradled the newborn and gave a shout for joy. His jubilation was cut short when the ewe's insides flooded out behind her, gleaming like wet gems in a growing pool of blood. He sat wide-eyed, holding the damp lamb in his lap. The ewe gasped for breath, her side contracting with spasms. Jesus stared in disbelief. In all the births he had witnessed, he had never seen the ewe expel her guts. He did not know what to do. And her blood kept spilling, the stain spreading fast across the ground.

In a moment, it was over.

Tears welled in the young shepherd's eyes, pooling thousands of stars into a single blaze just beyond his eyelashes. He felt the lamb's tiny head drop against his knee. He looked down and was shocked to discover that it had stopped breathing. Trying to remember what he had seen Solomon do, he wiped the stringy mucus from its muzzle and held it upside down by its back legs. He then spun in place, twirling the lamb as high above his head as he could, hoping the force of motion would draw the mucus and water from its lungs.

Jesus felt his heart lift when, after only a few moments, the animal's legs begin to kick. At this he slowed his pace and gently lowered the creature to the ground. The lamb coughed and shook its nose, slinging mucus and water into the air. When its airway cleared, it found Jesus's fingers and began to suckle.

"No, no, there is nothing there," the shepherd said. He brought the lamb to its lifeless mother and placed it before her. The lamb gently rut its head into her belly, drawing the milk, which it sucked noisily from her teats. Jesus sat back on his heels and marveled at the mother's power, even in death, to nourish.

As the lamb continued to drink, Jesus worked his eyes deep into the nest of stars overhead. Nearby, obscured by the darkness, he heard a second pack of wolves cast its howls into the night air. The first pack echoed in reply. The wails floated like eerie ribbons wrapping about themselves. The predators were closing in.

Jesus shuddered and gazed down.

The ewe lay against the dirt, her one eye wide and unblinking. Having failed to save her, he could not bear to leave her to the wolves. With tears streaming down his cheeks, he slipped his knife from its sheath.

Before wielding his blade, he gave thanks to the ewe, and to his own mother, for their sacrifice. Then, with a heavy heart, he bent to his difficult work, praying he could finish before the wolves attacked.

Keeping watch on a hilltop above, Rahim spotted a slow-moving figure emerging from the dark. Certain that a lone wolf had drifted from the pack, the shepherd leapt to his feet. He prepared to shout out a warning. Then paused. As the figure drew closer, its shape began to crystallize. And, to Rahim's surprise, the figure had not four legs, but two.

"The boy arrives!" he yelled.

Dumbstruck, the shepherds leapt to their feet. Together they watched in disbelief as Jesus lumbered toward them, emerging like a spirit from the dark. The young shepherd's shoulders bent under the weight of the ewe's glistening, freshly skinned carcass. His legs trembled beneath its weight. His tunic hung loosely, splattered with blood.

"What in the name of . . . ?" someone whispered.

When he reached the fire, Jesus bent and let the carcass slip to the ground. It landed with a muffled thud.

Peter stared in awe, then rushed to embrace his friend. "You did it!" he cried. "You vanquished the wolves!"

Exhilarated, the other men circled the young shepherd, slapping his back and tousling his hair.

Judas appeared suddenly. His eyes, hazy and red, flitted from Jesus to the ewe's body and back again, confounded by the sight.

When Solomon arrived, the circle opened to receive him. He looked over his youngest shepherd. Saw his pale expression. The tears in his tunic. The gashes running along his cheeks and hands. He then saw the lump at his stomach, settling just above his belt. Mathias saw it, too. "The boy is with child!" he cried.

The shepherds stared in puzzlement as the lump began to wriggle and rise. Soon a small black head poked out of Jesus's collar.

When the lamb let out a weary bleat, the men laughed aloud.

Solomon stepped forward smiling and laid a hand on the boy's shoulder. A deep knowing passed between them, from one motherless child to another. "You have done well," he said.

Relieved by the young shepherd's safe arrival, the men's attention quickly returned to their gnawing hunger. One by one they circled the fresh meat.

"There is not enough to feed us all," Mathias said, sniffing at the carcass. "How shall we divide it?"

Rahim's eyes fell to the lamb. "The newborn will slow us," he said. "We should divide it, too." He made for the tiny sheep.

His nerves stretched taut, Jesus sprang in anger and shoved the shepherd back. Something about his efforts to save the ewe, and his battle with the wolves, had unleashed a new ferocity inside him. Rahim gasped, falling backward. "Curse you!" he breathed, regaining his balance. He then lunged at the young shepherd's throat.

Jesus struggled to fend him off, cradling the lamb close to his heart.

Enraged, a glassy-eyed Judas slipped his dagger from its sheath and bolted into the fracas. Butting his way toward the young shepherd, he rose before him, brandishing his weapon to keep Rahim and the others back.

"Hold still!" Solomon commanded, seeing the situation spinning out of control. Thinking quickly, he turned to Peter. "Throw the meat on the fire and we shall each enjoy a mouthful," he told him.

"No," Jesus said.

Everyone turned.

"I will make a meal for us," he said, his gaze steady as the rocks.

Solomon's eyebrows rose at the boy's sudden declaration.

"But you do not know how to cook!" Akbar protested.

"If what I make does not feed us well, I will divide my earnings among you," Jesus replied.

Solomon took a long look at his youngest shepherd. After a moment he said, "So be it."

The others backed away.

Peter joined Jesus near the fire. The crackle of the flames rose between them.

"I am sorry . . . that I left you . . ." Peter began, but could not finish.

When Jesus said nothing, Peter gathered himself and whispered, "What happened out there? We heard the wolves—"

"Cut the meat into small chunks," Jesus told him. He did not wish to speak of the dark. Or the wolves. Instead, he wanted to appease the men's hunger so they would leave him, and his lamb, alone.

Ashamed, Peter nodded and turned to his task.

Taking a deep breath, Jesus let his mind return to his childhood. To preparing meals with his mother. His hands began to move with the memory. No longer thinking, he filled a pot with water and set about boiling all the leftovers they had—bones, browned vegetables, a handful of rice, fruit rinds. When the broth boiled, he added the chunks of meat and cooked them until they were tender.

Peter watched and was amazed.

The men smacked their lips as they circled the fire, feasting on the thick stew. Later, their bellies satisfied, they cheered Jesus. "He has fed the masses with a single loaf of bread!" they joked. Drunk with satisfaction, no one thought to ask how he had learned to prepare a meal.

Solomon noted the sand and sweat caking the boy's arms and legs. "Come with me," he said, getting to his feet. "I know a small spring where you can bathe." When Jesus hesitated, he added, "You may bring the lamb."

Jesus held still as Solomon poured ladles of water over his head and scrubbed his limbs with a cloth. He wondered if the elder shepherd thought it strange that he did not disrobe. But if Solomon did, he did not show it.

Solomon took a deep breath. "Tonight you faced grave adversity," he said, "and I feel certain you fought bravely."

Jesus looked up. Awash with pride.

Solomon continued to scrub him. "But, my brother, there was no need to fight."

Jesus's mouth fell open in disbelief. In anger. "But the wolves . . . I had to stop them—!" he began to protest.

Solomon shook his head. "You had to stop them because you did not seek to understand them."

Jesus frowned.

He had saved the lamb's life! And brought back the ewe!

Why now did he suddenly feel chastised?

"I do not understand," he grumbled.

Undeterred by the young shepherd's resistance, Solomon went on. "Wolves are powerful creatures," he said. "They therefore respect power."

"But that is why I fought!"

"No. You fought because you were at their mercy."

At his words, Jesus recalled the terrifying confrontation—the closing circle, the ferocious snarls, the snapping teeth. He had been lucky to escape.

His tunic drenched, Jesus began to shiver.

Solomon handed him a dry cloth. "I have a powerful secret to share with you," he said. "A shepherd's secret."

Jesus wrapped himself in the cloth and kept silent.

"The time to protect yourself and your sheep from a wolf begins when the animal is at a distance."

Chilled and exhausted, Jesus found himself struggling to understand.

"Remember this. The next time you encounter wolves, and you are injured or have something to protect, do not pray to avoid them. Instead, *call out to them.* In their language. Just as you try to call the birds."

"What?" Jesus gasped.

Was he suggesting that he should intentionally draw *the wolves?*

Solomon smiled. "Yes! And only after you have invited them close—on their terms—do you show your strength. If you do this, you become not prey, but a member of the pack. It is then and only then that you load your sling. And fire your shots. Coming from a powerful member of the clan, this admonishment will subdue them. And you will see then how they respect you. How they fall back and await your next command."

Jesus stared in wonderment. "Is that the secret?"

"Yes. And having been in a situation like yours many times, I have used it to survive. Never once have I had to flee for my life."

Jesus gazed up at the stars. He took note of Solomon's teaching. Though, secretly, he could not deny the rush he had felt upon realizing that his new identity granted him permission to use force. And this privilege he hoped to explore more fully.

Solomon put his arm around the young shepherd. Holding him close, he sensed that something inside the child had changed. That a shift had occurred toward self-assurance. Toward deeper strength and confidence.

Perhaps he would be ready sooner than Solomon had initially believed?

Beneath them, the lamb bleated and wove between their legs.

Jesus knelt to lift her.

Solomon chuckled. "And what will you call your little one?"

Jesus gazed at the animal draped in his arms. He rubbed a finger along the fuzz drying between her ears. He thought for a minute and waited for the answer to come. When it did, he said, "I will call her Anna."

Solomon nodded. "Anna," he whispered. He gazed into the distance and said, "Have you ever heard the story of Anna of Asher?"

Jesus shook his head.

"She lived day and night in a far-off cave. Praying and fasting in worship." He paused for a moment, then said, "So great was her faith that she was able to cultivate the gift of foresight. Of prophesy." He took Jesus's eyes into his own. "And you know what she foretold?"

"No."

Solomon smiled. He remembered his mother telling him the story of how Anna of Asher had predicted the return of a force to the earth. A force that would reawaken humankind and restore the balance of The Way. Solomon's eyes fell again on the young shepherd. A look of temptation rose and then dropped suddenly from his face, as if he had decided midstream to withhold a great treasure. "Anna is a good name," was all he said, nodding as if someone had spoken wisely.

Later that night, after the others had fallen asleep, Solomon walked through the camp to where Jesus slept. Keeping still, he let his eyes wander over the boy's features. After a moment, he sunk to his knees until he was close enough to see the slow pumping of the vein embedded in Jesus's neck. Careful not to awaken him, he let one hand fall toward the boy's throat. Parting his collar, he reached inside and found the copper medallion. With great care, he pressed his fingertips along its face. One by one, he divined the raised lines of the great sycamore. Even in their silence, they spoke to him, like a missive from his mother.

Feeling suddenly uplifted, he gazed deep into the sky and scanned its silvery lace. As he watched, a comet streaked across the dark, soundless, as if someone had dipped a quill into light and sketched it.

In that moment, he allowed himself to rejoice at the boy's survival. For he knew that his facing the wolves alone could have ended in tragedy.

And though glad for the boy's success, the elder shepherd felt troubled by another concern. He wondered if the boy's reckless need to protect others, and his willingness to risk his own safety to do so, might endanger his journey—or his future.

But Solomon also knew, intimately, the root of the young shepherd's desire. For he, too, carried the unbearable shame of having failed to protect his mother from harm. And, for this reason, he doubted that he himself could alleviate the tendency within his charge.

Repairing such damage, he thought, was better left to the Sisters.

CHAPTER 6

South of the Sea of Galilee—14 A.D.

Wind drove across a flat, open field, rolling broad waves through a sea of scarlet anemones. The shepherds led their flocks through the brilliance, clicking their tongues to keep the animals moving. It had been a good year. Both the shepherds and their charges had put on weight. With the annual celebration of Passover approaching, they made their way toward Jerusalem, where they would find a ready market for their sheep. And a world of sensual delights for their travel-weary souls.

Peter leaned against his staff and stared northward. He was excited by the prospect of the city. He told Jesus what he remembered: the chaos, the streets littered with smells, carts spilling with teas and herbs and unusual sweets, musicians on every corner, and the Temple's looming columns. He could not wait to share the adventure with his friend.

Later in the day, the shepherds gathered at the edge of the sea. It was the largest body of water Jesus had ever seen. It was clear in the shallows but toward the middle its color darkened to silver blue. Every so often, the splash of an overzealous fish rippled the jewel-like surface. In the surrounding hills, men tended terraced olive groves and barley fields with hoes and sickles. Oxen stumbled through rich, brown soil. Women, veiled in long, black shawls, balanced jars of water on their heads. Children scampered after butterflies. Birds darted between trees. Flowers carpeted the hillsides. The rich smells of earth and salt and fish rode across the water in every direction.

Hot from their travels, the shepherds stripped off their tunics and dove into the sea to cool and wash their bodies. Jesus remained on the shore, gathering wood for a fire. The men taunted him, trying to get him into the water. Mathias and Peter leapt onto Rahim's shoulders, pretending to drown him. "Jesus!" they shouted. "Come save Rahim!"

But Jesus waved off the challenge. "Rahim can save himself," he said.

Peter snickered at his friend from the water. "Let us grab him," he whispered to the others.

Judas, who was standing nearby, let go a loud whistle. Upon hearing the signal, Solomon shouted, "Jesus! Go to the fishermen and get our evening meal."

Relieved at his narrow escape, Jesus bolted down to the shore, where he found two fishermen standing by their wooden boat. A haul of small, shiny *mousht* snapped inside their nets. Jesus returned to camp carrying a full sack. The shepherds gathered around the flames and sharpened sticks. They ran the pointed ends through the fishes' mouths and lay them across the flames. As the flesh sizzled, the men's banter turned lascivious.

"I must find a woman to lie with," Rahim told the group.

"I must find two!" Mathias boasted. "It has been a long time."

"Perhaps not long *enough* for some women!" Akbar shouted.

The men howled.

Jesus and Peter sat next to each other, listening to the men's lurid talk.

Lowering his voice so that the others would not hear, Peter said, "Why would anyone want to lie with a woman? They are nothing but clots of filth and treachery."

Jesus gaped at his friend. "Brother? Why such anger? They speak of women, not serpents!" he joked, hoping to lighten Peter's mood.

"Women *are* serpents!" Peter roared. "Who slither on their bellies and trick you into hideous acts! But what would you know about such things?" he spat. Having said this, he leapt to his feet and dashed off.

Jesus made to follow, then thought better of it. Having witnessed his friend's tempers, and knowing them to be short-lived, he felt certain it would not be long before Peter returned, acting as if nothing had happened.

Hidden in a copse of trees, Peter felt his breath tighten as he constricted around his darkest secret. Up until now, it had remained safely buried. But something about the men and their talk had loosened its grave. And he could feel the awful rot seeping out.

He wanted to tell Jesus. Wanted to reveal what had happened when the woman his father had laid with in a dark and sour-smelling place had come to find him. And the unspeakable things she had done with him. Even at six years of age, he had known what they did was evil. But he could not stop her. And when he tried to tell his mother, she did not believe him.

Soon after, his father had stopped speaking to him. Then, without any explanation, his father had sent him away with the shepherds, telling him never to return.

When Peter had recovered his breath, he peered through the branches and saw Jesus whittling an olive switch. He thought once more of confessing. Of sharing his secret. Then he imagined the look of disgust that would flood his friend's face.

How could he have been so weak as to let a woman overpower him? Jesus would demand to know.

And, to his profound shame, Peter had no answer.

The walls of Jerusalem rose before them like fallen giants regaining their feet. Jesus had never seen such massive structures.

Solomon leaned on the back of a sheep to deliver the day's schedule. "No sheep is to be sold within the gates, lest we owe tax to the Romans," he said.

The men nodded. Jesus scanned their faces and noticed one missing. Judas was nowhere to be found.

"Once the animals are sold, we will be free to enter the city," Solomon continued. "I will take charge of whatever flock remains."

"How long do we stay?" Mathias asked.

"We will gather before sunrise tomorrow," Solomon answered. "Those who are not with us will be left behind."

Jesus turned to Peter and whispered, "We have only one day?"

His friend shrugged. "Better make the most of it then!" he said with a wink.

When the last sheep was sold, Solomon divided the coins among the shepherds. Jesus and Peter stretched out their hands and had their palms filled with copper. "Exchange these inside the city," he told them. The boys jumped in excitement and bounded down the path leading to the great bronze gates. Anna nickered and followed at their heels.

Closer to the city, they heard shouts and whistles and the grinding of stone. From behind, a group of dark men, clad in loincloths, led a team of oxen pulling an enormous cart. On the cart's bed, a gigantic block of limestone had been laid on its side and anchored with thick ropes. As the stone's shadow passed, the crowd parted to allow it passage. Jesus held his breath and Anna crouched in fear as the cart's great wheels rolled past, crushing rocks under its round, intrepid feet.

"How much for your lamb?" a man shouted when the crowd reassembled itself.

"Not for sale!" Jesus shouted back. He pushed forward, barely able to keep his eyes on Peter. The air was thick with smoke and the scent of burning flesh.

Just inside the gate, an altar rose atop marble steps. Priests were taking lambs, pigeons, and other animals from hundreds of supplicants who wanted their sacrifice roasted in the Temple. The animals' heads dangled in the men's arms, gaping red smiles slit neatly across their throats. The altar stairs were awash with blood and the sticky magenta footprints left by the priests.

The sounds of chanting and the clanking of ongoing stonework mixed in the air and reverberated off the walls looming above. Scanning the ramparts, Jesus noticed Roman soldiers posted on every turret. Their presence made him nervous. He whistled for Anna to come closer.

"Give this man your money," Peter told him as they stood before a wooden table on which sat a brass scale.

"What will I do with a scale?" Jesus asked, misunderstanding.

Peter laughed. "No, you fool! Give him your money so he can exchange it. They do not accept shekels here." Peter dropped a handful of coins onto one side of the scale.

The man tossed small silver coins, one at a time, into the opposite basket until the scale balanced out. Peter then scooped the silver coins into his hand.

"But now you have less," Jesus observed. "He has cheated you!" Letting his anger slip free, he pushed his face close to the man's. "Give back what is his!" he yelled, gripping the top of the table.

Peter struggled to pull him back, impressed by his friend's strength.

"Enough!" the grizzled moneychanger spat, pointing to the line forming behind them. "Tell your brother to give me his shekels or leave my table!"

After receiving further explanation from Peter, Jesus relented. When they left with their new coins, Peter poked him in the ribs. "So you do not like moneychangers," he laughed. "For a minute, I thought you were going to overturn his table."

Jesus laughed, too, his temper waning. "He thought we were brothers!"

"Are we not?" Peter asked. "If not by blood, then certainly in spirit!"

A woman covered from head to toe in dark fabric floated by carrying a tray of pomegranates.

"I am hungry," Jesus said. "Let us find something to eat."

An instrument, like a metal horn, sounded from above.

"First let us pray," Peter said.

Jesus frowned. "But we have so little time," he said. He did not want to pray. He wanted to explore!

Peter threw an arm around his friend. "Do not look so distressed. You will have your fill of this city, and all its hidden treasures. I promise!"

The two shepherds arrived at the bottom of the Temple's great marble staircase. Still irritated, but unable to deter Peter, Jesus lifted Anna onto his shoulders and began to climb toward the sacred building. At the top was an entrance. Inside, Jesus saw groups of women, their heads bowed in homage. He moved to join them.

Peter grabbed him by the shoulder. "Not there!" he scoffed. "That is the *women's* area," he said. "Follow me."

At a second entrance, Jesus smelled sweetness in the air and heard the wooden chanting of male voices. The boys removed their keffiyehs and prepared to enter along with a crowd of men. Without warning, a blond-headed priest stepped in front of Jesus and drew him aside. "No animals inside the Temple," he said.

Jesus pulled himself from the priest's grip. "But she is with me," he challenged.

"That may be true," the priest said, "but the Lord has forbidden animals inside His house."

Jesus scowled at his assailant. "But does God not allow lambs inside the Temple in sacrifice?" he asked, having seen the animals' bodies roasting on pyres.

Peter winced. He knew nothing good would come of questioning a priest. Especially during Passover.

"Of course!" the priest answered. "As offerings. To return to God what is rightfully His."

"Then, by your reasoning, a lamb is fit to be in God's house only when it is dead and cooked?" Jesus asked, goading him.

A group of men on their way inside turned to listen, curious that an adolescent, a simple shepherd at that, would question a priest.

Peter grew worried.

Jesus saw the crowd forming and became emboldened by the attention. Never before had so many people, so many *men*, taken notice of him. Or listened to what he had to say.

Peter leaned toward his friend. "All right, brother. You can have your way. We will pray some other time. Just follow me. And keep quiet!" he hissed, and tried to lead Jesus away.

"No, I want to know the answer," Jesus said, holding his ground. His desire to protect, to defend, overriding his reason.

Peter panicked. "Why does it *matter*?" he hissed.

Jesus ignored him.

"According to Scripture," the priest began with rising frustration, "a lamb is fit for God's house only when offered in sacrifice."

"And does the Scripture not also say that we are lambs of God?" Jesus said, recalling the topic from Peter's morning prayers.

"Yes, of course," the priest said with annoyance.

"Then are you saying that we should also be dead and cooked before entering God's house?" he asked, his wit having been sharpened on the whetstone of shepherd banter.

The crowd roared. "Here *here*!" someone shouted. There was much anger brewing against the priests whose high taxes and misuse of Temple Law had upset the faithful.

Several men patted Jesus on the back. "He is wise beyond his years!" one of them said. "The Lord shines through him!" another cried. "Let him speak!"

Jesus's heart pounded in his chest. In all his years, he had never spoken out against so powerful a figure. (And as a girl, it would have been unthinkable!)

The young priest was seething. His face gone purple. He wiped sweaty palms against his robes. He refused to have his intelligence and authority questioned by the common rabble. "What is your name?" he demanded.

"I am the same as this one," Jesus said, raising Anna from his shoulders. "I am a lamb of God."

The crowd burst into more laughter. Jesus cheered aloud, playing up the approval.

"How old are you?" the priest demanded. "You cannot be much more than twelve," he guessed, wringing his hands to contain his fury.

"If you say so," Jesus replied, not bothering to correct him.

"Then you are too young to know of what you speak, but old enough to know better," the priest said. He raised a fist and within seconds a Roman guard appeared at his side. The crowd pulled back. Peter stepped in front of Jesus.

"Remove him from the Temple!" the priest demanded.

"By your command, Caiaphas," the soldier answered.

An elderly man, bent as if forced to carry the heft of his years, reached through the crowd and gripped Jesus by his tunic. "Are you the Chosen One?" he asked. "The Messiah for whom we wait?"

Before he could answer, Jesus was dragged away. He fought to free himself, but the soldier held fast to his collar. In one swift motion, he tossed Jesus down the stairs. Peter and Anna descended after him.

"If you know what is good for you," the soldier yelled, "you will stay away from here!"

"What is good for me is *not* in there!" Jesus spouted, hoarsely.

Peter arrived and bent over his friend. "Are you hurt?" he asked, dusting him off.

Jesus struggled to regain his breath. A grin split his face. "Ha! Maybe now they will think twice before bullying a little lamb!"

Peter was appalled. "Are you mad?" he asked. "You cannot talk to a priest as if he were a fool!"

"Why not, if what he is saying is foolish?"

Aghast, Peter could find no retort. Still, he berated Jesus for his poor judgment, and for misbehaving inside the Lord's house. Secretly, though, he could not stop his blood from racing.

The two friends sought a patch of shade in which to calm their nerves and collect themselves. Then, aware that their time was dwindling, they rushed out to explore the famed Jerusalem. They listened to musicians. Drank lemon water with honey. Haggled with vendors for new sashes, keffiyehs, and sandals. They watched the builders lift marble blocks and felt the thud inside their chests when the stones dropped into place. They tasted roast pigeon, citrus fruits, unfamiliar spices, and bread soaked in scented olive oil. They listened to new languages and imitated the strange guttural sounds of exotic-looking families. They circled the city, examining each of the gigantic gates, and counting the soldiers who guarded them. Every direction held a treasure for the senses. There was danger, too—thieves waiting down narrow passageways. Corrupt vendors. Charlatans who vilified God. Plumes of oily smoke. The acrid smell of death. Whores. And drunkards. But Peter, having come across such unsavory types before, made sure to avoid them.

At the end of an alley, the boys found themselves in front of a large man with a moon-sized face. He held a short length of knotted cord before their eyes. The boys passed questioning looks between them. When their eyes were averted, the magician twisted the cord into his fist. He shook his hand five times and then released the cord with a grand gesture. To their amazement, the knots were gone!

A thin man with a long beard and a crazed look in his eyes approached from behind. "Follow me! The end is coming!" he shouted into the boys' faces. "We will all be judged! Save yourselves!" He ran off, his white linen robe billowing behind him.

Peter and Jesus stepped aside only to run headlong into another man wearing the same white linen robe. "We have sinned against the Lord! The end is near!" The boys turned again and again only to find themselves surrounded by more long-bearded men dressed in white, imploring them with wild, crazed eyes. "Save yourselves! The prophet has spoken! We have angered the Lord!"

Jesus was amazed by their tenacity. "Who are these men?" he asked.

"They are the crazy ones who live in the mountains," Peter told him. "They do not eat, or drink, and they perform secret rituals that drive them insane."

Jesus wanted to know more about the doomsayers, but was distracted by a man dressed in stripes who ran past playing a flute and tossing dates into the air. "Let us follow him!" he shouted.

Leaving behind the magician and his mysterious knotted rope, they laughed and ran in pursuit of the sweet fruits that had fallen in the wake of the man wearing stripes. The chase ended quickly, the flute player being much swifter of foot and, perhaps, intoxicated. Out of breath, the shepherd boys found themselves beneath scaffolding left behind by the stoneworkers. They climbed the narrow wooden slats and from there leapt onto a turret high above the city. Their jaws dropped at the view of the activity boiling below them. Jesus knelt and lowered Anna to the ground.

Beneath, they saw a middle-aged woman standing at the top of some steps. Her dark hair was long and braided. She wore a brilliant robe the color of ripened plum. Around her neck hung a coppery medallion amidst several chains that clinked together as she spoke. A group had assembled around her, pushing in close.

"You must not give away your power!" the woman called out, lifting her voice above the clanking of stoneworkers and donkeys. "The light you seek, the Messiah you await, is *within* you. It is *you* yourselves who are The Way!"

A buzz moved through the crowd.

"Who is she?" Jesus asked. The strange woman reminded him of Zahra.

"A charlatan," Peter sniffed. "Speaking against our Heavenly Father. Surely you know her kind? The ones who keep the old ways? Who refuse to acknowledge our God as the one true Lord?"

Jesus nodded. His hand drifted, almost unconsciously, to the medallion around his neck. Nearly seven years had passed since Zahra's murder. Yet the memory of her rose within him as if he had seen her only yesterday.

Peter snorted. "My uncle said such women gather in secret hiding places and cast evil spells on people to make them forget God." He shrugged. "Whatever they do, they are most certainly not welcome *here,*" he added. "Someone will remove her soon."

Jesus turned aside to hide his look of dismay.

Peter spat a pit down at the crowd. He drew back giggling when it ricocheted off a bystander's nose. He was preparing to spit another when a swarm of soldiers, guided by two Temple priests, suddenly lunged up the stairs toward the woman in the plum-colored robe.

Alerted to the ambush, those who had congregated around her dashed away, while others linked arms and formed a barricade between the soldiers and the woman.

A second wave of soldiers arrived, this group shoving its way into the crowd and ramming through the barricade. The air filled with screams and shouts of terror. The people struggled to keep their arms linked. They fought with fury, kicking at the soldiers and their weapons. Jesus saw one girl leap onto a soldier's back and dig her fingers into his eyes. Enraged by the resistance, the soldiers grabbed anyone they could lay hands on, men, women, children, beating them into submission with clubs and chains.

Jesus held his breath and scanned the crowd for the woman who had been speaking. But he could not find her. Soon the people's barricade broke apart. A dozen or more soldiers rushed through the gaps seeking the perpetrator.

"Seize her! Seize her now!" a priest cried out.

But when the soldiers could not find the woman, the priests threw up their hands in frustration.

Furious, the soldiers began stripping garments off the onlookers. But none was found wearing a plum-colored robe.

"She is gone!" Jesus cried.

"Who is gone?" Peter asked.

"The woman who was speaking. She has vanished!"

Amidst moans and clanking chains, the angered soldiers led away naked and bleeding onlookers.

Jesus looked on with concern. "What will happen to them?"

"To who?"

"The people they are taking away . . ."

Peter shrugged. "I hope they will be made an example of," he said and stuffed another date into his mouth.

Night fell on Jerusalem like a blanket knit with torch flames. Flickering shadows distorted faces and narrowed alleyways. The smell of burning oil weighed down the air, making it harder to breathe. Exhausted from their adventures, Peter and Jesus went to find a place to sleep. On the way, they wound through the priests' richly appointed houses, built around courtyards filled with fruit trees.

"I am thirsty," Jesus said, making his way toward a well.

"Hurry," Peter urged, "or we will not find a place to sleep."

Jesus dropped the bucket into the water. When it splashed at the bottom, he heard something move nearby. "Who is there?" he asked into the dark, keeping his voice firm. When no one answered, he crept around the well. On the far side he found a girl cowering behind the stones. "Bring the torch!" he called to Peter.

The girl flinched, afraid for her life.

"Be still," Jesus said. "We will not harm you."

Peter held the torch to the girl's face. She swiped a veil of matted hair from her eyes and faced the boys head-on. Her eyes were large with fear and laced with cunning. She was scared, but clearly not out of options. Looking her over, Jesus suddenly recognized her. She was the girl who had leapt onto the soldier's back! To protect the woman in the plum-colored robe!

Jesus recalled her bravery and felt an instant affinity with the girl. As he was remembering, her gaze fell upon him. When it did, he felt his insides spark with flame, then settle into a profound calm. Her look was not casual. But piercing. Her eyes, carved broadly in her face, shone with the silver of mirrors. Beneath the right one rested a handsome birthmark that rose and fell as an accent to her every expression.

Gazing upon the shepherd, the girl struggled to conceal her emotion. Then, despite her efforts, her lips surrendered into a smile.

Anna the lamb tentatively approached the strange girl, sniffing. She lowered her head and gently butted her knees.

Jesus swallowed with difficulty. "That is Anna," he said. "I think she likes you." He continued to stare into her silver eyes. It had been a long time since he had been so close to a girl his own age.

The girl dropped her gaze. She blushed like a garden.

Peter saw the exchange pass between them. He noted the stillness they shared and felt his chest tighten.

"What is your name?" Jesus asked.

The girl said nothing.

"We have to go," Peter growled.

"But why is she alone here at night?"

"That is not our worry," Peter said. "If it were left up to *you,* we would sleep on a dung heap!"

A door on one of the priests' houses flew open with a crack. The girl and the shepherds ducked behind the well.

A large man with a greasy face stepped into the courtyard and threw a woman into the street as if tossing out a bucket of slop. The woman landed hard but scrambled to her feet. She spun and charged back at him.

"Give me my money!" she hollered. "Your master owes me!"

The large man threw her back down with little effort. Again, she rose and charged. Again, the man threw her down. He seemed to be making a game of it.

Above them, Jesus noticed the Temple priest with golden hair who had accosted them peering down from a balcony. He was busy retying the sash around his robe.

Across the courtyard, the woman leapt onto the large man's back, sinking her teeth into his ear, poking at his eyes. "Give me my money!" she screamed.

The man roared in pain and charged into the courtyard, the woman clinging to his flesh like a burr. Enraged, he sunk to his knees and rolled over to crush her against a low wall. He forced his weight onto her again and again. She groaned and gasped for breath, eventually releasing her grip. The man staggered to his feet. He wiped blood from his eyes. "I swear I will tear you limb from limb, you filthy whore!" he bellowed and reached over to grab her by the hair.

"Mother!" the silver-eyed girl groaned.

Jesus sensed her tensing for an attack. Knowing she would be beaten to death, he grabbed her and held fast. She screeched in protest, but before she could bolt, Jesus shoved her to the side and charged forward. Solid as a bull, he rammed his full weight into the large man's gut. The sudden attack knocked the assailant off balance so that he tripped and tumbled over the low wall behind him.

"Do not lay another hand on her!" Jesus roared, standing over him.

The brute leapt to his feet. When he saw the young shepherd, he began to laugh. "What is this?" he cried. "Would you defend a whore, little man? Have you already developed an interest in her wares?"

"Leave her alone."

Peter stared, aghast.

The man wiped a sleeve across his bloody face. Then, without warning, he lunged forward. Jesus raised his fists and stood his ground. The man stopped short. He looked his young challenger in the eye and then, after a moment, waved a hand. "Aw! You are not worth the trouble," he said, dusting himself off. Having had enough, he turned to walk back to the priest's house. "But a word of advice, little brother," he called over his shoulder. "You should have chosen better for your first!" He snorted at his own remark then slammed the door behind him.

Peter dropped to his knees. His entire body shaking with fear.

The young girl dashed from behind the well. "Mother! Mother!" she cried.

Jesus stood back, his face covered with disbelief.

Had he really turned back the giant?

He turned to see the girl helping her mother to her feet. He rushed over to assist her.

"Do not touch me!" the woman hissed, swiping a hand at his face. Jesus toppled back, startled. When she was upright, the mother hurled insults at the house. "May God curse every one of you! May your fruit shrivel in the heat of hell!"

Jesus tried again to help the woman but again she struck at him with her fists. "Be gone from me!" she shouted. She looked blindly through bloodied eyes. "Mary! Where is that useless child of mine? Mary! Come help your mother!"

The daughter struggled to support the woman as she swayed from side to side, dizzied from the beating. She managed to secure an arm around her mother's waist and led her, limping, toward the dark.

Jesus made to follow the women, but Peter held him back. "Enough!" he snapped, keeping his grip firm.

Just before the mother and daughter disappeared, the girl turned back to look at Jesus once more. Holding him in her blazing gaze, she mouthed the words "Remember me."

That night, as the two boys prepared for sleep, Peter grumbled about Jesus having put their lives in peril. "Why must you always do that? Why must you always take such great risks for so little gain?" he asked, kicking leaves and sticks across the ground to clear a spot for his bed. "Your life, *my* life, for the daughter of a *whore*?" He rambled on, cursing the woman and her child with a litany of ugly names.

Jesus remained silent through the tongue-lashing, allowing Peter to vent his anger. He could already hear the wheezing between his friend's words and did not want to further upset him.

When Peter finished his tirade, he flopped onto the ground and turned his back. He had been alarmed at how much Jesus's interaction with the young girl had upset him. He could not define the emotions that quickened his blood whenever he thought of his friend doting on another. But he suspected that such an attachment was wrong. Perhaps even ungodly. And so he buried such feelings alongside his other secrets, hoping to keep them hidden.

When Jesus heard Peter's breathing return to normal, he rolled over and let his thoughts drift again to the young girl. He had been taken aback by the powerful sense of peace that had passed between them. Standing before her, he had felt seen in a way that he had not been seen since the time with his mother. As if the truth of him were laid bare. And he no longer needed to hide.

That night, under the stars, sleep did not come easily to either boy. And in the morning, neither dared speak of his dreams.

The day of their departure arrived. Jesus leapt up at a rooster's insistent crowing, startling Anna. He wrapped his keffiyeh tightly around his head and nudged Peter awake with a foot.

The boys made their way to the main gates and stopped just inside to have tea. The vendor, whose skin matched the color of his roasted leaves, poured a high, thin stream of liquid from a silver samovar. Having slept poorly, Peter said little to his friend. He returned to the vendor for a second cup.

"Excuse me," a voice said from behind.

Peter turned around as the shadow of a hulking man passed over him. His face was huge and round, like the moon.

"Was your brother not the boy who spoke yesterday at the Temple?" the man said, nodding toward Jesus.

Peter shrugged. "Perhaps, perhaps not," he said vaguely.

The man grinned. His eyes drilled into Peter's. With a grand motion, he swept his hand alongside the boy's ear. When he withdrew it, a shiny coin twirled between his fingers.

Peter gasped in recognition. He was the magician they had watched in the alley!

"What do you want with Jesus?" he asked, taking his tea from the vendor.

"Ahh . . . Jesus," the man pronounced slowly, as if he had heard the name before. He moved in close, alarmingly close, and whispered into Peter's ear, "Your brother has a natural charm about him. It engages people and disarms them. If he were to become my assistant, I promise there would be great riches for you both." He dangled the coin before Peter's eyes.

But Peter only scowled. Still smarting from Jesus's interaction with the girl, he was not about to let someone else steal him away. "Jesus is a shepherd, not a magician," he told the man. He then spun on his heels and went to find his friend.

"Who was that?" Jesus asked.

"No one. It is time to leave," Peter said and trotted for the gate.

Having arrived at the gathering spot early, the two shepherds sat in the shade of the great wall to wait for Solomon and the others. To pass the time, they made a game of counting camels.

"There is one!" Jesus shouted.

"Look over there!" Peter countered. "That makes two for me!"

Without warning, a sharp cry rang out behind them. Those standing nearby turned their heads to see what had happened. In that same instant, a man with a mask burst through the crowds and headed straight for the gate. Behind him, a mob of angry men gave chase, howling like a pack of wild dogs. Startled, the boys leapt back as the man ran past, close enough that they could hear him panting. As he fled, the fugitive threw down his dagger, its blade smeared with blood.

When the clouds of dust settled, the two boys stared down at the weapon. Though it had been trampled halfway into the ground by the mob, there was no mistaking the distinct sickle shape of its handle.

When Judas did not return in time for the appointed departure, Solomon grew worried and dispatched the shepherds to search the city. One group overheard gossip that the shepherd had killed a man. Another heard he had killed three. Solomon himself was escorted to a lightless den by a shopkeeper who claimed Judas had smoked bad opium and run screaming into the night.

Despite the number of witnesses claiming to have knowledge, no one could tell the shepherds where to find their missing man. It was as if he had vanished.

Having delayed their departure as long as he reasonably could, Solomon finally relented, and the shepherds made their way out the gates. Gathering their remaining sheep, they drove them on toward open terrain.

As the din of the city faded, Solomon trailed behind, his step halting, reluctant. Later, at mealtime, he maintained his distance from the others, refusing to eat, his face drawn and strained.

For weeks afterward, the shepherds often found their leader staring expectantly into the distance. Seeing Solomon's acute distress, and fearful that it might jeopardize their safety, the men decided among themselves never to speak of the incident in Jerusalem, or of Judas, again.

CHAPTER 7

Somewhere outside the Great Desert—16 A.D.

Peter helped Akbar roll the boulders away from the cave's mouth to release the herd from its nightly shelter. The animals tumbled out and lined up along a stagnant tributary, pressing their noses into the warm water. The season had brought an exceptional lack of rain; some waterways and streams had evaporated entirely leaving only tepid puddles thick with mud and pollen.

Normally the stretch of land the shepherds had come to, a sweeping plain bordered by mountains to the north and vast desert to the east, was fertile and welcoming. One of Solomon's favorite places, he often grazed his flocks there. But the recent drought had withered his paradise, and the shepherds found themselves forced to travel directly from one water source to the next in order to ensure that they, and their animals, did not die of thirst. Several of the shepherds had traveled this route with Solomon before, but as they drew deeper and deeper into the desiccated land, and the rain's mercy continued to elude them, they expected Solomon to announce that they were turning back.

He did not.

Instead, much to their surprise, he insisted that they push ahead.

"Now that we have come to the center of the plain, the journey back would prove just as difficult as the one ahead," he told them one night as they gathered around the fire.

The men groaned, knowing it was true.

"But at least we know for certain where the springs are in the land we have already crossed," Akbar suggested.

Solomon nodded. "True. But many of them have begun to dry up. And I believe that when we arrive at the mouth of the Great Desert, and begin our southward descent along its border, we will find the springs there more enlivened."

Hearing this, the men exchanged looks in the firelight. Though some harbored doubts, none dared openly express them.

Jesus lay on his mat, reluctant to rise. He had slept well but felt an unusual lightness in his head and a thickness inhabiting his limbs. The strange sensations had affected him for several mornings and he had begun to wonder if the symptoms were due to lack of water.

But then why were the others not suffering the same?

Remaining still, he listened to the tent flap snapping in the wind. Outside, he heard the men rousing the sheep with clucks and whistles. Soon came the crackle of the fire and the smell of its heat. Then the low murmur of the men's prayers.

Just as Jesus lifted himself onto his elbows, Peter burst inside the tent. His face appeared pale, his expression drawn.

"What is it?" Jesus asked, alarmed by his friend's pallor.

Peter glanced over his shoulder and drew closer. From behind his back he drew a goatskin pouch. Confused, Jesus glanced inside its opened mouth. At its bottom, he saw four or five handfuls of lentils. Still baffled, Jesus asked, "Is something wrong with the beans?"

Peter nodded. "This is all we have left," he whispered. He bit his lip. "I thought we had more, but I misjudged."

Jesus frowned. "Perhaps you did not account for the ewes' reaching the end of their cycle? Without their milk, we are eating more of our stores."

Peter nodded again. "It is true. I did not take that into account." Again, he glanced behind him, as if fearing they had been overheard. "What will I do?" he whispered.

"You will have to tell Solomon, of course!" Jesus said, shaken from his listlessness.

Peter shook his head. "I cannot. He will be furious. And the others, too!"

Jesus hopped to his feet. "Then I will tell him," he said. He saw a look of dejection crossing his friend's face. Jesus slapped him on the back. "Do not worry. It is not your fault. And Solomon will know what to do."

Peter glanced up. His features lightened. "Thank you, brother," he said. "I owe you."

Jesus laughed. "That is not the half of what you owe me!" he joked, then threw back the tent flap and stepped into the day.

Jesus found Solomon standing atop a buttress of stone, gazing northward toward the distant ripple of mountains. When he approached, the elder shepherd flinched, as if taken by surprise. Jesus noticed his reaction. Normally it would not be possible to startle Solomon, so keen were his senses, so open his attention.

"I am sorry, I did not mean—"

Solomon shook his head as if to clear a disturbing thought. He lifted a hand. "Do not apologize," he said. "I was lost in thought. That is all."

Jesus nodded. He looked up at his leader and noted the odd and far-off expression hazing his features.

"You came to ask a question?" Solomon said.

Jesus started. "Uh, yes," he said. "Well . . . *no*." He felt Solomon's gaze upon him. Usually the older shepherd's attention felt soothing, but, for whatever reason, in that moment it felt as if Solomon was taking stock of him. The young shepherd drew a slow breath. "We have nearly come to the end of our food supply," he said.

Solomon's gaze narrowed as if he had not understood. When he said nothing, Jesus tried again.

"Peter showed me the last of the lentils—"

"Yes," Solomon said, cutting him off. Laying a hand on the young shepherd's shoulder, he said, "Tell the men to gather."

Back at camp, the men circled the fire, waiting for Solomon. Peter took Jesus aside and asked how their leader had taken the news. Jesus only shrugged, for truly he did not know.

When Solomon approached, his step was quick. In his arms he carried his staff, two sacks of wool, and a goatskin rounded with water. The men looked from one to the other. For what was he preparing?

"Brothers, now that the ewes have reached the end of their milk cycle, we need more provisions to sustain our journey. I know of a village to the north where I can trade our wool for dried fish, cheese, and lentils. I will depart immediately and will return in no more than eight days."

The men grumbled with surprise, but did not protest. Given their circumstance, they had little choice, and Solomon's solution seemed the most prudent since, alone, he could travel much farther and faster than with the flocks.

"And in your absence—?" Akbar began.

Having anticipated the question, Solomon said, "In my absence I leave Jesus in charge."

Someone gasped.

The young shepherd felt the moisture wick from his mouth.

The others whispered among themselves.

But before anyone could object Solomon turned to his journey.

The next morning, while Peter built the fire, Jesus waited for the men. As he did, he draped himself along Anna's back. His lean body stretched with a blend of ease and awkwardness that marked widening adolescence and the approach of young adulthood. His arms and thighs bowed with obvious strength beneath broad shoulders. His cheekbones cradled an intensifying gaze, his look having ripened with maturity. And, as if his body had understood his choice of gender, a soft down crept across his lip and shadowed his sideburns. Even his voice had settled into a deeper pitch.

As the men gathered in a circle about him, Jesus felt awash with pride and fear. He knew Solomon to be wise in his judgment, but felt uncertain that he, Jesus, was capable of handling the enormous responsibility. As for the men, they seemed to have come to terms with the decision. Though it was unusual to entrust a junior shepherd with such a great duty, they, like Solomon, had long ago acknowledged the young shepherd's unique abilities. In addition, just the prospect of fresh food had cheered their spirits and settled their nerves.

Raising himself, the young shepherd pointed toward the horizon and said, "Today we will journey to the fan of red rocks." He knew that the distance was not great and that his shepherds could easily travel farther, but he also judged the red rocks to be the most likely source of water, perhaps for miles. It was a conservative plan, the older shepherds realized but, given the increasingly dire conditions, a wise one.

"Simon, you will lead your flock to the east, bordered by Akbar and his flock to the west, and Mathias to the south," Jesus commanded. The men nodded and turned to their duties.

As they retreated, Jesus felt a sharp sting at his calves. He whirled to find Peter grinning up at him, an olive switch dangling from his hand.

"You may be the leader now, but I can still outsmart you!" his friend taunted.

In a blinding flash, Jesus loaded his sling and ricocheted a stone off Peter's chest.

Peter yelped.

"But I can still *outshoot* you!" Jesus countered.

Peter laughed and threw his arm around Jesus. "Here, I almost forgot," he said, reaching into his sleeve. He lifted out two dried dates. "Save these for later."

Jesus squirreled away the fruits then, glancing ahead, noticed the flocks beginning to outpace them.

"We must move on to our separate duties," he said.

The afternoon heat grew as the flocks fanned across the landscape. Soon the last traces of cypress and cedars gave way to scrub and cactus. Jesus climbed up a ridge to scan the flocks. He noted how the sheep gathered in tight clusters around patches of dried grass and wilting shrubs. The mouths of the darker animals, including Anna, hung open as they panted in the heat. The men moved slowly, their faces tucked deep inside their keffiyehs to shade their cheeks from the sun.

Jesus, however, did not need to see their features to recognize them. He knew every man by his posture and stride.

Over the last two years, some members of their group had changed. Rahim had been crippled with fever and returned to the town of his birth. A month later, Eliah, Rahim's nephew, had arrived to replace him. For every shepherd who had left, a replacement had arrived. Except for one.

No one had replaced Judas.

Jesus stepped along a ridge, careful to avoid a tawny cobra sunning itself. As he continued, a raven glided overhead. Tossing back his head, Jesus opened his throat and called to the animal. Displeased with the quality of his call, he prepared to cry out again when he spotted a sheep straying toward the cobra. He loaded his sling and fired the stone at the serpent's head. But the missile missed its mark. And not by a little. Jesus stared in shock.

He reached for a second stone, but when he did, his arm brushed against a new angle, a different shape clinging to his body. He glanced down and found a nub of soft flesh protruding from his chest. He rubbed a hand across his upper body and easily found its twin.

He marveled at the change. And his failure to notice it. But his wonder quickly transformed into fear.

Was his body going to betray him?

Dropping between two boulders, he tore a strip of linen from his keffiyeh and bound the growing buds of his breasts. He then arranged his tunic more loosely about his torso. He waited for the pounding of his heart to slow before emerging from the rocks. Standing tall, he drew a gaze about his person, assuring himself that all appeared as it should. From now on, he realized, he must take great care.

On the edge of the desert, among men, he would not survive discovery.

As the sun drowned into early dusk, the air cooled. In the distance, Jesus could just barely make out the scalloped edge of the desert's tongue to the east. He then scanned right, to the bouquet of red rocks jutting from a crest of white limestone. He let out a crisp, looping whistle that signaled for the group to turn. A chorus wove through the air as the other shepherds spoke to their sheep. Peter lifted his head at the call. He redirected his own flock and searched the horizon for his friend. He found his long, proud body silhouetted against a cherry sky. He could not drop his eyes from the sight.

Once the animals had watered at the spring, and all the goatskins been filled, Jesus went to find adequate shelter for the sheep. Simon accompanied him in his search. Lighting a torch, the one-eyed shepherd led the way into a dark cave. Inside, their sounds grew muffled and close. The reddish brown walls flickered in the firelight as if they were made of flesh rather than stone. The smell turned musky and sharp like sweaty camel hide. Toward the back, they discovered a deep hole. Simon lowered his torch inside it, but they could not see the bottom. He dropped a rock into the darkness, but they did not hear it land. Jesus grunted, signaling that they would have to continue their search.

Picking their way out, Simon caught his leg on a stone and tumbled to the ground. Following just behind his fall came a shattering sound. Like a bowl dropped to the floor.

A chill scurried up Jesus's spine. "What was that?" he asked, kneeling to help Simon. Simon leapt to his feet and lifted the torch. Jesus saw that his hands were shaking. "Simon?" he whispered, holding down the fear rising in his throat.

Simon said nothing. He pointed to their feet. Scattered beneath them lay the broken shards of a large ceramic jar and the dusty remains of its contents. Jesus put a hand down to lift a shard.

"No!" Simon yelled, his eyes growing wide.

Jesus retracted his hand as if from an open flame. "What?" he gasped. "What is it?"

"The cave belongs to the jinn," Simon said. "We should not be here."

"The who?"

"We must find another cave," Simon said and hurried out.

That night the men gathered close around the fire as the air turned cold. Peter distributed the remaining scraps of food among them.

Jesus took his share and sat next to Simon. He waited for the older shepherd to speak about what they had seen in the cave. Simon tugged nervously on his faded eye patch. His hands were dry and wind-beveled. "My father told me that this area is home to the jinn," he said, pointing into the dark with a long, dirty fingernail.

Peter sat to join them.

"But what are they?" Jesus asked, making room for his friend. "Angels?"

Simon shook his head. "No. Not angels. More like demons. For the words they speak are evil."

"And what do they look like?" Jesus asked, his imagination conjuring images of snarling beasts.

"Who can tell?" Simon shrugged. "No one has seen them and lived."

"Then how do you know they exist?" Jesus challenged, detecting the curly scent of superstition.

"To be sure, they exist," Simon insisted, leaning in and lowering his voice. "They are said to be headless and bloodthirsty. With a special desire for young boys."

Jesus frowned. "But how can you know this if no one has survived to tell of them?"

Simon threw up his hands. "Do not question what I say!" he said. He looked about for a moment and then whispered, "But I am not surprised to see evidence of them now that we have drawn close to The Narrows."

Peter winced as if they should not be speaking of such things.

Jesus squinted into the fire. "The Narrows?"

Simon tightened his lips. "We have talked enough. I wish to smoke." He turned to stand but Jesus grabbed his arm. "No, Simon! You must tell me. What are The Narrows?"

The man lowered his aging body back to the ground. He wrapped a blanket around his shoulders as if the subject were chilling his bones. "The Narrows is the desolate and God-forsaken corridor of land that runs between the plain and the mountains to the north," he said. "God willing, neither of us will ever see it." Simon fell silent, but Jesus waited, sensing he had more to say.

Simon shook his head before continuing. "Rahim's older brother once became separated from the main herd in a dust storm and unknowingly led a small flock of goats up into The Narrows. When the others discovered where he had gone, they searched for him night and day but found nothing. He disappeared without a trace." Simon shuddered. "No more," he said, rising to his feet. "I say no more."

When Simon was gone, Peter and Jesus leaned closer to the flames.

"Do you think what he says is true?" Jesus asked.

Peter shrugged. "I do not know about the demons. But I *do* get a strange feeling whenever we pass close to The Narrows. As if it harbors some kind of wickedness. But who knows? Maybe it is just the crazy ones they say live there. Those who hide in caves and waste away."

Saying this, he lifted a cloth from inside his tunic. He spread it open on the ground, revealing a handful of dried figs. "For you," he said.

Jesus hooted with delight. "Thank you, brother," he said and knocked an affectionate fist into Peter's shoulder.

Peter rubbed his arm in mock pain. Then, sensing that he was blushing, he turned to hide his face.

As he chewed up the fruits, Jesus's mind returned to what Simon had said. Over the years he had grown accustomed to the shepherds' outlandish tales and nomadic superstitions. But he found something about Simon's story, and the discovery of the broken jar, unsettling.

It was the sound of the wind, dry and tinny like the inside of an empty kettle, that startled Jesus. Seven days had passed and Solomon had still not returned. During that time, Jesus had managed to find water for the animals, but many of the springs he had located had long ago stopped bubbling. And, as their food supply dwindled, so did the men's morale. Being shepherds, they were not strangers to hardship, but their souls had grown scarred from many difficult hours. And though the men did not complain openly, Jesus and Akbar had had to step in between two small skirmishes, spurred on, no doubt, by the stresses of thirst, hunger, and heat.

Jesus pushed back the tent flap and scanned their camp. None of the others had risen. He stepped outside, folding his hands inside his tunic. The night's chill still crinkled the air. Three buzzards circled in patient, languid curves overhead. Two of them had been following the group for several days. The third bird, Jesus noted with concern, was new. Slipping on his sandals, he wandered to the sheepfold they had built out of tangled branches. Anna saw him approaching and tottered to the edge of the enclosure. She bleated softly and pressed her nose into the thorny wall.

"Good morning, little one," Jesus said, petting the downy fur around her muzzle. She licked his hands free of salt and rolled her brown eyes. The shepherd felt grateful for the animal's show of loyalty and confidence. Still, he prayed that the day would bring Solomon's return.

The shape on the horizon appeared suddenly as if poured from the shimmering heat. Attuned to the landscape, Jesus noticed it even before his sheep did. The form appeared to be moving slowly, almost as if it were not moving at all. He knew from the apparent lack of motion that it was heading straight toward them. He shielded his eyes against the sunrise and tried to ascertain the shape's identity.

Was it a wolf? A bandit? Perhaps a lion?

He knew he should wake the others but decided to wait. He wanted to be sure before sounding the alarm.

As the wavy shape moved closer, its edges hardened. The figure moved with a long step that favored the left leg. He recognized the gait.

Solomon!

Jesus tossed a vibrant whistle into the air. The men stumbled, weak and thirsty, from their tents. Soon the air reverberated with the cries and trills of various languages as the shepherds welcomed their leader back into the fold. In no time, they unloaded the sacks and pouches strapped to Solomon's shoulders. The containers brimmed with dates, olives, dried fish, roots, spices, bread, and wine.

Jesus and the red-bearded shepherd embraced and kissed each other's cheeks.

"I thought you had forgotten us," Jesus said, fighting back tears.

Solomon let his gray eyes soak up the boy. "The flocks are well?" he asked. Jesus nodded. The elder shepherd smiled. "I believe, then, that you are ready," he said and turned to greet the others.

Despite their leader's return, the shepherds' anxiety continued to escalate as they approached the edge of the Great Desert.

To make matters worse, Solomon told them he had heard that rains had not come to the southern plain to which they were journeying, but had arrived in the lands far to the east. This news worried the shepherds as they feared Solomon would decide to cross the desert in search of more succulent lands. No one, however, despite his thirst and hunger, welcomed the idea. For such a crossing—many months in length—was among the most grueling journeys a shepherd could make.

One evening, shortly after his return, Solomon climbed up the rocky escarpment to relieve Simon of his duty.

"But I have not yet done a full watch," the shepherd said. He pointed upward. "The stars have yet to cross the sky."

Solomon nodded. "I know."

The shepherd let his one eye roam over his leader's face. "You have some thinking to do, is that it?" he asked. He squirreled two fingers beneath his eye patch to scratch at the empty socket beneath.

Solomon gave a tired smile. "I do."

Simon nodded. Then, without another word, he lifted his staff and turned to join the others.

The red-bearded shepherd sat and pressed his back against the rocks. He gazed up at the stars and wound his eyes between them until he found nests of smaller stars. To these he gave his full attention. Until his body became still. And his mind opened.

Held in contemplation, he thought first of his mother. Of her nimble hands and throaty laugh. He smiled to remember these details. Urging his mind forward, he recalled his final visit with her. In Nazareth. As they had sat leaning against the well, she had told him of the child who needed to be delivered. And he had given his word.

But with Judas gone, how would he carry out his duty?

With only himself remaining, the plan to transport the young shepherd had been gravely imperiled—it now being necessary for Solomon to concoct a reason for the shepherd to make the journey *alone.*

He then recalled that their mission had been endangered once before—with Zahra's unexpected death.

Yet he had still managed to retrieve Jesus.

Perhaps it was destiny?

Either way, Solomon knew he had to devise a strategy. For the last several weeks, since guiding the flock along the plain beneath The Narrows, he had been unable to think of a way to transfer his young charge.

And time was running out.

Soon they would travel beyond the secret entry point, and all hope would be lost.

Solomon returned to the fire and took up his pipe. Smoking with the others, he watched Peter arrive and lay his mat next to Jesus. Keeping silent, the shepherd studied the air between the two friends. As was his custom, Peter lifted his flute to play. Solomon noticed how his adolescent body swayed, rhythmically, toward Jesus. And how his flute's arching, woody melody floated like an unanswered question between them.

Seeing their interaction, the elder shepherd contemplated the plan he had envisioned and decided to carry it out. Immediately.

Despite the dangers involved, he felt certain that a far worse tragedy would result if he let the young shepherd stay.

He only hoped Jesus could endure the trials that lay ahead.

As the sun rose, Solomon gathered the men around the fire. Everyone remained silent as the flames crackled. They were anxious to hear what he intended. More than a week had passed since his return and already their supply of food was dwindling. Over the last few days, the hot smell of desert had grown on the wind, hovering, like the smell of the sea before it comes into view.

"I have reached a decision, brothers. And not an easy one," Solomon began.

The men dropped their eyes to the dust, knowing what they would hear.

"We have waited long enough for the rains to come to us. It is time now for *us* to follow *them*," he told them.

The men grumbled among themselves, their worst fears confirmed.

"I wish it could be otherwise," Solomon continued. "But at this point we have little choice left."

No one took comfort in his conclusion. Yet how could they argue against it? As it stood, they were blocked to the north by the mountains, by desiccated land to the west, from whence they had come, and now Solomon had learned that the path they had intended to follow southward was just as bleak.

When no one spoke up, Solomon continued. "As you know, our journey across the great sand will be difficult. But I promise you that we will be well stocked with food before our departure."

The men struggled to calm their nerves. They knew that Solomon had led his sheep across the difficult terrain before.

"But Solomon, with all respect, I must ask you, from where will this new supply of food come?" Akbar asked. "We have already traveled well beyond the last village I know of."

The shepherds' eyes grew wide as the ramifications of Akbar's question settled in.

Anticipating their concern, Solomon said, "Tomorrow, I will leave for the village of Kerek. And in ten days' time I will return with the necessary supplies. Then we will undertake our crossing."

A silence fell among them.

Simon nudged a stick into the fire. "But Solomon," he said, "the only way to Kerek from here"—he gazed off, swallowing—"is through The Narrows."

The men's eyes darted haphazardly from one face to the next, like flies fleeing the whip of a camel tail. Jesus held his breath, hoping he had not heard right.

Solomon raised a hand. "There is no need for fear," he said.

Resistance rumbled around the fire, quiet at first, but rolling and gathering like thunder. The men had held down their fears for too long. And the worsening conditions had weakened the last of their resolve. Before anyone could stop it, the thunder gave way to lightning.

"This is unjust!" Mathias blurted. "No man has ever returned from The Narrows. If you disappear, we are doomed!"

"How can you so readily put our lives in jeopardy?" Akbar demanded.

"You should have told us long ago that this was your intention!" Eliah complained.

The questions and doubts tangled into a clamor that silenced the fire and startled the animals. Anna jumped from Jesus's side and skittered behind the bushes.

"Silence!" Solomon roared. The crackling of the fire returned to prominence. He began again in a calm voice. "If I have not come back after ten days, there are provisions enough for you to attempt a return."

"Attempt a return?" Akbar cried. "We already know how barren the land from which we have come! And we have barely enough food to make it back to the last spring!"

"Barely enough is still *enough*," Solomon countered. "And, you should remember, Jesus led you on a safe journey here. He can lead you back, if he must."

Jesus felt the men's eyes boring into him, questioning his mettle. The young shepherd did not like the feeling but kept his composure, hardening his face with confidence so as not to jeopardize Solomon's authority or bring his wisdom into question. But despite his calm exterior, doubt echoed through the valleys of his heart.

Could he really lead them back?

After the men had gone muttering to their mats, Jesus approached Solomon where he sat smoking and mending a tear in his tunic. "Solomon?" he asked.

The elder shepherd nodded but did not lift his eyes from his work.

Jesus stumbled over what to say next. The questions and fears rose quickly to the surface and clogged his throat.

Solomon let the tunic fall from his hands. He then knocked his pipe against a stone, emptying it of ashes. "You will know what to do when you know what you are facing," he said, as if reading the young man's mind.

Jesus looked down. He then wondered if he should tell the shepherd what he had seen his father and the men in his village do. To Zahra. In all the years he had spent with Solomon and the men, he had never uttered a word of it, for fear of his own safety.

But what if Solomon did not return from The Narrows?

Solomon gazed at the young shepherd, as if waiting for him to speak. But Jesus held his breath. He did not feel ready to take so great a risk.

Solomon set off early the next morning while it was still dark. He walked nearly two miles before sinking to his knees. He looked to the sky, to the light seeping between its tawny folds, and called for his mother. When he felt her near, he began to speak. He told her of his plan for the crossing. Of the challenges that lay ahead. Of the need for strength and courage. He asked her to send these in abundance. And he asked for her blessing.

As he spoke, he opened the small bag he kept, always, inside his tunic. He poured a trail of small yellow seeds across his palm. He put three into his mouth and chewed. He took a deep breath and made a space in his mind for the pain. He thought again of his mother, of her gray eyes, her knowing hands, and his days as a boy listening to her, and her sisters, tell stories of ancient sycamore trees and of his grandmother, Orpah. He held onto these memories as he made the long walk back, knowing that by the time he arrived, the seeds' effect would be upon him.

When he returned to camp and lay down on his mat, Solomon felt a pang of doubt pinching his heart. "Mother," he whispered, "show me. A sign. That I have served you well." And with that, he fell into delirium.

Jesus was out collecting stones for his sling when he heard Akbar yelling for Peter. He then heard the slosh of water being carried in a goatskin and the pounding of someone's feet. He dashed over to find the other shepherds gathered around Solomon's mat. Jesus pushed his way through and found the elder shepherd lying on his side, a trail of vomit clinging to his beard. His color had faded to a sickly pale. Peter lowered a ladle of water. Solomon drank, but the liquid came back up as quickly as it went down.

Simon knelt and placed his hand on Solomon's forehead. It felt cold and clammy, though his cheeks glowed with heat.

"What is wrong with him?" Jesus asked, trying to contain his panic.

Simon shook his head. "A snakebite, perhaps."

"Check him," Jesus cried. "Check him for marks." The search of Solomon's skin turned up nothing. No rash or blemishes or bites.

"Solomon," Jesus asked, kneeling beside him, trying to keep his voice steady. "What should we do?"

"Let me rest," the shepherd wheezed and grit his teeth in agony.

"He is better!" Akbar called, having been given the duty of watching Solomon through the night.

The men gathered and waited for their leader to speak. The fallen shepherd rubbed his eyes and wiped the crust from his cheeks. His color, though better, remained unhealthy. A slight tremor shook his limbs. They wrapped him in blankets and sat him closer to the fire. They then waited, but the shepherd said nothing.

Eliah grew despondent. "What will we do?" he asked. "Which way should we go now that you are unable to make the journey through The Narrows? Either way, without provisions we will suffer mightily!" The questions hung in the air.

The shepherds looked to one another for answers but found only empty stares. Solomon remained silent. It was almost as if he had surrendered. Jesus could feel the shepherds' unrest. He looked into their eyes. Profound hunger and thirst could make even the most seasoned among them mutinous. And while he had never witnessed an uprising, he had heard the stories.

Why does Solomon not speak up? What is he waiting for?

"Solomon," Simon begged.

But Solomon said nothing. His eyes remained fixed on a point above their heads. One by one, the shepherds rose to depart.

If they left, Jesus realized, Solomon's authority would be compromised. And anyone might step in to fill the vacuum. Jesus looked down at Solomon's trembling hands, his crusty lips, and the sickened yellow of his skin. In these details, Jesus realized the finality of the moment. Watching the others turn to go, he knew that within seconds the fulcrum would shift, the balance would be lost, and the opportunity, the opening into freedom, would likely never come again. He stood and felt his years as a shepherd rising behind him like a wave. He steeled his courage and said, "I will go."

The men froze in their tracks.

"What?" Akbar blurted.

Solomon lifted his eyes to meet those of his young shepherd. And in the gaze that passed between them, each received the sign he was seeking.

CHAPTER 8

Somewhere near the Great Desert outside ancient Palestine—16 A.D.

Mathias packed the last of Jesus's supplies into an old pouch. Simon then handed him a short dagger and told him to keep it close and always at the ready. "The jinn are powerful and devious spirits. Do not let them tempt you," he warned.

Jesus lifted his staff and goatskin of water and faced the first landmark Solomon had indicated—a long, slanted ridgeline of columnar rocks far in the distance. "Keep the crest of the ridge always in front of you," Solomon had said. "If you do this, you will arrive at your destination."

Jesus turned back to his fellow shepherds. Reluctant tears clung to the corners of every eye. Lips quivered in sorrow and silent prayer. No one knew when, or if, they would see their trusted companion again. As Jesus scanned the faces, he found Peter's. His friend had begged Solomon to let him accompany Jesus on his journey, but Solomon had refused, saying that he could not risk the loss of two shepherds. Trembling, Peter knelt and cradled Anna, unable to lift his reddening eyes. He did not have the strength to say good-bye.

For the first time since accepting his mission, Jesus felt overcome with regret. And fear. It started in his toes, numbing them, and twisted its way up each of his legs until his knees shook.

"Peter," he whispered. The weight of his decision dropped on him like a sudden stone—the thought of leaving behind all he knew. The surrendering of his safety. And the family of men who loved him.

What if he never saw them again?

His arms began to shake. He wanted to call the whole thing off. To unpack his pouch and run laughing through the flocks with his friend. But when his eyes fell to Solomon, lying weakened on his mat, he knew his fate was sealed.

Anna kicked free from Peter and ran to her shepherd. Jesus read the confusion on her face. He struggled to contain his emotions. He shifted the pouch on his back and tightened the cord. He turned to face his journey and began to walk.

Peter stared into the sand and clenched his fists.

Jesus had just hit his full stride when someone shouted, "Wait!" He turned as Peter fell into his arms, wheezing. Their embrace was deep—the first of its kind. They held tight with the fervor of an uncertain future. Overwhelmed with the sensations of skin, scent, and breath, each waited for the other to pull back. But neither did.

After a moment, Jesus felt a surge, like a hot fist, pushing from beneath Peter.

Behind them a shepherd coughed sharply. The duration of their embrace had crossed an unspoken line.

Peter pulled away. His face flushed with embarrassment. His eyes dropped toward the sand. "I will . . . miss you," he whispered. He lifted Anna quickly and jogged back to the others. Bewildered, Jesus watched him go, his friend's stride fractured through a prism of tears.

Simon pierced the air with a rousing whistle and the shepherds jumped to their flocks. Akbar and Eliah bent to help Solomon stand. If all went according to plan, they would meet Jesus in a valley several days away. Like the young shepherd, they needed to be on their way.

Two days after his departure, Jesus felt the landscape shift beneath his feet. Plants disappeared. Scents vanished. Even the wind had stilled, and the air thickened with an eerie silence. The ground rolled and unfolded in monotonous, endless waves. Every bank, every rock, seemed to be the same ones he had passed hours before. He rode the waves up and down, stumbling his way toward the ridge with a constant sense of déjà vu.

At night, the silence continued, and Jesus found it even more unsettling than if a pack of wolves had been howling nearby. A strange haze blotted out the stars, heightening his disorientation. He built a fire, not only for warmth, but for companionship. He could not remember a time when the land had felt so desolate.

He slid closer toward the fire. Flames licked the air like quick tongues. He laid his head against the cold ground, longing to feel Anna's breathing at his side.

In his loneliness, his mind turned toward his final moment with Peter. He felt again the surge that had rushed up between them.

Drifting farther back, his mind returned to the first occasion when he had felt so altered by another.

It had been in Jerusalem. When he and Peter, on their way to bed for the night, had spotted the young girl by the well. Her mother had called her Mary, and she had held Jesus in the light of her silver-eyed gaze. He recalled how the girl's look had produced a peace, and a stillness, within him. Though each of the memories left him somewhat bewildered, he let their recollection keep him company, until sleep came, finally, and took him.

Jesus did not rise until long after the sun. He berated himself for oversleeping. As he stood, a heaviness weighed down his limbs. He rubbed his eyes and found them puffy with sleep. Perhaps, he thought, he had been keeping too rigorous of a pace.

But what was too rigorous when men's lives depended upon his return?

He shook off the sluggishness and gathered his belongings. He would forgo his morning tea.

After several hours' travel, he paused to slip open his tunic and relieve himself. Before the liquid had soaked into the sand, Jesus felt eyes upon him. He gasped and spun around. Fear snaked up his back. He scanned the horizon but found it empty.

Easy, easy, he whispered to himself.

He was well versed in the ways in which constant sun and lack of water could turn the mind against itself. He scanned the land once more, just to be sure. When he was certain there was nothing, he lifted his staff and continued his journey. But he continued to sense that he was not alone.

By the afternoon, a thirsty heat had pried its way under his skin, reaching in to wick the moisture from his bones. Jesus knew he would have to find water. He had not rationed as well as he might have, relying instead on Solomon's assurance that he would find springs in the lower depressions. As yet, however, he had not discovered any water sources, and his meager supply was running low.

The first layer of skin began to peel from his lips. Though he had faced stronger sun in the past, for some reason Jesus felt particularly susceptible to the heat. He searched several low spots for a spring. But found nothing. The extra exploration delayed his journey and he was frustrated by the slowed progress.

Pausing to confirm his bearings, he watched the distant horizon ripple upward in waves. He perceived the usual mirages: a giant lake stretching between crests, a lush green jungle sprouting from nowhere. His mind struggled against the temptations. But his thoughts began to fray.

Why had Solomon allowed him to take such a dangerous and hopeless journey? Was it revenge? Could he possibly have wanted him dead?

The land began to tilt. He tried to still his mind, but the questions spiraled. He was just on the verge of losing control when a bloodcurdling scream pierced the air. The cry flattened him to the ground. He pressed his lips into the dust, too scared to look up. He waited for another scream. But only silence followed. He held still for several minutes, wondering what he should do. Slowly, he lifted his head and wiped the sand from his cheeks. He scanned the horizon, expecting to see the headless bodies of the jinn. But he saw nothing. Only the columnar ridge, looming closer.

Unable to sleep, Jesus struggled to remember Solomon's instructions, and the landmarks and timetables he had given him. Staring through the dark, he could make out the ridgeline. He knew he would cross it by the end of the next day.

But was he behind schedule? Should he have already crossed?

His mind fumbled. He rose and built a small fire. He poured the last water from his goatskin to make a cup of tea and gnawed on a handful of dried dates. His stomach growled for more.

Finally, he arrived at the bottom of the ridge. Anxious to have the journey behind him, he scrambled up its side. His feet slipped on the loose rocks and crusty soil. At the top, he felt as though he was standing on the slicing edge of a knife. The land on the opposite side dropped too abruptly to be traversed without the risk of broken bones. He knew that going straight down would be the fastest way, but Solomon had warned him against this temptation. "Keep to the top until it is safe to descend," he had cautioned.

Jesus found the thin trail that ran atop the crest and knelt to tighten his sandals.

He walked cautiously, stabilizing each step with his staff before proceeding. He kept his mind fixed on the terrain and did not permit his thoughts to roam. Though he did wonder, briefly, how he would manage to carry a full load of supplies back across the ridge.

Toward the hottest hour of the day, the trail descended beneath the crest so that a wall of stone rose on one side. Jesus skimmed his hand along the wall as he walked, finding temporary relief from the vertigo.

He stopped when a sudden blast of cool air chilled his skin. Enticed, he took a few more steps and found the mouth of a cave. The air issuing from inside the mountain felt refreshing, and delectably damp. His body craved the relief. He took a step inside but froze. Memories of the cave he had entered with Simon rose in front of him: the fluttering torchlight, the crack of ceramic, the chill, and the strange presence.

What if this cave were home to evil spirits?

His spine shuddered, tossing his shoulders like the wings of a bathing bird. He passed the cave, afraid to look back.

The pain began as a dull ache in his abdomen. Hunger was finally getting the best of him. He reached for the pouch inside his tunic. The one Solomon had given him. "When the hunger begins to weaken you," the elder shepherd had said, "eat a handful of these."

Jesus poured the reddish seeds into his palm. He had been eating them every few hours since early morning. At first, they had brought relief to the cramping in his stomach, but this more recent pain, duller and lower in his gut, refused to be soothed. He continued his steady pace, hoping to push through the discomfort. But the harder he strove, the more light-headed he became. The pain blossomed wider, spreading into his thighs, tightening the muscles, making his legs ache with every step. He looked ahead, but the ground rose and fell like water.

A sudden flash of brilliant color shone before him. Then, just as quickly, vanished.

Had it been a bird? A mirage?

A coppery taste coated his tongue and the back of his throat. He swallowed against it.

Was he going mad?

The pain shifted and sharpened. It drove like a spike into his bowels. He fell to his knees. He reached inside the pouch of seeds but the sight of them brought on a wave of nausea. Sweat soaked the hairline of his keffiyeh. He knew he had to find shelter. He would never make it through the night exposed on the ridge. Through the haze of ache, he remembered the cave. If he could make it back, he could rest safely until the pain subsided.

He turned, careful to keep his balance on the narrow trail. He took an unsteady step. A rock dropped out of the sky and skimmed along the path behind him. He spun around, raising his staff to fend off whatever was tailing him. But again found nothing.

The sudden movement dizzied him and brought on a sickening bout of vertigo. He took another step. The ground beneath his foot crumbled. His right leg slipped out from under him. His weight transferred to his left leg but it was too weak to hold. For a brief moment, he felt weightless and knew he was falling.

It is over. I am done.

Just before his body hit the ground, Jesus felt a strong and steady force, like the palm of a giant hand, cradle him and lift, ever so slightly, upward.

Then the world went dark.

CHAPTER 9

Somewhere within The Narrows *outside ancient* Palestine—*16* A.D.

Jesus could not yet open his eyes, but his other senses had become alert. He heard dripping water. And hurried whispers. The air felt cool and moist. A sweet smell tickled the insides of his nostrils. He struggled to open his eyes. The whispers rushed and grew louder.

A sudden golden light suffused the space, pushing back the darkness, and he realized his eyes had been open all along. At the edges of his vision, he could discern the interior of a cave. He smelled the acridness of burning oil. Someone had lit a torch. The light steadied. But he saw no one.

He tried to sit up but two hands pressed him back down. He was startled to feel the hands touch his bare skin. He looked down and saw that he was naked. Terrified, he sprang back up, reaching for anything to cover himself. A bolt of pain seared through his leg. Through the flickering light, he saw his shinbone protruding from a deep gash below his knee. Blood pooled between his thighs.

Out of nowhere, a shrill scream pierced the air and reverberated along the stone walls. Jesus went cold. The hurried whispers increased, but he could not understand the words. A hooded figure carried a small torch to the end of the table and touched his broken leg. The pain rang bells in his head.

"No!" he cried. A second figure stood near his chest, holding him down. "No, please!" he cried again, afraid the jinn would kill him. The spirit twisted his leg bone, sending throbbing shards of pain in every direction.

Another scream pierced the darkness, followed by a series of moans.

Had they captured another hapless shepherd?

Jesus felt sick to his stomach. A hooded figure lifted a blood-soaked cloth from between his legs. The horrific sight stole his consciousness and his slackened body fell against the stone slab.

Jesus flinched at the beating of nearby drums. A dull ache pounded in his leg and stomach. He heard the voices of the jinn, singing a strange, high-pitched song. He turned his head and in the murky light saw a group of hooded figures.

Hooded, no doubt, to hide their headlessness.

The tempo of the drum increased. The pitch of the voices rose. A tambourine-like clanging joined the din. The crazy sounds echoed throughout the cave, scattering in every direction.

They are going to sacrifice me!

He remembered Simon's warning that jinn were bloodthirsty for young boys. This new fear reinspired his need to escape. He tried to sit up, tried to locate the dagger Simon had given him, but found his wrists and ankles tethered to the stone slab with straps of goat gut.

The music's tempo sped to a frenzy. The voices chanted and wailed. Jesus yelled for help. He panicked and struggled against the straps.

Then the music stopped. Jesus held his breath. He heard low whispers speaking in quick, ardent tones. The strange smell returned to the air. He craned his neck to look at the entrance. He saw a coven of jinn cloaked in long robes walk past carrying a figure draped in a white sheet. The sheet was stained with copious amounts of blood.

A corpse! A sacrifice!

Jesus thrashed in terror, knowing that he would be next. As the group disappeared into another chamber, they took the light with them. He was left, again, in the dark.

The next time he woke, Jesus found himself in the light. He could hear someone speaking in a distant chamber. It was a soft voice, but commanding, and though it rose and fell with strength, and a certain infallibility, there was compassion behind the words. The voice of a leader. "Go!" the spirit ordered. Someone sprinted past the entrance. The leader's tone reminded him of another.

Solomon! he thought with a jolt. *And Peter and the others. They were waiting for him—*

"You are awake!" someone said, interrupting his thoughts.

Jesus stiffened. He could not see who had spoken. He twisted his wrists and found them still tied. His leg no longer ached, but his stomach felt swollen and tender. He looked down and saw that his lower body had been covered with a linen cloth. His upper body was naked. He saw the nubs of his breasts, fully exposed, and felt a mixture of fear and shame. His captors knew his secret. And would kill him.

A hooded figure walked alongside him. Jesus wanted to close his eyes, so as not to see the jinn's face, or lack thereof. But he could not resist peeking into the emptiness.

"Calm yourself," the spirit said. The voice was strange, warbling at a high pitch, more of an echo than a voice. "Drink this," it said, holding out a clay cup.

Jesus closed his lips.

"No?" the spirit tried again. It set down the cup and rubbed its hands together quickly, as if trying to start a fire between its palms. When they were well heated, the spirit lowered them onto Jesus's abdomen. He flinched, but the spirit pressed its fingers into his flesh. Its hands were strong and accustomed to the task. Jesus heard a low hum and felt a rush of heat spread throughout his torso. The jinn held its hands still, as if to listen for something through its fingers. Jesus felt the pain in his abdomen subsiding. In its place, a warm glow spread within his body.

A second spirit entered the chamber. This second jinn was also cloaked and hooded. The first spirit removed its hands and left the chamber. The second figure came and loomed over Jesus. "What is your name?" the second spirit asked in a stern, hoarse voice.

Jesus said nothing.

"I ask you again, what is your name?"

"Untie me," Jesus replied.

"Tell me your name, now."

"There are shepherds waiting for me," Jesus countered.

The spirit rocked back and forth. Irritated. "Why were you traveling in disguise?"

Jesus shook his head.

"You were traveling as a male. Why?"

Jesus felt prickles rising up his neck. "My name is Jesus," he said.

"Enough! What is the name your mother gave you?"

"Untie me!" Jesus cried.

The jinn's voice grew impatient. "Your life is in our hands. You will answer me! How did you find your way here? Who sent you?"

Jesus struggled against his ties. "Do not hurt me! Let me go!" he cried out.

"Who knows you are here?" the spirit demanded.

"Please," Jesus stuttered, weeping from fear and pain. "I am a poor shepherd. I was crossing The Narrows to bring back food from the village of Kerek. If you do not release me, six men will die."

The spirit pressed in and lowered itself close to his face. "If I release you," it hissed, "*thousands* will perish."

The first jinn returned to the room. "Enough!" it said. "She needs her strength."

Jesus frowned, unsure who the spirit was referring to.

"We need answers," the second figure said. "Or would you rather that our lives were put in jeopardy?"

"You know the answer to your own question," the first jinn shot back. "And your tone has become unproductive."

The second jinn stepped back. Jesus sighed with relief.

"What you say is true," the hoarse-voiced spirit said. "Forgive me."

Jesus shuddered at its exit.

A third hooded spirit, a smaller one, entered the room carrying a bowl.

"You may clean her," the first jinn said.

Jesus reeled in confusion.

Who was it talking about?

He winced upon realizing that the "she" they were referring to was *him*! It had been a lifetime since anyone had referred to him as "her." He had all but forgotten. The reference sounded false, like a lie. His heart hardened in resistance.

The smaller spirit peeled back the warm linen that covered him. Jesus saw that his broken leg had been straightened and neatly bound. The jinn lifted a damp cloth from a bowl. It rubbed it between Jesus's thighs. When the spirit removed the cloth, it was soaked with blood! Jesus's eyes flew open. The blood had not issued from his injury. So where had it come from? He felt panic rising.

What had they done? Where had they cut him?

He struggled again to free himself, but was weak from loss of blood. Dizziness pulled him down.

"Calm yourself," the larger jinn said in its high-pitched voice. The smaller jinn continued to draw blood from the invisible wound. Jesus felt a tremble in his thighs and a momentary shame, sensing that he was wetting himself.

"Do you not know what is happening to you?" the first jinn asked.

Jesus said nothing. He was drawing inward, preparing to fight against death.

"Do you not know about the monthly renewal?" the spirit asked.

Jesus stared blankly.

"So," the spirit said, nodding, "you do not."

Jesus felt his head lighten.

"You are tired," the jinn said. "We can speak more of these things later. But I promise you this, your days of living as a shepherd are over."

Jesus felt a wail building inside his body.

No! It cannot be true. It cannot. Solomon! Save me!

Another jinn laid its hand across his eyes and said, "I will give you rest." In an instant, Jesus fell again into darkness, a desperate cry caught in his throat.

Two of those who dwelled in the caves stepped outside to look up at the stars. One had a slight stoop in its shoulders and appeared to be the elder of the two. In its hand it held the medallion that Jesus had worn around his neck. "Travel to the outer perimeter," it told the other. "Find out where the shepherd came from. We must be absolutely certain that she did not follow Samara here."

The taller one nodded. "I will do as you say," it said in a coarse voice and left to gather supplies for the journey.

Several days later, the cave dweller with the coarse voice returned. Upon its entry, it lifted a bucket of water and drank greedily. Its travel through The Narrows had been difficult. Its cloak was torn and smelled of sheep urine. It found its elder and stood before it.

"I located the source of the shepherd," it said. "They did not follow Samara and have no intention of attacking."

The elder sighed with relief.

"But there is heavy news still," it said, lowering its gravelly voice.

The elder lifted its fallen shoulders as if to brace for what it would hear. "Tell me what you know."

Jesus lay on his back and endured the slow passage of hours. His body ached with pains both sharp and wide. He spent days slipping into and out of consciousness. Even in the darkness, he had sensed spirits gathering around him, and with the last of his strength resisted their every attempt to harm him.

"How is she?" Jesus heard a spirit voice ask. The voice had a timbre that was deeper than the others. It was the leader he had heard earlier.

"She refuses to eat or drink," another spirit answered.

"Or answer any questions," another added.

"Bring her to my chamber," the elder jinn commanded.

"But if we untie her she will try to run away," the younger spirit warned.

The elder approached Jesus. The spirit stood before him, silent. Even though Jesus could not see inside its hood, he could feel its eyes upon him.

Weakened from hunger and thirst and defeated from days in the dark, Jesus could only whimper.

"Bring her," the elder repeated.

When the tethers were untied, Jesus expected to find his wrists and ankles rubbed raw. But to his surprise, his skin was supple and free of lacerations. After dressing him in a lightweight tunic, the two jinn carried him down a corridor. As they headed toward a distant chamber,

Jesus could see the layout of the caves for the first time. As they advanced, he noted a honeycomb of rooms cut into the rock. The air in the corridor smelled leafy and full, reminding him of an oasis.

"Leave us," the elder jinn requested when they arrived at its chamber. The two spirits laid Jesus on a mat. They did not release their hold. "You may let go of her," the elder assured them.

The others retreated and Jesus remained, alone, facing the spirit through murky light. The elder jinn lowered gently to the ground. The space behind it was lined with jars and manuscripts.

How could a headless spirit read?

The elder faced the young shepherd. Though a distance of nearly twelve feet separated them, it felt to Jesus as if the spirit were seated next to him. After a few minutes, a deep calm washed over him.

Do not be fooled, Jesus told himself. *Stay alert. Do not fall under its spell!*

When the spirit leaned forward to adjust its position, Jesus's eyes shot toward the entrance. As soon as he was able, he would escape. He would find Solomon and the others and warn them. As he contemplated crossing the desert, he noticed a stiffness gripping his legs.

How long had they held him captive?

The jinn cleared its throat. "You have been here thirteen days," it said.

Jesus gasped.

Thirteen days! The others were expecting him to come back in ten!

The spirit spoke again. "Your friends left to make their return yesterday," it said. "They were well stocked for the journey."

Jesus flinched.

Return? Without him? It was impossible!

His mind raced. In his distress he had failed to notice that the jinn had been reading his thoughts.

The spirit lifted an object from its cloak. Jesus froze. He recognized it immediately. It was Zahra's medallion. He pressed his fingers to his chest. He had not even realized it was gone.

The spirit rose and lit another torch. Jesus squinted against the brightness. When his eyes adjusted, he could see the jinn more clearly. The spirit was smaller than Jesus had originally perceived. And its cloak was not black, but the color of ripened plum. The light cast a long shadow into the hole where its face would be. Jesus watched in horror as the spirit lifted its hands to remove its hood.

"No!" Jesus shouted. But it was too late. The hood came down. Jesus stared, petrified by the sight. To his shock, there was a *face.*

It was *Zahra*!

The old woman's gray eyes bore straight into him. Jesus could not breathe. It felt as though a snake were constricting around his throat.

Zahra lifted her medallion and dangled it in front of him. In that instant everything became clear. The past and the future circled to meet before him.

Solomon had known all along who murdered his mother! And, wanting to deliver Jesus to his mother's spirit for retribution, the elder shepherd had sent him through The Narrows knowing Zahra would find him and take her revenge.

Jesus thought back to that horrible night. The violent memories broke loose and ran rampant through his mind: Zahra's warning. Her slap. His hiding place behind the bushes. The mob of angry men. The false charges. The crack of rock on bone. Zahra's blood and her slow fall.

Jesus shook his head, trying to stop the memories. When they would not relent, something inside him broke, and he began to sob.

The old woman watched and waited. Jesus fell forward, folding onto his knees. "I am not the ghost you fear," she said. "I am Mother Susana."

Jesus heard her, but could not respond. He lay motionless on the floor. The pain in his leg and the reliving of that violent night having wrung the last strength from his bones.

In the silence, Mother Susana wrapped her hand tenderly around the copper piece. At first she could only suspect the circumstances under which the strange shepherd had come to possess Zahra's medallion. But, from what Sister Joan had managed to discover, Mother Susana was beginning to understand.

Though Sister Joan had been able to speak only briefly with Solomon, the shepherd had managed to convey that Zahra had, in no uncertain terms, instructed him to deliver the child to the Sisters. He had just begun to explain *why* his mother had made this request when the other shepherds had drawn near, forcing Sister Joan to flee back into The Narrows.

Jesus lifted himself slightly from the floor. Straining to wipe his tears along a shoulder.

As Mother Susana observed the young shepherd, her brow furrowed. Despite Solomon's assertions, Zahra's choice confused her. From what she had observed, the child lacked any grounding that would enable her to embrace the life of a Sister. After all, the child clearly knew nothing of The Way or its guiding principles. And, stranger still, having spent her formative years disguised as a boy, she appeared profoundly out of touch with her own feminine power.

Given this apparent unsuitability, and without having the benefit of Solomon's full explanation, she could only wonder what Zahra had seen in the child. But because Susana had fled to The Narrows so long ago—shortly after Solomon's birth—she had not seen her twin in many, many years.

Perhaps she had merely taken pity on her? Perhaps she had been unwell and her judgment impaired?

Mother Susana shook her head. Given the loss and trauma that she and the Sisters had recently sustained, she could not afford to spend time deciphering the peculiar new arrival. She had many more vital matters to attend to first.

Jesus shifted his weight and moaned at the pain in his leg.

The elder woman gazed over at the shepherd. "You need not be afraid," she assured her. "You will be safe here. But," she added, drawing herself upright, "you must know that you are forbidden to ever leave." Saying this, she lifted a small bell. "Go now in peace."

The other spirits arrived and stood in the entrance. Seeing their elder without a hood, they felt safe to remove their own. As Jesus was lifted from the floor, he found himself staring into the faces of two women. One of them possessed the same full lips and high cheekbones as his mother.

That night Jesus lay on his back thinking over all that had happened. He could not decide if any of what he had experienced was real or the delirium of hunger and injury. But whether actual or imaginary, he feared that unless he escaped, he would slip into irreversible madness.

Alone in the dark, Jesus contorted his forearms and twisted his elbows until he loosened the ties at his wrists. With great discomfort, he sat up and broke the straps off his ankles. He slid down carefully from the stone slab. When his feet hit the floor, a bolt of searing pain shot through his leg and up into his temples. He wanted to scream, but swallowed his cries.

He had determined to escape.

When the pain relented, he hopped on his good leg, making it through the door and into the corridor. In the dark, he skimmed his fingers along the wall for balance and direction. He froze when his fingers slipped across a fold of linen and then, the warmth of a body. Jesus spun and tried to run. Unable to see, he crashed headlong into a wall and tumbled to the ground. His leg rang with fresh pain.

The figure whose robes he had felt came and stood over him. "It would be wise not to try to leave," the coarse voice warned.

CHAPTER 10

Somewhere within The Narrows *outside ancient* Palestine*—16* A.D.

Following his failed escape attempt, Jesus was left in the dark for several more days. His ties had been redoubled. And not a single person visited his chamber, even at night.

Had they left him for dead?

Lying along the cold stone, he shouted at the top of his lungs for help.

Perhaps Solomon and Peter were searching for him?

When he had shredded his voice into a raspy hoarseness, Jesus felt his heart beginning to break. He longed to be back in the open, tending his sheep. He longed for his life's freedom and simplicity, the notes of the flute and the smell of grass. He longed for Anna and her soft muzzle. And, most of all, he longed to be Jesus.

Sister Ruth found Mother Susana sitting in the dark,.her eyes closed in contemplation. The elder woman had sequestered herself to replenish her spirit and meditate on the future.

During this time, she had instructed the Sisters to leave the young shepherd in solitude. Having been alarmed by her urgent need to escape, and knowing that such an attempt would gravely imperil their lives, Susana hoped a short period of deprivation would soften the young woman's will.

"Mother," Ruth whispered.

The old woman nodded but did not open her eyes.

"It has been three days," Ruth continued.

Mother Susana nodded slowly.

The old woman's heart, Ruth knew, was heavy and preoccupied with serious matters. First, there was the recent loss of Sister Samara. When she had returned from the outside world, broken and bloodied, they had tried to heal her, but to no avail. The injuries, from knives and stones, were too grave. But her unwarranted return had also sparked fear for the safety of the other Sisters. And just when that worry had reached its peak, the strange young shepherd had appeared, unescorted, leading them all to believe that an attack upon the caves was imminent. Then, Sister Joan had returned from her journey with news of Zahra's strange request—and of her murder.

It had all been, Ruth thought, *too much.*

Watching Mother Susana's eyes wander behind closed lids, she wondered if the old woman would be able to rise under the weight of such tragedy. An ordinary human would have been knocked to the ground. But Ruth knew better than to question the woman whose strength had been forged in a fire hot with faith and reverence. She was therefore not surprised to see the elder woman open her eyes and stand, effortlessly, as if lifted by a large hand.

Mother Susana walked to a nearby lamp and lit the wick. She turned to face her visitor. "You speak the truth, Sister Ruth," she said. Her eyes burned with conviction. "It is time that we gather." She nodded. "Call a Circle."

Sister Ruth lifted Jesus's head and held a liquid-filled sponge above his mouth. She let the water drip between his lips. Jesus woke to the sensation of falling raindrops.

"Hello," Ruth said, smiling when she saw his eyes open.

Through the haze of pain and hunger, he glimpsed her clearly for the first time. Her body was stocky and round. Her chest ample beneath the folds of her robe. Large dimples bore into her cheeks, especially when she smiled or laughed, which she did with relish and a toss of glistening auburn hair. Her eyes were a plain, ordinary brown, yet they danced with a spontaneity that Jesus found disarming.

"My name is Ruth," she said, breaking the spell. "Keeper of the Tree of Life, Sister of The Way."

Jesus wrinkled his brow. He had no idea what she was talking about.

Maybe she was demented?

Ruth continued her ministrations. She lifted the sponge again and squeezed it above his mouth. "You must drink as much as you can," she said, as liquid streamed between his lips.

Jesus felt the room dip and spin. But he tasted sweetness in the water and could no longer resist. He drank with fury.

"Good." Ruth nodded. "Very good." She pulled the linen cloth from his body. He lay naked before her. She filled a copper bowl with water and mixed in two drops of flowery-smelling oil. She lifted his foot. He struggled to protect himself.

"Trust me," Ruth said.

Jesus held still. Almost against his will. The water felt warm as she rinsed the dust from between his toes.

"Why do you not just get it over with and kill me?" he asked, watching her with suspicion.

Ruth smiled, amused by the youngster's brashness. "How old are you?" she asked. "Fifteen? Maybe sixteen?"

He glared at her.

She laughed. "Oh! Those eyes!" she said. "They have a life of their own." She moved the sponge up the calf on his good leg. She massaged the liquid deep into his muscles. While she worked, she considered his face. "You know, you really *do* look like a young man," she said. "And a handsome one, too!"

Jesus blushed at the word. *Handsome.* His mother had first called him that.

"But from where I'm looking," Ruth continued, nodding between his legs, "you are, in truth, a young *woman.*"

Jesus snapped his legs shut.

Ruth let out a deep, rolling laugh. "You certainly *act* like a young man, though!" She gently lowered his legs. "Mother Susana was right, we will have our hands full with you." She sponged his arm, taking time to massage his palm and fingers. The gentle touch loosened his tongue.

"Why did you kill the other shepherd?" he asked.

"Kill?" Ruth blurted, her eyebrows reaching for the sky.

"I saw them taking his body away. I saw the blood," he challenged.

Ruth frowned. Her cheeks reddened. "That was Sister Samara," she said with quiet deference. "And we did not kill her. She was murdered. By someone outside."

Jesus watched her round eyes fill with tears. He followed one as it trailed down her cheek and dropped onto her chest. It was then that he noticed the medallion around her neck. It held the same likeness of the sycamore as the one he had worn!

Ruth saw the recognition come into his eyes. "You have much to learn," she told him. "But not today." She finished washing his neck and tossed the dirty water down a hole in the floor. She knelt and uncovered a plate of olives, bits of bread, and plants Jesus did not recognize. She placed an olive near his lips. He wanted to resist but his hunger was too great. She smiled as he chewed the small fruit. "There are those among us, those in the Circle, who do not want to heal you," she admitted. "They feel that you threaten our safety. They worry you will try to escape if you are made well." She sighed. "But after intuiting you, I said you would eventually decide to stay." She threw him a wink.

Jesus felt his distrust faltering. It was hard not to like Ruth and her dimpled cheeks.

"So tell me," Ruth said. "Deep in your heart. When your leg is better, will you try to escape?"

Without a thought, Jesus said, "Yes." And knew it was true.

Ruth laughed again, deep from her belly, sending rolls of mirth down the corridors. "I thought you would say that!" she said and offered him another olive.

During the next month, Jesus heard the caves buzzing with activity. There was much to be done, it seemed, though he could see nothing of what was transpiring. He had also noticed that the women had stopped questioning him and rarely visited his chamber. Even Sister Ruth had ceased to come any longer, having passed his care onto a younger woman. Tabitha was her name, and she arrived every morning to rub a sour-smelling oil into his leg and manipulate his joints.

"You are healing f-f-fast! D-does it feel b-better?" Tabitha asked through a pronounced stutter.

Jesus nodded. Noting her simplicity, he decided to try to wheedle information from her. Clues that could help him escape.

"Have you lived here a long time?" he began.

Tabitha looked up in surprise. The shepherd had never spoken to her before. She responded with an enthusiastic nod. "W-w-when I was a g-girl, S-s-sister Joan brought me here."

Jesus frowned at the mention of the giant woman who had foiled his escape. "Why did she bring you here? Did she capture you, too?" he asked. He wondered if all of the women were prisoners like himself.

Tabitha smiled and wagged her head. "No. Not like that. I lived with my b-b-brother. Joan took me away because he w-was not k-kind." She tipped her head forward. "He gave me this," she said, parting her hair to one side. Jesus gasped. Underneath the wisps lay a thick, knobby scar. Ruth would later tell him that all the beatings Tabitha endured had left her unable to speak with clarity.

Jesus lifted a hand to his cheek, his fingers playing along the scar his own father had inflicted.

Tabitha blushed and pulled her hair back down. "I do n-not t-talk about that."

Returning to her task, she pressed her palms along Jesus's calf, kneading the muscles underneath. As she did, Jesus prepared to ask her about the location of the cave's entrance. But when he opened his mouth to speak, he spotted a tall shadow darkening the doorway.

One morning after Tabitha had come and gone, Jesus heard a strange sound coming from down the corridor. It began as a low hum but gradually increased in volume. The sound slipped around the walls and funneled into his room, where it concentrated and blossomed with alarming power. He could feel the tone buzzing in his breastbone. Frightened, he rolled onto his knees. For the first time in what felt like ages, he pushed himself to a standing position. His leg held the weight, though the effort made it ache. He hobbled around the room, his hands gliding along the wall for support.

The intensity of the sound increased.

He found that by leaning against the wall, he could move with surprising ease. He hopped to the door and looked outside. Down the hallway, to the left, he saw a glow, the color of pear, spilling from a side chamber. It was the place from which the sound came.

Driven by curiosity, he hobbled toward the vibration. As he drew closer, the sound changed. Its pitch reached higher and its edges smoothed.

It was nearly perfect.

When he arrived at the door to the side room, he wiped the sweat from his forehead and peered inside. What he saw held him in amazement.

The walls of the chamber had been carved into a nearly flawless sphere. A group of women sat in a circle on the floor with their eyes closed. They were all holding hands and intoning a single sound. Each wore a plum-colored robe and a copper medallion. It then occurred to him that, with all the women gathered in one place, he might be able to bolt out the entrance unnoticed.

But for the moment, the magic of the scene held him transfixed. Jesus had never seen women gathered in such a way. And he had never heard a group of people produce such a pure and seamless sound. The individual could no longer be distinguished from the group.

Seated at the center of the circle was the woman who had reminded him of his mother. Sister Shereen, he thought was her name. From what he had observed, she served an important role among the women, though he did not yet understand what it might be.

The volume of the tone increased and the vibration widened as if it were coming alive. From her central position, Shereen served as the tone's fulcrum and her body shimmered. Jesus gasped at the phenomenon. He slapped a hand over his mouth, hoping the others had not heard. Much to his relief, no one seemed to notice and the sound continued unchanged. Soon a feeling of lightness and buoyancy surrounded him as if he were being lowered into a body of water. His skin felt crisp and sparkly. He smiled as a strange giddiness overcame him. Entranced, he spread his arms wide and was surprised to find that he could stand without support.

He felt like he could fly!

Just when he was certain he would lift into the air, a heavy hand dropped onto his shoulder. When he turned, he was staring into the angry eyes of Sister Joan.

"I am told you can walk," a voice said.

Jesus looked up from his mat and saw Sister Ruth. His eyes searched for Sister Joan but did not find her. She had been guarding his doorway ever since apprehending him. He looked again at Ruth but said nothing. Even if he would not admit it, he was glad to see her dancing eyes.

"I am glad to see you, too," Ruth said with a nod. "Come follow me," she said and disappeared out the door. Jesus remained on his mat. Her invitation had startled him.

Was it a trick? Had they set a trap? Why after all this time would she suddenly entice him to leave the chamber?

Minutes passed. Ruth did not return.

Jesus wondered where she had gone but feared what might await him in the corridor. He struggled to contain his curiosity. But when she still did not return, he surrendered. He pressed his palms into the ground and lifted his torso above his stiff leg. The maneuver hurt his injury, but not like before.

He limped toward the entrance and fell against it. The rock was cool to the touch and calmed his nerves. He took a few unsteady steps around the room. His body's confidence returning. Using the wall for balance, he followed in the direction he had seen Ruth turn. When he caught up to her, she appeared to be standing at a dead end. His senses leapt to full alert.

Why had she brought him there? Was he to be cornered and killed like an animal?

Ruth pretended not to notice his anxiety. She lifted her hand and placed it against the wall. "Close your eyes," she instructed.

Jesus balked.

"Close your eyes," she repeated.

He did as she asked but kept one eyelid cracked. He wanted to see the enemy's approach. He watched as Ruth pressed her palm against the immovable stone. To his amazement, the entire wall rotated on a hidden axis and light from the outside world spilled into the corridor.

A sharp pain filled his head as he encountered the full intensity of daylight. During his period of confinement, his eyes had become accustomed to nothing more than the unsteady glow of torches.

"Keep your eyes closed," Ruth said again. "But lift your face."

Jesus tipped his head and watched the inside of his eyelids stain magenta. After another moment, Ruth said, "Now open your eyes partway."

He did as she said and felt a sting. But less sharp.

Ruth coached him further and soon he was staring into the hot, bright world of The Narrows. The sight elated him. He began searching for a route of escape, but realized he would never be able to outrun Ruth. He decided to wait for a better opportunity.

"This way," Ruth said, fully aware of the young shepherd's intentions.

They slipped out of the caves and the door swiveled to a close behind them. From outside, Jesus noted, one could not detect the slightest seam in the rock.

"Watch your footing," she cautioned.

Jesus looked down. He was standing on a narrow ledge. Much like the one he had been walking on just before his fall. Ruth saw the color wash from his face.

"Take my hand," she instructed.

When the sureness of her fingers twined with his, the fear began to dissipate. Together they made their way along the edge. As they walked, the taste of freedom sweetened Jesus's tongue and his soul yearned to return to the life he knew. Looking across the sands, he could see how far the desert stretched. Every direction appeared endless. He knew that once he broke free, the crossing would be difficult. But he felt his leg remembering more with each step, and grew drunk on thoughts of escape.

Ruth looked over her shoulder at her young charge. Jesus quickly erased the enthusiasm from his mind, afraid that she might sense his desire.

After a few minutes, Ruth released his hand. She lifted her palms to the cliff side. As before, she leaned into the rock and an unseen door swiveled open. She led Jesus into the new chamber. He hobbled behind her, down a slight incline.

Then he heard a sound that made his heart freeze. He stopped and balanced on his good leg. His mind could not trust his ears. But his heart wanted to believe.

Could it be?

It was the bleating of sheep.

Soon the familiar scent of wool wafted to greet him. A thin blade of light cut through a crack in the ceiling and filled the space with a dusty glow. In the middle of the chamber, Jesus saw a woman standing before a small flock.

"Greetings," Ruth called.

"Greetings," the woman returned.

Jesus then recognized her. It was Sister Shereen, the one who had been seated in the center of the circle. Ruth would later tell him that it had been Shereen who had laid her hands on him after the fall. He recalled the warmth that had spread from her fingers, like rivulets of water seeking out his injury.

Like his mother, she stood dark and slender, with glittering skin of the same cocoa color. Beneath her plum-colored hood shimmered waves of cinnamon-colored hair. Her golden, almond-shaped eyes dripped with wisdom. And when she smiled, she left no corner of the room unlit.

Moving closer, he felt suddenly humbled by Shereen's presence. It was impossible to deny the power that radiated from her. Unable to hold her gaze, Jesus let his attention fall to the sheep. They were worn and thin, as if they had been on a long journey without enough to eat. Their hooves were splitting, their wool dry and frizzy. His heart went out to them. One of the animals began to struggle and bleat insistently in a loud, pleading mew. The others shifted as the one butted its way out. Jesus dropped to his knees, instantly recognizing the blackened face. The lamb wedged itself between his legs and nuzzled its head along his shins.

"Anna!" he whimpered. He fell across her back and ran his fingers through her wool. Her oils softened his palms. She was leaner than the others. The bones beneath her eyes protruding like shelves. "Anna . . . my Anna," he stuttered through tears.

Shereen smiled. "Sister Joan brought them back from the flatlands," she said. "Not without great difficulty, as I understand," she added with a comical tip of her head.

"But . . . but how—?"

"They were a gift to Mother Susana. From her nephew."

Jesus gawked. "Her *nephew*?"

Shereen nodded. "Solomon sent them. Just as he sent *you*."

Jesus could not believe his ears. His mind reeled. He grabbed at the possibilities spreading before him.

What was happening?

Desperate and contradictory thoughts pelted the inside of his head.

Had Solomon sent him here intentionally*? Or had the women killed the shepherds and stolen their sheep?!*

And how could Solomon have been Susana's nephew, unless . . . ?

"Zahra was Susana's sister," Shereen told him. "Her twin."

Jesus gaped. Inside he heard Solomon's voice.

Sometimes we are called upon before we are ready.

His mind spun.

Had the gray-eyed shepherd somehow known his secret all along?

The wet touch of Anna's muzzle on his cheek steadied him.

Shereen observed the young shepherd intently. "We have not kept sheep here in years," she said, "and are very much in need of milk and wool. We have decided to ask if you would stay and tend our flock."

Jesus bent to press his face into Anna's woolly back.

Somewhere inside himself he heard the tearing of a seam.

"We cannot pay you with coins," Shereen added. "But you will be well cared for and this will be your home," she said, indicating the large cave. "Are you willing?"

He looked up and mistook Shereen for his mother.

How he wanted to hear her call his name! To feel her arms enfold him. How he—

"Are you willing?" Shereen asked again.

Jesus peered through dual rivers of tears. He nodded.

Ruth shared a smile with the others.

Sister Shereen came and knelt before him. She glanced from shepherd to lamb and back again. A sudden spark lit her expression. She gazed intently into the shepherd's eyes. "Anna?" she whispered. "Is that you?"

Jesus swallowed hard.

An invisible door swiveled inside him.

"Yes," she answered.

PART THREE

SISTER

CHAPTER 11

Somewhere within The Narrows *outside ancient* Palestine—*17* A.D.

Early dawn paused before flushing across the desert. The sun, still dressing in her illuminated robes, remained hidden. The air rustled with dry scents. A raven alighted on a crag, hunting for lizards. A lone shepherd stood against the horizon, her leg crooked to rest one foot on the other knee. At her waist hung a leather sling and a pouch full of stones. Beneath her a small flock of sheep spread across the valley floor. In a single flash, quick as lightning, the shepherd loaded her sling, set her target, and fired. She watched with satisfaction as her stone ricocheted off the ground just inches below the sheep's nose, changing the animal's course and diverting the flock away from the snake-infested rocks.

Living separately from the others, Anna had sought to establish a routine designed around the needs of her animals. Each morning she rose before the sun, built a fire, washed her hands and face in a small bowl, and ate the meal left by Sister Ruth.

It had not taken her long to train the animals to negotiate the ridge down into the valley. There she would let them mingle in the fresh air and sunshine. Sometimes she could even find a fresh spring. The landscape, despite its barrenness, bubbled with many hidden water sources.

Although the animals had adjusted to their new surroundings with relative ease, Anna's adjustment had come more slowly. It had taken months for her disguise to unravel. At first she had felt awkward shepherding the flock as a young woman. And it had seemed stranger still to adjust to her body's new shapes and cycles. Since the start of her monthly renewal, her hips had widened ever so slightly, and her breasts had begun to announce themselves more prominently, though they remained considerably smaller than most. Despite the changes, Anna noticed that her shepherding skills had sharpened rather than declined.

Perhaps since she no longer feared discovery, or struggled against the developments of her body, she could better focus her energies on the tending of her flock?

Whatever the reason, her efforts had begun to pay off handsomely. Within months of their arrival, the sheep had begun thriving and providing the Sisters with skins full of milk.

Stepping out of the caves to rest from their labors, Sisters Shereen and Ruth climbed to a summit above the caves. From this vantage they could observe the young shepherd tending her flock in the valley.

The two women felt particularly vindicated by Anna's success since it had been they who had helped calm the Circle's initial concerns about her.

Shereen turned to Ruth. "Has she yet shared anything of her past with you?"

Ruth shook her head. "Just a few stories from her life among the shepherds. For the most part, though, she has remained preoccupied with her animals and their comfort."

Shereen nodded with a smile. "You will have to share her stories with the others. I gather they are curious to hear about her adventures as a boy!"

Ruth chuckled in agreement. She then grew serious. "But I would expect, now that she has gotten the sheep settled, her mind will turn to other concerns."

Shereen lifted a hand. With the tip of a finger, she traced the lines creasing her palm. "She will have many questions for us," she said.

"Yes."

A gentle breeze swept around them, bringing the scent of sage and lifting the hair about their faces.

"Do you think Zahra was wrong to send her?" Ruth asked.

Shereen gave a slight shrug. "I do not know," she said. "Though I can understand why Mother Susana and the others might think so," she added. She watched the shepherd's stride. Noted the graceful, almost floating gait. "There is something so different and . . . *unknown* . . . about her. And yet"—her voiced dropped to a whisper—"and yet she possesses qualities that are so *familiar*."

Ruth turned to Shereen with a questioning look. Knowing the older Sister to possess extraordinary powers of intuition, she wished for her to elaborate.

But Shereen interrupted. "Can you imagine the courage and cunning it took for her to endure life as a male shepherd?"

Ruth followed Shereen's gaze back down to the strapping young woman. Together they watched her effortlessly steer the sheep through an outcropping of rock.

The wind carried the sound of mewing to their ears.

"It is strange," Shereen continued. "But I cannot help but draw a comparison between Anna's journey and that of the Awakeners."

Ruth gasped, startled that Shereen would compare the strange young shepherd to those most revered Sisters.

"Consider this—both have left behind all they know to fend for themselves. Both have traveled the world in secrecy. Both have endured the knowledge that their lives were forever at risk should their identity be discovered. And both have survived by the strength of their wits and bravery."

Ruth held still.

Shereen gazed into the distance. "And none of them," she added wistfully, "no matter the success of their endeavors, can ever return home."

Ruth could sense the sudden shift that had occurred in her friend—her thoughts having moved inward to dwell on her own future. For Shereen, too, would one day make the arduous journey across The Narrows to re-enter the world as an Awakener.

Ruth took her friend's hand.

Peering again at Shereen, at the amber light gleaming in her eyes, she thought she detected something more: another set of thoughts looming above the concern for her future.

Perhaps a further suspicion about Anna? Or an inkling of Zahra's intent?

Ruth took a deep breath and let her mind settle. Whatever Shereen had seen, she felt certain it would reveal itself when the time was right.

Anna woke to the clip-clop of hooves and the crackling of a fire. Opening her eyes, she found a jagged pane of light reaching deep inside the cave's throat. For some reason she had slept later than usual.

Sitting up, she saw that Ruth had already come and gone. The fire had been stoked and Anna's breakfast—a bowl of porridge and a chunk of dark, seeded bread—set on a nearby rock.

But Ruth had also left something else.

Lying alongside her breakfast was a small pile of greenery. Anna looked in disbelief, then rubbed her eyes and looked again.

It was a stack of live sycamore branches!

She leapt to her feet and drew the knobby limbs through her fingers in amazement. She supposed that Ruth wished for her to give them to the sheep.

But from where could she have possibly obtained green sycamore branches?

She brushed the mysterious branches along her palm. Their sudden appearance only served to increase the agitation she had felt growing inside her.

Though she had adapted well to her new life, even come to take pleasure in it, Anna found herself increasingly haunted by questions about the Sisters—and recollections of her past. Her dreams, in particular, had taken on a frenetic pace, stitching together distant memories that came in rapid flashes—her mother's unusual songs; Zahra's medallion and her ragged plum robes; Solomon gazing into her eyes and saying, *I believe, then, that you are ready*; the woman who had spoken out in Jerusalem being hunted down by soldiers; and the revelation that Mother Susana was Zahra's twin.

Then, as she was having these dreams, live sycamore branches had appeared in her cave, reminding her of the great old sycamore in her village, and the one on Zahra's medallion.

To Anna, it seemed as if connections must exist among all these things.

The next day, intent on learning more, she approached Ruth.

Having expected the shepherd's question, the round Sister replied, "So you knew the limbs were from a sycamore?"

"Of course!" Anna spouted. "There was such a tree in my village."

"What village was that?"

"Nazareth."

Ruth frowned. She knew nothing of that place. She pushed in a different direction. "Did Zahra, perhaps, teach you of the tree's healing abilities?"

Anna's face twisted up. "Of its what?" she asked.

Ruth nodded. "Then she did not."

A silence fell between the women.

Ruth's eyebrows drew together in consternation.

If Zahra had wanted Anna to join them, why had she not begun to teach her?

"And what of your mother and father?" Ruth asked, digging deeper.

Anna shrugged. "My father was a carpenter. My mother was"—she choked on her words and lowered her face to hold down the pain—"my mother was *beautiful*," she whispered.

Seeing that their talk had upset the shepherd, Ruth decided not to press further. She placed a hand on her friend's shoulder.

Anna collected herself, wiping a sleeve across her eyes. "I am sorry. It is just that . . ."

"You are confused as to why you are here?"

Anna nodded.

Ruth smiled. "I promise. You will have your answers. When you are ready."

Anna balked. "But I am ready *now*," she said.

Ruth tipped her head with understanding but said nothing further.

Anna took a deep breath and crossed her arms. "Sister Ruth," she began, "you know now that I am not a danger. That I will not run away. I have tended the sheep as you have asked, and provided good milk for the Sisters. Why then will you not answer my questions? Or, at the very least, tell me from where you have obtained live sycamore branches?"

In reply to Anna's question, Ruth asked one of her own. "If you had a ball of yarn, could you unwind it from the middle?"

"What?" Anna said, baffled.

"Of course you could not! And if you tried, you would ruin the entire ball."

Anna shook her head in frustration. "I do not understand—"

"Just as you cannot take yarn from the middle, so I cannot tell you of the sycamore branches. Or of the reasons you have come here. But trust me when I tell you this: The answers *will* come. You must learn to be patient." Ruth said this despite knowing that no one could answer *all* of Anna's questions. With Zahra gone, so much about the young shepherd, and her reasons for being among them, could never be known.

Anna frowned, dissatisfied with Ruth's response. Realizing she was not to receive any of the information she sought, and still feeling uneasy from her dreams, she grabbed up her sling and pouch of stones. "I must tend to my sheep," she muttered and departed without looking back.

As was their custom, the Sisters gathered for evening tea. Sitting in a circle around a fire, they sipped from their cups and shared news and insights of the day. Behind them sounded the click-clack of Tabitha's loom as she wove a new tunic.

Sister Ruth approached the fire and sat next to Shereen.

"Greetings of the night."

"And to you," Shereen said. Her eyebrows lifted. "Well?" she said, eager to hear what more Ruth had learned from the young shepherd.

Ruth shrugged.

"What did she tell you?" Shereen prodded.

Ruth gazed into the hazy surface of her tea. "That she lived in Nazareth. That despite being friends, Zahra taught her nothing of The Way. And that her father was a carpenter. Quite a bit older than her mother, I think."

Ruth sighed and blew the steam from her cup. To her the information carried little import. Which was why she was startled by the look that shattered Shereen's face. A look of utter surprise and . . . anguish.

"Shereen?" she asked, bewildered. "Did I say something to upset—?"

"No," she said. She held up a hand. "It is nothing."

Ruth watched Shereen realign and regain her composure.

Shereen glanced quickly about the circle. Relieved to find that no one had noticed their interaction, she drifted slowly to her feet. "It has been a long day," she said. "I think I will retire."

CHAPTER 12

Somewhere beyond the Great Desert—17 A.D.

The men's laughter rose to Peter's ears but in it he found no joy. From a distance, he watched the others dancing around a limber fire, wine in their hands, women on their arms, a goat sizzling above the flames.

Having successfully crossed the great sands, the shepherds had stumbled into the village tattered and bone thin. The people's hospitality had been a welcome relief.

But Peter did not have the heart for celebrating. Ever since the loss of his friend, he had found the world a dismal place. His life devoid of meaning.

Gazing across the barren landscape, it seemed impossible to him that a spirit as vibrant as his friend's could have been extinguished.

And yet Jesus had not returned.

Long after Solomon had declared Jesus dead, Peter had spotted his friend everywhere—rising atop ridgelines, drifting through bobbing flocks, approaching camp at mealtime. He would even have sworn he had heard his voice—calling out to the birds, to the sheep—and to Peter.

Worse still, Peter's growing despair had led to dangerous oversights. On one occasion, only a few weeks into their arduous crossing, he had allowed his lead sheep to wander straight into a cobra's nest. His error had resulted in the animal's agonizing death. Afterward the shepherds missed no opportunity to berate him. Chastising him for his idiotic and costly mistake.

As a consequence, the self-assurance that his friendship with Jesus had helped instill had begun to fade. Leaving him vulnerable, once again, to the voices from his past. During the long lonely nights, he found his father's disapproval intruding ever more into his thoughts.

How could my loins have issued such a weak and pathetic son? he remembered his father crying in anguish, the night before he had sent Peter away forever.

Peering through the smoke, thickened with burning fat, he spotted Solomon sitting on a distant ridge. As of late, the men had noticed that their leader had again become preoccupied and distressed, just as he had outside Jerusalem. Most assumed it was because he blamed himself for the loss of their best shepherd. Others were not sure what had caused his fresh apprehension. And still others stewed over what their leader's anguish might portend for the future.

As for Peter, he did not care to trouble himself with Solomon or his woes. He hoped, in fact, that the elder shepherd *did* blame himself for the loss of Jesus. A loss from which Peter felt certain he would never recover.

CHAPTER 13

Somewhere within The Narrows outside ancient Palestine—20 A.D.

Sister Ruth ambled down the narrow path that led to Anna's cave. She had set off earlier than usual and the pre-dawn air felt soft against her skin.

When she arrived at the chamber, she found the shepherd already gone. Only a ring of bright coals remained in the place of her morning fire. Setting down the meal, Ruth went to a small stone enclosure. She knelt down and drew away its heavy, flat top. In the cool cavern underneath, she found goatskins full of milk. This morning the skins were three in number rather than two. Ruth smiled at the ample supply. The sheeps' bounty, and Anna's gift for tending them, had added much-needed flesh to the Sisters' bones.

Ruth had just bent to heft the skins of milk onto her shoulders when she heard loud mewing. The animals sounded close. This was unusual since Anna normally led them toward a distant valley. Curious as to why the flock remained nearby, she replaced the stone lid and left the cave.

Outside, the sun was just peeking over the horizon, firing bright, dusty arrows across the desert floor. In this early light, Ruth spied Anna laying a set of shears flat along the flank of a sheep. Rolled onto its back, the animal remained calm, its head lolling to one side, while

Anna loomed above, pressing one knee gently into its chest. In a single, seamless motion, the shepherd grabbed a fistful of woolly rings and slipped the blades beneath, working her shears in a scissoring motion. After a dozen or more snips, the animal's coat began to lift off its body in a single, thick blanket.

"Easy, little one," Anna whispered to the sheep as she rolled the fleece toward its front legs. "Almost done now," she added.

Then, as if they had shared a silent communication, both Anna and the animal rose to their feet. The fleece slipped loose from the sheep's body and Anna billowed it into the air. Judging the cut to be good, she tossed the woolly blanket onto a nearby pile, where it landed with an airy bounce.

"Oh! Look at all that beautiful wool!" Ruth cried out. She wound her way down the pathway and rushed to the stack of buoyant fleece. She wove her fingers between the plush curls. "This is the softest I have ever felt. And just look at the size of the pile. It is as tall as you!" she remarked.

"Yes," Anna said, smiling broadly. Glancing over her shoulder, she whistled for the next sheep. It came trotting over and lay at her feet.

Ruth shook her head in disbelief. "I never tire of seeing how your animals trust you," she said.

Anna blushed and leveled her shears along the animal's flank.

Fascinated by the shepherd's work, Ruth sat on a nearby rock to observe. Reveling in Anna's skill, she said, "You must have enjoyed your life as a shepherd."

Without hesitation, Anna said, "Yes."

Ruth dropped her chin into her hands. "What about it gave you the most pleasure?"

Anna thought for a moment. A sudden light came into her eyes. "The freedom," she said.

Ruth nodded as though she understood. After some time her eyes drifted toward the horizon. She sighed as her expression took on a hazy glow. "What was the most beautiful city you ever visited?" she asked.

Anna glanced over in surprise. Ruth never spoke about the outside world. Anna returned her attention to the blades and gave the situation some thought.

"I would be happy to answer your question," she said, "if you will answer one of mine."

Ruth started.

Anna looked over with a grin. Ruth's dimples drilled into her cheeks. "Ha!" she spouted. "You are far too clever for your own good! And so *tenacious.*" Her body shook with a deep chuckle. After a moment she said, "I promise to answer whatever question you may ask—if I am able."

Anna frowned and set down her shears. "That is not a fair bargain."

Ruth nodded. "True. But it is the best I can offer."

Anna released the animal beneath her and billowed out its shorn fleece. She tossed the coat onto her growing pile. Scowling, she said, "Then I shall only tell you about the *second* most beautiful city."

Ruth burst out laughing at the defiant retort, her mirth nearly toppling her backward.

Anna laughed, too. "You were not expecting me to say that, were you?"

Ruth grabbed at her sides. "No!" she admitted. And realized that, for the first time since her arrival, Anna had caught her off guard.

Clearly the young shepherd possessed a fiber that ran deeper than she had estimated.

Pleased with herself, Anna took up her shears and called the next animal. As she snipped its coat, she began to tell Ruth about Dara, the city of orange spires and lyre makers.

Ruth's eyes lit up at her vivid descriptions. "And did you have dates stuffed with honey and almonds?" she asked. "Those were my favorite."

Anna nodded, recalling the fruit's sweet, buzzy flavor.

When she had finished with her tale, Anna grew quiet. She signaled to the next sheep. It was her namesake. Anna's woolly black body bobbed forward. The shepherd drew her palm along the sheep's back. Then, without seeming to have intended to, she said, "Aside from being beautiful, Dara was also where I discovered my name."

Ruth's eyebrows drew close. "The name you took as a shepherd?" she asked.

Anna nodded. The black sheep knelt and rolled onto her back.

Ruth held still, gauging the moment. She did not wish to press the shepherd until she was prepared to reveal more of her past. Still, if she were to approach Mother Susana about Anna's future among them, as she and Shereen had planned for her to do, Ruth needed a clearer understanding of the young woman's early character. Proceeding with care, she asked, "And how did you come to choose the name Jesus?"

Anna leveled the shears along the sheep's hock. "It was to have been my brother's name," she said. "But he . . . did not survive."

Ruth watched Anna's demeanor change. Saw how a cloud seeded with sorrow drifted before her eyes. Although she did not know the particular circumstances under which Anna had joined the shepherds, she had divined some idea by stitching together her unusual appearance and the little Solomon had told Sister Joan—that Anna's mother had died tragically, and that her father had disguised and sold her. Knowing now that Anna's only brother had perished helped expand Ruth's understanding.

Seeing that Anna had reached the end of her tale, Ruth cleared her throat and said, "Now it is your turn. What question do you wish to ask of me?"

Anna looked up. Knowing that Ruth would not address her most pressing question directly—of why she had been brought to them—she decided to come at it from another angle. "I want to know about your medallion," she said. "Why do you wear it? And what does it mean?"

Ruth tipped her head. "You ask because Zahra gave you hers and you want to know why?"

Anna nodded. "Yes."

Ruth took a moment to think. Drawing in a deep breath, she said, "The sycamore is an ancient and enduring symbol of what we believe. The values that inspire and comprise The Way."

Anna held still, listening intently.

"We wear the medallions," she went on, "in honor of what we believe, and as a token to prod us into remembrance. Especially when we are faced with adversity."

Hearing this, Anna's eyes grew wide. "So Zahra was a Sister of The Way, too?" she asked.

Ruth nodded.

Anna's eyes narrowed. "But just what *is* The Way? Are you the ones who practice 'the old ways'?" she asked, remembering the disdain with which her father, and Peter, had spoken of such people.

Ruth smiled and wagged her finger. "I promised to answer *one* question," she said. "As it is, I have already answered two!"

Anna sighed. Though Ruth's answer had proven somewhat unsatisfactory, she felt relieved by the Sister's sudden willingness to entertain questions. And she hoped that, perhaps soon, Ruth might agree to answer more.

Ruth turned to observe the growing pile of fleece. It had begun to lean to one side. "I will go and collect others to haul away your treasure," she said. She looked again at the young shepherd. Studying her, she sensed the eager force of her curiosity. Wanting to put things in perspective for the shepherd, Ruth stepped forward and laid a hand on her shoulder.

"How long does it take a ewe to produce a lamb?" she asked.

Anna shrugged. "Almost a year," she said.

"Ah," Ruth said. "That is a long time to be patient. But not the longest I know of."

Anna's forehead wrinkled. "What do you mean?"

Ruth smiled. "Do you know how long it takes before a fig tree can bear its first fruit?"

Anna shook her head. "No. But why are you asking me—?"

"Five years."

"What?"

"A fig tree must patiently wait five years before bearing its first fruit."

Anna kicked at the stones beneath her sandals. "Are you saying that—?"

"I am saying that every creature must endure some period of waiting before the longed-for moment of fruition arrives. For some, the wait is longer than for others." She paused, then asked, "Do you understand?"

Anna's lips tightened. "Yes. You are saying that *my* wait is to be long," she mumbled.

"Perhaps," Ruth said with a nod. "But let us hope not."

Sister Joan traveled several miles from the caves to a distant pinnacle high above the valley floor. From there she could scan the entire horizon unseen. In years past she had usually climbed to the spot once every lunar cycle, but ever since Sister Samara's dangerous return, she had taken to making the journey every three days.

She shielded her eyes and scanned the valley's perimeter. She saw nothing, but felt a tingle in the hairs at the back of her neck. Perhaps it was only a wolf or a passing sandstorm. But she sensed an incongruity in the landscape.

To relieve her anxiety, she methodically double-checked her preparations to secure the caves in case of an incursion. She mixed the blinding powders of capsicum and turmeric into leather strips that could be used to hurl a stinging cloud into an intruder's eyes with a single snap. She also reinforced the false ceiling above the central chamber. With the slip of a hidden lever, several weighty stones would tumble down and seal off the cave.

She knew that an unexpected attack was unlikely, and practically impossible, given their barren surroundings and her constant surveillance. But she also knew that it would be foolish, and perhaps deadly, to be caught unprepared.

CHAPTER 14

A village at the northeastern border of
the Great Desert—20 A.D.

Nearly four years since parting ways with his youngest shepherd, Solomon found himself leading his flocks back toward the Great Desert. As of late, he had been troubled by a sense that he needed to return.

His apprehension had only mounted when he began to overhear threatening banter in the villages that skirted the desert. Banter that suggested a rising resistance to The Way and a fresh desire to root out its proponents at whatever cost. And while murderous enemies had gathered before, never had Solomon encountered such a great number of them so close to the secret caves. And it was their rising clamor that made his sleep restless.

The women in the marketplace sat on the ground in front of their wares. One held a basket brimming with lentils.

Solomon approached carrying sacks of grain and fruit. He glanced down at the basket of beans. "Have you no more than that?" he asked.

The woman shook her head. "I began with five full bushels this morning, but a group of explorers bought nearly all I had."

"Explorers?" he asked.

"Yes," the woman replied. "The men who have gone to search the northern plain."

Solomon froze. His face drained of blood. For it was fissures in the northern plain that opened into the Sisters' domain. "Why would they wish to explore such godforsaken land?" he croaked.

The woman glared up at him. Shrugged. "How should I know?" She poured the remainder of her lentils onto a scale. "If you are interested in more beans, I can ask my neighbor."

Unable to gather himself, Solomon nodded slowly.

"Eh! Terese!" the woman cried out. "The one here wants more lentils."

Within moments, her neighbor gimped over dragging a full sack. When she arrived, she poured what she had onto the scale.

"So the explorers did not buy all you had?" the first woman asked her friend.

The neighbor shook her head. "Not of these. But they took every leaf of tea I had."

The first woman turned and spit. She then set the weights on her scale. "This one here wants to know why they are searching the northern areas," she said, tipping her head toward Solomon.

The neighbor tossed her hand and let out a grunt. "It is the priests," she said. "They are the ones riling everyone up." She tightened the cinch on her sack. "They come visiting our villages, telling the men they need to root out the pagans and heathens and barbarians. It is *they* who have the men running about like chickens without their heads."

Solomon frowned. "But why search an area where even the crazy ones cannot survive?" he asked.

The neighbor shrugged. "I only know what I hear," she said.

CHAPTER 15

Somewhere within The Narrows *outside*
ancient Palestine*—20* A.D.

Anna scaled the narrow precipice and teetered along its crumbling edge. Above, the noonday sun cast its baking heat downward. Her tenuous route took her past several caves. Their ragged mouths gaped to her left, exhaling icy air that lifted bumps along her flesh. Having spent countless hours exploring the area, she had discovered all of its secret cave systems and had ventured inside every one. Though she had found nothing of particular interest, aside from occasional evidence of rodents, she had noted that each cave faced a slightly different direction and was therefore useful for providing shelter from the sun at certain times of day. Such was the ideal place she was seeking, as her flock drifted along the valley floor.

Once she had selected her spot, Anna set down her staff and opened the linen cloth inside which she had wrapped her afternoon meal. As she nibbled on the hunks of cheese and bread, the cave's chill tingled the sweat along her back. Anna liked to have her meals in this particular place as it allowed her to observe not only her flock, but the Sisters' caves as well. And it was from this vantage that she had begun to decipher repeating patterns in the women's activities.

First, Mother Susana would rise, well before the sun, and depart from the main entrance. Dipping into the far valley, she would set off toward an elongated slope of craggy rock. Anna had tried to track her on several occasions, but despite her advanced years the elder woman always managed to disappear, leaving Anna breathless and unable to discover her final destination.

Later, but still before sunrise, Sisters Shereen, Helena, Irene, Naomi, and Rachel would walk from the main entrance to a smaller one farther west. This cave also possessed a seamless entrance that yawned silently as the Sisters slipped inside. Anna had noted that the five Sisters spent the majority of their time within that separate cave and were visited frequently by Mother Susana. At day's end, they would all emerge looking tired but exuberant—their skin dewy, their cheeks glowing. Together they would journey back to the main caves, whispering among themselves. Anna longed to know what occupied these Sisters and what it was they pursued with such vigor.

As for Sisters Ruth and Tabitha, Anna noted that they rarely left the main caves during the day. When the two *did* venture outside, they either slipped into the smaller cave for a brief stay, or journeyed into the valley, carrying baskets, to collect bits of plants and, occasionally, insects.

Perhaps for eating or flavoring their meals?

As for Sister Joan, Anna could rarely track her comings and goings. Like Mother Susana, she seemed to travel along routes as unseen and irregular as the wind. But Anna knew that the towering Sister remained suspicious of her and was never far away. Sometimes, when she was leading her flock, she would swear she felt Joan's gaze upon her.

Though Anna had memorized the pattern of the Sisters' movements, she could not for the life of her imagine what sorts of activities might so intently preoccupy them. Nor how such activities related to the practice of the old ways. If that was indeed what they were doing.

Several years had passed since Anna had first approached Ruth seeking answers. Yet since that time, and much to Anna's disappointment, the Sister had offered no further insights. No additional information to explain the mystery of the Sisters' endeavors nor of Anna's presence among them. For months after her first attempt, Anna had continued to try to pry answers loose from her friend, but when those efforts proved fruitless, she eventually relented. Not because she no longer desired to know, but because, remembering Ruth's words about patience, she had become concerned that if she were to persist, the

Sister might withhold the truth out of principle. Anna had also noted that the more she insisted, the less often her friend would visit. And given how much she relied on Ruth's company, she decided against doing anything that might damage their friendship.

Across the canyon, the door to the main cave heaved open and a figure slipped out. Anna immediately recognized Tabitha's halting gait. As usual, she was carrying her basket and following the path down into the valley.

Anna took another bite of bread and felt a breeze rustle the edges of her tunic. She gazed out along the horizon and smelled the air. She detected the faintest scent of salt mixed with iron. Her lush lips compressed into a line. She sensed a storm.

The flash of movement caught Anna's eye just as she was gnawing on her last crust of bread. Given the velocity and location, just south of the Sisters' caves, she assumed it had been a bird or something lifted by the breeze.

Then came a yelp.

Anna leapt to her feet. She fixed immediately on the sound, seeking its source. Within seconds she caught sight of a wolf, perched along a ledge. She held still to observe the creature and noted the dull and dirty condition of its coat. She noticed too its rib bones rippling beneath taut skin.

Anna stared in disbelief. The animal's close approach was unprecedented—as her constant presence and surveillance had rendered the area free of major predators. Or so she had believed.

Though the creature remained a reasonable distance away, Anna did not wish to chance that it might launch an attack, especially given its desperate condition.

Remembering Solomon's advice, she cupped her hands about her mouth and let out a mournful wail, seeking to engage the creature. Hearing the call, the animal spun on its heels and cocked its head to one side. Anna let go another cry. Hearing this, the wolf dropped its head and, seeming curious, made its way toward her. As it drew closer, it leapt onto a boulder.

Loading her sling and lifting it into position, Anna fired several stones arcing toward the animal's perch. The stones ricocheted off the rock with loud bangs sending the wolf skittering for cover. When Anna launched a second round, the wolf dropped to the ground and streaked into the distance.

From her outpost, Anna tracked the animal's departure until it had fled to a safe distance. When satisfied, she hooked the sling back inside her belt.

She then detected more movement.

She looked up.

The wolf could not have conquered the distance back to her that fast!

Her gaze then lighted on a human figure. Fleeing deeper into The Narrows.

Tabitha!

She had forgotten all about the younger Sister. She watched as Tabitha dashed from rock to rock, her steps frantic and uneven. Anna thought her movements indicated fear.

But to where could she possibly be running?

Her current path would only take her farther from the caves.

Perhaps she had become lost?

Dashing back along the precipice, Anna charged down into the valley. Strong in her stride, she scrambled over sharp lips of rock and tore through brambles and tight crevices until she caught up to the fleeing Sister.

When Tabitha spotted her, she yelped and ran off in the opposite direction.

"Tabitha! It is me!" Anna called out.

When Tabitha kept running, Anna sped after her.

"Tabitha! Stop! It is Anna!" she cried again.

When the young woman still would not relent, Anna surged forward, looped her arms around Tabitha's waist, and yanked her body back against her own. Tabitha fought like a wildcat, screeching and kicking. But Anna held tight. She had long ago learned how to restrain creatures that did not wish to be caught.

When the outburst had exhausted her, Tabitha sagged and slid to her knees.

"Easy, easy there," Anna said and turned the Sister around to face her.

Tabitha's entire body was shaking, her eyes widened in shock, her breathing shallow and quick.

"Deep breaths, take slow, deep breaths," Anna urged. Tabitha's clipped breathing reminded Anna of Peter's affliction. In all the years she had known Tabitha, she had never noticed that she suffered from the same symptoms.

"Oh Anna!" Tabitha cried, grabbing the shepherd's tunic in her fists.

"It is all right now," Anna told her. "You are with me. You are safe."

When a sudden swirl of wind whipped at the ground, Tabitha cringed and tried to dash.

Anna held her fast. "It was just the wind!" she said.

Tabitha held still, trembling. "But I heard him," she whispered, her eyes darting about.

"Heard who?" Anna asked, puzzled.

"A man," she said. "I heard him grunting."

Anna glanced over her shoulder. "No one is here, Tabitha. I have held watch the entire day and the only thing I have seen—" She stopped short, her mind making the connection.

Perhaps Tabitha had seen the wolf?! Or heard it rustling about?

She was about to offer this explanation to her friend when she thought better of it. Knowing she had encountered a predator was unlikely to make Tabitha feel more secure.

The wind's pace increased. Its bursts coming with more frequency. Glancing up at the sky, Anna said, "Let us get you home."

"But what about the—"

"I think you heard something else," Anna told her. "There is no one here but us." As she was saying this, the wind drove past. Anna's head snapped up. She had caught an odor in the breeze. Not like the earlier scent of salt and iron. But something entirely different. A scent that was strange, yet familiar. Without warning, shivers shook her spine.

Whatever it was, it had gone too quickly for her to identify it.

"Let us hurry," she told Tabitha.

The two bent against the oncoming wind, lifting their tunics to protect their faces.

As they made their way, Anna felt a hum rising through the soles of her feet. It rose gradually to nibble at the skin of her bones.

She turned to look behind, toward The Narrows. Though she could perceive little through the gritty wind, she sensed a great storm billowing overhead.

"We have to go *faster*," she told her companion.

But Tabitha was drained from her imagined calamity and began to stumble at Anna's quickened pace.

An eerie roar rose in the distance.

Alarmed, Anna grabbed Tabitha's elbow and pulled her near. "There is not much time until the storm is upon us. Let me carry you," she urged.

Tabitha shook her head. "I am too big!" she said.

The roar increased behind them.

"I can carry a full-grown ram," Anna insisted. In a swift motion she hefted Tabitha up and draped her along her shoulders. "I will get you back!" she assured, the muscles in her thighs swelling with effort.

The roar had approached a deafening level by the time Anna and Tabitha reached the caves.

When Anna climbed the last embankment, she spotted Ruth pacing outside the main entrance.

"Tabitha!" she cried. "We were looking everywhere for you!" She helped lower the younger Sister from Anna's shoulders. "Come inside quickly!" she told them.

"No," Anna said above the wind. "I need to return to my sheep."

"But the storm! It is too dangerous!"

Anna shook her head. She helped rotate the great stone at the entrance then urged the women inside. Ruth's hand then shot out to grab Anna's tunic before she could depart.

"Be careful, my friend!" she shouted, her expression pained.

Anna nodded and nudged her inside. When they had rotated the stone back into place, sealing the caves, she sprinted back amidst the roiling clouds to find her flock.

Anna sat up at the sound of crackling flames, her eyes swollen from windburn, her tongue thick with thirst. She looked about quickly, uncertain where she was.

Focusing in the semidarkness, her gaze fell on two faces flickering in the firelight.

"You are awake!" Ruth said, her cheeks dimpling with joy.

Anna licked her lips and found them coated with sand. Remembering the storm, she said, "My sheep . . ." She tried to stand.

Sister Ruth held her down. "The flock is safe," she told her.

Joan knelt by the fire, her expression drawn and serious. "Tabitha said she heard someone grunting. Did you hear anything?"

Anna wiped the back of a hand across her eyes. "I think she heard a wolf," she said. "I encountered one and scared it off just before I saw her fleeing."

Sister Joan persisted. "And you are certain you saw or heard nothing else?"

"I am certain," Anna said.

Exhaling with relief, Joan sat back.

Ruth bent to uncover Anna's morning meal. "You must be hungry," she said.

Anna nodded and broke off a hunk of cheese. "Thank you."

Joan took Ruth aside and the two spoke in whispers while the shepherd ate. When they had finished, Ruth turned to Anna and said, "You exhibited extraordinary bravery yesterday. Not only in bringing Tabitha safely home, but in returning to save your sheep from harm. And we are all very grateful to you."

"A shepherd takes care of her flock. First and always," Anna said, repeating the oft spoken phrase.

Joan cleared her throat. "In that same vein," she began, "I have a request to make of you."

Anna glanced over, curious as to what the Sister might want. It being rare for Joan to address her.

"I would like to ask that you keep a regular lookout while guiding your flocks. And scan the different directions at regular intervals." She leaned in further. "Should you see anything unusual, like the wolf, for example, I would ask that you report it to me *immediately*."

Anna's eyes sought Ruth's.

"Will you be able to assist Sister Joan?" Ruth asked, ignoring the young shepherd's bewilderment.

Anna frowned. She suspected that she was meant to be looking for men like those who had killed Sister Samara. And Zahra.

Men, she thought shamefully, *like her father.*

Aware that the women were waiting for an answer, she nodded.

"Good," Joan said and rose to her feet. She then drew a breath and wrinkled her nose. "Is that unbearable stink coming off of *you*?" she asked.

Anna dropped her eyes. She glanced down and saw that her arms and legs were smeared with hair, oils, and urine from the sheep. And, to make matters worse, her monthly renewal had come. A sour combination.

Joan's eyebrows rose as a thought came into her mind. "You need a proper cleaning." She and Ruth exchanged looks. "Perhaps she could join us at the next Cloud Bath?"

Ruth smiled. "An excellent idea!"

"What is that?" Anna asked.

"I must return to my duties," Joan said and excused herself.

Ruth looked over at Anna. "It will be more enjoyable if it comes as a surprise," she said with a wink.

Anna squinted against the sun as she struggled to retrace the steps Tabitha had taken. The task was proving infinitely more difficult than she had imagined. In the storm's wake, the landscape had completely altered itself. Having peeled itself free of its rough outer tunic, it now seemed to recline in silky undergarments. Not a single sharp edge remained, every crack, crag, and thorn having been softened with a glazing of sand. Even the trails Anna and her sheep had carved into the land had been erased—as if they had never been followed.

After several hours, Anna managed to locate the area in which she had met Tabitha but, as she had anticipated, no trace of that day remained.

Discouraged, Anna turned around and headed back toward her flock. Her limbs heavy and spent, she decided to lead the animals back toward her cave so that she might rest.

Firing a whistle into the air, she signaled to her sheep. She watched as those who had scattered began to gather.

She had bent down to tighten her sandals when a color too brilliant for the land caught her eye. She turned to look and saw a bit of deep blue tangled in the thorny branches of a low-lying bramble. She scrambled over and grasped the bit of color between her fingertips. To her amazement, it was a small swatch of woven fabric. From a tunic, perhaps, or a blanket. Colored a bright indigo blue.

A dark cloud settled along Anna's face. She had never seen any of the Sisters wearing such a color. Nor did she know how they would produce the dye necessary to stain wool that particular hue.

She glanced into the sky.

Perhaps a bird had carried the bit of fabric? Or it had ridden on the storm?

Perhaps the wolf had dropped it from an earlier conquest?

Refusing to believe that anyone could approach the area unseen, and not wanting to arouse needless panic among the Sisters, she decided not to mention the strange swatch of fabric—unless it became absolutely necessary.

CHAPTER 16

Somewhere in The Narrows outside ancient Palestine—25 A.D.

Ruth found Mother Susana in her chamber refilling a lamp with oil.

"Mother?" Ruth asked.

Susana directed a narrow stream of golden liquid into the lamp's mouth. Without lifting her eyes she said, "Ask your question."

Ruth took a deep breath. "As you know, it has been many years since Anna's arrival. In that time, she has proven her loyalty and purposefulness. In caring for her sheep, she has provided us with a generous supply of milk, cheese, and high-quality wool, which we have spun into numerous blankets and tunics. Never once has she attempted to leave, nor has she mistreated a Sister in any way. She has shown extraordinary patience by continuing to live apart from us without any understanding of our purpose, or the reasons for her being here. She has even agreed to assist Sister Joan with her duties. And, of course, you know of her exemplary rescue of Tabitha and the sheep . . ."

Saying this, Ruth fell silent. She did not wish to overstep her bounds.

Mother Susana remained focused on the oil and nodded into the silence. "Go on," she said.

Encouraged, Ruth continued. "In her time here, Anna has clearly absorbed much wisdom and equanimity, yet, as Shereen and I have observed, she lacks the spiritual foundation necessary for strong self-knowledge and growth. We do believe, however, that her internal confusion would be diminished, and her self-knowledge strengthened, if she were granted more exposure to the philosophy and practices of The Way. Up until this point, she has been absorbing the knowledge by living among us, but her learning has not been at all guided."

"I see," Susana said, interrupting. "But was it not a question you came to ask?"

Ruth broke into a guilty smile. "Yes, Mother, it was," she confessed. She took a moment to gather her thoughts. "What I wanted to ask is . . . has not the time come to bring our young shepherd into the fold?"

Susana frowned and wiped the excess oil dripping down the side of the lamp. Ruth knew that she was not ignoring her, but considering the question.

The elder woman slowly set down the lamp and placed her hands in her lap. "I, too, have observed our young shepherd from time to time," she said. "And she certainly does possess the admirable traits of which you speak." Her forehead wrinkled with thought. "My sense, however, is that she suffers from a lack of confidence in her female identity as well as a tendency to put herself in jeopardy for the sake of protecting others."

Ruth's eyes widened. She, too, had noted the second tendency. And had only to recall the great risks Anna had taken in rescuing Tabitha and the sheep. But of the first—a lack of confidence in her identity—she had seen little evidence.

Susana lifted two flints from a table. She held them up to eye their sharp, scalloped edges. "I must confess, though, that I have not engaged our most recent arrival with the fullness of my attention."

Ruth's brow furrowed. "Then you have not been able to determine the reason that Zahra sent her?"

Mother Susana closed her eyes. "It still eludes me," she said. "But I *have* intuited, as I believe my sister did before me, that Anna possesses a very particular, and perhaps powerful, destiny. One that would appear to converge with that of The Way."

Ruth's cheeks dimpled in surprise. She had not imagined Anna serving a greater purpose than her current one. Her curiosity piqued, she waited for Susana to elaborate.

Susana struck the flints near the lamp's wick.

"Unfortunately, the particulars of the convergence remain unclear to me, and as indecipherable as Anna's gender sometimes appears."

A spark shot from the flints. It hit the wick and fizzled out.

"But while the lack of clarity around her future path disturbs me, I think you are right to conclude that it would be better for all if she did not remain an outsider."

A second spark shot against the wick. It burst into flame.

Susana gazed up at Ruth.

Ruth's eyes twinkled, having intuited Susana's answer before she spoke it.

Mother Susana smiled. "Your vision has improved," she said. A sudden look of regret darkened the old woman's face. "Perhaps we made a mistake in not choosing you to become an Awakener?"

Ruth shook her head. "Our paths flow from deep wisdom. I trust in what has yet to come."

Susana stared into the flame. "I assume, then, that you wish to be in charge of preparing our newest apprentice?"

"I would be honored," Ruth said.

Susana then tipped her head, as if having heard someone speak nearby. After a moment, she said, "When she is ready, I think it wise to introduce her to your work."

Ruth raised an eyebrow.

Susana lifted a hand. "I cannot tell you why I think this. But it seems important," she said.

Ruth smiled. Having received an answer to her question, she planted a kiss on Susana's cheek and left her chamber.

Alone, the elder woman gave a deep sigh and bent over the light. She had always trusted in the source of her decisions, and in those of the Circle. But, with all that had transpired—all the deaths and rising threats—she had developed grave concerns regarding the future of their mission. In particular, it worried her that a new and grave possibility had arisen—that everything they had so carefully tended could be swept away.

Contemplating this, Susana closed her eyes as a shudder shook through her.

Anna had cornered a sheep and was tugging nettles from the bandaging on its hock when she heard Ruth calling. She glanced up and spotted her friend ambling down the ridgeline. With an exuberant yelp, Anna jogged up to greet her. Seeing her rapid approach, Ruth laughed and reversed her course, running back up the ridgeline. Anna pursued. Ruth looked over her shoulder and saw the young shepherd gaining quickly, her long muscular strides covering the terrain with ease. Before Anna could catch up, Ruth ducked between two boulders. But Anna had foreseen the maneuver and turned up a shortcut. Without warning, she leapt in front of the elder Sister. "A-*ha!*" she shouted.

Ruth squealed with fright and the two fell down laughing. She gave Anna's leg a playful slap. "Are you busy with your tasks, or do you have some time to spend with me?"

Anna glanced over her shoulder. "One of the sheep injured a hock this morning and I have set a poultice on it."

"Will it be all right for an hour or two?"

Anna raised an eyebrow, considering. "Yes, I suppose."

Ruth smiled. "Good. Then come. There is something for you to see." She led Anna up the ridgeline to a deep crevice. They sat inside its cooling shade and fanned themselves. From under her robes, Ruth produced a linen kerchief. She held it before Anna and slowly peeled back its corners. Inside the folds lay a handful of fresh figs. Anna's eyes grew wide at the sight of the plump maroon fruits. She could hardly believe her eyes!

"Where did you get those?" she asked, astonished.

Ruth held her gaze. "It is time for me to tell you a story," she said. She took a deep breath, crossed her legs, and sat up tall. "We who live in the caves, and who are called Sisters, are among the last keepers of The Way."

Anna kept silent and did not move.

Was she finally to receive answers to her questions?

"Those who live in accordance with The Way," Ruth continued, "live by simple yet universal truths. We believe in a divine and ever-present Creator. We call her the Great Mother. And sometimes we call her by other names. The Queen of Heaven. The Most High. The Source. The Spirit. Maker of All that Is Seen and Unseen. Other peoples refer to her according to their own custom and language."

Memories of the words in her mother's hymns leapt into Anna's mind. "Queen of Heaven" and "Bless the earth that is to be blessed."

Had her mother somehow known of The Way?

Ruth took a breath and continued. "We believe that every form of life and the very earth itself is a sacred manifestation of the Mother. We believe that daily and direct contemplation of the source of our life, through conscious and creative means, is the way for humans to remain spiritually connected to the ever-present miracles around them. We further believe that the highest human power, and that which should be cherished above all, is the female capacity to create and nurture life. And, lastly, we believe that human suffering arises, one way or the other, from a spiritual separation between individuals and the Mother from which they arise."

Anna swallowed the information eagerly along with a fig's sweet flesh. "But how did The Way come to be?" she asked.

Ruth chose a fruit for herself. Felt its weight in her palm. "The Way has existed since the beginning," she said. "Since the time when people bowed before the awesome power of Creation. When divinity and spirit dripped off every leaf. When each star was counted and loved. When people took what they needed, but no more. When life was treasured as a gift, not a promise.

"It was then that people revered the Great Mother, *not* because she symbolized a literal being, but because she represented and embodied the beauty, mystery, and sanctity of life. For them she personified the intrinsic and bountiful force that surges through everything, connecting the known and the unknown, bringing hope of renewal. And since women were the earthly beings who most clearly manifested the awesome power of Creation—by generating and sustaining new life from within their own bodies—they held positions of honor in both worship and community life. Simply put, it was a time when people understood that if women and the life-giving source of the Mother did not exist, neither would they. And they bowed down before that simple truth in endless gratitude and awe."

Anna frowned. "So, at that time, women did not live separately as the Sisters do?"

"Oh no!" Ruth said, raising her hands. "There was no need to. Unlike today, no one group was trying to dominate or subjugate the other. Rather, men and women respected and honored each other and participated equally in all aspects of life. The focus of their communities, therefore, was to collaborate and cooperate—enabling all to thrive and raise their children in peace."

"Does that mean that daughters were as valuable as sons?" Anna asked, her curiosity piqued.

"Of course!" Ruth chimed. "When one lives according to The Way, *all* children are cherished and encouraged to flourish."

Anna drew back, unable to believe her ears. "Then why did things change? And become so different?" she demanded.

Ruth closed her eyes above a smile and thought for a moment.

"Let me first tell you another story," she said. Anna refolded her legs and listened with eagerness. "When Susana and her twin, Zahra, and their younger sister, Maya, were growing up, they lived on the outskirts of a village with their mother. Orpah, as they called her, was a widely acclaimed healer, just as her mother had been before her, and her mother's mother, and so on.

"Stories abounded of Orpah's vast wisdom, and the circle of respect for her was wide. Her three daughters accompanied her everywhere, and it was under her influence that they imbibed knowledge of The Way."

Anna tried to imagine the young daughters shadowing their mother. She had never thought of Zahra, or Mother Susana, as having once been girls.

"But by the second half of her life, Orpah had grown concerned," Ruth continued. "In her many travels, she had learned of a fledgling but potent movement to degrade the inherent sanctity of life, and the female, and instead to instill a thirst for domination and warfare, and the hoarding of material possessions, thereby closing people's hearts to The Way."

"But *why*?" Anna asked.

Ruth shook her head. "Fear. Greed. Envy. An empty need to control. And a misunderstanding of the nature of true power."

"What do you mean? By who?"

"It was a small group at first. Men from the outskirts of the community who, for whatever reason, lost their sense of gratitude and purpose. Instead of respecting themselves and others and participating in the communal life, they began to steal."

"Steal what?"

"Food. Shelter. Women. Children." Ruth winced. "They came to see how much easier it was to take rather than create. And their appetite soon grew beyond them."

"So what happened?"

Ruth shrugged. "When the communities became tired of the thievery and tried to protect what they cherished, the men attacked."

Anna's eyes widened. "But why did the people of The Way not join together to stop them?"

"Oh, they did!" Ruth said. "Especially the men and women who had lost children in the rising violence. They protested adamantly in the name of the Mother and did all they could to resist. But this only infuriated the men, who then sought a way to undermine the people's power so they could continue their plunder."

Ruth went on to explain that it was then decided among the outcast men that the best way to weaken the people was to destroy the Mother.

Anna gasped.

"But knowing that it would be difficult, if not impossible, to force themselves between the people and the Mother, they decided to simply create a new divinity—a male."

"A male god?" Anna asked. "Like the one my father always called out to?"

Ruth nodded. "Yes, but rather than upholding the value of life and cooperation, this new god, in various texts the men produced, espoused domination and destruction. In one story after another, he favored some people over others and declared that only those he deemed worthy were entitled to life and its bounty. He called for death to those who were not chosen. And belittled the life-giving capability of women, first by saying that only men could wield spiritual power, and second by claiming that women had arisen from men, rather than the other way around!"

"But all those things are insane!" Anna protested.

"True," Ruth sighed in agreement. "Which is why the outcasts eventually had to enforce their beliefs with blades."

Anna's skin went cold.

"Quickly becoming intolerant of anyone who defied them, and of those who practiced what they called 'the old ways,' the men began killing and torturing resistors. This new movement soon ushered in a period of catastrophic violence. And, in their efforts to undermine all earthly symbols of the Mother, the proponents of the male god eradicated untold numbers of priestesses and female healers, along with all evidence of their existence. Entire villages were slaughtered. Vast stores of manuscripts burned."

Anna shuddered at the thought of Zahra's ghastly murder being repeated over and over. She then realized that her father's hatred of the old woman had arisen because he, too, had been persuaded to trust in the male god and the proponents' need to crush dissention.

Ruth nodded, seeing that Anna was drawing connections. She then continued. "The new movement has had many names and incarnations. But its every form revolves around a central, irrational myth: that a single male god independently generated life on earth." Ruth shook her head at the perversity. "Have you ever seen a male bird or bee or fish or man generate new life from its own body alone? In fact, I am not even sure a *female* could do this. Though no female would be so arrogant as to claim that she could!"

Anna's eyes widened, astounded by Ruth's words. "But why does not anyone other than the Sisters denounce this?" she asked.

"Oh, some do," she said. "There are those in the outside world who believe as we do, who turn to Creation for answers and not to other men and their false notions." She then lifted her face toward the sky. "But over time, and under the pressures of terror and greed, most people's spirits have been cleaved from the world and the wonders around them. And because they have been told what to think—instead of trusting what is before them—they have fallen into forgetting. They no longer *remember*." She dropped her eyes. "Where separation and forgetting have been planted, connections to reality dissolve. Anxiety sets in. People ask, *Who am I? Where do I come from? What is my purpose?* And so, seeking to fill the emptiness in their souls, they embrace lazy beliefs, which eventually lead them to violence, war, gluttony, and other vices—particularly those that involve victimizing women and children—until finally they sink into maiming and destroying without remorse." She looked straight into Anna's eyes. "Such violent and dangerous times are upon us," she said.

Anna nodded at the solemnity of her words. After a long silence she asked, "But are there no longer any men who practice The Way?"

"Of course there are!" Ruth said. "Though, at the moment, they are few in number." She paused before continuing, as if selecting her words with care. "Men today have a greater struggle to realign themselves with The Way," she said. "The new movement has bestowed upon them a false sense of power and most are too afraid to relinquish it. They are too afraid to honor the true, life-enhancing power of the Mother. Unfortunately, many men would rather possess easily what is false than hazard the journey to what is real." She nodded. "It is therefore up to women to lead us back into remembrance."

Anna held still.

Ruth's face suddenly brightened. "But your friend Solomon lived according to The Way," she said.

Anna sat up eagerly. "He did?" she asked, excited by her newfound understanding.

"Yes," Ruth answered. "And Solomon's cousin, the man who escorted me to The Narrows many years ago, was another." She lowered her voice. "Though we learned from Solomon that he has since fallen away."

Anna's mouth fell open. "*Judas?!!*" she cried.

Ruth burst out laughing at the young shepherd's surprise. "Yes. Judas was Maya's son," she confirmed. She gazed down into her fig's seeded heart. "He was a good man. At least when I knew him. I understand that Solomon was very saddened at his loss."

Anna took a deep breath and let Ruth's words sink in. Her mind was roiling with revelations. She knew that she needed to return to tend her animals, but her heart felt jittery and her questions would not be still.

"What happened to Orpah?" she asked.

Ruth glanced over. "Are you certain you are ready for more?" she asked.

"Yes! I am!" Anna assured her.

Ruth laughed and lifted another fig. "Orpah," she said, "became convinced that the growing influence of the male divinity foreshadowed a slow and painful suicide for life on earth. After all, she reasoned, to devalue the Mother was to disparage the source of life and, therefore, one's own existence."

Anna nodded.

"And so, in the deepest love and gratitude toward Creation, Orpah vowed to spend the time until her last breath renewing the memory—and influence—of The Way."

Ruth went on to explain how, over the years, Orpah's convictions grew more fiery and vocal. As a result, she had numerous conflicts with proponents of the new movement and its male god. And although she pitied them for their spiritual impoverishment, they hated her for the unshakeable strength of her beliefs. For years they plotted to kill her, but hung back for fear of retribution by the faithful crowds that attended her.

"Years later," Ruth said, "a hired assassin found her alone in the woods, resting under a tree. It was he who slit her throat."

Anna drew back in horror.

Ruth nodded. "When the daughters received word of Orpah's death, they knew there were many seeking to destroy them. That was when they decided to go into hiding, to preserve the legacy passed down by their mother, and the many mothers before her."

Anna's forehead wrinkled. "But Zahra was living in my village," she said. "And what about Maya?" she asked before she could stop herself. She then recalled Judas's fury and Peter's story about the murder of his kin.

No wonder he had been so profoundly traumatized!

"Never mind. I know what happened," Anna confessed with a shudder.

Ruth nodded solemnly, then tipped her head. "Susana was the first of the three sisters to seek seclusion," she said. "It was she who chose The Narrows. And she who found the caves. When she had secured the location, she asked Zahra to join her, but for reasons I do not know, Zahra stayed behind." She took a breath. "I believe this separation was a source of great pain for Susana," she said quietly. "As for Maya, she chose to wait until her daughter, Delilah, had reached an age where she, too, could make the journey."

Anna drew back. She then asked, "Was Judas's family killed because someone found out about their connection to The Way?"

Ruth shrugged. "It is possible."

Saying this, Ruth leaned back and measured the sun's position in the sky. "We have been talking a long time," she said. "I had not planned on telling you so much, especially not all at once," she said, chiding gently. She scooped up her empty cloth and began to push herself to her feet.

"No! Wait!" Anna cried, grabbing the hem of Ruth's robe. The story of the caves had her riveted and she was desperate to know more. "Tell me what happened next," she pleaded. "What did Susana do when she got here?"

Ruth settled back down to a sitting position. "Should you not check on your flock before we continue?" she tried.

Anna shook her head. "I can tell the sheep's location and condition by the sound of their hooves. They are content."

Ruth chuckled and leaned again into her tale. "Wanting to preserve the ancient wisdom passed on by her mother, Susana gathered a group of women to become apprentices of The Way. Sheltered here within the safety of the caves, these young women pursued a rigorous program of study and expansion."

"Is it the same as what you have learned?" Anna asked.

Ruth nodded. "Yes. Though there have been changes made to integrate new knowledge, the path an apprentice takes is still much the same. First, upon arriving here, she must spend several years rinsing herself of the poisonous and often degrading influences of childhood—influences from adherents of the male divinity who taught her to belittle or deny her female powers and to defer to authority rather than rely on insight.

"In place of this poison, an apprentice learns to reconnect with the profound power of Creation that lives within her own mind and body. Slowly she learns to fuse her creative powers with the corresponding ones in the mysteries around her by attuning herself to the lunar and tidal cycles of which she is physically a part. Then, through direct and creative contemplation of objects in the world around her, she reopens her heart and mind to the vast and infinite power of the Mother and learns to draw upon her limitless forces."

Anna leaned in, fully absorbed.

"During the second phase of her training," Ruth continued, "an apprentice hones her skills of Communion and intuiting through chanting, poetry, and contemplation. And, perhaps most important, she grows to understand the complex and various reasons for illness and masters the application of natural and energetic cures for the body and mind.

"Then, after many years, when she has attained a certain level of skill and awareness, and gone through the ceremony of Sisterhood, she might then be called into the world as an Awakener. Such women travel from village to village, much like Orpah before them, to affect cures and share knowledge of The Way in the hope of reawakening people to the sacredness of the world around them. Sisters

Shereen and Naomi will be the next two sent out as Awakeners," Ruth confided.

Anna was not surprised by this news. She had recognized the considerable powers of both women. "But when do they come back?" she asked.

Ruth shook her head. "Only Sister Joan is permitted to come and go from The Narrows. Once a Sister has left the caves," Ruth continued, "she is never to return, nor reveal anything of our hidden location. Doing so would endanger all our lives." She paused before adding, "That was why there was so much fear when Sister Samara returned unexpectedly. How could we know that her murderers had not followed her? This was also why, initially, we were so terrified of *you*."

"Because you thought I had been among those who murdered Sister Samara?" Anna asked, beginning to understand.

Ruth nodded. "Sister Joan's sole duty is to protect the caves, their occupants, and their secrets from intruders. She discovered you crossing The Narrows—without an escort—shortly after Sister Samara's return, which was why she dealt so harshly with you." She chuckled. "Most believe Joan has a sixth sense and can smell danger on the wind!"

"But I never even saw her!" Anna exclaimed. "I only remember a rock dropping from the sky, then I fell off the—"

Ruth grinned. "Her methods are clever, and many," she said.

A lull fell into the conversation as Anna thought about what she had learned. After a few moments, she asked, "Do you think The Way will ever flourish again?"

Ruth laced her fingers together in her lap. "The Way has continued to survive through consciousness and spirit, and it thrives wherever these do," she said. "Like all living things, The Way has its seasons and its cycles. You have come upon it in a quiet, contemplative season. As with a plant in winter, it is a time for inwardness, anticipation, and enriching the roots upon which the plant will rely for future growth. It is a time when all of us, especially the Guardians, must remain vigilant. Because as time cycles, a new season will come and it will again call The Way into blossom."

"Wait," Anna said, eager to understand everything. "Who are the Guardians?"

Ruth smiled. "The Guardians are those who protect the Sisters in the outside world—much as Sister Joan protects us here."

"Were Solomon and Judas Guardians?"

Ruth nodded. "Yes."

"I knew it!" Anna said, brightening. She leaned forward. "But why must they be particularly vigilant during this time? What are they watching for?"

Ruth laughed. "Never an end to your questions, is there?" Taking a moment to gather herself, she considered telling Anna about the cyclical arising of The Way's most powerful figure, and the attending resurgence, but decided against it. It was not that she did not trust Anna—she emphatically did—but the sacred being was not usually spoken of until she became apparent.

Having conversed with great intensity for quite some time, Ruth felt the need to rest. She glanced down at the last fig. "I believe I have said all I wish to today," she said.

Anna sat back. She realized that Ruth's story had begun to explain many of the things she had been aching to know. And suddenly felt the need to sit and consider all she had heard. Still, there was one phenomenon about which she remained baffled. "Would you tell me just one more thing?" she asked.

"Yes?"

Anna reached down and lifted the last pink fruit. "I want to know where *these* come from."

Ruth let out a merry laugh. "I knew you would ask that!" She leapt to her feet, her rotund body animated by a mixture of excitement and anticipation. "First, tend to your injured sheep, then join me outside the center entrance."

When Ruth saw Anna coming, she started down the ridgeline.

Anna's face fell. "Are we not going into the main chamber?" she asked.

"No," Ruth said.

Anna tried to hide her disappointment. She had not gone inside the main caves since her arrival and was eager to explore them.

When they were a short distance from the main entrance, Ruth stopped and pressed her palm against the face of rock. Within a moment, a seamless door rolled open. It was the westernmost entrance that Anna had seen the Sisters passing through each morning.

As they stepped inside, Anna swooned in the embrace of lush, humid air. The extravagant dampness was in stark contrast to the barren terrain's dry breath.

She hesitated.

How could the air be so full of life in the middle of a desolate land?

"This way," Ruth said.

At the end of a narrow corridor to the right, Ruth again turned another invisible door. The air that rushed out felt invigorating and *alive*. Ruth lit a lamp and led Anna down a tight passage. At Ruth's urging, Anna bent to slip through a tight doorway. Once through, she found herself standing inside a voluminous chamber. When her eyes adjusted to the light, her mouth fell open.

The great spherical room throbbed with the luxuriance of leafy green life. Rising from the center, anchored by a web of serpentine roots, was an ancient sycamore fig tree. Its massive moss-covered trunk, like the tree Anna had known in her youth, divided early and launched a flock of great, knobby arms into the sky. Its swollen and generous canopy pressed upward as if it wanted to lift the roof. Narrow shafts of sunlight spilled through cracks in the ceiling and sparkled along the dark green leaves. Clusters of pinkish fruits flamed along the branches. Wasps circled between the upper branches, performing their ancient and instinctual dance. A dazzling yellow snake slithered around an outer limb and dropped gracefully to the one below.

Anna could not believe her eyes. Even in her wildest dreams, she could not have imagined such—

"The Tree of Life," Ruth whispered.

"But . . . how . . ." Anna stammered. Her eyes fanned across the room.

Beneath the great sycamore grew an intricate system of well-tended gardens that engulfed the room like a jungle. Fruit-laden olive and pear trees stood like Roman sentinels along the high walls. Carpets of grasses, barley, grains, and mysterious herbs of every description cushioned the floor. Flowering grapevines spun up the walls and across the ceiling. Bees danced through multicolored petals.

"Let me show you something," Ruth said.

Anna followed her to the back of the chamber where a spring bubbled into a ceramic holding jar. Anna could see that when the water reached a certain level, it would spill through holes at the top of the jar. From there, it followed a web-like system of channels carved into the floor, thus delivering a steady supply of water to thirsty roots and stems.

Anna spun around when she heard a humming sound behind them. She was shocked to discover Sisters Shereen and Naomi rising from beneath the lush undergrowth. Each carried a small basket.

"Greetings, Sister Anna," Shereen said.

Anna's ears flushed with heat.

Sister Anna. It was the first time anyone had called her that.

Anna watched as the Sisters slipped gracefully between rows of plants to harvest herbs, seeds, and flowers. These they would distill, she learned later, into balms, elixirs, teas, and ointments used to combat specific ills and injuries. The expertise with which their hands wove through the tapestry of rampant growth was astonishing. As was the ease with which they could identify and select from hundreds of different species. She came to realize that each woman, like Orpah before her, carried a veritable wealth of healing remedies within her memory. And each accepted the notion that the land from which she rose contained every ingredient essential to nurture and promote life.

Farther away, Anna spotted Sisters Helena, Irene, Naomi, and Rachel milling through the vines. She knew that they were also apprenticing to become Awakeners. While the women continued with their work, Anna's eyes strayed again to the great tree dominating the room.

"Still hungry?" Ruth asked.

Anna nodded.

"Have as many as you like," she said, indicating the figs dangling seductively from the branches. "The only promise you must make is to plant the seeds of whatever you consume, or tend to the garden's other needs for an equivalent amount of time. By returning as much or more than what you take, the flow remains infinite. As in nature. For every tree that dies, another grows. For every life created, another dissolves and returns its life force to the whole. Nothing is removed from this cycle. Nothing wasted. It seems so simple. But that is how one lives according to The Way."

Anna nodded and trotted to the tree. She ran her palms along its ever-molting, cream-colored bark as if greeting an old friend. She felt its dusty balm coat her fingers. With a single pull on a lower limb, she lifted herself along the trunk and disappeared high in the branches.

Boosting herself into the tree's emerald canopy, she hollered for joy. Beneath her, the Sisters passed smiles among themselves.

When Anna leapt back to the ground, she held a cluster of figs in the belly of her tunic. Before eating the fruit, she offered her harvest to the others. The Sisters gathered to admire what she had found. Each pulled a single pink heart from Anna's store and marveled at the skin's silky texture. Together they gave thanks to the mystery that had assembled the fruit's intricate beauty and with that, sunk their teeth into the syrupy, seeded middles.

"Sister Anna?" Shereen asked. "Would you be able to assist Sister Rachel and me in the collection of the Seven Cures?"

Anna looked to Ruth for guidance. Ruth nodded. Sister Rachel then put a basket into Anna's hands and led her back into the aromatic garden where they began to unveil its secrets.

CHAPTER 17

Somewhere in the mountains north of the Great Desert—25 A.D.

Solomon approached the village on foot. Alone. His cheeks burned by the sun. His gingered beard in straggles.

He emerged from the dark like a spirit.

"Greetings," he croaked in a hoarse whisper.

The men around the fire assessed the lone traveler with suspicious eyes.

"May I sit, brothers?" he asked.

The men said nothing, but made a space between them. The one seated closest handed over a skin of water.

Solomon drank. The liquid stung his throat.

"Have you traveled far?" one of the men asked.

Solomon nodded. He had, in fact, journeyed back through the Great Desert. This time he had exited from the sand where its northernmost border brushed against the mountains.

After learning of the movement to exterminate those who kept the old ways, he had disbanded his group of shepherds, selling off the sheep and paying each man his due. Although the others, even Peter, had little difficulty securing new positions, their having crossed the Great Desert being proof enough of their worth, Solomon had abandoned his life as a shepherd.

He turned instead to traveling between the villages scattered in the foothills, determined to assess the rising threat, and do all he could to thwart it.

Handing back the skin of water, he asked, "Brothers, tell me. Am I near Kerek?"

The men's faces widened in the firelight.

"Why do you seek to go there?" one of them asked through a suspicious squint.

Solomon prepared to answer, then stopped himself. His eyes swept across their faces. The direct and empty stares caused the hair to rise along the back of his neck. He was not among friends.

"Why do you think?" he said gruffly, hurling an intimidating gaze back at them.

One of the men leaned forward with a wide grin. "You have come for the hunt, then?" he asked.

Solomon gritted his teeth. Nodded. "Yes."

Someone slapped him on the back. "I *knew* you were one of us!" he said. "We ourselves have only just met," the man said, indicating the others. "But you are welcome to join us."

"You must be hungry. Share in our feast," another said, handing over a plate of olives and flatbread.

Another man stepped from the dark to throw wood on the fire. As the flames licked higher, Solomon and the others dug into their meal.

"Kerek is less than a day's journey from here," the grinning man said. "But I was told that a band of us has already begun to gather there."

"Then we must leave *tonight*!" Solomon urged, throwing down his meal.

The others looked up in surprise.

"An eager one, are you?" the grinning man said through laughter. "Have no fear, there will be enough throats to slit for every man to have his share."

Solomon struggled to mask his rage. Holding tight, he drew in a deep breath and collected himself. In order to succeed in his mission, he would need to set his emotions aside. "In that case, we can afford the delay," he said, digging back into his meal.

Confident that his outburst had gained the men's trust, he kept still. Listening.

Soon the grinning man took out a pipe. He leaned back and nodded toward one of the younger men. "My son and I used to be farmers," he told the group. He turned to face Solomon. "What was your work?"

Without looking up, Solomon said, "Shepherding."

The man's eyebrows rose. "Ah, a shepherd! Now that is a hard life. Almost as hard as a farmer's," he added with a chuckle. When no one spoke, the man went on. "I myself am glad to be done with it. Back-breaking work to tend the land!" he said. "And not nearly as *rewarding* as serving God's call," he said. "Am I right, brothers?"

The other men's eyes sparkled as they nodded in agreement.

Another spoke up. "It is far easier to slaughter a heathen than a hog, as I used to do," he said. "And the last one I took kept a stash of coins under her tunic. The sum totaling far more than I could have ever earned at my trade."

Aroused by their talk, the eldest man among them lifted his voice. "Brothers! You speak only of earthly rewards, but you would do well to remember the honor of serving our Lord. For it should be the act of ridding the land of the unholy ones who deny Him that inspires you."

Their faces riddled with guilt, the others agreed quickly, saying, "Yes, you speak the truth!" and "Of course that is so!"

Solomon held his tongue. He again observed the circle of men. Some were young, some old. All were the sons of women. Not one of them had begun life as a killer. And yet they had become so.

It never ceased to amaze him how easily ordinary people could be led into treachery. All that was required, it seemed, was teaching them from a young age what to see and think and feel—to believe, for example, that a flower was not a wonder of its own accord, but the act of a singular god. Taught, then, to stop looking and to rely instead on others for one's perceptions, a person could be led to see—and believe—almost anything. No matter how destructive. No matter how divergent from their actual experience.

As his grandmother used to say, *Divided from one's own sight, a person is rendered a tool in the hands of another.*

"But why must we gather in *Kerek*?" one of the younger men asked. "It is such a barren place and the villagers there are few in number."

The old man opened his eyes and raised a hand as if to share a surprise. The others leaned in, listening intently.

"Kerek is not the final destination," he told them. "Word has come that a father and son from that village stumbled upon a discovery, by chance, in the desolate corridor to the south."

"But that would mean . . . *The Narrows*," one of the men blurted.

The others drew back in fear.

"Yes," the old man said with a nod. "And though I do not know the extent of the discovery, they say it is *astonishing*."

Later that night, when the others had fallen asleep, Solomon gathered his provisions and fled into the dark. He traveled swiftly toward Kerek, his thoughts snagging on sharp edges of panic.

CHAPTER 18

Somewhere within The Narrows *outside ancient* Palestine—25 A.D.

"Anna. Anna! Get up! *Get up!*" Ruth called out, rushing into the cave.

"What? What is it?" she muttered through a daze.

"Have you not heard me calling?" Ruth asked, propping hands on hips. "They have prepared the Cloud Bath!" She tossed Anna her tunic. "Come now," she insisted. "We should not be late."

"But my sheep . . . will be hungry . . . I must take them out—"

"The animals will be fine. It is *you* who needs some tending to," she said.

Ruth led Anna into the northernmost valley. Given its lack of vegetation, Anna rarely traveled through it.

"Where are we going?" she asked.

Ruth smiled. "To a very special place," she said.

"Will you still not tell me what it is?"

"Why do I not show you instead?" Ruth said, and with that turned toward a solid bank of rock. Anna stopped in her tracks, expecting her friend to crash headlong into stone. But, to her surprise, Ruth simply vanished—seeming to have passed straight through!

"Ruth?" Anna called out. "Where did you go?"

Ruth laughed and reappeared instantly, seeming to have poured herself out of the rock. "Look here," she said. "The stone is cracked but the seam overlaps itself. Creating a hidden passage through its center. You cannot see it unless you know where to look."

Amazed that in all her explorations she had never noticed this feature, Anna stepped forward and found where Ruth had slipped inside. As she followed behind, the walls of stone retreated and rose, creating a spacious cavern. As they moved deeper inside, Anna sensed heat issuing from the rocks.

They soon entered a dim vestibule, its walls shivering with torchlight. Anna paused, letting her eyes adjust. To her right she noticed an animal hide hanging before an opening. Behind it she heard the whispers and occasional giggles of other women.

Eager to begin, Ruth pushed through the animal skin. When she did so, Anna caught sight of the other Sisters. They were undressing. Some were already naked.

Anna felt her entire body freeze.

When Ruth realized that her friend had not followed her into the changing area, she returned and took her by the hand. Laughing, she led the reluctant shepherd inside. "Come now, I have never known you to be *shy*!" she said.

Ruth led her across the threshold. Embarrassed by the show of flesh, Anna dropped her eyes.

Sister Rachel stepped forward and held out a cloth. It was wet and warm. "Welcome, Anna. This is for your hands and face," she said. "It will help you acclimate to the temperature." When she saw Anna's look of shock, she said, "Let me help you." With that she began tugging at the cord on Anna's tunic.

Anna stepped back, but before she could protest, a loud hiss echoed from farther inside the chamber. Soon thereafter, a minty-scented steam began to billow underneath a second animal hide, rolling across their ankles like hot fog.

When the hissing sound diminished, a bell sounded, and the women stepped through the second doorway. Ruth and Rachel escorted the reluctant shepherd through.

Inside, Anna found the rest of the Sisters seated in a ring around a mound of glowing coals. It was difficult to distinguish faces through the thickening steam.

"Sit here, Anna," someone said. It was Tabitha. Without looking up, Anna turned and sat beside her. Tabitha took Anna's hand in hers.

The other Sisters smiled over at them.

After a time, the women's whispers fell into silence. The steam rose steadily to curl along the rounded ceiling.

Feeling protected within the cloud-like veil, Anna lifted her eyes to peek out at the circle of women. Living in her separate cave, she rarely found herself among them. Much less among them *unclothed.* Across the way, she spotted Shereen. The curls of her cinnamon hair spilled like water over her shoulders. Beneath, her breasts hung like soft fruits. Below these lay the gentle curve of her belly and the dark fur hovering in the valley of her hip bones. Anna marveled at her sheer beauty. She dropped her eyes when a gush of heat rose into her cheeks. Forced to look down at her own body, she felt the familiar shame at its inadequacy. Hers exhibited none of the lushness of the other women's bodies. Nor the soft, lilting grace. Hers, by contrast, was a lanky affair of angles and sharp edges.

But it was not just Anna's physical appearance that made her feel uncomfortable. It was also the women's ways—their gentle aura, their intimacy with one another, and the ease of their spirits—that turned Anna's mind back to how she had felt as a child. To her strong sense of not being able to relate to other girls. And of being somehow different.

Women possess a gracefulness in their being that I do not. And that I could never imagine possessing.

As she was thinking this, Anna felt someone's eyes upon her. She turned and found Ruth seated nearby, watching her. She tipped a knowing nod. Anna froze.

Had Ruth been reading her thoughts?

Ruth leaned forward as if she might say something when another woman stepped through the door. Anna looked up and caught the eyes of Sister Joan.

Two Sisters scooted over to clear a space. "Here, Sister!" they called.

When Joan sat on the stone bench, the silence returned. Only punctuated by the hiss of water drops hitting hot coals.

After some time the women began chatting with one another in hushed tones. Their talk seemed easy and light, laced with laughter.

Feeling awkward in her body, Anna did not wish to speak with anyone. Watching the others mingle freely, she felt the sudden urge to leave. When her eyes cut to the doorway, Ruth spoke up.

"Everyone, I would like to welcome Anna to her first Cloud Bath," she said.

The entire chamber fell silent. One by one, the women turned toward the shepherd.

Stunned by the sudden attention, Anna's ears began to ring. Loudly.

"We most certainly have much for which to be grateful to our shepherd, do we not?" one of the Sisters said.

"Yes, to be sure. For she has brought much bounty to our lives," several voices chimed.

Then Sister Joan spoke. "And I truly believe our well-being is enhanced by her presence," she said.

Anna cast her eyes down in disbelief.

Then another woman spoke. Her voice rose with authority above the others. "On the day she arrived, I felt our young shepherd would bestow great blessings upon us. And over time my belief in her, and her destiny among us, has only strengthened."

Anna could not believe her ears. She looked up to see who had spoken and found herself floating in Shereen's gaze.

Ruth glanced over to see the exchange. Seeing the look that passed between them, she felt something fizz beneath her skin.

Was there not something that ran between the two women? A joining? A connection deeper than anyone realized?

At that moment, a bell rang in the next chamber, signaling that the baths were ready. The Sisters stood and shuffled into the next room, where they passed bowls of cool water.

Numb from all that had transpired, Anna followed Ruth toward a far wall.

"Hold still," Ruth told her. She then began to scrub Anna's limbs with oils and a rough stone. Soon the room filled with the sound of brushing as the Sisters proceeded to scour one another clean.

That night, unable to sleep, Anna restarted the fire in her chamber and sat on the ledge looking up at the stars. Down below, she heard her flock milling about, forming and re-forming groups as some sought warmth while others braved the chill to continue grazing.

But Anna's thoughts were far from her sheep. Shereen's words in the Cloud Bath had left her restless.

Did she really believe that Anna possessed a destiny among them?

The possibility made her heart sing. Then, just as she began to wonder what her particular destiny might be, she felt a pain stab her heart.

Wincing, she looked up into the stars and saw her mother's face forming between the lights. Mari's eyes shimmered between those Anna could remember and those of Shereen—the two gazes blending into one.

Anna's eyes filled with tears and the vision began to swirl.

How she wished her mother could be there to see what she had become.

CHAPTER 19

The Village of Kerek—25 A.D.

Descending into the valley well before dawn, Solomon hoped his arrival would go unnoticed. As he made his way toward the village, he was shocked to discover its sky alight with fast-moving torches. Rushing into the streets, he found the villagers dashing from house to house and streaking along the perimeter. Behind them, an ungodly wailing rose into the sky.

Solomon grabbed hold of a young boy.

"What is it?" he asked. "What has happened?"

The boy pointed back toward one of the houses. "Someone has killed Jaruk and his son. The women woke to find them still on their sleeping mats. Drowned in their own blood!"

Aghast at the news, Solomon released his hold.

"Watch yourself!" the boy cried over his shoulder as he fled. "The murderers still wander free!"

As the men sped about the alleyways, Solomon went to the house of those who had been killed. There he found the village women gathered, their mouths opened toward the sky, howling in anguish. Nearby he saw two elder women seated upon a rock, too old to join the others. He went to them.

"Greetings," he said. "I am sorry for your loss."

The old women stared out through milky eyes. Chewing their empty gums. After a moment, one of them shook her head. "I told them not to go. But would they listen?" She snorted. "Ha! Not to an old woman. And see *now* what has come of it."

Intrigued by her comment, Solomon spurred her on. "And to where was it that they went?" he asked.

The old woman's blind eyes went wide. "Where, you say? To The Narrows, of course!"

Solomon froze. He looked about. Cautiously he asked, "Was it they who made the discovery?"

A man dashed by, waving his torch. He threw Solomon a suspicious look.

The old woman nodded. "It was," she said. "And now the old ones have taken their revenge."

Solomon was glad the women could not see the look of surprise that came to his face. "The old ones?" he asked, feigning ignorance.

The woman grunted. "I am only the great-grandmother," she griped. "What do they tell me? But I am more clever than they!" she cackled. "And from my great-grandson's whispers I learned that they found a clan of women, of healers, hidden away."

Solomon's head went light.

The other woman spoke up. "The men do not think them dangerous. But, I tell you, their powers are great!"

The great-grandmother nodded. "Yes! That is so! And now they have taken my beloveds!"

Overcome, Solomon excused himself and wandered off. The others dashed wildly about him as he trod with heavy steps, his mind a blur. He was glad that those who had discovered the caves could not share what they knew with others. Yet he was also saddened by the loss of life.

But who had really taken the men's lives? he wondered.

He knew it could not have been the Sisters.

And he could think of only one other.

But was it possible?

The men's shouting grew louder. A mob formed and came storming toward Solomon and the women. Above their heads they held a young boy aloft.

"He saw the killer! The boy knows the truth!" the crowd was shouting. They stopped before the house of the victims and called inside. After a moment, a thin woman with tear-stained cheeks emerged.

Someone lowered the young boy and pushed him forward. "Tell her what you saw," another whispered.

The boy fiddled with his fingers.

"Tell her now!" they urged.

Keeping his eyes on the ground, the boy said, "I could not sleep. And was looking out my window. I saw a man come out of the house. He was not tall. He had a knife. With a strange shape. Then he ran off. And I went back to sleep."

"Which way?" someone in the crowd shouted. "Which way did he run?"

The boy put a finger to his mouth, then pointed west.

"Let us be off! Let us track him down!" someone cried out.

The men jostled into a pack and, brandishing their knives, fled toward the horizon.

Solomon kept still, watching the light of their torches shimmer into the distance.

If his assumption was correct, they would not find their man. For Judas knew better than anyone how to disappear.

CHAPTER 20

Somewhere in The Narrows outside ancient Palestine—30 A.D.

Anna finished washing her face then strode out her cave's entrance. Climbing to her usual stone perch, she surveyed the perimeter. The dawn's powdery light illuminated the new angles sculpted into her body by the hammer and chisel of time. During the past several years, her entire frame had lengthened, growing to a respectable height that rivaled even that of Sister Joan. Her shoulders had filled out broadly above narrow hips and long, powerful thighs. Her skin had darkened to a chocolate color even darker than her mother's. And her green eyes, if it were possible, had grown more captivating and cat-like. Bejeweled with flecks of gold, they seemed able to compel the truth from all who looked into them. Beneath, her cheekbones rose like confident mountain peaks that sloped down to meet the broad river of her nose then the full delta of her mouth.

Ruth and the other Sisters had expected Anna's masculine appearance to fade with age. But, to their surprise, it had only amplified. Her wide jaw, strong eyebrows, and trace of dark hair along her cheeks served to further confuse the appearance of her gender. She was, by all accounts, a handsome woman, who could easily have been mistaken for a beautiful man.

Despite Ruth's having invited her to live among the Sisters, Anna had declined. She had told Ruth that she felt better being close to her flock. But the truth was she did not want to live with the others. It was not that she did not love the Sisters—because she did. And would give her life to protect them! But *living* among them, and sharing the intimacies of such an arrangement, would only increase Anna's discomfort at being unlike the other women.

Anna stood before the great sycamore and held her breath. Slices of early sunlight poured through cracks in the cave's roof.

Beneath the tree, and throughout the gardens, she could see the Sisters already at work. Some were tending plants. While others sat in contemplation. Not wanting to disturb them, she quietly made her way to the spring bubbling near the center of the foliage. In order to give the Sisters more time to perform their duties, Anna had taken on the responsibility of maintaining the garden's irrigation system. Kneeling beside a broad-leafed plant, she checked the spring beneath the ceramic holding jar and found its flow active and gurgling. From there she shuffled on her hands and knees along the path of ever-narrowing channels that fanned like a spiderweb throughout the garden. Using a wooden trowel, she tended to each, clearing debris from some while digging out others to restore the proper flow. Her careful path took her in an ever-widening swath designed to ensure that no waterway went untended.

Losing herself in the task, she ruminated on how a single source of water could be divided over and over to nourish far more than a single stream ever could. The amazing power of division, she thought, was not unlike how the sycamore supported itself. Such a great tree could not rely on a single root, no matter how giant, but could flourish, instead, atop a fanning of the many.

Anna snapped from her reverie when she felt a hand press along her back.

"Good morning, Anna," Rachel whispered.

Anna looked up with a smile. She never interrupted anyone in the sycamore cave, but more often than not, Rachel would find her.

"I just planted a new row of herbs. See them there?"

Anna marveled at the feathery plants.

Rachel's smile disappeared behind a frown of concern. "Perhaps they will not receive enough water in that location?"

Anna dropped to her knees and surveyed the nearby channels. "The soil *is* a bit dry. Even for young anise."

A look of surprise came to Rachel's face. "How can you know it is anise?" she said. "The seedlings do not even yet resemble their adult form." She shook her head in amazement. "You have very keen powers of perception," she said. "And very big ears!" she added, knowing Anna had gained the knowledge by listening to their conversations.

Anna grinned. "I will dig a new channel to water your plants," she said.

"Thank you, Anna. You are most helpful—as always," Rachel said, tipping a warm smile toward her friend. Her eyes then glanced toward the other Sisters. "I must get back to work," she whispered. "For I think today will prove to be of enormous significance." She then disappeared into the green before Anna could ask *what* significance the day might bring.

Leaving the sycamore cave, Anna made her way to the center entrance. She hesitated before rotating the stone. Despite the fact that she visited the cave on a daily basis, she still felt a bit awkward whenever entering the Sisters' domain.

Inside, she heard the click-clack of the loom. She followed the sound and found Sister Tabitha sitting before the warp and weft of a half-finished blanket. Tabitha beamed when she saw Anna.

"Do you like it?" she asked.

"It is a beautiful pattern," Anna assured her.

"These are my f-favorites," Tabitha said, indicating the scarlet and golden mustard colors she had chosen.

"I can see why," Anna offered. "The loom is still working well for you?" she asked, running a hand along its wooden frame.

"Oh yes! B-better than e-ever!" Tabitha replied, passing a woolen thread through the weave.

Having fashioned some rudimentary tools, like those she remembered watching her father use, Anna had begun making small repairs for the Sisters—most recently carving a new warp beam for Tabitha's loom.

Tabitha paused in her labors. "I almost forgot! I was to t-tell you that Sister Ruth wishes to s-s-see you," she said.

Anna nodded. "Do you know where she is?"

Tabitha went suddenly still. "Sh-sh-she is—" she stuttered, unsure whether or not she should reveal the Sister's location.

"Who are you looking for?" a voice demanded from behind.

Sister Joan filled the doorway.

"Greetings," Anna said. "I am looking for Sister Ru—"

Joan lifted a hand, silencing her. She leveled a sharp stare. After a long moment she said, "Follow me."

Keeping up a brisk pace, Sister Joan led Anna down to a dead-end passage. When they stopped at the wall, Anna expected her to press a palm against the rock and open a secret door, but instead she said, "Close your eyes."

Anna heard Joan rustle in her robes. Then she heard the sound of metal scraping metal followed by a loud click. She felt the cool breeze of a doorway being opened, and Joan led her forward. "You may now open your eyes."

Anna stood in an unlit passageway. Joan remained on the other side of the door. It did not swivel like the others, but opened at one side as if on a hinge. "Continue walking forward," Joan said. "Toward the light." Without further instruction, she closed the door and left Anna in total darkness. A loud clank sounded from the door, followed by complete silence.

Anna felt her throat constrict.

Where was she?

Then, from somewhere in the dark, a voice.

"Hello?"

Anna recognized Sister Ruth's lilting tone. "It is me. Anna."

"Come in, come in!"

Anna tried to follow Ruth's voice but got trapped behind a maze of rocks that blocked the passageway. Whichever way she went, she found herself at a dead end.

"Go back to the beginning and always choose the left," Ruth called.

Anna did as instructed and was soon standing in a room filled with tall clay jars. Ruth stood at a narrow table and balanced a thin stick between her fingers. "Welcome to the scriptorium," she said, smiling.

Anna stared in wonder.

"Sit with me." Ruth pulled a stool next to her. Anna jumped up and sat. On the table beneath her, Ruth had laid open a sheet of almond-colored parchment. The letters she had scratched across its surface, black as raven feathers, were still wet.

"What *is* all this?" Anna asked, her eyes scanning across the tops of thick earth-colored jars laid in rows along the floor.

"This," Ruth indicated with a sweep of her arm, "is a record of our foremothers' knowledge." She pointed to a grouping of the tallest jars. "The volumes stored in these vessels catalogue the known healing efficacies of thousands of plants and other natural substances. The information they contain has been compiled by a limitless number of women over many, many years."

Ruth watched Anna's eyes widen. "You want to see?" she asked.

Anna nodded eagerly.

Ruth stepped down and lifted the tops of the taller jars. Inside the first were rolled scrolls of goatskin. The others contained sheets of papyrus bound together with leather.

Anna looked across the vessels' gaping mouths and thought back to when she and Simon had stumbled upon the mysterious jars in the caves.

"But texts kept in jars do not last forever," Anna said, recalling the disintegrated remains that had spilled from the shattered vessels.

"You speak the truth," Ruth chimed. "Which is why it is my duty to protect and maintain them. If time or pests damage any manuscript, it is my job to reproduce it with the greatest precision. From time to time, I will also script additions into particular manuscripts to record recent discoveries, as we continually improve and perfect various cures."

Anna stared at the rows of jars, saying nothing.

Ruth smiled. "Would you like to stay and watch me work?" she asked.

Anna looked up in surprise, and then replied, "Yes!"

Ruth returned to her table and stirred a pot of ink.

"Please bring a sheet of parchment from that pile," Ruth instructed, pointing to a stack of papyrus sheets.

Anna did as she was told, remaining near the table. But when Ruth dipped her quill into the ink, Anna backed away, as if from something powerful she did not understand.

Ruth laughed. "No, no," she teased. "Come close so you can watch," she said. "Who knows? Maybe one day this will be *your* duty!"

Anna lifted her eyebrows.

Ignoring her disbelief, Ruth rubbed the tip of her quill along the blotter to clear the excess ink. She then bent to her work.

Anna stared in awe as Ruth placed familiar yet, to her, indecipherable marks onto the parchment. Anna had never seen a woman who knew how to write.

"When I was growing up," Ruth said, her eyes never leaving the parchment, "I used to watch with envy as my brothers received tutoring in the art of letters. Every day when the old man arrived with his fistful of quills and inkpots, I would slide my weaving loom closer to my brothers so that I might overhear their lesson."

As she scripted word after word, Ruth took care to reveal the manuscripts' content and meaning. "This passage toward the bottom describes how to collect the Seven Cures and how to apply them," she would say. Or, "This passage describes how to prepare an antidote for beestings."

Turning to another sheet, Ruth said, "Ah! Now this is an important section. This describes how the mind's health affects the body." She pointed to the page as she read from it. "This says that grief can cause all the same symptoms as illness. And that it takes sensitivity to divine the actual cause of someone's suffering. It further says that sometimes a cure can be affected by simply listening."

Anna thought back to the night Zahra had healed her neighbor Daniel. She remembered how the old woman had listened as the boy spoke, until his breath miraculously returned.

Had Daniel been grieving?

In a cautious tone, Ruth then added, "But the passage further reminds us that not all pains can be soothed and not all lives saved. After all, it says, the beating of our hearts is not promised, and our breath is as fleeting as the wind," she said. Ruth gazed into the distance and shook her head. "So many have forgotten this," she said. "And so many act in ways that presuppose ownership of their existence. But our life truly is a *gift*."

"That is what Shereen says," Anna noted. "She says that gratitude is a far more reasonable approach to life than presumption."

Ruth returned her gaze to the young shepherd and smiled. "Shereen speaks with wisdom. And you have listened well," she said.

Encouraged by her words, Anna then asked, "But Ruth? If all these books contain knowledge of various cures, then where is the book that talks about The Way? In which jar do you keep it?"

Ruth's eyes glimmered. "I suspected you would ask that," she said. She drew her pen down the parchment, leaving a black vertical line in its wake. "There is no such book."

"What?" Anna squinted with suspicion. "But why not?"

Ruth leaned back and laid her quill in its trough. She set to the task of making more ink by mixing water with pulverized soot and tree gum.

"The Way is not a law or a formula that can be captured in the static pages of a book," she began. "The Way, as you are beginning to see, is a living, breathing spirit. It is a manner of walking in the world. The Way revolves around conscious and truthful experience, not man-made laws. And from this experience, you come to understand what is rightful living and what is not.

"Because of its fluidity, The Way is not a practice that can be learned by rote. Nor by repeating specific prayers or invocations. Thoughtless repetition and blind obeisance are, in fact, anathema to the basic tenet of The Way."

She gave the mysterious black mixture a final stir and then poured it into the inkwell.

"After all, if you are forever referencing the same text, because someone tells you to, you shrink your spiritual experience of the world. Your senses are deadened to the bounty around them. Imposed or mindless reiteration, by its very nature, numbs the spirit and closes your heart to the world around you. And, unfortunately, when people are told what it is that they see, they can be easily misled."

She looked again at Anna, fixing her eyes on hers as if she were going to reveal the most important secret. "The Way," she said, "lives inside the heart. It is free to all. It requires no hierarchies or prophets or tax. No one, therefore, can own The Way nor can anyone withhold it. At any given moment, a person is free to live into the miracles of the life around them and, having received this experience, to take appropriate action. And, most important, because The Way is born of the eternal whole, it can never be destroyed and will exist into eternity, world without end."

Saying this, Ruth went quiet, though she knew she had not spoken the entire truth. There did exist one circumstance, and only one, in which the physical recording of The Way's basic tenets would be justifiable. But to even contemplate such a situation made her shiver, and she did not wish to speak of it.

Anna sat still and let the new ideas settle around her. After a moment, she glanced over at the jars of scrolls. "Is every plant mentioned in the writings?"

"If they have healing qualities, yes," Ruth said.

Anna reached between the folds of her belt. "What about this one?" she asked, holding a small bit of green aloft. She had pinched the leafy stem from an unusual plant she had discovered.

Ruth squinted at the stem then took it gingerly into her hands. "Where did you find this?" she asked, her eyes widening.

"Growing near the western perimeter."

"Have you shown this to any of the other Sisters?"

Anna shook her head. "I did not wish to disturb them."

A light came into Ruth's eyes. "I have not ever seen this plant here in The Narrows," she said.

Anna grew excited at her friend's enthusiasm. "What is it?" she asked.

"It is called *haoma,*" Ruth told her. "When crushed with mint and olive oil, it provides an excellent cure for ailments of the breath. Can you take me to see where it is growing? Perhaps we can cultivate it in our garden."

Anna was preparing to answer when someone began shouting in the corridor.

Ruth's head snapped up. Anna's heart skipped a beat as a look of fear shattered her friend's face.

The shouting grew louder.

Ruth leapt up and rushed to stack the parchments in her arms. "Help me hide these," she commanded. Together they slipped the manuscripts back inside the jars and sealed them. They worked quickly as the shouting increased.

Were they under attack?

Anna nearly jumped out of her skin when Sister Tabitha burst into the chamber. She was carrying a torch and grinning from ear to ear.

"Come quickly, come qui-quickly!" she repeated, stuttering in her excitement.

Ruth laid a hand against her heart. She, too, had been terrified. Unaware of having caused a disturbance, Tabitha led them to the great round room where they found the Sisters and Mother Susana sitting together.

Susana greeted them, smiling. "Join the Circle," she said. "We have gathered to decide whether or not to send Sisters Shereen and Naomi as Awakeners."

Anna felt hesitant as she sat down among the women. On either side of her, Sister Ruth and another woman gently lifted one of Anna's hands into theirs. Anna gasped at their touch and her mind raced.

She was not qualified to join the Circle! She was not even a Sister, not officially. And she was nowhere near as wise or knowledgeable as the others. What if—?

Sister Ruth gave Anna's hand a firm squeeze, bringing a quick end to her rampant self-doubt. Ruth then leaned over and whispered, "Breathe deeply and try to clear your mind of distracting thoughts. Concentrate on listening with all your senses. On connecting yourself with the others and allowing their thinking and intentions to enter you."

Nodding, Anna tried to do as she was told. As the silence expanded and deepened, she began to feel a light buzz coming through the fingers of the women's hands. It was like a binding force, a uniting, as if many splinters were joining to form a single board.

After a few moments, Mother Susana spoke. "We have entered the silence before Creation. We have entered the ground of the Goddess. May our bodies be still. May our minds be peaceful. May our hearts be open. May all that we realize today benefit all of Creation."

Sisters Shereen and Naomi stood and moved to the center of the Circle.

What followed was an orderly, though sometimes heated, discussion of the arguments for and against the Sisters' departure. Most spoke of the two Sisters' dedication, achievements, and preparedness. But Joan, and even Mother Susana, issued words of caution.

"Ever since the death of Sister Samara," Joan began, "I have detected rumblings in the distance. Resistance to our ways grows stronger. It might be unwise and dangerous to send them into the world at this time."

"But if we do not send out our Awakeners when they are most needed," Sister Shereen began, "why send them at all?" It was clear she felt ready to begin life outside the cave and was growing anxious to fulfill her purpose.

Mother Susana counseled, "To have both of our most highly trained Sisters leave us might slow the development of future Awakeners. For this reason, would it not be wise to wait? Or if not wait, then to send only one Sister at a time?"

When the debating had finished, Mother Susana closed her eyes and said, "Enter the silence."

The women in the Circle grew still. Anna could feel the strength of their thoughts reaching into her mind. She tried to clear a space to accommodate both their thinking and her own. She soon found herself changing her mind several times as she allowed the different points of view to flush through her heart unhindered.

Spontaneously, the women began intoning a sound, like the one Anna had heard when she first arrived. As before, Anna felt a hum inside her bones as the tone ran through her body. The sound grew in strength and unity. The creation of the tone, she realized, joined the women together, despite their differences, and solidified their intention to pursue the right and wise choice, no matter whether it was theirs or not. After several minutes, the sound began to subside and silence again ensued.

A second round of discussion followed. It was unanimously agreed that Sister Naomi would enter the world within the next two months. Sister Shereen, however, would remain in the caves for another three years to continue training the other apprentices.

When Mother Susana announced the decision, Anna looked to Shereen, expecting to find her disappointed. Instead, she saw an expression of contentment cross her face. Despite her personal interests, Shereen recognized the wisdom of the decision and how it ultimately benefited the life and mission of the Sisters' cause. With this understanding, she accepted the necessity of her sacrifice and its sting was lessened.

Anna found herself wishing that someday she would be as wise and courageous as Shereen.

CHAPTER 21

Somewhere beyond the Great Desert outside ancient Palestine—30 A.D.

Peter gazed across the rocky landscape. Beneath him hobbled a group of three sheep. They were old and infirm. Up ahead, the other shepherds led their large flocks toward the setting sun.

Since joining the new group, Peter had felt belittled and demoralized by his reduced status. The head shepherd, a wiry man with an ear torn to rags during a fight with a wolf, had so far entrusted him only with the weakest animals.

Still, Peter was glad to be free of Solomon and the others. They only reminded him of his great loss. Often his mind turned to Jesus. And to how his friend had believed in him.

But what would he think of me now? Peter wondered.

He cringed at the thought.

Just ahead of his lead sheep, a snake slithered out to sun on the rocks.

Spying him, Peter loaded his sling and fired a deadly shot. The stone hit the snake in the head and he flew, lifeless, from the rock.

Smiling at his deadly shot, Peter reset his sling and puffed out his chest.

He then decided to do all he could to lift his status among the new shepherds. And to earn the ragged-eared man's respect.

In so doing, he would make himself worthy of his friend's memory. And impress him, even in his death.

CHAPTER 22

Somewhere within The Narrows *outside ancient* Palestine*—*30 A.D.

Anna led the sheep down into the valley. Standing guard over the flock, she heard the swift whistle of air rushing along a raven's wings as it glided above. She turned and caught sight of the onyx bird drifting overhead. She watched the glow of dawn powder its feathers with silver. Though it had been some time since she had practiced, she tossed back her head and cawed a coarse call into the air. The raven tilted its wings, driving itself higher, then circled back on a wide arc of sky. Startled by the creature's overt response, Anna concentrated and called again. The raven drifted closer and she could see its shiny marble eyes watching her. Anna called again and, this time, the raven called back.

Anna's mouth fell open.

Finally, she had mastered the call!

She hardly had time to digest her success when another raven cried out. The second bird's call echoed with a deeper authority than either the first raven or the shepherd had been able to summon. Anna turned and, to her surprise, found Mother Susana standing on the ridge. It had been *her* call. The raven floated toward the old woman and spiraled above her. Mother Susana waved her hand and the bird flew off, disappearing as quickly as it had appeared. Susana stepped down from her perch. She lifted her staff and gestured for Anna to follow.

Anna bounded up the ridge to join her.

The two women walked together for several minutes, silent but for the whisk-whisk of their sandals across stone. Arriving at a crest of dark red rock, Susana indicated that they should sit. Together they watched the first shadows of morning appear on the sand like pale ink stains.

Anna noticed how a feeling of calm overcame her. Just from being in Susana's presence. It was the same feeling she had when sitting in the arms of the great sycamore.

But a small part of her mind could not help wondering why the elder woman had called to her. They rarely spoke.

Had she done something to displease her?

Mother Susana chuckled to herself, sensing the young shepherd's fears.

"I am told you have recently been of enormous help in acquiring special herbs," she said, her voice clear and steady.

Anna glanced over. It was true. Since stumbling upon the haoma, she had set her sights on uncovering ever more rare finds. Her efforts had resulted in the collection and cultivation of several new varieties.

"Yes," Anna said. "And Rachel has told me that the haoma is growing well and should, one day, be hearty enough to provide a consistent harvest."

"Is that so?"

Anna frowned. "At first we struggled with its needs, having overwatered it, I fear. But now the plant is well established and will soon bloom."

Mother Susana allowed herself a smile. Both Shereen and Ruth had kept her apprised of the young shepherd's progress—from tending sheep to making repairs, from gardening to copying scrolls. And, the elder woman could see, their claims that Anna possessed a keen curiosity and capacity for learning had not been exaggerated.

The young shepherd boy had truly grown into a remarkable woman.

Though she had left Anna's guidance in the hands of the other Sisters, Mother Susana had felt propelled as of late by a sense that her turn to participate in the young woman's development had come.

Staring into the distance, the elder fell into a deep silence. After several moments, she said, "When Zahra and Maya and I were young, our mother taught us a game," she said.

Anna watched the old woman's eyes grow hazy with internal focus. Her fingers curled around her staff.

After a minute, Mother Susana said, "Would you like to try it?"

Anna nodded.

"First," Mother Susana began, "find something."

Anna looked around her.

"It can be anything. An object, a scent, a sound."

The pale green shoot of a small plant poking from the rock caught Anna's eye. She had not even noticed it before.

"You have chosen?"

Anna nodded.

"Now," Mother Susana intoned. "Take slow, deep breaths and focus on what you have chosen. As you breathe, let your mind slip from its hinges. Let it go out and greet what you have chosen. Let your heart set its cares aside. Let it also go out and greet what you have chosen. Introduce yourselves and discover all you can."

Anna looked down at the shoot. It seemed so plain. She wished she had chosen something more interesting.

"Do not judge, simply discover."

Anna frowned and returned her focus to the stem. With her second glance, she noticed two small leaves, like blades of grass, splitting from the central stem. One of the blades was green while the other was pale yellow.

Probably because the first blocks sun from the second, she thought.

"Good," Mother Susana whispered.

At the base of the stem, she noticed a fuzzy web of roots that wound down into the rock, holding it in place and mining for food.

What does it find to eat? she wondered.

"Good. Now close your eyes. Go deeper."

Anna closed her eyes. The image of the stem glowed inside her eyelids. Without any prompting, her mind traveled backward, to the time when the stem was merely a seed, deep in the belly of another plant. She saw how, when the wind rose, the seed was thrown into the air and tossed on erratic currents until it landed with a merciless thud against dry rock, not a speck of soil in sight. A locust clicked on a nearby ledge.

Would the insect eat the seed? she fretted.

"Good. Go deeper."

Anna heard Susana speak, but the words felt more like vibrations than language. Her body, she realized, had moved to a different plane. She was no longer wrapped in the shell of Anna but joined with the entirety of the world. It felt like floating.

"Live yourself into the miracle of what you have chosen."

Anna's awareness jumped inside the seed itself. There she felt the hum and presence of life. Untapped life. Waiting to be born. Throbbing against the husk that contained it. From inside the seed, she heard a gentle pattering. After a moment, she realized it was the sound of raindrops. She felt the entire globe lurch as the seed rolled. Just before she turned upside down, she pulled her awareness back outside the seed and saw it floating on the tip of a tiny tongue of water. The water whisked the seed toward a crack in the rock and finally over the edge!

"Live into the miracle."

Anna considered the impossibility of the seed's situation. After its harrowing journey on top of the winds, after avoiding a hungry locust, it had fallen into a deep, dark crack. But the crease formed by the crack, she realized, acted like a cup to capture and hold water and soil. Soon she heard the crack of husk as the seed burst open beneath the water's soft touch. From between its two halves, a pale gold shoot, impossibly tender, reached skyward, drawing water into its core to lift it . . . up . . . up . . . toward the light far above.

"Good, Anna," Mother Susana whispered. She laid a hand on her knee.

Anna jolted as if wakened from a dream. When she opened her eyes, her vision was blurred.

"Have you seen?" Mother Susana asked.

Anna nodded. She felt strangely lightened. Peaceful. And whole.

The sun began to rise behind them. The desert's colors dazzled Anna's eyes as if unleashed for the first time. She looked back down at the shoot. Her vision, she noticed, had sharpened considerably.

"My mother encouraged us to play that every morning before we began our day. Even if only for a moment or two. The game, she said, was more vital to our lives than food. And when we were older, she revealed the game not to be a game at all, but the art of Communion. The practicing of eternity. The secret of joy."

Anna kept still.

"Do you understand where you have been?" Susana asked.

Anna nodded.

"Carry it with you in your heart. Always remember."

After a while, Mother Susana leaned on her staff and stood. She tapped Anna playfully on top of her head with a finger. It had impressed her how instinctively the young shepherd had sustained Communion. And enticed the raven!

Truly the young woman possessed a great potential, she thought. As they returned together to the valley, Susana noted how Anna walked more thoughtfully, planting her feet so as to avoid the tiniest shoots and lichens.

CHAPTER 23

A village on the outskirts of The Narrows*—30* A.D.

Solomon rested in the shade as the women's wailing rose to his ears. To him it had become a familiar sound. And, once again, he had arrived too late to prevent it.

For years he had pursued his cousin from village to village, skirting along the perimeter of The Narrows. Though a capable tracker, Solomon was no match for Judas. At times he had felt certain he would come upon him, only to have all traces vanish. Yet, whenever word arose of a group planning an incursion into The Narrows, his cousin would strike, killing all who claimed to have knowledge of secret lairs or caves.

In this way, Solomon knew, Judas was striving to ensure the Sisters' safety.

But at what cost?

Not only had blood been shed and lives shattered, but through his awful deeds, Judas was ruining his soul.

How Solomon wished he could find his cousin. And return him to his senses.

Exhausted, the shepherd leaned back against a rock. Soon his eyes closed. When he had entered the dreaming place that arises just before sleep, his mind drifted back to his childhood. It was a happy day. The morning sun glinting along the walls. Seated by the fire, his mother was baking bread with her sister, Maya, and best friend, Alawa. Nearby, Solomon and Judas sat together carving whistles with Alawa's eldest daughter, Shereen. Behind them, two infants lay swaddled in a corner, Shereen's sister, Yadira, and Judas's sister, Delilah. The three mothers and their children had lived together almost as if a single family—the fathers' trades taking them to distant lands for long stretches at a time.

Though not related to her by blood, Solomon and his cousin loved Shereen as though she were their own sister. And their childhoods were integrally woven by days of play and song and wonder. He recalled, too, how his mother, Zahra, had adored Shereen. For, even at a young age, they could perceive an eminence and a dignity about her. A vital force. A destiny. Something beyond sheer beauty and equanimity. The future of which, perhaps, only Zahra had an inkling.

None of them was therefore surprised when, years later, Shereen began to prepare for her journey into The Narrows. Despite its inevitability, however, her eventual departure tore a great hole in their hearts. A gash that had already begun when, a year earlier, Shereen's younger sister, Yadira, a far more restless and rebellious child, had abandoned the family to marry an aging carpenter.

A frown darkened Solomon's face as he recalled the implications of Yadira's reckless choice, and how deeply it had affected them all—most especially Yadira's daughter.

Shereen had been deeply troubled by her sister's departure. More so than anyone had anticipated given that she, too, would one day leave the family's fold. And Solomon vividly remembered overhearing Shereen ask his mother to give her word that she would travel north to watch over Yadira—and her future children—and safeguard them from all harm. Having trusted in Shereen's intuition, and believing it to be her duty, Zahra had given her promise. And it was for this reason, which perhaps only Solomon knew, that his mother had never joined her twin in the caves.

On this last thought, Solomon's eyes flew open. For his thoughts had turned to the Sisters. And to Shereen and the young shepherd in particular.

When Sister Joan had come upon him and his flocks all those years ago, shortly after they had parted ways with their youngest shepherd, he had wanted desperately to convey the truth to her. But when the other shepherds had grown suspicious, Joan had fled back into the desert before he could reveal what he knew.

Having left the outside world at such a young age, he knew that Shereen could have no idea as to the young shepherd's identity.

But had she somehow sensed their connection?

Had she realized that Zahra had honored her promise—for all those years?

Shaking his head to clear his mind, Solomon let his eyes drift along the horizon. Training his vision, he sought movement of any kind. For he, too, had made a promise to Shereen—that he would safeguard Judas. And it was the troubling sense of having failed them both—the two he loved so dearly—that stirred him to his feet and propelled his aching body back to his quest.

CHAPTER 24

Somewhere within The Narrows *outside ancient* Palestine—33 A.D.

Late one night, when the others had retired, Mother Susana sat alone beneath the great sycamore, listening.

It had been almost three years to the day since Naomi's departure.

Fortunately, the time had passed without incident. In the peace of those years, Shereen had continued to train Sisters Helena, Irene, and Rachel. As each cure, value, and philosophy of The Way was passed down to the next generation of Awakeners, Susana's mood had lightened and her faith in the future blossomed. Once again, she dared hope that the survival of their foremothers' wisdom would ensure a future for all living things.

Looking up into the great tree's canopy, into the patterns woven by its leaves and branches, she further sensed that the time for Shereen's departure was upon them.

The lamp next to Anna's hand began to sizzle. As her gaze lifted from the parchment she found that the lamp had nearly burned out of oil.

How easily she had lost track of time!

She wanted to keep working, to keep proofreading the parchment that Ruth had given her, but it was late. And her eyes were heavy.

Leaning over the table, she lifted Ruth's quill from the inkwell. With it, she made a small mark in the margin to show where she had stopped. Through the dimming light, she looked down at the passage and reread the last part. It described some of the healing powers and cures that could be rendered from the sycamore—a tea that could be distilled from the bark to relieve chest pains and lung troubles, and an ointment from the sap that removed warts and soothed ringworm. Anna nodded at the text's accuracy, for she herself had witnessed such cures being mixed and utilized by Shereen and the other Sisters.

When Ruth had offered to teach her how to read in exchange for her proofreading efforts, Anna had eagerly accepted. However, having read hundreds of texts, and having never once discovered even the slightest mistake, Anna wondered why Ruth had asked for her help.

Careful to use only her fingertips, Anna rolled the parchment into a tube and replaced it inside the correct jar. Standing among the vessels, she double-checked that each was properly filled and sealed. Satisfied that all was in order, she extinguished the torches and headed into the maze.

Outside, she found the air drenched with moonlight, a silver piping glazing every edge. On the way back to her cave, she climbed on top of the ridge to survey the valley. Midnight was, she thought, the most magical of hours. Facing the moon, she inhaled a slow, deep breath. She then closed her eyes—and listened.

Below, she could hear the scurry and scamper of nighttime creatures embattled in nocturnal skirmishes—the drama of hunters and hunted. When she was younger, she would have perceived these sounds, as she had always possessed keen senses, but would have only sifted through them for signs of danger.

Was a predator afoot? A storm approaching? Were any of the sheep in distress?

Now she listened differently. No longer a bystander, she immersed far deeper. Listening not only with her ears, but with her heart, her mind, her skin.

Though Anna did not perceive a change within herself, by reading and upholding the values of The Way, her experience of life had been unalterably transformed. Communion had become an instinctive state. No longer did she merely watch the moon; she traveled moon. No longer did she mimic birdsong; she inhabited birdsong. As her body had attuned more intimately to the cycles and wonders around her, so had her soul's roots deepened, and with them, her contentment.

Heavy with exhaustion, Anna slipped into her cave. She smiled to see that someone had tended the fire. She unrolled her mat and was about to lie down when she heard a clatter behind her. Looking up, she saw a dark body rushing toward her.

"Anna!" she cried out.

The sheep rushed upon the shepherd and butted its head into her belly. Anna rubbed her hands up and down the animal's woolly flanks.

"Were you missing me?" she asked.

As if having understood, the animal lay down with the shepherd, pressing its back along hers. Settling in, Anna gazed into the glowing coals and imagined how, when she opened her eyes in the morning, their hot ginger blaze would have traveled to the sky to become sunrise. Drifting to sleep on this thought, Anna could dream of nothing finer than spending the rest of her days in The Narrows serving the Sisters of The Way.

Late one night, after finishing her work with the scrolls, Anna wove her way through the caves toward the Sisters' sleeping area. Earlier that day, an idea had come to her.

Not wanting to wake anyone, she sat outside the doorway, waiting. She soon heard someone rustle and get to her feet.

"Greetings of the night," she whispered to Tabitha when she emerged, as she always did, to get a drink of water.

"Oh!" Tabitha gasped, putting a hand to her chest. "Anna, it is only y-you," she said, relieved.

"I did not mean to frighten you, but I have something that I think might be of help."

"W-what is it?" Tabitha asked.

"Come with me."

Anna led the young woman into a separate room and lit a candle. "Lie down here," she told her. Tabitha stretched out along a mat.

Anna held up a jar. "This is a remedy that I saw Sister Shereen make out of the haoma plant. If you do not mind, I would like to apply it to your chest."

"W-what will it do?"

"I am hoping it will help make it easier for you to breathe," she told her.

Tabitha smiled. "I w-would l-like that!" she said and parted her robe.

With strong and supple hands, Anna smoothed the buttery oil between the channels of Tabitha's ribs. While she worked, she encouraged Tabitha to take long, slow breaths. When her inhalations and her exhalations began to regulate, Anna spoke in a gentle, whispery voice.

"Will you tell me something, Tabitha?"

"Uh-huh," she sighed, her tone relaxed and easy.

Anna swallowed. "Will you tell me about your brother?"

Tabitha's eyes flew open. Her breathing began to catch.

"Shhh," Anna whispered. "You are safe here. And I am listening. To *you*. Tonight it is *your* turn to speak," she said, hoping to reassure her.

Anna waited until Tabitha's breath began, again, to settle. She knew she was taking a great risk in trying to help her friend. But for some reason she thought that the sorrow Tabitha carried led to her tendency toward quick, shallow breathing. And that, if she could instill a sense of ease into her breath, Tabitha could feel and learn again the rhythm of speaking fluidly.

"I d-do n-n-not want to t-talk about th-that," Tabitha said, her stuttering more pronounced than ever.

Anna's heart fell as her confidence wavered.

Perhaps her instincts had been wrong? Perhaps she was causing her friend more harm than good?

She felt stones roll in her belly.

What would the others say when they found out?

Tabitha began to weep. Her tears came reluctantly at first, then burst wide in a rushing flood.

Seeing her friend's distress, Anna cried out an apology. "I am sorry, Tabitha!" she said, desperate to stop what she had begun. "I am so very sorry for—"

"He w-was so mean to me!" Tabitha bawled, her fists clenching in anguish. "I l-loved him *so m-much* . . . and he only *h-hated* me."

Silenced by Tabitha's unexpected confession, Anna reached down and, before she could think about what she was doing, continued massaging the remedy across her chest.

Beneath her, Tabitha's eyes burned with a fiery light. Then, like an animal slipping free of the hunter's hand, the story she had resisted rushed from her mouth. As it did, her breathing came deeper. And gained power. Her words coming quick and clear. Laced with hurt and anger.

When she had finished describing what her brother had done to her, she closed her eyes and grew quiet. Finally, she said, "If I had a younger sibling, someone looking up to me, I would never bring them harm. It would never even *occur* to me!" She then opened her eyes and gazed off, as if into a remembered room. After a moment, she whispered, "To do what he did to me, he must have been in great pain himself."

Anna's eyes grew wide, amazed by her friend's capacity for compassion. And her willingness to let go.

In the silence that followed, Tabitha closed her eyes and whispered, "Thank you."

But Anna could not say for certain to whom she was speaking.

Ruth sat up, unable to sleep. The night had been unusually cold and she felt a chill in her bones. Wrapping herself in a robe, she headed toward the main chamber. As she glided down the torch-lit passageway, she heard the click-clack of the loom. She thought that odd.

"Sister!" Ruth said when she spotted Tabitha hard at work. "What has got you up so late in the night?"

Keeping her eyes on the weave, Tabitha took a long breath and exhaled slowly before saying, "I am making a new tunic for Anna."

"I see," Ruth said, nodding. Her features then shifted with disbelief. "*What* did you say?" she asked.

Tabitha took control of another breath and said, "I am making a new tunic for Anna."

Ruth's jaw dropped. "Tabitha," she said. "You are not stuttering!"

A smile spread across the young woman's face. "Anna has been teaching me a special way of breathing," she said, then emitted a slow, controlled exhalation. "And made a special remedy to help me."

Ruth smelled the scent of mint and haoma and a realization struck her between the eyes. Before she could speak, the door inside the scriptorium closed with a loud clank. Shortly afterward, Anna appeared before them.

"Why is everyone awake?" she asked, appearing confused. "Is it already morning?"

Ruth rushed up to Anna and threw her arms around her. "You have done very well, my friend," she told her. She nodded toward Tabitha. "Tell me, what made you think to use the haoma remedy?"

Anna glanced down at her feet. "I could not say, really. Just a feeling I had after seeing Shereen make the mixture. Something about it reminded me of a time in my childhood. When I had seen Zahra using it."

Ruth nodded thoughtfully. "From what I have heard, she was a gifted healer," she said. She gazed down again at Anna. "And now it would seem that you are following in her footsteps."

"Oh no! Not at all," Anna said, taking a step back. "It was just something I thought might help," she added. But inside she felt lightened by a sense of accomplishment . . . and purpose.

Ruth pressed a finger to her chin. Though not entirely certain why, she felt it imperative to inform Mother Susana of Anna's achievement.

Ruth lifted a pitcher and poured three cups of water. "We should all be going to sleep now. Tomorrow will be a momentous day," she said.

"Yes it will!" Tabitha chimed.

Anna tipped her head. "Why will it be momentous?" she asked.

Ruth glanced over. "Have you not heard?"

Anna shook her head.

Ruth frowned. She knew the news would be difficult for her friend to hear. And she should have thought to make sure Anna knew ahead of time.

Unaware of Ruth's thoughts, Tabitha said, "It is Shereen's final day among us. For tomorrow she will depart to begin life as an Awakener!"

Ruth cringed and watched the realization hit Anna's heart, swift and sharp as an arrow.

CHAPTER 25

A village on the edge of the mountains—33 A.D.

Having arrived at first light, Solomon approached the elder men in the village while the women huddled off to the side, tending to their morning chores.

The men's talk rose in a clamor as each struggled to lift his voice above the other's, eager to explain to the gray-eyed visitor what had happened.

"He came at night!"

"We were sleeping!"

"We pounced upon him!"

"He fought like a wildcat!"

"But we got our knives into him!"

"Just before he fled!"

"See here? See his blood?"

Solomon looked down. Beneath their feet appeared a crimson trail that stretched into the wavy sand.

"We would have pursued him, but decided to let the wolves do our work," one of the men said.

Solomon knelt and pressed his fingertips into the bloody dust. It still felt moist to the touch. He knew then that he could not be far behind. Rising to his feet, he dashed from their sight, tracking the one who had left the jagged path.

As he traveled farther into the barren terrain, Solomon felt a knot tightening in his stomach. For just ahead the vultures had begun circling. Bracing himself for what he might find, he pressed onward, despite the staggering heat.

But just before he arrived at the center of the vultures' circle, the trail of blood ended abruptly.

Startled, Solomon scoured the ground for any tracks or sign of Judas. After an hour of searching, he found nothing, no footprints or pools of blood. Only the broken strap from his sandal.

If the wolves had attacked, Solomon knew, he would have found his cousin's clothing—and the goatskin pouch he kept ever on his back.

But if not wolves, what had taken him?

Only one grisly possibility remained—that Judas had been taken by a lion and, too weak to fight, had been carried off to the animal's lair.

But if so, where were the animal's tracks?

Perhaps a passing windstorm had erased them?

Exhausted and sensing that a vital part of himself had been lost—Solomon fell to his knees and wept.

CHAPTER 26

Somewhere within The Narrows *outside ancient* Palestine*—33* A.D.

In the hush before dawn, when the air in the caves moved only on the breath of the sleeping, Mother Susana sensed the tight clasp of fingers gripping her neck. She choked and gasped as the bony digits pressed down her windpipe. Her eyes flew open to locate her attacker but she saw no one. The space around her reflected only darkness. Not even the moon spoke that night.

She bolted upright and sputtered to regain her breath. As she drew in long, ragged mouthfuls of air, the situation became clear. The attack had been only a dream. She sat in the dark and calmed herself. She knew of no reason that she should feel agitated. The last three years had been peaceful and productive. Sister Joan had traveled to several villages and had found no news of Sister Naomi. That was taken as a good sign since word of capture or murder, they knew, traveled quickly.

But as the hour of Shereen's departure drew near, something made Mother Susana anxious.

Recently, while taking her morning walks, she had felt her mother's presence close. Then Zahra's. As if they had something they needed to communicate. As if they had a warning.

Mother Susana breathed deeply and settled into the darkness. She held Communion with the air around her and its soundlessness. Her body dissolved and she drifted into the future like a boat slipped from its moorings. She watched the time unfold and people play their parts. She saw Shereen going forward into the world, as intended. Then the time beyond that began to blur. And she could not decipher beyond that part of her vision. Something within it remained ambiguous and confusing. Something about the future of The Way. And the path yet to come.

Why could she not see it more clearly?

"Mother?" someone spoke in the dark. It was Sister Joan. She had risen when she heard Susana's quickened breath. The two women sat and joined their intuitions. Their minds raced forward, propelled by their connection. But, hours later, after traveling forward and back, neither knew how to interpret the strange wonders they had seen.

Dressed in their finest robes, the Sisters gathered in the garden. The time had come for Shereen's last supper.

The women sat down to form a plum-colored circle around the trunk of the great sycamore. Anna and Tabitha entered the chamber carrying a warm loaf of bread, a plate of wheat grains, and a jug of wine. They laid these offerings before Mother Susana and placed small cups in front of the others.

Following a long period of silent reflection, Mother Susana took the bread and lifted it above her head. "Let us give thanks to the earth and to the Mother of All for her generosity and sacrifice."

The Sisters in the circle nodded and whispered, "We give thanks."

"Let us also give thanks to those whose hands tilled the soil, planted the seeds, tended the plants, harvested and ground the grain, stoked the fire, kneaded the dough, and baked the loaf."

The women whispered, "Yes, yes, we give our thanks."

Mother Susana broke the bread and laid the halves on the plate of grain, saying, "Take this all of you and eat from it. This is the body of the Mother, source and life of us all. From her womb we draw life. From her breast we draw strength. To her womb we shall return and yet be born again. For all that we take, may we plant new life in kind. Do this in remembrance of Her." She then passed the bread around the circle. As each woman took a piece of the bread, they lifted a grain of wheat from the plate. When they had finished eating, they pressed small holes into the ground before them and planted the grains.

Then Mother Susana lifted the wine and gave similar thanks. "This is the blood of the Mother, source and life of us all." She passed the jug and allowed each of the Sisters to pour a cup. After drinking their fill, they each poured the remaining liquid on top of their newly planted seeds, thus reuniting the body and blood of the Mother.

Mother Susana pulled a single ripe fig from the folds of her robe. She held the fruit up high and gave thanks to the Mother of All. She then added, "We give our word that the Mother's gifts, and the miracle of life, will not be taken for granted nor mistreated nor forgotten." She passed the fruit to Shereen, who dug a deep hole into which she placed it. She covered the fruit with dirt and watered it with wine, saying, "May all that proceeds from my journey be of benefit to all of Creation."

Sister Joan stood ready at the door. In her hands she carried a staff. On her shoulder hung two skins of water.

Sister Shereen floated into the entranceway, her steps buoyed by the honor of her future, her golden eyes burning within the shadow of her hood. In the folds of her garment, she carried several small pouches containing the Seven Cures as well as other precious herbs and seeds that could be transformed into a variety of remedies.

As the Sisters gathered, Anna kept her gaze lowered. While the faces of the others were lit with joy, hers was stained with tears. Her heart aching inside her chest.

She knew that as an Awakener Shereen could never return to The Narrows. And, since Anna herself would never become an Awakener—those doors not being open to a mere shepherd, much less a woman of dubious gender—she knew that she would never *leave* The Narrows. That being so, she would never see Shereen again.

Joan placed her hand on the hidden stone to open the entrance door. As she did, a shaft of sunlight flooded the room. When it struck Anna's eyes, she felt a temptation she had not felt since her arrival. The temptation to leave.

She gazed out the entrance.

As if reading Anna's thoughts, Sister Shereen stepped forward. She drew Anna off to the side. Kneeling down, she took the young woman's gaze into her own. "Listen to me, Anna. It is not for you to go. You must stay. And you must believe in the rightness of your remaining among the Sisters," she told her. She then lifted Anna's hand and drew her closer. "But know this," she added, dropping her voice to a whisper. "The blood that runs through my veins, runs also through yours. Be assured of yourself and of the path that lies ahead."

Anna was startled by her words. And by the force with which Shereen had spoken. She started to ask Shereen what she had meant, but Sister Joan stepped forward and guided her charge through the doorway.

Anna stood high on a rock promontory. From there she watched Sisters Joan and Shereen making their way toward the distant horizon. Seeing them so exposed, it suddenly dawned on her that the Sisters would do better to put more resources into protecting those who traveled to the outside world rather than into those who remained within the safety of the caves.

Thinking this, she grew agitated and began to pace as anguishing thoughts crept through her mind.

Why had she not offered to travel with Sister Shereen?

Could she not have helped her fulfill her destiny?

Could she not have protected her from those who wished to suppress The Way?

But now it was too late!

Furious at her failure, Anna slapped a handful of stones into her sling and was about to fire them off when a hand fell along her shoulder.

Spinning with a gasp, she found Mother Susana standing alongside her. She marveled that she had not heard the old woman's approach.

Mother Susana gave a smile, but she looked tired.

Anna felt the thoughts roiling through her mind grow still.

Together, they stared in silence, watching the women depart. Beyond them, the vista unfolded like a fabric sewn with muted colors—chalk, sand, and clay. Above the land, the sky was inking from silver to blue.

Finally, Mother Susana spoke. "Some days I feel so uncertain," she said.

Anna started. She could not imagine Susana being doubtful. "About what are you uncertain?" she asked.

The old woman closed her eyes as if trying to see beyond the present. She bit her lip with anxious teeth. "I am uncertain about the future of The Way. And whether or not I am serving it honorably. And effectively."

Anna's eyebrows rose in surprise. "But what about all the Awakeners you have sent into the world?"

"Yes," Susana mused. She ran thoughtful fingers around the perimeters of her two medallions—hers and Zahra's. "Sometimes I worry that all we are doing is sending sheep to the wolves," she said.

Anna gazed toward Shereen. But the Sister was gone from view. Anna shuddered.

Closing her eyes, her mind then fell to the shepherd's secret Solomon had taught her. "If you want them to be safe, perhaps it would be better to send the sheep dressed as wolves," she whispered, almost to herself.

Mother Susana stopped breathing. All expression drained from her face.

Anna's own cheeks flushed with shock and embarrassment.

What had come over her? She had not even meant to speak!

The look of bald astonishment on Anna's face amused Mother Susana. The seed of a smile took root in the elder's lips and soon lifted her cheeks high in joy. A rich laughter rumbled up from the old woman's belly. Her outburst was as much a release of pent-up worry as it was sheer delight at the revelation. Laughter continued to shake the old woman's shoulders until Anna could not help but giggle herself. The looks on their reddened faces made each of them laugh even more. They bent over themselves, caught in hilarious spasms. Finally, after several minutes, the mirth drained away, leaving them spent and wiping tears from their eyes.

When she could again speak, Mother Susana said, "You are wise beyond your years."

Anna blushed again, this time with pride.

Mother Susana stared across the landscape. She watched the light shift in degrees. She then returned her attention to the remarkable woman before her. She wondered at the strange and indecipherable visions she had had of Anna's future.

Had she missed something? Or misunderstood? Was it possible that the shepherd's destiny lay beyond the caves? In the world from whence she had come?

But at no point had she ever considered selecting the shepherd to become an Awakener.

This was not because Anna was incapable of practicing The Way. On the contrary, Susana had seen the woman demonstrate an impressive degree of compassion and creativity. From living among them Anna had developed inner strength, patience, and the ability to listen deeply. From tending the manuscripts she had imbibed a great store of knowledge. And from assisting the Sisters in the garden she had developed a healer's instinct—which she had then used successfully to restore Tabitha's voice!

But Anna had lived her formative years in a manner that had denied her true self. Despite her obvious progress, she still did not seem entirely comfortable in her own skin. And while the young woman could flourish within the compassionate and encouraging world of the Sisters, Mother Susana doubted that she could similarly flourish beyond the caves. After all, the female Anna had existed in the world for only a brief time, and as a child. There was too much about the adult Anna that was unknown and untested.

Taking the sum total of Anna into consideration, Mother Susana believed that the risk of sending out a spirit that had not yet fully emerged was too great.

Having renewed the conviction of her decisions, she returned to the matters at hand. "Speaking of wolves," she said, facing Anna head-on, "did Sister Joan not ask you to stand guard over us in her absence?"

Anna leapt to her feet. "Yes, Mother Susana, she did. Thank you for reminding me!" she said.

Susana smiled. "And thank *you* for speaking with me today. Your particular wisdom never ceases to refresh."

Anna nodded, though she could not imagine how anything she might say could impress Mother Susana. Still, it made her feel happy to think it possible.

CHAPTER 27

Somewhere within The Narrows *outside ancient* Palestine*—33 A.D.*

As the days following Joan and Shereen's departure passed, the routine within the caves returned to normal. From her perch, Anna watched the sheep spread on the dark valley floor. A gentle breeze lifted their musky scent to her nose.

In the quiet, she listened for the voices of predators but heard none. She found a reference point on the horizon and scanned the desert, methodically sweeping her gaze. She anticipated sighting the lone figure of Sister Joan, but so far had seen nothing.

Her return was not expected for several more days.

The lizard squirmed inside the cup of Anna's hands. She had found the bright green specimen sunning on the rocks. Taking a break from her morning watch, she brought the animal into the central chamber to show Tabitha, who she knew had a passion for the creatures.

"Oh!" Tabitha cried with delight as the tiny green beast sauntered up her arm and nestled on her shoulder.

Mother Susana and Sister Ruth sat over a fire, letting the flames ease the morning chill from their bones. Susana seemed genuinely tranquil and undistracted by her recent worries. They all laughed when the lizard perched on top of Tabitha's head.

Ruth lifted the pot of water from the coals to fill everyone's cups with tea, but her pour cut off midstream. A guttural sound, like a deep groan, rolled down the cave from the front entrance. Mother Susana's eyes snapped into Ruth's. No one moved. The groan rose again. It did not sound human. It lifted the hairs along their arms. They heard a great crash and the chamber floor shook beneath them. Tabitha was knocked from her feet. The lizard scampered through a crack in the wall.

Anna looked to Ruth, "What was *that*?" she whispered.

Ruth lifted a finger to her mouth. "Shh!" she warned.

Mother Susana listened with an air of extreme calm. As if she knew what was coming. But Anna did not feel so calm.

The sound of falling rocks echoed through the chamber. The groan grew louder.

Sister Ruth barely had time to lift Tabitha before a different sound pummeled their ears. At first Anna had trouble recognizing the strange utterances. But her body soon remembered.

They were the voices of men.

The shouting came sharp and serrated with anger. Tabitha began to whimper. Sister Ruth held her firmly by the shoulders. "Tabitha," she said. "Go warn the others! They are in the gardens."

Anna could see Tabitha's eyes register the words but her body remained limp. The men's voices strained as they dug through the rocks at the entrance.

Ruth held Tabitha tight and demanded her full attention. "Their lives are in your hands," she said. "Go!"

Tabitha jumped up and ran.

"Mother," Ruth commanded. "We need to move you to your chamber."

But the old woman did not move. She sat still as if someone were telling her a vital story.

"Mother," Ruth insisted as the shouting grew louder.

A giant figure, torn and bloodied, toppled into the room. Everyone jumped until looks of recognition crossed their faces. The figure was Sister Joan.

"We were ambushed," she gurgled through a mouthful of blood.

"They . . . they knew the way to the caves . . . and hid themselves. I took a shortcut but . . . they are here," she said, then stumbled forward.

Sister Ruth ran to help her.

"No! Leave me. Get Mother to her chambers!" she moaned. After issuing her warning, she fell to the floor, weakened from her efforts and loss of blood.

The first man burst into the chamber in a whirlwind of dust. His eyes widened in amazement beneath a bright blue keffiyeh. For a moment Anna thought how strange the sight must seem to him—a group of women, warming themselves around a fire, drinking tea, in a remote desert cave. Gathering himself quickly, the man turned toward Mother Susana and whipped his saber high over his head. The blade whistled like a raven's wing cutting the air.

"Noo!" the Sisters screamed in unison.

Mother Susana kept still as the man advanced.

Before he could reach her, Joan's arm snapped like a cobra and sprayed a handful of hot powder into his eyes. The man screamed in pain and dropped to his knees. His saber clattered to the floor as he beat his fists against his eyelids.

Sister Joan lunged toward Anna and seized her by the tunic. Despite her blood loss, she mustered the strength to pull Anna's face close. "Take Mother to her chamber, now!" she hissed through bloody lips.

Anna's insides turned to ice.

The man with the blue keffiyeh heard their voices and lunged blindly. He screamed at them, hurling obscenities that Anna had not heard since her time among the shepherds. The other men, having dug their way into the entrance, called out to their comrade.

Terrified, Anna tried to take Mother Susana away, but the man's violent thrashings were unpredictable and blocked their escape.

Sisters Ruth and Joan distracted him by throwing stones while Anna led Susana toward the door. They had nearly escaped when the man heard their footsteps and leapt toward them, knocking his entire body into Mother Susana. The old woman's frame crumpled beneath the blow. Her head cracked against the wall as her body hit the ground.

"Mother!" Anna shouted. Finding a resurgence of strength, she lifted the woman's broken body onto her shoulders and carried her off like a wounded sheep.

"Run, Anna, run!" Ruth yelled, following behind her.

The men's shouting echoed off the walls in sharp angles.

Anna was certain more of them had entered the chamber. "What about Sister Joan?" she asked, her thighs pumping beneath the load.

"Keep going," Ruth said, with an air of calm. "She knows what she must do."

Back in the central chamber, the men descended on Sister Joan like locusts clinging to a stalk. They grabbed at her ears, her eyes, her breasts. She shrieked and fought like a wildcat. In the scuffle, she managed to fling her blistering powders into the eyes of two more, bringing them to their knees, howling. She fought with the last of her strength and struggled to get to the far wall.

The men surrounded her and just when she thought she was done for, they suddenly pulled back. Confused, her eyes flew from man to man. Her gaze then fell on the intruder with the bright blue keffiyeh. As he rose to his feet, his puffy eyes burned an angry and luminous red. His nose ran. His mouth twisted into a wiry grimace. His saber gleamed in his hand. He took a step toward the unarmed woman, licking his lips. "May God torment you for denying Him," he hissed. The others held still waiting to relish his revenge.

Joan whispered her final words as the man's shadow crept across her. His comrades moved in to watch the slaughter.

The bloodied Sister closed her eyes and, in a single motion, reached up and pulled the lever. The support beams slipped and the false ceiling came crashing down. Sister Joan and her assailants vanished instantly under the giant stones.

When the dust settled, the men who had escaped the rocks fanned out over the rubble looking for their fallen comrades. Finding them crushed and lifeless, they became enraged and zipped down the passageways like angry wasps, swinging their sabers before them.

Anna stumbled into the chamber, out of breath, and laid Mother Susana on her mat. Sister Ruth leapt to the door. She yanked on a leather strap and a huge stone that had sat motionless for years rolled across the door, dropping with a thud into a deep groove. With their location secured, Ruth lifted a flint from her tunic and lit the torch alongside the door. Bringing the light, she knelt quickly next to Anna. Looking down, they considered Mother Susana with concern. The gash on her head had swelled and was bleeding badly. Her skin had turned the color of ash.

Without a word between them, the women burst into a flurry of activity. Ruth pulled a pouch of herbs from inside Mother Susana's robes and pressed two seeds under the old woman's tongue. Anna tore a strip of material off the bottom of her tunic. She gave the fabric to Sister Ruth, who slathered it with a poultice of bay laurel mixed with olive oil. She gently pressed the dressing onto Susana's wound. Anna then lifted Susana's head and Ruth laid a pillow beneath it.

In their urgency, neither woman noticed how seamlessly they worked—almost as if of one mind.

Then the first scream hit their ears. A woman's scream. One of the Sisters.

More terrifying sounds snuck through cracks in the walls. Men's crazed laughter. Bloodcurdling wails. The clashing of rock and metal and flesh.

Anna cringed at the horrid sounds. Ruth pressed a finger to her mouth, signaling that they should keep silent. Another scream. More laughter. Then moans and cries. And pleading. Anna pressed her hands to her ears. She could not stand the madness anymore.

Ruth took Anna into her arms when two men started shouting outside the door and grunting in their efforts to roll back the stone. The women heard the crack of metal on rock and more yelling. They clung to each other as the men sniffed around the doorway, hurling taunts and threats through every seam.

Anna winced as the sounds of torture and devastation continued to echo down the corridors. Clutching Ruth, her mind turned toward Sister Shereen. Joan had returned without her. And that could only mean that Shereen, the great Sister of the Way, the woman of knowledge and infinite golden eyes, was dead.

As if she had read this dreadful thought, Mother Susana twitched beneath them.

The men strained a second time against the stone but could not move it.

As they waited in horror, a thought suddenly occurred to Anna: If the men could not roll the stone to get in, how would the Sisters ever roll the stone to get out?

CHAPTER 28

Somewhere in the desert outside ancient Palestine—33 A.D.

Anna jerked up with a start.

Had she fallen asleep?

How much time had passed?

She lifted herself from the floor. Her head fuzzy. Her lips dry.

Holding the torch aloft, Ruth stood at the door, peering through the cracks for any sign of movement. Beneath them, Mother Susana lay on her mat, looking like a bird that had unexpectedly dropped from its nest. Anna watched the quickened rise and fall of her narrow rib cage. Despite their ministrations, her breathing had become shallow. Anna feared that the next time she peered down, her breath would have ceased.

Ruth lifted two more seeds from her pouch. She placed them under Susana's tongue. Lowering the torch, she sparked a small pile of dried herbs on the floor. The room filled with thick, spicy smoke. She came and sat next to Anna. "Let us join," she said. Anna was unsure what to do as they held hands over Mother Susana. She remembered what Shereen had told her to do when working to heal someone.

Listen, she had said. *But not just with your ears. Listen with your whole body.*

Anna felt her soul expand and open to the two women before her. She sensed her own thoughts rushing out and theirs rushing in. Her fingertips buzzed and she knew that something of significance was passing among them.

Mother Susana's eyes opened slowly as the women leaned over her. Her tongue worried at the seeds beneath it. She and Ruth linked eyes. The expressions on their faces widened with disbelief.

"I have seen things. Things I wish I could tell you," the old woman said. "All has become clear. And I have seen the sycamore rising."

Ruth nodded.

Anna looked from one to the other in confusion.

Was Susana hallucinating?

Susana continued to hold Ruth's eyes. "The Way is in your hands, daughter," she said.

"I understand," Ruth whispered.

Anna wanted to protest. She wanted to say, *No, Mother Susana. You will get better! The Way is still in* your *hands!*

Mother Susana turned her eyes on the young shepherd. Anna melted beneath the benevolence of her gaze. The old woman lifted a shaky hand to her own throat. She struggled to pull Zahra's medallion from inside her robe. "This was meant for you," she told Anna.

Ruth helped the old woman place the chain over Anna's head. Anna stared in disbelief.

Why should she be the one to wear the medallion? It was not right! She did not have the wisdom of an Awakener. She was not even truly a Sister!

Susana scooped Anna's gaze into her own. "Wear it always. So that you will remember who you are, no matter who you must become," she whispered. A wet cough hacked at the old woman's chest. A trickle of blood spilled from her lips.

Anna did not understand.

What was happening? What did she mean?

A river of questions rose within her. She lifted the old woman's hand, but as she did, it went limp. Anna's own hand began to tingle.

Ruth said nothing and gently lowered Susana's eyelids with her fingertips. Silent tears streamed down and pooled in the wells of her cheeks.

Ruth and Anna spent another two days in Mother Susana's chamber. They wanted to be absolutely certain that the marauders had left. During the wait, they collected every useful thing they could find. They gathered herbs and flints, goatskin pouches, quills, ink, blankets, dried dates, and a jar of olive oil. Ruth said it was important to take all they could since she did not know what they would find on the outside. She said this as though she knew they would get out of the chamber, though Anna had yet to understand how.

On the third morning, Ruth and Anna held Communion. They said blessings over Mother Susana and buried her, as best they could, with a sycamore seedpod in her hand. Then they sprinkled her body with wine.

When the ceremony was complete, Ruth stood and walked to the door. Anna expected to see her miraculously roll away the large stone. Instead, the Sister lifted a hand and pressed it against the wall alongside the stone. Anna recognized the motion. A secret entrance! The slab of rock rotated on an axis to reveal a long dark tunnel. Ruth lifted her lamp and motioned for Anna to follow.

Within minutes, the women found themselves back in the main chamber. They pulled torches from the walls and lit them. The flames cast an eerie light over the giant pile of rubble before them.

"Look!" Anna gasped. Sister Joan's hand protruded from the rocks. Nearby, they could discern the dusty arms and legs of several men.

Sister Ruth knelt and held the hands of Sister Joan and one of the men. "May you all return to the Great Cycle, and yet be born again," she whispered.

Farther ahead, the corridor echoed with an ominous silence. Gone were the sounds of conversation, the mortar and pestle, crackling fires, drums, the clack of the loom, song, and laughter. Anna's scalp began to hum.

They approached the pantry with caution. When certain that it was empty, they stepped inside. Ruth gasped. Every jar, bowl, and pot had been smashed against the ground. Dark stains spread on the floor where milk and oil were soaking into the dust. A few dried figs and olives rested among the shards of broken pottery. The men had taken everything.

"Gather what you can," Ruth said as she bent to the floor.

As they headed toward the great garden, fear wrapped like a collar around Anna's throat. Sisters Helena, Irene, and Rachel had been collecting herbs when the marauders attacked. At the entranceway, Ruth paused to take a deep breath. She then lifted her torch and proceeded into the room. A hazy light filtered through cracks in the roof. When Anna's eyes adjusted, the sight before them yanked at the back of her tongue. She dropped to her knees, gagging. Ruth helped her back to her feet. She pressed a small seed into Anna's palm and told her to suck on it. "It will strengthen your stomach," she said, her voice hoarse with shock.

When Anna faced the room again, the first thing she noticed was the wide, empty space above them. The men had hacked down the great sycamore. It leaned, awkwardly, on its side like a great fallen beast.

The air smelled of blood and freshly cut greens. With their blades, the men had slashed every vine, tendril, and sapling. Entire plants had been torn up by the roots. Containers of seedlings trampled.

The bodies of Sisters Helena, Irene, and Rachel lay in tangled heaps among the greenery, their blood mixing with the shredded leaves.

Behind them, the spring bubbled water into the ruin.

"Stay here," Ruth instructed. She knelt to touch each body and whisper a blessing. She struggled to hold down her stomach. It was not that she was unfamiliar with the sight of violence. But it had been a long time. She stood before the jagged trunk of the sycamore. She could see milky sap leaking from the gashes left by the blades. She held her tears and let her mind move forward. In her vision, she saw the Sisters' bodies returning to the soil and their life force being drawn up by the tree's great roots. From this exchange, she could see bright green shoots rising from the broken trunk and running up toward the sky. Then she saw the bees returning. And the birds. The Sisters, she knew, embodied in the tree, would rise again—world without end.

But what of her and Anna?

"Let us go from here," Ruth said.

Despite the silence, more horrors awaited them in the passageways. Fallen bodies lay around every bend. Bracing, Ruth led Anna through the tangle of arms and legs. Beneath them the Sisters' plum-colored robes were darkening with one another's blood.

After what seemed to Anna an eternity, they arrived at the scriptorium. The door had been heaved open and the entire room plundered. Every jar had been smashed and every manuscript burned to ashes. Ruth knelt and ran her fingers over the broken shards and shattered inkpots. Anna expected her to break down sobbing. But she did not.

Instead, she rose and said, "They were only words. We must remember that the knowledge and Spirit still live within us."

Ruth turned to leave the room when something rustled behind them. Both women flinched and prepared to fight. Their eyes fell on a figure hidden within the shadows.

"Show yourself!" Ruth demanded.

The figure whimpered unintelligible sounds.

"Come out now!" Ruth tried again, though she feared what might appear.

The figure slipped into the circle of light cast by Ruth's torch. Her face was stained with tears, her nose running uncontrollably. Her upper lip, cut and bleeding, trembled with fear.

"Tabitha," they whispered and took her into their arms. The woman's body shook as if from cold.

"You are safe now, Sister," Ruth whispered, wrapping Tabitha within her robes.

Outside the caves, Tabitha and Anna waited on the ridge while Ruth went to see if anything remained of the sheep. Anna hoped with all her heart that the men had not discovered her separate chamber. But when Ruth returned, picking her way carefully along the narrow trail, Anna could tell by her expression that all was lost. Her black sheep, her friend and namesake, was gone.

Little was said among the women as they made their way across the endless plain, as they pushed through rippling mirages and hot gusts that blew sand into their mouths. Only during the heat of the day would they stop to sip water, share figs, and repair their battered sandals.

Anna felt as though her heart were breaking. As they walked, she fought against sickening waves of guilt.

Why had she left her post?

If she had not, surely she would have seen Sister Joan running and been able to warn everyone of the men's approach.

Was she not to blame for all the loss?

She tried to banish the visions of violence from her mind but could not. When lifting her eyes to scan the horizon, she saw a limp arm lying among the rocks. When warming her hands at the fire, she saw manuscripts smoking among the coals. When turning into the wind, she heard terrifying screams.

The sting of tears burned her cheeks. Though her feet moved her farther away, she felt a longing to return to the caves, to the Tree of Life, and the place where she felt inextricably connected to all Creation. But nothing, she knew, remained.

How could these things have come to pass?

As they traveled farther from their home, skirting the Great Desert, Anna wondered at Ruth's thoughts. She seemed particularly difficult to read.

Was she angry with Anna?

Did she, too, yearn to return?

Or was she preparing herself for the inevitable?

For, eventually, they would cross out of the plains.

Then what would become of them?

Many days into their journey, when the women had paused to pluck nettles from Tabitha's tunic, Anna lifted a hand against the sun's glare and scanned the horizon. Far in the distance behind them, her eyes fell on a slanted ridgeline of columnar rocks. She recognized it immediately. It was the landmark Solomon had pointed out at the start of her journey into The Narrows. She looked around them and recognized the familiar sand formations at the mouth of the Great Desert to the east. A chill ran down her back. It had been here, in this exact spot, that she and Solomon had parted ways.

You will know what to do when you know what you are facing, she heard him say.

The voice in her head was so loud and real that she spun around, certain she would see the gray-eyed shepherd standing behind her.

"Anna?" Ruth asked.

"It is nothing."

Ruth's eyes squinted. She could easily discern that it was more than nothing.

It was dusk when the women, with weary steps, came upon a village. The first thing Anna noticed was the smell of camel dung and the sound of the animals' burnished complaint. Their comical groans had been missing to her for years. A whirled cloud of birdsong followed. Anna's heart lifted on the climbing harmonies. In an instant, she recognized the various dialects: sunbirds, bee-eaters, swifts, larks, and flycatchers.

The shifting surface of sand gave way to rocky soil. Soon thereafter they came upon a village of small mud and straw houses. Scrawny guinea hens strutted unceremoniously down the main road. Without warning, a group of young boys dashed past. Two of them chased a third who was waving a shriveled pomegranate. When they saw the three women spit out by the terrain, they stopped cold in their tracks. Their young eyes stared sharply. Anna's ears began to ring.

"Cover your faces," Ruth urged as she tightened the linen about her cheeks. Tabitha did the same. Though neither of them had been in the outside world for many years, they knew that women should not be traveling without a male escort.

But Anna hesitated. The once required motion of concealing herself, of lifting fabric to face, had become foreign to her. In her years as a shepherd, and even among the Sisters, she had learned that she could stand tall and face the world head-on.

The boys gawked at the strange dark woman—alone, defiant, handsome, her face exposed before them.

"Anna, cover yourself!" Ruth hissed.

Shaken, Anna reached for her shawl and awkwardly wrapped it about her face. She felt the rough material scratch her skin. For the first time since she was a child, she felt invisible.

The two groups continued their face-off. The boys seemed to be making a silent decision. Should they ignore the women? Or alert the adults? The one holding the dead fruit stepped forward. He stared at Tabitha with cold, reptilian eyes. "Who are you?" he demanded. Tabitha said nothing. Anna could see her friend's hands trembling beneath her tunic. The boy picked his nose. "Who are you?" he whined, taking a challenging step forward.

Anna felt her hands tightening into fists.

"Ta-ta-tabith-th-th—" she stuttered, shaking from limb to limb.

The boys howled.

"Did you hear that?" the boy with the pomegranate shouted. "She's a half-wit! A ha-ha-ha-half-wit!" He exploded forward in a punctuated lunge. Tabitha tumbled back. Her fear elicited another round of bawdy laughter. Without thinking, Anna took a step forward, positioning herself between flock and predator. Startled by her sudden move, the boy tripped backward. His comrades laughed at his frightened stumble. Anna held her ground.

The boy became enraged at having been made to look foolish. With a single burst, he hurled his shrunken fruit at Tabitha. It smacked her forehead with a hollow thud. The boys broke into hysterics. Ruth pulled Tabitha to her. She had been dizzied by the blow. Anna knelt to grab the pomegranate. But before she could get her hand on it, a torrent of stones assailed them.

"No!" Anna shouted between salvos. She hurled stones as fast as she could, but the boys fired incessantly, pelting them with a rain of rock. When Ruth and Tabitha started running back into the plains, Anna followed.

The boys hurled insults and errant stones. "Sinful women! Do not ever come back! You half-wits! You freaks!"

The hollow within the rock was so small that the Sisters' legs overlapped when they lay down. Despite the discomfort, they were too afraid to leave the hiding spot, lest they be discovered.

Anna stared at the cave's ceiling and said nothing. She kept her arms wrapped tightly around her chest. She tried to steady her nerves by practicing Communion, but failed. Her mind would not leave the confines of her head, and her painful thoughts wound around themselves like pot-bound roots.

"Would you like a sip of water?" Ruth asked. Anna did not respond. Ruth watched her friend fall deeper into a rut of torment. She knew that no words would suffice or still the storm inside her. "Anna," she tried. "You could not have prevented what happened. You did everything you could to protect us."

There was no response.

"We need food," Ruth said, two days later. Their supplies had dwindled and the grumbles of their stomachs echoed against the rock.

"I will go," Anna said. She uncoiled and slipped out of the hollow like a snake let slip from a sack.

"We will come with you," Ruth insisted.

"No. Stay here. I will be back."

"But what if—?"

Anna departed before Ruth could follow. "I will be back," she called over her shoulder. Ruth held her breath as Anna disappeared into the dark.

Once she was a good distance away, Anna looked up at the stars, marked her location, and turned toward the shepherd routes she had seen. She braced against the evening's chill and sped her pace. Toward the desert.

CHAPTER 29

The western edge of the Great Desert *outside ancient* Palestine—33 A.D.

The shepherds had a saying that no lie can survive the desert and no trouble can overwhelm it. The sand's insatiable thirst seeks to drink whatever it can from those who enter—sweat, tears, saliva, blood, lies, illusions, and longings. All are drained from the traveler and soak into the ground without trace. One is never quite as clean, the shepherds' wisdom continues, as upon one's return from the desert.

It was this saying that Anna remembered as her feet swept briskly across the sand. She had no idea where she was going. She only knew that she could not stay where she was. Something inside her wanted to move. And something in the desert was calling her. She could only hope that Ruth and Tabitha would understand.

The first day was hard. With each step the ache in Anna's heart spread and her stomach rumbled. She cursed herself for leaving without a food stash. Having failed to find any tracks before sunset, she nestled beneath a ridgeline and built a fire. The flames crackled. In the distance, a lone wolf threw its long, sad plea to the stars.

How easy it would be just to keep on going and never look back. How easy it would be to live on her own again. In total freedom and without care.

As quickly as these thoughts arose, she chastised herself for having them.

What was wrong with her? Had she forgotten everything? Had she forgotten her life in The Narrows? Had she forgotten the example of the Sisters and Mother Susana?

Had she forgotten The Way?

The desert's monotonous heat and Anna's repetitive thoughts began to fuse one day to the next. Her hunger increased along with her thirst. It seemed as though she had been wandering for forty days though, in reality, it had been only a few.

She had searched and searched the sands but failed to uncover tracks of any kind. Once, when she had come upon a set of human footprints, she shouted for joy, only to discover that they were her own and that she had been walking in circles.

That night, too tired to build even a small fire, she rolled onto her back and considered the vast dome above her. Tears welled in her eyes, extending bright legs from each star like lighted sea urchins. She had come to the desert seeking something. Answers? Guidance? Yet all she felt was aimless and alone. The lone wolf sighed again into the sky. The sound broke her heart.

"What am I to do?" she bellowed into the cold night. "Great Mother, why do you not answer me?"

Anna's heart sank with the knowledge that she had disappointed all those she loved.

Had she not failed to protect the Sisters? And Mother Susana? And Zahra? Even her own mother?

She felt utterly unredeemable.

Her mind heaved like a heavy door and opened onto the darkest human thought. She no longer wanted to breathe. She no longer wanted to see. All that loomed before her eyes was death. She wished suddenly that she had never come into life.

My poor daughter! I wish that you had never been born.

Without warning, a galloping herd of sobs shook her body. From the wells of her eyes and throat and ears leaked the poisons inside her—anger, shame, confusion, regret, grief, and fear—all spilled onto the sand and were instantly absorbed. She curled into a ball and was wracked with even greater sobs until, many hours later, a final, feeble moan escaped her lips.

Lying against the cool sand, her face damp and raw, Anna stared into the stars with relief and wonder. A cool breeze floated over her skin. She felt rinsed from within. She noticed that the stars were closer and brighter than ever. Communion came quickly and without effort. She rose toward the heavens. Her limbs separated from her body and dissolved into the limitless space around her. No longer could she discern the distinction between skin and starlight, breath and wind. Everything, she felt, had become a part of the other. The sensation of floating into the world seemed suddenly funny and she laughed aloud.

It was then that she heard the whistle. The sound was faint at first. And high-pitched. Too high-pitched, she thought, to be human.

An animal?

Her being returned solidly to earth. She stood and directed her every sense toward the sound. It came again, carried on the breeze. She walked toward the whistle as it quivered in the air. When it grew louder, seeming to rise almost from beneath her, she scanned frantically for the source, but saw nothing. With a whoosh, the ground gave way beneath her feet and she plummeted down a sharp slope. Her fall ended quickly, leaving her on her back. Stunned, she kept still, mentally searching to determine if she had broken any bones. A breeze rolled up her robe and the whistle again pierced her ears. She turned her head and came face to face with a shepherd. She leapt to her feet and bellowed in fear.

The figure on the ground did not move. Nor would it. Peering through the starlight she could make out two desiccated eye sockets staring from beneath a plain white keffiyeh. Swallowing her fear, she turned the hollow body over with her foot. The bones lay in the shape of a young man. He was dressed in an indigo tunic, the color of midnight. At his waist hung the tools of his trade: a slingshot, a goatskin pouch, and a tall, crooked staff. Like Anna, the young man had fallen down the slope. But in his tumble, it seemed, he had landed on his knife. Its bloodless blade was still planted firmly between his ribs. The wind rose again and a whistle emanated from between cracks in the blade's handle.

Like a bolt of lightning, Anna heard the call. She knelt and stretched a trembling hand toward the body. She slipped the knife from between its bones. With a heart pounding in both sorrow and joy, she closed her eyes. For the first time in her thirty-three years, the torrents that had carved her life ran with a single purpose. Mother Susana's last words echoed in her ears.

So that you will remember who you are, no matter who you must become.

Finally, Anna understood.

Keeping her eyes closed, she twisted a fistful of hair between her fingers and pulled back her head. As she lifted the blade toward her throat, a steady calm overtook her.

Crouched within the hollow, Ruth had begun to lose hope. She knew the depth of the struggle in Anna's soul, but had believed that her young friend had the strength to resolve it.

Perhaps, in their weakened state, she and Mother Susana had misjudged Anna's destiny? Perhaps the shepherd had not imbibed as much of The Way as they had believed? And had no intention of returning?

Ruth shook her head against such thoughts but could not escape them entirely. She looked down at two dried dates, untouched, on the ground behind Tabitha. She had stopped eating. Ruth could feel the despair gaining a greater and greater foothold within her companion's heart. Against her better judgment, she lit a small fire, hoping to reignite Tabitha's will.

We must leave here. We must try to survive, said a voice inside her head as the flames licked the air. She felt a pulsing in her knees. Something was asking her to rise. To find a way. Later that night, she said, "Gather yourself, Tabitha, we are leaving."

Tabitha stayed crouched as if she had not heard her.

Ruth tugged at her sleeve. "We are keepers of The Way," she said. "We cannot give up hope."

At the mention of The Way, a glimmer swam through Tabitha's eyes.

"Let us go," Ruth said.

They turned toward the ragged entranceway only to find it blocked by a man peering inside. Tabitha gasped and fell back. Ruth held her ground, though her legs shook like boiling water.

"Do not be afraid," the man said. He pushed into the hollow. Ruth glanced at the fire.

It was the light that had given them away!

She berated herself for setting the blaze.

The man knelt, sturdy and broad-shouldered beneath his tunic. His face remained hidden within his keffiyeh.

Like a cat, Ruth pounced and lifted a burning branch. She swung it at the man's face with all her strength. Having anticipated her move, he caught her wrist in the clamp of his hand and held the branch inches from his face. It was then that Ruth saw his eyes. They shimmered like heated emeralds before the flame. Her hand released its hold. The man held her eyes as he removed his keffiyeh.

Tears of recognition streamed down Ruth's cheeks.

"Do not cry," the man said. His voice was strong and kind. He took her hands in his and held them steady. He then took a deep breath as if anticipating a long and arduous journey. "Sometimes," he said, "if they are to survive, the sheep must dress as wolves."

PART FOUR

HEALER

CHAPTER 30

Somewhere within ancient Palestine—33 A.D.

When they arrived at the village, Jesus approached a farmer's wife and asked if she could provide him and his sisters with shelter for the night. The woman eyed the handsome brother with suspicion. He and the women were desperately thin, their bones protruding from their faces. Jesus told her that they were making a long journey back to the place of their birth and needed rest. Too tired to listen further, the wife agreed to let them stay in the storage shed. The year's harvest had been scarce, she explained, so there would be room for them inside. She decided, however, not to tell her husband about the visitors.

The shed's interior echoed with the timbre of stone. By the light of a single oil lamp, Jesus and his sisters divided the small meal provided by the wife—a crust of bread and some olives. They gave thanks to the Mother and the work of human hands. Then they ate. Despite the danger that hovered nearby, a smile passed among them—they were glad to be alive.

Through the flicker of lamplight, Ruth marveled at Anna's transformation. Having cut her long black hair and donned a shepherd's tunic, she looked as handsome and confident as any man. The shorter length of her hair accentuated the square ridgeline of her jaw. Her green stare blazed out from her dark skin, heightening the air of self-assurance and intensifying her masculine charade.

But beyond the obvious physical alteration, Ruth sensed another more profound change.

Was there not a new vibration emanating from Anna? Were not her thoughts and intentions fully aligned and unshakable?

Ruth found the entire effect captivating. And though she harbored reservations about the disguise, there was no doubt that Anna could, once again, thrive as a man called Jesus. And for now, she hoped, he would keep them safe.

After the meal, the sisters' eyes grew heavy and Tabitha fell quickly asleep. But Jesus could not rest. His heart raced with the rush of his new identity.

The farmer's wife had not even given him a second glance!

He felt a strong desire to roam in his disguise. To know, again, the freedom and the world's sanction. When Ruth fell asleep, he slipped outside.

The night drifted down to meet him, bathing his indigo tunic in starlight. In the distance, an owl questioned the dark. The crisp air woke Jesus further and he decided to walk the village's perimeter. After a time, he came to a dwelling set at a distance from the others. Its roof sagged with age, threatening to collapse on its occupants at any moment. A soft light ruffled the window frame. Voices whispered inside. Unable to deny his curiosity, Jesus snuck up to the dwelling. He peered inside and saw a woman bent over a small boy. She was laying strips of damp linen on his forehead. Her husband stoked a meager fire nearby. The mother placed a hand on the boy's cheek. She looked back and whispered, "Abel, his fever is rising. What shall we do?" The father's face fell for lack of answers.

Jesus observed the boy closely. His color was sallow and gray, his forehead fevered, his arms clutched tightly at his stomach. Jesus recognized the symptoms. He had once seen a Sister suffer in the same way when she accidentally consumed spoiled milk.

Perhaps, in his hunger, the boy had eaten something rotten?

Taking care to remain hidden, Jesus's hand drifted down to the pouches in his tunic. Among the many cures he had gathered before their flight from the caves were the seeds used for stomach ailments. His fingers danced over the small pods. He knew that he could help the boy.

But should he risk exposing himself? What if the parents discovered his secret and sounded the alarm? What if the villagers sought out Ruth and Tabitha and attacked them while they slept?

He looked again into the woman's eyes and saw the look of desperation he had once seen in the eyes of his own mother. He felt his heart ripping in two.

How could he put his friends at risk? Yet how could he turn away?

Without another thought, he wrapped his tunic about him and walked to the dwelling's entrance. He lifted the camel hide and said, "Blessings on your house."

The father stood and lifted a pot over his head. The mother spread herself across her son.

"Who are you and what business have you here?" Abel asked, shaken by the intrusion.

Jesus swallowed his fear. "My name is Jesus," he began. "I am a poor shepherd traveling with my sisters to the village of our birth. I saw that your son was ill and thought I could help."

The father raised the pot higher. "Help how?" he asked with suspicion.

"I am familiar with his illness and carry a remedy for it."

The husband turned to his wife. She gazed down at her son. The boy shook with pain. Jesus knew if the child did not get help soon, whatever he had eaten would begin to poison him. The mother turned her eyes up to Jesus, imploring.

The father swiped his arm across a tear. "This is my only son," he said. "He is all we have left in this world. I beg of you. In the name of God, please help us."

Jesus nodded. "Let me fetch my sisters."

Ruth's anger at Jesus for having put them at risk vanished when she saw the boy curled on the floor. She knelt and smelled his breath. Jesus's suspicion was correct. "Do you have the seeds?" she whispered.

Jesus reached into his pouch and brought out a single green pod. Ruth nodded and watched as he placed the pod in the boy's mouth. She then gathered a bowl and a cloth.

Within moments, the boy began to convulse and groan with pain.

"What is it?" the father shouted. "What have you done to him?"

The mother reached for her son and sobbed.

Jesus held the woman back. "Wait," he told her. "He must expel the poison."

The mother shook her head from side to side. "No! My child! What have you done to my child?" she screamed.

The father rushed upon them when suddenly the walls reverberated with the boy's forceful retching. Tabitha dutifully held the bowl before him until he had nearly filled it. When he was done, he fell back onto his mat, exhausted. Ruth wiped his mouth clean and Tabitha disappeared outside to empty the bowl. The smell of rotting meat hung in the air.

The mother and father gathered close to the boy. "Nathaniel?" his mother whispered. "Nathaniel, my son, what do you feel?"

The boy opened his eyes and looked up at his mother.

Jesus turned to Ruth. She nodded toward the door, indicating that they should depart.

"We will leave your family in peace," Jesus said.

Overjoyed at their son's recovery, the mother and father paid little attention to the departing visitors.

Jesus accompanied his sisters to the shed, his steps lifting with confidence.

As they lay down to sleep, Ruth glanced over and saw the light in her companion's eyes. She knew something of the exhilaration he was experiencing—she too had felt a rush the first time she was able to effect a cure. But Jesus's elation was no doubt far more potent given that he had taken action in the outside world—in full view—an experience that circumstances had never allowed her.

Despite the success, however, she thought it unwise—and dangerous—for them to draw such attention to themselves. Given their vulnerability, maintaining anonymity seemed the only way to ensure their safety. Thinking these things, she said, "I am glad we were able to help the boy. But I think we should avoid exposing ourselves until we better understand our circumstances."

Jesus frowned. "Do you think they saw through my disguise?"

Ruth sighed. "No, I do not," she admitted. She gazed down his lean, masculine frame. "But still, it would be foolish of us to risk—"

"Ruth," Jesus interrupted. "If they believe I am a man, we will be safe," he said, his confidence fortified by the evening's events.

Frustrated by his assuredness, Ruth held her tongue and kept the rest of her thoughts to herself. It was then that she noticed a trickle of fresh blood running down his leg. She quickly pulled a rag from within her robes and held it out to him. "You must wrap yourself more carefully from now on," she cautioned.

Jesus looked down and saw the blood of his renewal. His poise and confidence wavered as a grave worry struck his heart.

Had anyone seen?

The rooster had not yet crowed when the yelling began. Ruth and Jesus woke with a start. The voices were coming from the farmer's dwelling. "Where are they? Do not let them leave the village!" they cried out.

Ruth shook Tabitha from her slumber. "We must leave," she said. "They have discovered Anna's charade. Come quickly!"

Jesus pushed through the door while his sisters covered their faces. They were met instantly by a large crowd of villagers. The farmer who owned the shed stepped to the front. His wife cowered behind him. "Are these the people?" he asked in a gruff voice.

Nathaniel's father, Abel, nodded and said, "Yes, these are the ones who came into my house last night."

The farmer cast a sharp eye on the strangers. The other villagers pressed behind him.

Tabitha grabbed Ruth's robe, terrified.

Even in her fear, Ruth noticed the lack of flesh on the man's bones and the patches clinging to his clothes. He had clearly been chosen as the one to approach them, though for what purpose she could not yet tell. She feared the worst.

Jesus took a step forward. "We come in peace," he said, having difficulty steadying his voice. "We mean you no harm."

Whispers flew among the onlookers. Then a motion began in the center of the crowd. People began to shift until a body emerged from their midst. It was an old man. His arms and neck were covered with sores. The villagers backed away, afraid of his affliction.

The farmer took a hesitant step toward them. "My name is Esok," he began. "Please. He is my father."

Jesus looked to Ruth and then to the farmer. "I do not understand," he said.

Esok dropped to his knees before him. "Please," he begged. "Sweet angel of God, please, I beg of you. Make my father well." So saying, the farmer and the crowd shuffled back to a safer distance.

Ruth felt Tabitha's grip loosen. She looked down at the old man, standing alone before them. She could tell by his wandering eyes that he had poor vision.

Jesus held still, uncertain what to do.

"Can you see from here what ails him?" Ruth whispered.

Jesus narrowed his eyes. "Is he a leper?"

"*They* seem to think so," Ruth said, nodding toward the crowd. "But what do you notice about his lesions?"

Jesus observed the old man carefully. He saw him scratch furiously at the wounds around his neck, scraping them raw. "His wounds seem to gather at the edges of his tunic," he said.

Ruth nodded. "His skin reacts badly to wool. Tell them that he is not dying. And that he will not make them sick. But we need to get him inside a dwelling."

Trembling, Jesus stepped forward. "Esok, your father will not die. And he will not make anyone ill. We need you to take him to your house where we can apply a remedy."

Esok nodded to two men and they came forward to carry his father.

Inside the mud dwelling, Jesus requested that the old man exchange his wool tunic for a linen one. The eyes of onlookers, bunched like seeds in every window and crack, widened with befuddlement at the strange request. Undeterred, he and Ruth set about mixing a balm that would ease the man's itch. Tabitha helped to wrap the most infected sores and laid the man on his mat to rest.

"He will be better in a few days," Jesus told Esok. "But he must never wear the skin or wool of any lamb."

"Thank you, thank you," Esok repeated. "Our great Lord has shown His mercy."

Jesus looked to Ruth. She sensed his desire to correct the man's misperception and tell him that it was gifts from the *Mother* that were responsible for his father's healing. But Ruth lifted a hand as if to say, *Not now. Not yet.* Seeing her signal, and knowing that his actions had already caused her distress, Jesus held his tongue. But not without effort.

"This matter had delayed our journey," he told the villagers. "And our family is expecting us. We must offer you final blessings and depart."

Without warning, Esok leapt in front of the door to block them from leaving. Jesus's heart skipped a beat. He remembered what had happened to Zahra after she healed Daniel.

"Please," Esok began. "Let us show our gratitude by sharing a meal with you. We know many hidden paths that will shorten your journey."

That night a guinea hen was killed and fresh bread baked for the evening meal. As they sat to eat, Esok told them, "We have little to offer, but what we have is yours."

The following day, the people gathered to wish their guests farewell. As promised, one of the villagers, a wiry man with gray hair, stepped forward to guide the travelers. He asked Jesus to where they were headed. Jesus thought for a moment and then, without consulting the others, answered, "Nazareth."

Ruth looked up in surprise. When Tabitha and the guide walked ahead, she drew Jesus to her. Knowing that the village he had chosen lay several weeks away, she asked, "Why Nazareth?"

Keeping his pace brisk, Jesus looked into the distance and said, simply, "Because my mother lies there."

Hearing this, Ruth observed her friend closely. Seeing his eyes mist with longing, she asked no more.

As their group traveled westward, Ruth dropped behind to consider the future.

Ever since being forced from the caves, she had been contemplating what they should do. She knew that the other Awakeners had most likely been killed, which meant that she, Jesus, and Tabitha were, perhaps, the only Sisters who remained. The most critical thing, therefore, was to find a means of preserving their knowledge and understanding of The Way. While crossing the desert, Ruth had considered several possibilities: They could return to the caves and attempt to rebuild them. They could find a new refuge. Or they could try to restart the Sisterhood in a distant land.

But she doubted if these things were possible. And she wondered, too, if the destruction of the caves had not signaled that the time for seclusion was over.

Then, just as she had been considering these things, Anna had once again become Jesus, and further possibilities had arisen.

As the men walked ahead, Ruth noticed how easily Jesus initiated conversation. It was obvious he had become fluent in the language of men during his years as a shepherd. And she could not help but marvel that a Sister could—at last—roam freely in the world.

Could not his disguise, and the freedom it afforded, play a role in the protection of The Way?

Was he not, hiding safely in the skin of his disguise, potentially the most powerful of all Awakeners?

She watched Jesus stroke the soft down along the sides of his face. His self-assurance restored.

In her heart, Ruth understood why Jesus felt lured by his homeland and the memory of his mother. She remembered that he had lived most of his life in the skin of another. No doubt the fractures caused by his disguise had enflamed his desire to be near the one who had known him first, and most truly.

Breathing deeply, and walking with even steps, Ruth dissolved into the sun's waves and sought guidance. Her skin softened as the premonitions came, quick and strong. Since Susana's death, she had noticed a strengthening of her own intuitive powers. Her step faltered under the surge. Jesus strode back to help her.

"I am all right," she assured him. "It is only the heat of the sun."

Jesus nodded and shared his water with her before retaking the lead.

Recovering her balance, Ruth considered her visions in silence. Because of what she had seen, she decided that it was right for Jesus to lead them into the world, and so she supported their journey to Nazareth, assured that the destination would not deter their efforts to preserve The Way (though the details of how they would accomplish this remained as yet unclear).

But as they traveled on, Ruth remained deeply troubled by another aspect of her vision—a suggestion that Jesus would never return to the place of his birth.

CHAPTER 31

Somewhere within ancient Palestine—33 A.D.

The main road by which traffic moved was a broad path trodden into the soil by the crossings of feet and hooves. Finding the road consistently occupied by merchants, bandits, fanatics, shepherds, and madmen, Jesus and his sisters sought to avoid confrontation by traveling at night. Doing so, they believed they could remain invisible and safe from suspicion.

But word of Jesus's powerful abilities had already begun to spread.

"I am hungry," Tabitha confessed as the sky began to lighten, shedding the first layer of night.

Ruth turned to Jesus. "We have little food left and should refresh our supplies."

Jesus scanned the distance. "I believe there is a village just ahead," he told them. "Let us make our way there."

A young woman with a badly soiled tunic stepped into the early dusk to check on a newborn calf. On the way, she spotted the silhouettes of three travelers on the horizon. She alerted the other villagers. "He is here!" she cried. "The healer has arrived!" As she ran from door to door, dots of lamplight poked holes into the dark like fireflies.

Tabitha was the first to notice the explosion of small flames. "L-look!" she cried.

Ruth and Jesus were shocked to see the sleeping town come alive.

"Will they h-hurt us?" Tabitha asked.

Ruth looked at Jesus. "It is too late to hide. And if we run, they will follow. Do you agree?" she asked.

Jesus nodded.

The crowd fell upon them. They braced for an attack, but none came. Only the clamor of desperate requests and invisible hands grabbing at their robes and feet. *Please help . . . My father is ill . . . My brother . . . The special herbs . . . My hand . . . She is blind . . . Evil spirits inside her! . . . Have you come to save us? Please, please . . .* The air hung heavy with the smell of filth and hunger and infection. Tabitha swooned under the onslaught. Ruth reached out to support her, fearing that the crowd would crush her.

An elderly woman entered the circle and batted the people away with a staff. "Get back! Get behind me!" she shouted until the villagers retreated. When she had cleared a space, the old woman stood before Jesus and his sisters. She knelt and bowed at their feet. "Forgive them," she said. "We are but poor people and our needs are great. We had heard rumors of your gifts—"

The crowd again pressed forward. The old woman turned to face them. "Have you lost your heads? Can you not see that our guests are weary from their travels? Let us first offer a meal before making requests of them."

She turned back to Jesus and his sisters. "Follow me," she said.

The old woman's son met them at the door to his house.

"Who are these?" he asked of his mother, casting a sharp eye on Jesus and the women.

"They are my guests," she told him.

The young man lowered his voice. "Mother, the women are pagans. I will not permit them inside my house."

The old woman looked him directly in the eye. "Son, I am old and my time nearly come. Surely you will not deny me the pleasure of a few visitors?"

"But, Mother—"

She threw him a powerful stare. He relented, stepping aside with disgust.

The old woman led her guests through the door. Together they sat inside her son's house while his wife and daughters stoked a fire and set thin loaves of barley bread to bake above the flames. Unwilling to join them, the young man loafed in a far corner, his brow drawn tight.

Outside the dwelling, Jesus heard whispers. He noticed, as before, eyes peering through every window and crack. The expressions were starved and desperate. The sheer number of onlookers and their intensity made him uncomfortable. In an attempt to remain calm, he told the old woman, "We must thank you for your hospitality."

The old woman smiled and leaned forward. In a whisper she said, "It is the least I can do for those who keep our wisdom."

Ruth and Jesus shared a furtive look.

What did the old woman mean? Was she referring to The Way?

Keeping his voice low, Jesus asked, "How is it that you seem to know us when we have never been here before?"

The woman chuckled and pointed to Tabitha. "It is the color of your robes," she said.

Ruth and Jesus flinched at their oversight.

How could they not have realized that others might recognize their dress?

Sensing her guests' sudden unease, the old woman held out a hand and said, "Perhaps I can provide your sisters with some fresh robes?"

Relieved, Jesus said, "We would be most grateful."

The wife and daughters approached to set fresh bread and a pitcher of milk before them. Jesus watched as they moved throughout the dwelling like spirits, attracting as little attention as possible and occasionally disappearing behind a wall of blankets to tend to a crying infant. Thick shawls covered their faces.

No one else seemed bothered by the women's show of obeisance. But it bothered Jesus. In his time with the Sisters, he had grown accustomed to living in a community of equals. His experience with them had revealed to him the true glory and wonderment of women. And though he knew it was a predicament upheld by tradition, the sight of women in subservient roles, covered and in silence, taken for granted and not honored, infuriated him. Perhaps what made him most angry was the knowledge that but for his odd looks, he too would be forced to live under the same restrictions.

While they ate, Ruth turned a strong eye toward Jesus. It was clear she had read the rebellious thoughts roiling in his mind. And her look was a warning not to express them.

Growing restless in his corner, the young man spat at the ground. It was clear he did not welcome the visitors and was accustomed to ruling his house.

Jesus leaned forward, irritated by the man's arrogance. "Your son does not seem to welcome us," he said under his breath.

The old woman rolled her eyes. "The young ones have become confused," she whispered. "Most know only the new ways—and prostrate themselves before a vengeful, intolerant god. It is the visiting *priests* who poison their minds. By threatening people with eternal damnation, they turn them against their own reason," she said. She scowled with sudden anger and lifted her voice. "But what has this new god brought us other than suffering, eh? Men who kill without remorse and women hiding in the shadows!"

The old woman's daughter-in-law gasped at her heretical words.

"Mother!" the young man roared.

She waved him off. "I am old. I am free to speak my mind!" she said.

Furious, the young man stormed from the house.

The next morning, Jesus and his sisters were awakened by an infant's cries and the anxious patter of footsteps outside the house.

Ruth sat up and leaned over her companions. "We must leave before the people wake," she said.

Both Jesus and Tabitha nodded and bent to tie their sandals.

When they stepped outside, dozens of villagers who had gathered in the early hours pressed in around Jesus. Some approached on their knees, others clasped their hands in pleading. The old woman was nowhere to be found.

Jesus was overwhelmed with compassion for the people afflicted with every imaginable ailment—boils, cysts, dog bites, blindness, diarrhea, arthritis, goiter, bloody urine, broken limbs, headaches, nausea, toothaches, and tremors. More than anything, he wished to begin helping them. But he was also mindful of Ruth's apprehension.

"Should I clear a path for us?" he asked her, thinking she would wish to depart immediately.

Startled, Ruth gazed across the desperate crowd. She, too, was deeply affected by their suffering. Though she continued to wish that she and her companions could avoid exposing themselves, she realized that was not to be. Something about their journey—and Jesus himself—was compelling them into the world.

But if they did *step forward, what would become of them?*

"Ruth?" Jesus asked, holding back the crowd.

Lost in thought, she glanced over and saw her companion—a handsome man with vibrant eyes, an island of stillness in a sea of need. In that moment she decided to release her hold and let the current take them. Rolling up the sleeves of her new robe, she said, "There is much work to be done. And not a minute to waste."

She looked up just in time to see Jesus breaking into a smile.

Ruth and Tabitha worked tirelessly to provide Jesus with dozens of pastes, tinctures, and powders prepared from their supply of herbs.

As they labored, Ruth noticed how skillfully Jesus observed afflictions and offered remedies to those who suffered. Having absorbed much in his years among the Sisters, he appeared eager to apply what he had learned and only occasionally needed to turn to Ruth for guidance. She also noticed how easily people opened up to him. Perhaps it was the dazzling pools of his eyes that put them at ease. Perhaps it was his innocence. Perhaps it was the simple fact that he was male. No matter the reason, she could not deny the soothing impact he had on those around him.

The phenomenon eased her worry over the risks they were taking, and the gnawing of her visions.

By the time the sun stood overhead, the three companions were exhausted. Their hands and robes sticky with salve, pus, and plant saps. They badly needed rest. But Ruth knew it would be unwise for them to stay in one place. And Nazareth was still far off. She expressed her concerns to Jesus and Tabitha and they agreed to depart.

While they were gathering up their belongings, a young mother approached them. In her arms, she carried her two-year-old son. Less bold than the other villagers, she did not press close, but stood nearby in the hope that they would notice. It was Jesus who spotted her. "Ruth," he whispered. "There is another."

The young mother set her son on the ground. He stood unsteadily on bare feet, a brown patch covering one eye. Black flies clustered along the damp rim of his good eye.

Out of nowhere, the old woman's son raced forward. "Do not bother with her," he scoffed. "She is but a whore. A blight on our village."

Having witnessed the young man's disdain the night before, Jesus ignored him. "Is there something you need, sister?" he asked.

The mother cast her eyes downward. "Please," she said. "I am deeply humbled before you. As he says, I am not worthy of your attention. Yet I do not ask for me—but for my son."

The young man grimaced and kicked dust at the child. "The calf is no better than the cow!" he growled.

Hearing the man's harsh words, Ruth spun to look at Jesus. She saw the burning in his eyes and felt his intention. She wanted to keep him from speaking out, but knew that her power to contain him was dwindling.

While the other villagers looked on, Jesus approached the woman. His steps laced with purpose. He knelt alongside the boy. "You are more than worthy," he told the woman. Lowering his voice so that only she could hear, he added, "We are equals in the eyes of our Mother. The Mother of All. Remember this."

The woman noticeably rose under the influence of his words. Her face turned upward like a plant seeking sun. "Thank you," she whispered.

Jesus marveled at the effect his words had on the woman and felt a charge run along his skin.

Why did Ruth insist on silencing him when speaking of the Mother could affect people in such a powerful way?

Inspired, he turned to the woman's child. "What is it that ails him?" he asked.

"His eye. Under the patch."

Jesus lifted the brown flap and gasped. The boy's empty and infected socket gaped at him. He suppressed his urge to recoil. "Who did this?" he asked, his anger sharpening.

The woman grew uncomfortable. She crumpled to the ground whispering apologies. Behind them, the old woman's son cleared his throat. Jesus whirled to face him, but the young man averted his gaze.

It had been he *who had gouged out the boy's eye! To punish the mother!*

Jesus visibly tensed. His fists clenching. Anger heating the spaces behind his eyes.

How could anyone damage the innocent beauty of a child? How could anyone strike against the holiness of another?

Graphic scenes of the devastation inside the caves flashed before him. He could make sense of none of it. He felt a strong urge to knock the young man down, to make him feel in equal amounts the pain he had inflicted. He moved to rise, to take revenge, but a hand pressed firmly on his shoulder. It was Ruth.

"We must do what we can to get the infection under control," she urged.

Jesus seethed beside her.

Ruth held him fast. "Turn the other cheek and put your feelings to better use," she counseled, echoing an important tenet of The Way.

Jesus struggled, tasting the metallic bitters of rage along his teeth. After a moment, his gaze returned to the boy. And to the desperation on the mother's face. Then, without further thought, he bent and lifted a palm full of dirt. He spat into the soil three times and blended the two ingredients until they formed a thick paste, having once seen Simon treat his own wound in this way.

Ruth stood nearby, marveling at his actions.

Jesus held the boy gently. Reaching up, he spread the cool paste inside his empty socket. "The clay will draw the infection," he told the mother. "When the redness is gone, apply a coating of olive and sumac oils until the skin heals."

The woman dropped her gaze to the ground. "But they say you can work miracles. Is it because I am not worthy that you do not restore his sight?"

Unable to believe her words, Jesus sat back on his heels. "Is that what you truly believe?" he asked, his brow furrowing.

The woman said nothing.

Jesus held still. Unsure what to say. He recognized that she, like him, had been raised according to the new ways—according to a belief that did not teach her to perceive her full beauty, nor honor her power.

His mind drifted back. To how his father had ignored him. And intimidated his mother.

Did he not, at that time, believe as this woman before him?

But what could he say that would show her otherwise?

Before he had any intention of speaking, Jesus leaned in and whispered, "Sister, you have already had many miracles in your life. The first was your birth into this world. The second was the birth of your son. The third is that your son will keep his life. Can you not see that you have already been found worthy?"

Saying this, he fell silent, startled by his own words.

The woman's face met his. She felt lifted by his clear gaze. And his conviction. She had never thought about her life as being filled with miracles. And in that moment, a great weight left her. "Yes, I can see that now," she whispered. She took her son into her arms and held him tightly. "Thank you, thank you, thank you," she repeated and smiled broadly into the day.

The young man's wife, who had watched the interaction from the window of her house, said to her daughters, "In all my life, I have never seen that woman smile." She shook her head in disbelief. Dropping her voice she said, "Truly, that man is an instrument of God."

Shortly after the three departed from the village, Jesus found himself stewing over what had happened, and confronted Ruth.

"You knew as well as I that the old woman's son injured the boy. And probably strikes his wife and daughters, too! Why did you stop me from challenging him?"

Ruth shook her head. She had sensed his anger. And knew to expect his outburst. But she was hungry and drained from the day's work and had little patience to spare. "I made a choice," she uttered flatly.

"What choice? To remain silent? To allow him to continue hurting people? How is that a choice?"

Ruth's lips tightened. She knew his sudden zealousness arose, in part, from experiencing how potent an impact The Way could have on people's lives. But there was also his unrelenting need to protect. Especially those who had been held down. And she feared that his growing fervor might come to endanger their lives—the very concern that Mother Susana had once expressed.

Frightened by this last thought, she blurted, "Have you already forgotten what happened in The Narrows?"

Jesus and Tabitha shrunk at the mention of their former home.

Ruth flinched, wishing she had held her tongue. "Forgive me," she said. She sighed and allowed her thoughts to settle. She turned again to Jesus. "You are eager to share. To right what is wrong. I understand that. But not every fight can be fought today," she said. "And not every heart opened in an instant. There were people who needed help. We gave them help. If you had confronted the young man directly, we would have been asked to leave. Or *worse*. So yes, I made a choice. I chose healing the sick over trying to break the hard and possibly paying with our lives."

They walked in silence for several minutes before Ruth spoke again.

"I share your frustration," she said. "But we are the only ones left, Anna, and—" Her breath caught. Her companions stared in horror. They well knew that such a slip in the wrong company would lead to death. Ruth recovered. "We are the only ones," she continued, her voice weighted with solemnity. "If we are killed, The Way may very well die with us. If this were to happen, the world would lose this knowledge, perhaps forever. And without this understanding, humanity would abolish itself. There could be no other outcome. Without imbibing The Way, the human spirit will rot beneath a plague of domination and war and greed. Do you see?"

Jesus nodded stubbornly. He understood her concerns. But could feel a wall rising around him, casting a long shadow, heavy as a shawl, across his face.

For how long could he remain silent?

"We may never be able to reveal all that we know," Ruth said. "Just as you may never be able to reveal all of who you are."

Her words fell along his shoulders, heavy as bricks.

Had he made a mistake in readopting his disguise? Would it not accomplish all he desired? Would he crumble under its constant burden?

Jesus knew he owed Ruth his deference. And knew her wisdom to be great. He wanted to rise above his anger. Wanted to live according to The Way. Yet he chafed against her words. As they walked on, the medallion hung about his neck like a stone. Weighted with frustration, he fell behind, scuffing his sandals in the dust.

CHAPTER 32

Somewhere within ancient Palestine—33 A.D.

Intent on their journey, Jesus and his sisters followed the winding footpath as it turned northward. They knew they were nearing the great Salt Sea when the scent of brine infused the air.

"C-can we go to the s-sea?" Tabitha begged, longing to see its famed expanse.

Jesus laid a hand on her shoulder. "Remember to breathe," he counseled. He knew that the stresses of their journey had made it impossible for her to pay attention to her breathing. But now that they were out of harm's way, he wanted her to remember.

Tabitha's forehead crinkled as she drew in a long, slow breath. "I have heard that one can float without swimming!" she said, her voice smooth as glass.

Jesus smiled and patted her back. "Well done!" he cheered.

But Ruth did not share their merriment. She nodded ahead. "I am told that up ahead the sea narrows into a river. When it does, we must cross to its east bank as soon as possible before continuing."

Ruth avoided her companions' bewildered stares and gazed toward the horizon. Though they had traveled in relative safety through the outlying communities (where some remained sympathetic to The Way), she felt increasing tension as they neared Jerusalem and the lands ruled by Temple authorities. These religious leaders derived their power from the people's blind deference and would therefore not look kindly on their example of spiritual independence. Nor Jesus's new insistence on speaking of the Mother. Her concern was heightened by the fact that their progress toward Nazareth had been slowed by the daily arrival of messengers imploring them to visit impoverished villages. Unable to refuse such requests, the companions had traveled to communities outside the river valley, bringing healing to the sick and hope to the despairing.

And word of their compassion spread.

Jesus woke in the small village of Zoar and went to sit under a cypress tree for morning Communion. Despite Ruth's warnings, it had become his habit to perform the daily practice with others. Having felt the transformative power of the practice in his own life, he could not resist sharing it. Soon a group of men, women, and children, compelled by the clarity of his eyes and the ease of his ways, broke away from the other villagers, who remained suspicious, and joined Jesus in the early light.

At first, those who had gathered found the ritual strange and unsettling. But, in the simple moment of connecting with their world, fully, directly, devotedly, they began to draw a new sense of strength and peace. Miracles, they realized, were not solely dispensed and controlled from the heavens, as the priests had claimed, but infused their entire world.

When they were finished, Jesus observed those before him anew. He noticed their jutting hip bones and sunken cheeks. Famished, they were pale and lacking in vigor. Even the effort of Communion seemed to have taxed them.

Lifting his voice, he said, "Is it not time for the morning meal?"

The people's eyes went wide, then their heads fell. A man sitting next to Jesus leaned over and whispered, "We are ashamed not to have enough sustenance with which to honor you," he said.

Jesus frowned. "The meal is not meant for me, but for all of us," he assured the man.

Then a memory came to him, and with it, an idea.

"Everyone. Go to your homes. Gather whatever food you have and bring it here," he urged.

The villagers exchanged baffled looks. One woman said, "But I have only a narrow strip of dried meat and some tallow."

Jesus held her eye. "Then bring that."

While the people disappeared inside their homes, Jesus asked for a fire to be built and a large pot filled with water.

Soon people returned and tossed their contributions into the circle—withered olives, a handful of beans, a block of pig fat, dried fruit, stale flatbread.

The people then retook their seats and, gazing upon the small heap of food, felt their mouths begin to water.

While they waited for the pot to boil, Jesus shared stories of his days as a shepherd. He told the villagers of wily cobras, endless caverns, and cities that rose into the sky like vines. As he spoke, a group of children gathered at his feet, their eyes lit by his tales. Jesus smiled at their enthusiasm and gave each a chuck under the chin.

Ruth noticed his tenderness and the smile that animated his face. Clearly he felt at home in his disguise. And no doubt was relishing the human contact that had been missing to him while living in the caves.

Jesus then told the crowd of the tragic night when the ewe that had birthed Anna had passed away. And how sorrowful he had been, but how equally amazed he was at the power of her body to provide life—going so far as to feed not only her own offspring, but eight shepherds as well!

As he spoke, Jesus diced the scraps of food and tossed them in the boiling pot. He then placed all the bread in a basket, which he instructed the children to pass around the circle.

Those villagers who remained skeptical of Jesus stood off at a distance, scowling at his words and speaking under their breath.

When Jesus was finished with his tales, those in the circle held up their bowls while Tabitha and the children ladled rich soup from the pot. When everyone's bowl had been filled, Jesus reminded them to give thanks—as he had learned to do from the Sisters.

As they ate, the people's eyes opened in amazement at the substance and quantity of the soup. Jesus told them, "It is just as it was that night!" he said. "Alone, we have little, but together, we are like the mother sheep—who can feed many!"

When they had finished their meal, some of the people asked Jesus if he would lead them again in Communion. Before answering, he turned to Ruth. In her look he read that she was anxious for them to move on. Knowing he had delayed their journey, and not wishing to upset her, he turned to the crowd to offer his apologies.

"And what do we have *here*?" a man's voice demanded before Jesus could speak.

Those who had gathered turned to see a priest from the Temple standing above them. His robes were finely woven and richly dyed. Though middle-aged, his straw-colored hair gleamed. Jesus looked down and observed the man's sandals. They were made of the finest leather and well crafted. His feet, and even his toenails, showed no sign of travel. Behind the priest stood two footmen. One knelt to hobble his camel, the other bent under the burden of sacks filled with coins. The villagers cast their eyes downward, unable to meet his gaze. For though they could not say exactly how, they knew that the priest would consider their gathering unholy.

"What brings us together so early in the day?" the priest inquired, eyeing the cypress tree with suspicion. Tabitha's eyes darted to find Ruth's.

Frustrated by the silence, the priest drove his neatly sandaled foot into the back of a villager. "You there," he asked a young man, "for what have you gathered?"

Jesus saw the villager's body crumple to the ground.

The priest stepped forward and rammed his toes into a woman's side. "Speak!" he demanded. "Why have you gathered in this way?"

The coals of rage began to smolder inside Jesus.

Who was this man and why should he threaten them?

He struggled to hold himself in check, recalling the severity of Ruth's warnings.

Eager to see the confrontation between the priest and the heretical young man, the villagers who had kept their distance rushed closer.

The priest continued his interrogations. He bent and shook one of the girls who had helped pass out the bread. When he did this, Jesus felt something crack inside him. He leapt to his feet and faced the priest head-on. Ruth's face went ashen.

Jesus ignored her signals. "Leave them alone!" he commanded.

The priest's foot froze in the crook of a boy's back. His face flushed a brilliant red, making the gold in his hair glitter. His eyes bore into those of the man in the indigo robe. "And just who are *you*?" he spat with disdain.

"Who do you say that I am?" Jesus retorted, goading him. He had no desire to make the priest's task easy. And he had kept his rage in check for too long.

The onlookers flinched. Ruth gasped.

The priest glared. Sparks issued from his eyes.

Had he not encountered this ruffian before? But where?

"Do not insult me!" he roared. He dashed around the circle and rammed his toes into a maimed villager's side. "Who is this man and what has he told you?" he demanded. "Tell me now!"

The villager listed to the side, trembling.

Seeing that the maimed man would not confess, one of the onlookers who had shunned Jesus's invitation called out to the priest, "He tells them godless nonsense such as to remember the life around them from which they rise and of which they are a part. He urges them to see with their ears and listen with their eyes. And goads them to be grateful and to find the miracles within and around, as if he were responsible for God's creation *himself!*" The man then spat upon the ground and fell silent.

No one dared move.

"Oh he does, does he?" the priest said. He trained his eyes again on Jesus. "Well then, I will tell you who you are," he snarled, staying on the far side of the circle. "You are a charlatan! A blasphemer! A worshipper of false gods! You are a feebleminded man preying on the weakness of others and smiting the face of the one true Lord. And worship of your 'miraculous' world is nothing but worship of a golden calf, a farce created to distract people from the truth!"

Cheers of approval arose from those outside the circle.

"You do not know of what you speak—!" Jesus countered.

But the priest ignored him and continued his tirade. "And as for your poor souls," he said, glowering at those seated on the ground. "Woe unto those who mingle with Satan's minions. Be assured that you are cursed to everlasting fire!"

"But sir," a young woman dared. "How can he be evil when he is able to heal our sick?" The villagers nodded their heads in agreement. A young mother hugged her boy close and looked up with grateful eyes toward Jesus. The rash that had infected her son's arms for years had nearly cleared.

"You ignorant fools!" the priest bellowed. "Who could exercise more influence over pestilence than a follower of Satan, the King of Pestilence? Can you not see? Who but a follower of Satan could say to an illness, 'Leave him!' and have it be so?" The priest practically spat the last words, but he observed the seated villagers out of the corner of his eyes. He could see by the adoring looks they cast toward the handsome green-eyed man that he had swayed them with his false prophecy. For the moment, the priest knew, they would not listen to reason. His mouth watered with the thought of ridding the world of the despicable blasphemer standing before him, but he feared inciting a riot amid desperate people. He would wait for a better time.

Stepping back, the priest made a quick signal to his footman. The man rushed forward. "At your service, Caiaphas," he said and forced the stubborn camel to its knees. The priest mounted the beast and, as its legs unfolded, he shouted down, "May God have mercy on your wretched souls!" And with that he departed.

The dust rose and settled on the path behind the three. As they walked, Jesus said nothing. He was too enraged over the confrontation with the priest to speak. His mind replayed the encounter over and over. As he did, his gut boiled with rage. He remembered Shereen's description of hypocrisy. "A hypocrite is someone who promotes one thing while doing the opposite," she had said. The priest, Jesus realized, had blamed Jesus for harming the people's souls, while he stood before them, burdened with finery and coins, and did nothing to relieve their suffering. It was madness!

Ruth, too, had been angered by the interaction. But her anger bent more toward Jesus and his stubborn refusal to hold his tongue.

How long would it be until his behavior and their teachings drew the Temple's scrutiny? How long until the authorities took action to silence them?

As for the light-haired priest, Ruth had seen enough. She knew all too well of such men's desire for power and control. And their taste for fine things. Like Jesus, she had wanted to speak against his venom—and that of the skeptical villagers. But before exposing themselves to any more risks, she wanted to ensure that the insights of their foremothers were protected and their future transmission assured. And so, despite the fact that her visions had yet to provide concrete solutions for accomplishing these goals, she drove them on toward Nazareth.

The fisherman leaned into his oars and rowed. A herd of goats standing on the river's shoreline diminished in size with each stroke. The fisherman's five-year-old daughter sat at his knees in the hull of the boat, tugging repetitively on a rope.

Ruth huddled with Tabitha in the stern. Jesus knelt in the bow, alone, watching the water slip past.

Tabitha smiled at the fisherman's little girl. "What is your name?" she asked. The girl's eyes widened with surprise.

"Aw, do not bother with Sophia," her father said. "She has been a mute since her mother died." He tousled his daughter's hair. She slipped behind his knee.

Jesus and Tabitha shared a look.

The opposite shore approached quickly. The sisters stepped from the boat and Jesus asked for directions. The fisherman pointed northward. "We will gladly accompany you," he added. He tied his boat to a tree. "Our home lies on the way to Nazareth."

As the men walked ahead, Sophia crept alongside her father, glued to him like a third leg. Intrigued by the girl, Jesus smiled down and pulled a silly face. When this failed to elicit a smile, he threw back his head and let out a corky raven's call. Within minutes, two glossy birds circled above them, calling out to their hidden companion. Sophia's face lit up at the ravens' arrival and she clapped her hands with delight.

"Do you want to learn how to call the birds for yourself?" Jesus asked her.

Sophia ducked again behind her father's leg.

Jesus extended his hand. "Have no fear, Sophia. Come with me and I will show you the way."

After several minutes of careful consideration, and much to the fisherman's surprise, Sophia slipped out, almost despite herself, and took Jesus's hand. In one fluid motion, Jesus lifted her onto his shoulders and hurled another cry skyward. Sophia clapped with glee as the birds echoed the cry. The others laughed in amazement at Sophia's sudden opening.

For the next several hours, Jesus spoke with the child and demonstrated various raven calls, showing her how to round her mouth and puff the air through a relaxed throat. Sophia was able to mimic his every move but never produced a single sound. Jesus seemed unbothered by this omission and praised her all the same.

By the time they reached the fisherman's village, Jesus felt his leg, the one that had been broken in The Narrows, stiffening. "Is it far to Nazareth?" he asked.

The fisherman peered toward the horizon. "It is far," he answered.

Ruth signaled to Jesus. She was eager to keep moving. Jesus thanked the man for his guidance, gave Sophia a chuck under her chin, and turned back to the road. The three had not taken ten steps when a raven cried out behind them. Confused, they turned to see Sophia, tossing her head skyward, her voice clear as glass.

Tabitha jumped up and down. She took a deep, careful breath before saying, "She can talk! She can talk!"

The fisherman dropped to his knees. "Most Holy Lord!" he shouted to the clouds. Sophia rushed into her father's arms. He held her to him and turned his eyes to Jesus. "I do not know who you are, or how you have done this. But with all my heart, I thank you for granting me this miracle." He wept tears of joy.

Jesus shook his head. "Do not misunderstand, friend. Your daughter's voice has been there all along. I simply asked to hear it." He gazed down at the young girl and felt suddenly emboldened by her courage and spirit. He took a deep breath and said, "Know this, friend. Your thanks is due to the Mother, who urges us to listen. Unlike the Lord you speak of."

Ruth gasped aloud.

The fisherman looked confused. He thought to ask more. Then realized he did not care for the reason. All that mattered was that his mute daughter could speak!

At the shore, Jesus and his sisters said their good-byes and departed for Nazareth. As soon as they left, the fisherman circled his village telling all those who would listen about the strange visitor and how he had miraculously restored his daughter's voice.

All who heard his story were amazed.

"I need to rest," Jesus whispered to Ruth as they walked up a gentle hillside sprayed with bluebells and limber grasses. He lowered himself carefully to the ground. The bones in his leg ached. The long days of walking were taking their toll on his old injury.

Ruth knelt alongside him. Without saying a word, she focused on applying a remedy, a balm of spearmint and arnica.

The silence between them hung weighted with unspoken words.

After some time, Jesus said, "I know you are angry with me for speaking of the Mother. And for challenging the priest. And I know you believe it puts us, and even The Way, at risk."

Ruth held her silence. She continued to work the balm gently into his leg.

"For that, I am truly sorry," he said. He stared into the distance and sighed. "But I can no longer keep silent. Not when I have seen, before my own eyes, the healing that can arise when people are freed from the chains of misperception. And given back their power. And their place in the world." He shook his head. "You know I have tried. But I can no longer bear to deny anyone this understanding. Especially when there are those who clearly hunger to possess it."

Ruth nodded. She still said nothing.

Jesus laid a hand on her shoulder. "Know that I will do all I can to keep us safe," he said. "It is the gift I have been given." He lifted her eyes into his. "Please," he said, "trust in me."

Ruth wanted to answer, wanted to temper his dangerous thinking, but something in the rawness with which he spoke made her hold her words. Made her want to spend time with what he had said. She nodded, to let Jesus know she would consider his thoughts.

She then turned her attention back to his leg. The muscles had loosened somewhat, but without rest, she knew, there would be little hope for improvement. And given Jesus's new inclination to speak out, they could not afford to bide long in one place.

CHAPTER 33

Somewhere within ancient Palestine—33 A.D.

The assassin kept himself hidden within a distant outcropping of rock. To pass the time, he wiped soap over his face and shaved his cheeks with the edge of a dagger. Ever since hearing of the healer's altercation with the golden-haired priest, he had begun tracking the man and his companions northward.

Though he had not yet approached his quarry, and did not yet know the details of his appearance, he felt certain he could learn all he needed to know from a distance. His employer, after all, required only a general description of the young healer's progress. To where was he traveling? Were the people made unruly by his words? Was the number of his followers growing?

As was his practice, the assassin would report on these things—though his personal concerns were different. Either way, he relished in the killing. And in that arena, his reputation was excellent.

Finished with his task, the assassin mopped the stubbly residue from his cheeks with his sleeve. Then, in a motion swift as the folding of a bird's wing, he slipped his blade back into its sheath.

CHAPTER 34

Somewhere within ancient Palestine—33 A.D.

The band of shepherds hunkered down just beyond the perimeter of the village. The men's tunics were stained with sweat, their faces burned with wind and sun. Each had a freshly sharpened dagger tucked into his belt.

"Is that his home?" one of the men asked, nodding toward a humble dwelling.

The head shepherd tugged on his ragged ear. "Yes, that is where his family resides," he said.

Peter glanced over at the men. His stomach churned with dread and anticipation. Ever since someone had stolen two sheep from the brother of the ragged-eared shepherd, the leader had been plotting revenge on his sibling's behalf. Having located the thief's village, they intended to retaliate by abducting his sister.

The group swept into the village on silent feet. Unnoticed, they slipped into the thief's home. A young girl saw them and let out a scream. Alerted to the intruders, the occupants cried out and sheltered the children beneath their robes.

Saying nothing, the men herded the women into a corner and began ripping the shawls from their faces.

Eager to prove himself, Peter reached out and uncovered the woman closest to him. She had unusually light hair. "Here she is!" he cried.

His cohorts rushed over, snarling with delight.

"Well done, Peter!" they cheered.

The man with the ragged ear grabbed the young woman roughly by the neck and dragged her from the dwelling.

"No! Setya!" the other women cried, lunging forward. The shepherds lashed out with their blades, holding them back.

Hearing the cries, the village men rushed toward the dwelling and, though unarmed, leapt upon the assailants. The villagers fought bravely but were soon thrown to the ground bruised and bleeding, no match for shepherds wielding rage and blades.

Those who had been injured writhed in the dust as the young woman's cries split the air, then faded in the distance.

Eager to enjoy their spoils, the shepherds quickly put up a tent. Tying the woman's hands behind her back, they threw her inside. Tumbling first to her knees, then to her back, she lay on the dirt floor trembling.

Removing the sash from his tunic, the man with the ragged ear stepped inside. The others wandered off to sit and smoke beside a pile of rock. Peter lifted his flute and began to play. They heard no sounds from the tent until the man with the ragged ear roared aloud. Then came the sound of two sharp slaps. Then silence.

Shortly afterward, the man emerged, his face sweaty and red. He stood outside the tent flap and retied his belt.

"Peter!" he cried.

Shocked to hear his name, the shepherd fumbled his flute. Slipping the instrument into his belt, he ran to his leader. When he arrived, the man swung an arm around Peter's shoulders.

"Since you found her, you may have her while she is still fresh," he said.

Peter stared agape. He wanted to protest but knew that would raise suspicions among his cohorts. To them he could not reveal his distaste for female flesh.

The man with the ragged ear slapped him on the back and pushed him inside.

Peter found the woman curled on her side, her teeth chattering. Her robe was pushed above her waist. Bloody handprints smeared on the insides of her thighs.

Peter winced. He wanted no part of her. Still he could not emerge from the tent without having done something. He could try to pretend otherwise but feared the woman might reveal his charade. Thinking this, his hands dropped to his belt. He stepped forward and nudged the woman onto her back with his toe. When she rolled over, her gaze rose into his.

"Why not be quick about it," she hissed.

Peter glared down but said nothing. He had worked hard to elevate his standing among the shepherds and did not want to risk putting his status in jeopardy. Still in all their travels he had managed to feign his experience with women. And had avoided lying with one fully. But his cohorts had never been lingering just outside the door!

"What are you waiting for?" the young woman asked, squinting through the sting of sweat.

Her words snapped Peter back to his predicament.

"Nothing!" he growled.

The woman's eyes ran up and down the length of him.

Her voice grew suddenly tender. "You do not wish to hurt me, do you?"

Peter stared, unsure what to say.

The woman nodded. "I can see that you are not like them." She closed her eyes. Whispered, "You are . . . *different*."

At this Peter's cheeks began to burn. "I am the same as any man!" he shot back.

The woman shook her head. "Of course, of course I can see that. I only meant—"

"Silence!" he roared. She fell silent. After a moment he saw her struggle against the ties at her wrists. Terror swelling inside her.

Something about the woman's subjugation unleashed a fury within him. Bound and trapped, she could cause him no harm. Could not inflict her wiles. Nor have her way. He grinned as a rush of power surged through his limbs.

"Roll over," he commanded. She did as she was told.

And upon her he exacted a lifetime of revenge.

When the band of shepherds entered the next town, the ragged-eared man sold the woman they had kidnapped for a good sum. Dropping a handful of coins into Peter's palm, he said, "Let us abandon our dirty trade and adopt a more lucrative one. For there is greater reward in women than in sheep!" He then swung an arm around Peter's shoulders and said, "Since you have proven your worth, you will now work beside me." He grinned before whispering, "And you shall have all the women you could ever want!"

Peter smiled at the flattery, but inside he wanted to scream.

CHAPTER 35

Somewhere within ancient Palestine—33 A.D.

A breeze blew between the stars as the three journeyed under cover of night. Though cloaked by darkness, they were not alone.

Having witnessed, or heard of, the miraculous healer, people from outlying villages had begun to accompany Jesus and his sisters.

Ruth glanced over her shoulder. "Their number has grown," she said.

Tabitha, too, looked back. "Yes," she confirmed. "Almost double since this morning."

Jesus shrugged. "What would you have me do? Their eyes have been opened. They are not mine to control."

Ruth frowned. "Yes, their eyes have been opened, but they need not follow us. They need only seek their *own* light, not that of another. And the crowd will attract unwanted attention," she said.

"But what am I to say to them? Be gone from me?"

"If you wish us to be safe, then yes," Ruth said.

Jesus sighed. He turned around and approached the crowd. There were men and women, young and old, some carrying children, others carrying meager belongings. As he drew closer, Jesus was startled to see how vast the crowd. At least one hundred strong, perhaps more.

Ruth and Tabitha watched as he spoke. Some people nodded their heads, others waved their arms.

After a moment, Jesus returned.

"What did they say?"

He let go a little laugh. "They say they are grateful for what they have been given and wish only to help spread the goodness of what they have received. They do not wish to serve. Nor to kneel." He lifted his hands in a gesture of defeat. "I was unable to persuade them otherwise."

Before Ruth could respond, the pounding of a runner's feet shattered the dark. The three fell back as a young man burst upon them. He tried to speak but was overcome with exertion.

Sensing that the man meant no harm, Jesus laid a hand on his shoulder, waiting for him to catch his breath.

Panting, the young man looked up. "You are the healer? The one with green eyes?"

Jesus and Ruth exchanged a glance.

"Yes," he said.

"Then please," he continued, struggling to slow his breath. "We are but poor farmers. Our village has been raided. Many were badly injured. Can you help us?"

Ruth stepped forward. "Where is your village?" she asked.

The young man pointed to the southeast. "Back in that direction, not far," he said.

Ruth's dimples drilled deep. "But that is where we came from," she said.

The messenger nodded quickly. "It is my fault. I did not know that you traveled at night. And lost track of you."

Jesus looked in the direction of the young man's village, then back at Ruth. When he did, Ruth could see that he had made his decision, and she had not the strength to dissuade him.

When Jesus saw her relent, he turned to the young man. "Take us there," he said.

When they arrived at the messenger's village, they saw no one about. It appeared as if the people had abandoned their humble mud dwellings. Then they noticed smoke rising from the chimney of the largest hut.

"They have gathered the wounded in there," the young man told them. When he led them inside, they found several men laid out on mats, bleeding from knife wounds to their faces, arms, and torsos. A group of women whispered among the men, changing dressings and offering water.

The messenger turned to Jesus. "They tried to protect us, but the bandits had weapons."

One of the men on the floor began to tremble. Ruth took Jesus by the elbow. "We must slow the bleeding, or they will perish," she whispered.

Jesus turned to Tabitha. "Gather all the spare linen you can," he said.

Tabitha nodded and ran off.

Ruth and Jesus then knelt to mix the necessary poultices.

Grateful for the help, the village women did all they could to assist.

When they were finished dressing the men's wounds, Ruth turned to Jesus. "All should survive, but for this one. Of him I am not yet certain," she said, pointing to the man who had begun to tremble.

Jesus nodded and addressed the village women. "These men will need to be cared for each day. Their dressings changed and a balm applied." The women nodded, their eyes wet with gratitude.

"Yes. Thank you," they whispered.

Then Jesus pulled the messenger aside. "All should survive," he told him. "But for the one with the deepest wounds, we can only wait and hope," he said, pointing to the trembling man.

The messenger drew in a heavy breath. "He will survive. He *must*," he said.

Jesus sensed the young man's sudden tension. "Why must he survive?" he asked.

Through clenched teeth, the young man said, "Because the bandits stole our sister. Together my brother and I must find them, and take revenge."

Learning of this horror, Jesus became enraged. Soon he found himself yearning to help the men seek out their sister and exact payment from her captors.

Across the room, Ruth sensed the coil tightening inside her friend. Rushing over, she pressed a hand along his back. "Let us go outside where the air is fresh," she urged.

Jesus sat with Ruth under the sea-green canopy of an olive tree.

His shoulders bent under an invisible burden. "I am losing my way," he told her.

Her eyes scanned the crowd of followers sitting at a distance. "*They* do not seem to think so," she said, tipping her head toward the people.

Jesus let his head drop into his hands. "But I *am*," he insisted.

Ruth nodded gently. Aware of his battle.

She drew a fallen leaf into her hand. "Your outrage is understandable," she said. "Living according to The Way does not mean setting aside one's emotions. Or turning a blind eye. Rather it means evaluating one's impulses for what they are, and what they might become, before taking action."

Jesus gripped his hands into fists. "I know that taking revenge is wrong. I *do*," he insisted. "But when I hear of such desecrations, I simply . . . cannot . . . think with my better self."

Ruth gave an easy smile. "It is because you realize this that I know The Way burns brightly within you." She gave his knee a pat. "Do not demand perfection of yourself. Only mindfulness. When the way seems unclear, or difficult, you must remember. And sometimes you must *remember* to remember." After sitting another moment, she glanced back toward the village. "They have built a fire and prepared a meal," she said. "Let us join them."

As Ruth stood to depart, Jesus tugged on her robe. "Ruth?" he said.

She looked down and saw a heaviness weighing his eyes. Part exhaustion, part despair.

"Help me, Ruth. Do not let me fail in this," he said.

Ruth folded him into her arms. Something then made her recall Shereen's final words to the young shepherd. "Be assured of yourself and of the path that lies ahead," she said. And held him close.

The villagers gathered about the fire, while those who were following Jesus sat in a larger circle around them. As the flames leapt higher, and food was passed, they despaired over the attack.

"It was premeditated," one man said.

The messenger nodded, his eyes filling with tears. "The shepherds thought our brother had stolen his sheep. But it was not so! He found the animals wounded and dying from a wolf attack. And slaughtered them to end their suffering. But they did not believe his story and took our beautiful Setya as compensation."

"Such a violation cannot go unanswered!" one of the older men said. "We must arm ourselves and seek them out!"

The others grumbled about the fire, their indignation rising, steaming toward violence.

"An eye for an eye!" another shouted. "That is the law!"

Jesus felt the men's anger escalating and shuddered. It reminded him of the night his father and the villagers had stormed off to kill Zahra—and the rage that had swarmed among them. It reminded him, too, of his own potent fury.

Unable to restrain the emotions tangling inside his heart, he cried out, "Listen to what you are saying!" The other men fell silent and turned to stare at the young healer. Jesus blinked as though surprised by his outburst. But, feeling their eyes upon him, he gathered himself. And let his mind soften. "You speak of murder as though it were an act of power," he said. "But I tell you this—whether it is the innocent or the guilty you kill, the act of destruction degrades the soul. And buries all hope."

When he paused, no one spoke, only the fire crackled.

Jesus glanced over at Ruth. She returned his glance with a smile. Knowing that he was seeking his center. And his better self.

"Friends," Jesus began again, gazing into his own hands. "Do not confuse destruction with power. They are opposites. Think of this: How long does it take to crush a butterfly with a stick?" He looked about. When no one spoke he continued. "I can tell you from experience: It takes no time at all. And yet what is required to create a butterfly? Nothing short of a magical transformation—a divine shifting of blood and sinew—a miraculous act that not one of us could ever dream of achieving! When you remember it this way, you can see that the act of swatting down a butterfly is a minor and inferior act—and one of great cowardice!—in comparison to honoring and sustaining it. So it is with *all* life."

Jesus reached up and laid a hand on his chest, feeling the medallion beneath his tunic.

Ruth smiled, sensing that he was trying to remember. And knowing that the words he spoke were as much to counsel himself as they were to guide the villagers.

Jesus went on. "Which, then, do you think is the more enduring, more honorable, and significant act: to murder a person or to nurture one? Whose action possesses the greater strength: the mother's or the murderer's?" When no one answered, he said, "You say nothing because the answer is as plain as the stars above us!"

Frustrated, a man shouted out, "But what should we do then? Surrender to the violators? Admit our inferiority?"

Jesus lashed out. "*Inferiority?!*" he cried. "You need to clean out your ears! Have you not heard a word I have said?"

The man sat back, startled at the gentle healer's sudden abruptness.

"There is nothing powerful nor redeeming about the violators' actions. On that we can agree. Unfortunately, many men would rather possess easily what is false than hazard the journey to what is real," he said, echoing the words Ruth had once spoken to him. "*You*, on the other hand, are farmers. You generate life where there is none. You tend what is precious and living. And in so doing you cultivate and sustain miracles that honor the source of life. Why then would you degrade yourselves to be *like* them?" he demanded.

The crowd grew uneasy at his words, seeing, for the first time, their foolishness.

"That they have no honor for life is evident in their decision to steal a woman," Jesus continued. "Does not this very act dishonor every female? Does it not reduce her to the status of mere property rather than a miracle before us? Does it not show a preference for destruction over creation? For coin over breath? And does it not also show confusion over the true nature of power?"

An older man stood up. "Healer, what you say may be true, but what about the words of the priests? And our great Lord? What about an eye for an eye?"

Jesus laughed and shook his head. "Where is the balance—or the hope—in such a counterfeit philosophy? If I cut out your eye, then you will cut out mine. But then I, who struck first, will feel that justice has been snatched from my jaws and so, to right the wrong, I must cut out your second eye. And, in retaliation, you must cut out the second of mine. Enraged, I will prepare to take another, but as I stand before you, what am I to do? My enemy has run out of eyes!"

A laugh rippled through the crowd.

Jesus laughed, too. "It is humorous, I know. But the outcome is far from glad. Think of it. What will I do? I must have an eye for the one

I have lost! What then is my solution? Only this: to steal the eye of another! Perhaps from my enemy's son. Perhaps from his daughter."

The crowd stopped laughing. The healer's story had cut close to their hearts.

"Yes," Jesus said, noting their response. "Just think of it. And what is far worse, is that if one follows such a law, there can be no end to the damage. Until every eye, on every living thing, is cut out and thrown away. And this, my friends, is the grave risk we face when we turn from the Mother."

When he was done speaking, Jesus dropped his gaze. He found himself humbled at his own words. And the great wisdom of The Way.

Wanting to be alone with his thoughts, he rose and drifted through the crowd. Then continued on into the distance.

Ruth watched his departure and felt lightened in her heart. For it seemed that her friend had fortified himself anew. But beyond that, she could see the momentous impact his words had had on the people.

And this made her wonder, again, at the future.

That night, as the villagers returned to their homes, they spoke among themselves of the healer's stories. Some dismissed him as a charlatan who spoke of perversities. While others, knowing full well that his words were dangerous, even heretical, could not help but feel elevated by his teachings and his ways.

In the morning, some of those who were not tending the wounded collected their belongings and followed the healer and his sisters as they headed north. For they were eager to witness more of the healer's wisdom, and to feel again that sense of connection and belonging that his words inspired.

CHAPTER 36

The City of Jerusalem—33 A.D.

The great wooden door groaned on its hinges. A Roman soldier released the iron handle with a clank. His sword slapped against his leather armor as he stormed into the room. He came to a sharp halt. "Sir!" he bellowed.

Farther inside the chamber, an exceptionally lean man stood at a high table, studying a scroll.

"One of the assassins desires to see you," the soldier reported. "He has brought news of a traitor."

Without lifting his eyes, the governor dipped his head. The movement was so slight that an untrained onlooker would have failed to notice. But the soldier observed it. "I shall bring him," he said. He clapped a hand on his sword and hinged in a bow.

Shortly thereafter, another man came and stood in the governor's doorway. His sun-baked cheeks and sand-beaten sandals branded him as a desert dweller. A dagger was tucked in the sheath laying flush at his side. A goatskin pouch hung tight along his back. When Pilate did not take notice of his entry, the assassin coughed to announce his presence.

Pilate smiled without looking up. "Welcome back, Judas," he said.

Judas bowed. "Your excellency," he said. He had learned long ago that the Roman leaders valued obsequiousness among their minions. When he stood, he noticed another man sitting in a far corner. Though older, his face carried a boyishness beneath a head of straw-colored hair.

"You have news?" Pilate asked, skimming his fingertips over the parchment.

"Yes."

Pilate waved an impatient hand. His mind was littered with pressing concerns and details. The time of Passover was fast approaching and soon the city would be overrun with pilgrims and heretics of every kind. Much planning needed to be done to reinforce the city's security, and he did not have time to waste on stories from the desert.

In hushed tones, Judas relayed to Pilate what he had learned of the new healer. "His following is mostly among the poor and downtrodden," Judas observed. "But it grows rapidly in number."

Pilate lifted his eyes from the parchment. The blond man in the far corner also looked up.

"And?" Pilate asked.

Judas described another rumor he had heard. "They say that people offer him gifts, but he refuses them."

"He refuses gifts?" Pilate asked. His eyes drifted to those of his companion.

Judas nodded. That particular detail pricked his conscience. It was unlike the false prophets he normally hunted. The ones who made his blood boil.

Pilate untied a leather pouch from his waist. There were four gold coins inside. He tossed the pouch to Judas. "Go back and learn more about this healer," he commanded. "But do not bother me again until Passover has ended."

Judas bowed deeply and departed. There was nothing unusual about a new healer in the land. Indeed, Judas had spent years hunting down messiahs, magicians, and soothsayers of every description. But what troubled him was this particular healer's refusal to accept gifts. Most of the mystical kind, he had found, were in the game for money, influence, or both. Those who were not were rare.

On his journey back to where he had last seen the healer, Judas spied a sizeable crowd gathering on the outskirts of a village. He knew that the charlatan he had been tracking could not have traveled that far in a few days; nevertheless, he drew closer to investigate.

The magician turned the great moon of his face toward the crowd that encircled him. He lifted a short, smooth section of rope from his pocket and dangled it before their eyes. When he was sure everyone had seen it, he folded the rope inside his fist. He shook his hand several times and told a child kneeling in front to blow on it. On the final shake, he opened his fingers and dangled the rope above the people's heads. To their amazement, five knots bulged along its length.

"Ohh!" the crowd gasped and broke into applause. A filthy boy wove through the crowd lifting an open pouch.

"Miracles are not bestowed on the tightfisted!" the magician announced. He pointed to a man dressed in rags who had let the pouch pass him by. "Surely you can offer a small token for these wonders performed before your very eyes?" he taunted. The young boy returned to the man and shook the pouch. The poor man hesitated before dropping in his last half-shekel.

When the magician heard the jangle of enough coins, he proceeded. "Blessings for your generosity!" he said. He then roved within the circle, pushing the people back. "Give me space!" he cried. "I need space in which to draw down the magic!" When the circle had widened, he threw a dramatic hand into the air and cried, "Bring in the afflicted!"

The onlookers gasped and fell back in horror as two men dragged a crazed young woman into the circle. She spat and foamed at the mouth. Her eyes rolled into the back of her head. Her matted hair clung to her face. She hurled obscenities at the quaking children in the front row.

"Behold a woman possessed!" the magician roared.

The woman screamed and lashed out at the audience. She struggled against her captors. The crowd drew back as if from a swarm of bees.

"Fear not!" the magician cried. "There is no demon who can defy this magician's powers!"

The men twisted the young woman's arms behind her back and forced her to her knees. Her head swung madly as the magician approached. He pressed a palm against her forehead. "Evil demon!" he cried. "Identify yourself! What is your name?"

The woman's eyes closed. "I am Korgina! Queen of Darkness!" she spat.

The magician appeared unfazed. "Korgina!" he commanded. "You do not belong here. Be gone from the innocent and return to your wretched queendom!"

The woman's body shook in a series of mad convulsions. Her eyes opened wide, unseeing.

"Be gone!" the magician cried and snapped back the woman's head with a sharp thrust of his palm. Seizures contorted her body and then she let out a bloodcurdling scream. She dropped to the ground in a boneless heap.

"Silence!" the magician warned the crowd. He knelt next to the fallen woman. He offered her a hand. The woman reached out and stood with his assistance.

"Where am I?" she asked in a sweet voice.

"You are among friends," the magician answered. "But tell us, what is your name?"

The woman smiled. "I am Rachel, daughter of Loch," she chimed. The crowd erupted in cheers.

Hidden from view, Judas frowned at the spectacle. Disgusted by the magician's performance, he felt the sudden desire to dispose of the man's life.

Was there no end to such imposters?

But, for the time being, he had set his sights on the new healer and so turned his back and continued on his way.

When the people had dispersed, the magician met Rachel behind a wall of shrubs. He reached into his jangling pouch and dropped three shekels into her palm. Rachel looked over his shoulder to where her hungry children tumbled in the dust. "What would you pay me to play blind?" she asked.

CHAPTER 37

Somewhere within ancient Palestine—33 A.D.

Her hands sticky with plant saps and her back aching from traveling and tending to the sick, Ruth sat to rest in the shade of an olive tree. Before her, great hordes of people milled along the reedy shore of the Jordan, seeking aid and words of wisdom. As the number of Jesus's supporters increased, Ruth had grown concerned that the three of them would exhaust themselves with the impossible task of healing and teaching such multitudes.

As if reading her mind, Jesus approached. His cheeks pale, his tunic smeared with grime, his hair tangled with salve and sweat. He sat by his friend, saying nothing. Together they gazed out upon the swelling crowd. As they watched, more people arrived, some limping, some blind. Others carrying sickly children.

Jesus glanced toward Ruth. He saw her exhaustion and sensed his own. "I have been thinking," he said. "And I fear we may not be doing the right thing."

Bewildered, Ruth looked over. "What do you mean?"

Jesus shook his head. "You have been asking me to help preserve The Way. And I have been leading us toward Nazareth. Collecting ever more followers. Depleting us of our strength and our focus." He sniffed with disgust at himself. "And those who antagonize us will only grow in strength and number as we approach Jerusalem."

"But we have helped many people," Ruth observed.

"Yes, but we cannot help them *all*," he said. He glanced down at his hands. They trembled with fatigue. "And even if we could, healing them does not preserve The Way. Nor does it ensure the safety of that which it is our duty to protect."

Ruth nodded but kept silent.

Jesus closed his eyes. "I had a dream last night," he told her. "It was exceptionally vivid."

"Tell me."

He swallowed. "I was back in the caves. Tending the water in the sycamore garden. Something had happened, some great shift, and a single powerful stream was issuing from the spring. It ran with such a concentrated force and fury that not only were the plants in its path destroyed, but those on the perimeter began to wither from thirst."

Ruth's eyes narrowed.

"Then someone put a shovel in my hand. It might have been Shereen," he said, his voice catching. "She told me to dig. And so I did. And as I carved more and more paths, the water began to flow in endless directions. Not just throughout the garden in the caves, but spreading through fields and villages and lands I had never seen. Yet the water's supply never dwindled. Only replenished. And everything within and beyond the web of its paths began to thrive."

Ruth stared in amazement. "What do you think the dream might have meant?" she asked.

Jesus shrugged. "I do not yet know. I only know that it left me with the distinct impression that my actions are not aligned with The Way. That I am making mistakes. And acting selfishly." He turned to face his friend. "And that I am most likely putting us all in jeopardy." Unable to hold her gaze, he cast his eyes downward and said, "I thought if we spoke the truth, if we spoke of the Mother, and refused to hide, that we could—" His voice failed him.

"I know," Ruth whispered, laying a hand on his. "I know."

CHAPTER 38

Somewhere within ancient Palestine—33 A.D.

Several miles downriver, a fisherman stood above his newest apprentice, watching him untangle the nets.

"Eh, there, not like that. You have to keep to the main strand," he said, correcting the young man's technique.

The apprentice frowned at being told what to do. His hands were scratched and scaly from hauling in the day's catch. His clothes and skin reeked of fish. Despite his filth, however, the young man was handsome.

The fisherman grunted. "When you have got them straightened, store them in the boat's hull. And be back before first light," he said.

The apprentice nodded but did not look up as the fisherman departed.

Despite several further attempts to unwind the tangles, the apprentice had little success.

Disgusted, he threw the nets into the boat and went for a walk along the river. Though he had told the fisherman that a chronic shortness of breath had forced him to seek more sedentary work, that was not so, and his legs still ached to wander.

Farther up the road, the fledgling fisherman was overrun by a group of boys and their father. On the man's shoulders rode a young girl with badly mangled legs. "What brings you in such a hurry, friend?" the apprentice fisherman asked, more out of irritation than real interest.

The father began to answer but when he saw the fisherman's face, his mouth fell open. The man dropped to his knees and grabbed at the hem of the fisherman's tunic. The fisherman drew back in annoyance. "Stand back! Why do you grab at me?" he demanded.

The father rose quickly, apologizing. "Forgive me," he said. "I . . . I thought you were one of them . . . I thought you were *he*."

The fisherman looked with disdain at the filthy boys and their mangled sister. "Whoever you thought I might be, I am not," he said sharply, wishing to be left alone. The father bowed in apology and, not wanting to be further delayed, hurried on his way.

A few moments later, a husband and wife came walking from the same direction as the father and his children. "Greetings," the young fisherman said, keeping his head lowered to avoid conversation.

"Glory be!" the husband blurted. "She could not move a single finger!" he beamed. "She dropped every dish and could not weave!" The husband lifted his wife's hand for the fisherman to see. It was gnarled, as if prematurely aged, but the joints seemed remarkably flexible. She moved her fingers gingerly and covered her smile.

"He is a mercy from above, my friend!" the man said.

"Who is?" the fisherman asked, annoyed by his own curiosity.

"The healer! He has surely come to save us all!" The husband and wife departed.

Eager for a distraction, and perhaps a chance to cause trouble, the apprentice decided not to return to his tangled nets. Instead, he would go see the mysterious healer for himself.

CHAPTER 39

Somewhere within ancient Palestine—33 A.D.

Ruth kneeled over a fallen tree, shredding the leaves of several herbs into a bowl. Her eyes stared wide, but seemed unseeing. Overwhelmed by the number of people who continued to arrive, it had been several days since she had had time to herself. And Jesus's extraordinary dream had left her bewildered, curious, and in need of Communion.

"Ruth?" someone said. She turned to see Tabitha kneeling by her elbow. Without another word, the younger Sister lifted the herbs from Ruth's hand. "Let me finish these," she said.

Ruth's eyes watered with gratitude. But, looking down, she could see the dark circles under Tabitha's eyes and knew that she was faring no better.

Tabitha smiled. "I am fine," she assured her. "Go."

Weary, but knowing it might be her only time alone, Ruth thanked her friend and slipped away.

Climbing a nearby slope, Ruth took refuge beneath an olive tree. Sitting, she drew in a deep breath and calmed her mind. Easing into the silence, she focused on a spray of olives dangling from a branch and let herself be drawn into the fruit, freeing her thoughts to wander.

Her mind drifted back to Jesus's description of his dream. She entered this memory until she, too, could see and feel his vision. As she gazed upon the boundless rivulets of water, rushing outward in every direction, images of a new possibility began to unfold.

Ruth swooned at the sight that rose before her.

After a few moments, she heard voices.

Woken from her vision, she opened her eyes to see a girl of perhaps four years walking alongside her older brother a little farther down the slope. Ruth noted the tangles in their hair and the hollows in their cheeks. She then overheard them speaking.

"Can we sit, brother? My stomach hurts," the girl said.

"We can rest for a little," he answered. "But we must be home before dusk." The boy glanced around them. Seeing a sage plant, he went to pluck a sprig from its middle. "Here, chew on these leaves. One of the healer's sisters said it is good for bellyaches."

The girl took the sage and popped it between her lips. After a bit, she asked, "Brother? Why does the healer say that our mother is a seed?"

The boy laughed. "That is not *exactly* what he says," he told her, grinning. He patted her on the head and went on to explain. "The healer says that knowledge of the Mother is like the seeds that farmers sow in the fields. And that the seeds' growth depends on the soil in which they land. Some of the farmer's seeds land in the shade, and are stunted. Some land in the thorns, and die soon after they sprout. While others land in good soil, and these take hold and blossom to great heights. That is like what happens when someone accepts knowledge of the Mother into their hearts. Do you understand?"

The girl frowned. "I suppose. But . . . what happened to the Father?"

Ruth smiled above them. Impressed.

"Nothing *happened* to him!" the boy replied. "It is just that some people have tried to raise the Father above the Mother, and some have even set out to extinguish her! They do this by making us afraid to acknowledge her—or to remember that we, like all of Creation, are born of a womb—and must honor this truth in our lives. And not forget."

"So is he saying we should be nicer to our mother?"

The boy nodded. "That is part of it. But it also means that we must treat all women, and all children of women, with greater respect. Just as we must treat that which brings everything into being, the Mother of All, with respect and gratitude. If we forget to honor that which nurtures life, then the Mother begins to wither, and we wither along with her, like the seeds that land on rocks."

The girl went silent. Her brows knit as she considered what her brother had said.

"Does your stomach feel better?"

She nodded. Then, without warning, leapt to her feet.

"Wait! Where are you going?" her brother cried as she darted off.

"We have to get home and find the farmer!" his sister called over her shoulder.

"What farmer?"

"The one with the seeds. We have to make sure he finds good soil so Mother can blossom!"

Ruth stared after the departing children, amazed at their interaction. And the ease of their understanding. She remembered having heard Shereen tell Anna that story when the shepherd had been younger and beginning to grasp The Way. Now, it seemed, despite his concerns to the contrary, Jesus had come to embody the teachings. And as the distance they traveled increased, and the number of people they met grew, his sight only continued to strengthen and with it his influence.

It was then that a realization struck Ruth so directly and with such force that she toppled back against the olive tree.

Ever since they had left the caves, she had tried to temper Jesus's sharing of his belief in the Mother and his knowledge of The Way. She had feared that his doing so would sound the alarm and draw their enemies. But all along Jesus had known intuitively that his remarkable appearance would cloak them in safety, and so he had insisted on leveraging his strange gift to its fullest. And now, having seen how the teachings could be spread by way of others, she suddenly understood that his instinct to reveal what the Sisters believed had been right all along!

His freedom in the world, Ruth could now see, had ushered an unprecedented possibility into the world.

A new time had come—a new cycle in which ensuring transmission of The Way did not require the Sisters to sequester themselves, nor even to serve as Awakeners, but to instill in the people *themselves* the ability to teach and heal.

As in Jesus's dream, the single stream of water must divide into endless channels—its life-giving powers thereby multiplied and spread to enliven the world.

Ruth chided herself for not having deciphered her visions—and Jesus's intentions—sooner. A key aspect of their quest, she realized, had been unfurling itself in front of her all along. And was, in fact, a much-anticipated phenomenon of The Way coming at long last to fruition!

Having been consumed with concerns about their survival, she could not have imagined that Jesus might come to serve as one of The Way's most sacred beings. One who would not only protect its truths, but launch a powerful and far-reaching resurgence.

I have seen the sycamore rising, Mother Susana had said.

Ruth shook her head in disbelief.

Suddenly certain of what they must do, she stood and raced to find the others.

But would they have time to reach enough people before the rest of her visions unfolded?

CHAPTER 40

Somewhere within ancient Palestine—33 A.D.

The following morning, Jesus and his sisters woke early and called their supporters to the river. The people gathered quickly, those who had been traveling with Jesus expecting that he would hold Communion or tell one of his illuminating stories.

Instead, Jesus and his sisters selected a small number of men and women, twelve or so, and asked the others to assist Tabitha in the collection of roots and herbs.

Taking the twelve they had selected farther up the river, Jesus and Ruth began to teach them the essential philosophies and remedies of The Way. Over the next several weeks, the twelve learned firsthand how to identify and collect plants and how to prepare remedies and apply them. They learned how to align themselves and their actions with the Mother's guiding wisdom and principles. And they learned how to experience the reverent connection of Communion.

The purpose behind the teachings was not, as Ruth had said when explaining her vision to Jesus, to create a new Sisterhood, nor to reproduce Awakeners—such things were impossible given the number of years required for such learning—but rather to instill in more people the knowledge of the power inherent in their being and their world. And to give them tools to remember and practice these truths.

Then, once the members of the group had a solid mastery of what they had been shown, each would go on to serve as a "keeper" or "teacher" who passed on the knowledge to other small groups, whose members then became new keepers who taught other small groups, and so on in an ever-widening circle—and through this dynamic process of sharing, the single stream would divide into an expanding web of channels—enlivening a lush and ever-renewing garden.

"Tell me how I can help," Jesus had said when Ruth first revealed her idea.

The round Sister had laughed at his words. "Help?" she had said. "It is *you* who has started this. And therefore *you* who must finish it," she added. They had then spent the evening devising a plan to teach the first keepers.

That night, as she slept, Ruth felt joy in what they were intending. Though she still could not silence the nervous buzz that ran through her bones (especially since the undertaking would require them to remain in one spot for a time). Nor could she ignore the strong sense that danger lay ahead.

While they continued to teach groups of twelve, Ruth kept a vigilant eye out for those who might bring trouble. She knew that the rapid spread of their teachings would inevitably draw attention. Fortunately, most of the people around them were welcoming and receptive.

Except for one.

Ruth had noticed a small, hooded figure traveling on a donkey. He had been following them like a shadow for several days. The person never approached, but lurked just beyond the edge of the crowds. Sometimes taking sanctuary in a tree. He seemed to be watching Jesus. Carefully.

When Ruth pointed him out, Jesus said he had already noticed him. But did not sense a threat. Ruth acquiesced, but kept a sharp eye on the stranger.

Having focused their efforts on smaller groups and watched, with delight, as knowledge of The Way began to spread rapidly through their supporters, Jesus and his sisters found their sprits much lightened.

With his strength and focus renewed, Jesus spent more and more time telling stories among the people and listening eagerly to theirs.

As Ruth and Tabitha watched him milling among their supporters, they shook their heads.

"He looks so at home among them," Tabitha said.

Ruth smiled. "It is as if he were born to this moment."

As they were saying these things, a ruckus erupted behind them. They turned just as a band of men catapulted toward them wielding scythes.

"There he is! That is the heretic!" the man leading the group roared. Gigantic in size, he wielded a blade in one hand and knocked people to the ground with the other.

Seeing the furious attack, Jesus's supporters rushed from every direction to form a shield around him. The assailants were forced to a halt at the ragged wall of people.

"Let us through!" they bellowed.

The supporters held their ground.

"You are harboring a heathen! A man who speaks against God!" they cried. They swiped at the crowd with threats and knives, but the people dodged the attacks and held their ground.

"May you all perish in everlasting fire!" one of the men raged.

"God will see that you suffer!" another said.

Recalling the violent scene he had witnessed in Jerusalem, Jesus tugged at the people standing before him, straining to push them to safety. "Leave here! Save yourselves!" he cried out. But his words could not be heard above the din.

As the number of supporters swelled, the attackers began to drift away from Jesus. Though armed, they were badly outnumbered. When the growing mass began to circle behind them, the assailants turned in retreat.

"We will be back!" they threatened as they fled. "God will not stand for such abomination near His Temple!"

When they had departed, Jesus's followers returned to their tasks as if nothing had happened. It was not the first time their group had been harassed—every village harbored those who defended the male divinity.

Still, this latest attack was certainly the most vicious.

Ruth looked over to where Jesus stood. He avoided her eyes, making an obvious effort to appear unaffected. Only his clenched fists gave him away.

Squinting into the distance, to where dust rose from the departing men's feet, Ruth wondered how much longer the sheer number of their supporters would be able to protect them. And keep Jesus from harm.

Toward the end of the day, when the shadows of the rushes grew long across the river, Jesus and his sisters took a short walk to clear their heads. As they went, they came upon a young boy crying near the shore. Jesus stopped and knelt. "Why do you cry?" he asked. A crowd soon gathered around them.

The boy lifted his hands. Inside them, he cupped a sparrow. Its feathered head lolled loosely to one side. Its small, pale eyelid was drawn, like half a seed, over its eye. A drop of blood stained the end of its beak. Tabitha wiped the boy's tears with her robe. He turned his face up to Jesus. "Can you bring him back to life? Like the magician?" he implored.

A gasp rippled through the crowd. Everyone knew that Jesus could not resist the request of a child. A charge ran from person to person. Surely their healer possessed more power than a magician! Everyone was convinced that soon they would witness a miracle.

Jesus patted the boy's shoulder. He caught Ruth's eyes and intuited her thoughts. They had heard much lately of a magician who performed amazing acts. His miracles were so impressive that he was attracting large crowds wherever he traveled. In their journeys, the three companions had encountered many prophets and profiteers. They knew that the parading of miracles greatly tempted the hungry and hopeless. This realization filled Jesus with an urgency to confront the magician's empty tricks. He cleared his mind, then turned to the crowd and began to speak.

"Friends, this child's desire is right in its innocence. But tell me, why do the rest of you seek vulgar miracles when you are blind to the genuine ones before you? It is not the raising of the dead that is miraculous, but the life of the living!"

The crowd became silent. Tabitha wrapped her arms around the boy as he clutched the dead bird.

"Everyone, please sit with me," Jesus requested. He lowered himself slowly. His leg aching from the strain of their journey. "We have spoken of Communion before," he began when all were seated. "But perhaps you think it is only a morning activity? Or something done at a designated time? I tell you, it is neither of these things. Communion is a way of being aware in your world that can become as natural and reflexive as your breath. All it requires is that you remember. And sometimes that you *remember* to remember all that surrounds us. When you do this, you will feel the power that resides within and around you. Then you will see the magician's miracles for what they truly are."

When everyone had settled, he encouraged them to "live into the miracle" of the bird, to run their thoughts along each tufted fiber of its feathers, to follow its flight backward over the valleys and treetops to the time when its very song had been hewn from sunshine and rain. After an hour, the crowd sat peacefully, rapt in their own experiences. The boy lifted the bird, eyeing it with attentiveness.

"Remember this, friends. Life is a gift. Not a promise. This being so, not every injury, not every illness, and certainly not death itself can be healed or reversed. To raise the dead would not be a miracle, but a degradation!"

The people nodded in understanding.

"To live in harmony with the earth is to accept that death is as much a part of the Great Cycle as life. To deny death is to deny life. To claim power over death, as some do for profit, is to doubt the rightness of the Mother from whom all life arises. Both life and death must be honored equally as each gives rise to the other. Does this not seem truthful?"

The people spoke among themselves. When they heard Jesus's words, they understood that they had been misguided. They could now see how foolish their expectations. Why should they seek resurrection of the *dead*?

When Jesus finished his story, the young fisherman standing on the outside of the circle stared in disbelief. Not at what Jesus had said, but at the man himself. Jesus felt the stare and turned in his direction. His eyes fell on the fisherman's white teeth.

"Peter!" he cried in shock. "Can it be you?"

Peter gaped as though confronting a ghost. "My God," he gasped. The friends rushed toward each other and locked in a warm embrace.

Ruth noted the insistence that passed between their bodies. The two men pulled back, blushing.

"I thought . . . I mean . . ." Peter stammered. "Solomon said that we must leave you. That you were dead."

Jesus smiled. "Are you happy that I am not?"

Peter stood still and tried to reconcile the memory of his childhood friend with the full-grown man before him. Gazing upon Jesus's handsome and confident face, he felt his admiration quickly rekindled. His mind returned to the day Solomon had announced that they could no longer wait for the young shepherd's return. Peter remembered the ache in his heart that had wedged in deep, draining his world of color and meaning. Since then, the pain had never diminished.

"By the stars above!" a bystander shouted. "Is he not your long-lost twin?" Those in the crowd gawked in astonishment at the friends' resemblance.

Peter and Jesus considered each other in the light of this new perspective. Indeed, it was true. Over time, their physical traits had grown more similar. Not just their vivid green eyes, coppery skin, and onyx hair, but the generous curves of their nose and lips. The only notable difference was Peter's greater height and breadth. His chest and legs having thickened with muscle from his labors and the urging of his gender.

Jesus faced the crowd. "Friends! Despite our similarities, we are not brothers by blood. Though we have always been brothers in spirit!" he said and swept a hand onto Peter's shoulders. Peter beamed, warming under the attention of his long-lost friend—the only one who had ever believed in him.

Peter and Jesus sat by the river eating a meal of fish and bread. Peter had told the crowd of supporters to stay back so that he and his brother could sup alone.

Ruth remained with the others, but could not settle her concerns. She watched as the two friends leaned intimately toward each other. She could feel Peter's need for attention.

But what kind of attention did he seek? Did he even know? Did Jesus?

Ruth worried that the ambiguity of their relationship might add further risk to their mission, and their lives. After all, Jesus was in all but name a woman. One whose passions remained supple and undefined.

Soon their bodies would seek to fulfill their needs.

What then? How would the attraction come to express itself? And how much worse if the attraction were thwarted?

With expert hands, Peter sliced a fish into pieces and regaled his friend with stories of their shepherding adventures.

"Remember when you tried to haul a jar of honey and it broke in your arms?" he chimed. "The goats would not stop licking you for a week!"

Jesus laughed at the tales as he watched his friend work. He could not help but admire the strength of Peter's hands and the muscles rippling his forearms. Peter, he could see, had grown into a strong and beautiful man. Jesus thought back to their final farewell and the surge that had passed between them. A heat invaded him at its recall. And a shiver tingled his belly.

Peter doted on his friend. He brought him fresh figs, washed his tunic, and repaired his sandals. He hung around Jesus, playing his flute, telling jokes, and sharing stories of his life since their separation. Though he could see that Jesus had duties to attend to, he seemed entirely disinterested in them. And constantly offered invitations to distract his friend. "The *mousht* are jumping. Let us go fishing!"

Peter's attentions and proximity soon began to inhibit those who wished to visit with Jesus.

"Wh-why does he stand so c-close?" Tabitha asked, obviously shaken.

Ruth did not answer. But her eyes narrowed as the two men walked off toward the river.

Jesus had been overjoyed at his friend's return. But as time passed, he felt himself becoming conflicted. It was true that he reveled in Peter's colorful retelling of their misadventures, and that he swooned at his sublime and seductive flute playing.

But why did he cringe when Peter called him "brother"? Was it because he wanted Peter to know the truth? Or was it because he wanted to be more than just brothers?

Still, Jesus was not unaware of how Peter hoarded his attention. Nor of the way Peter crowded out others from their private space. He, too, had noticed that Peter avoided the sick and those in need. He had also seen the way Peter asserted himself above his sisters and their supporters as if he were Jesus's most trusted confidant. As if all their teachings and healings were of no consequence.

Jesus recalled Peter's youthful disdain for females—his scoffing at Judas's loss of mother and sister, his contempt for the young girl hiding behind the well—and suspected that Peter's tendencies had only worsened during their time apart. But because of all he had learned from the Sisters, Jesus now knew the erroneousness of such disdain, and the truth of female power.

Yet when Peter pushed the others away, supposing himself intrinsically superior by virtue of his maleness, Jesus overlooked the behavior and did nothing to stop it. It was not that Jesus failed to recognize the injustice; it was just that he found himself more compelled by other aspects of his friend. By his hands, his shoulders, his voice.

At night, Jesus tossed in the midst of strange dreams unlike any he had ever had. Dreams of a new future. Of taking a husband. Of building a home.

And becoming a mother.

CHAPTER 41

Somewhere within ancient Palestine—33 A.D.

Peter hauled a net full of fresh catch onto his boat. The fish beat a desperate rhythm in the hull as he rowed ashore. He tossed the net onto dry land and began the grisly work of gutting and cleaning. The smell of fish innards stung his eyes, but he worked with a joy that had previously eluded him.

"Greetings," a man's voice said.

Thinking it was the old fisherman coming to assess his catch, Peter returned the greeting without looking up from his work.

"Are you not he?" the man asked. "Are you not the healer called Jesus?"

Peter started. He then smiled. His heart glowing at the man's mistake. "No," he said, glancing up. "I am not he. But his brother."

The man's eyes flitted mischievously within his moon-sized face. "His *twin* brother, no doubt?"

"Yes, his twin," Peter said. He did not hesitate at the lie. Almost believing it himself.

But the moon-faced man had known that Peter was not Jesus. "Are you, then, your brother's servant?" he asked, grinning in the shape of a wedge.

Peter frowned at the question.

Of course he was not his brother's servant! He was his equal. His confidant!

But the man continued before Peter could defend himself. "I am told your brother attracts many women," he said with a knowing nod. "Does he share their pleasures with you or hoard the flesh for himself?"

Peter squirmed as the question's implications took root.

The magician held his grin. He had long ago mastered the art of manipulating unspoken desires. And he had witnessed many between Peter and his so-called brother when he had first spotted the remarkable pair, as boys, in Jerusalem. Within the space between such desires, he knew, lay fertile soil for treachery. For in magic, as in life, it was not what people saw, but what they were *led* to see.

The man's question propelled an angry fist inside Peter, but when he looked up to refute him, he was gone.

As he carried his load of dead fish back to Jesus, Peter's mind spun with ugly thoughts. He had never questioned Jesus's love for him. Nor had he ever allowed himself to imagine Jesus choosing anyone above him. But now he could see that the possibility existed. And this simple fact pricked his dreams and soured his mood.

The notes from Peter's flute hovered like mist. The flames of a large fire flitted to the music. Jesus lay in a heavy sleep. He had spent most of the day wandering the riverside with Peter and ignoring the needs of those around him. When Tabitha had approached to ask for help, Peter had told her to go find Ruth. Jesus, for his part, had turned quickly so as not to see Tabitha's look of hurt. He knew he was being selfish, but he did not want anything, not even feelings of guilt, to blemish his time with Peter. Part of him wanted nothing more than to ignore his duties and walk for hours, side by side, with the handsome green-eyed fisherman.

But the other part of him, the part he silenced, did not know *what* he wanted.

Ruth approached the fire to let its warmth relieve the strain in her back. She swayed under a wave of exhaustion. She had spent a hard day demonstrating the mixing of various remedies to the next round of keepers. But had worked mostly alone as Jesus had become less attentive to his duties.

Rubbing her spine, she watched Jesus sleeping. They had not spoken in several days. His leg lay crooked on the ground. It had been too long since they had treated the encroaching stiffness. She knew that he would have difficulty walking in the morning if the balm were not worked into his bones. She asked Tabitha to bring the remedy and apply it.

As Tabitha approached, she nodded to Peter. He ignored her and continued to play his flute. Tabitha knelt alongside Jesus and lifted the indigo hem of his tunic, gingerly, so as not to wake him. Her hands froze when Peter's flute squealed.

"What are you doing?" he roared. "Get away from him!" Peter leapt up and swung the back of his hand across Tabitha's face. Ruth jumped to catch her. Anger darkening her eyes. Tabitha held a hand to her face.

Jesus was roused by the outburst. He sat up and saw Tabitha cowering in Ruth's arms. "What is it? What has happened?" he mumbled.

Peter pointed his finger at Tabitha. "She . . . she *touches* you . . . while you sleep!" he stammered, his cheeks puffing with anger.

Jesus and Ruth locked eyes.

Peter shook his hand in pain. "Why in the name of God do you tolerate these women?" he spat. "They are not worthy to tie the straps on your sandals!"

Jesus cringed. He did not want to believe his ears. Did not want to believe that there could be anything bad in the one who attracted him, like a moth that would not accept that the flame could burn its wings.

Ruth pulled Tabitha close.

Jesus turned to Peter. "What you have done is wrong, and cannot—" he began, but the shock and betrayal in Peter's eyes made Jesus's voice weaken. When he did not finish his rebuke, Ruth frowned and guided Tabitha away from the fire.

When they were gone, Peter continued to disparage the women. But Jesus did not hear his words. His ears were ringing too loudly. He felt a profound shame at his paralysis and his failure to confront the injustice.

Disoriented, he stared into the fire. In the distance, he could hear Tabitha weeping. His head fell and hung low.

What was happening to him? Why did his center feel misplaced? Why had he elevated a being of so little sight above his sisters? Above his very self? *Had he forgotten who he was?*

Or was he only now remembering?

Jesus lay down near the flames. He let his fingers wander over the medallion. The sycamore's jagged outline rose like a scar.

Remember who you are, no matter who you must become, Mother Susana had said.

Jesus closed his eyes and prayed ardently to remember.

After the night of Peter's assault on Tabitha, Jesus felt as though he was walled off from those around him. As though he could no longer navigate, or find his essence. He found himself avoiding the eyes and calls of his supporters and seeking only solitude. He could not bear to face Ruth or Tabitha.

His desire for Communion or any form of deep connection had diminished to almost nothing. He felt a keen sense of shame, of having failed to live up to the ideals he cherished, of acting with duplicity, and his shoulders bent under the heaviness of spiritual despair. Not even Peter's surprise of a litter of spotted puppies stirred more than a wan smile on his lips.

Why did the world seem suddenly pale?

At night, suffocated by the crowds, Jesus walked far from camp and climbed a hill. He lay on his back and watched the stars float across the sky. He recalled Solomon teaching him to divine shapes in the spaces between the lights. But, to his disappointment, he could discern nothing.

CHAPTER 42

Somewhere within ancient Palestine—33 A.D.

Judas staked out in the hills to get his first good look at the healer. He was shocked to learn that in his absence the number of followers had significantly increased. But there were other things that concerned him. Having moved in closer, he had noted several women working side by side with the healer. Mixing herbs and oils. This detail pricked his conscience.

Could it be?

He held himself in check. Perhaps his mind was playing tricks. He realized then that he needed to get closer. To see the healer's face and hear his teachings. Careful to keep himself concealed, he dropped down to the river. With caution, he mingled among the crowd, pushing through joyful people. He edged his way up to where the teacher sat, along with two women. He listened as the healer described the sustaining act of returning to the earth what one takes from her. Judas felt his ears burning at the familiar teachings. And the familiar voice.

Then the healer lifted his emerald eyes.

Judas gasped in recognition and fled. He ran for miles before crumpling beneath a boulder. His body shuddered with the effort of reluctant tears. His goatskin pouch dropped from his back. He could not bear to look inside it.

Out of nowhere the horrifying memory of his mother and sister's mutilation rushed before his eyes. Their slit throats. Twisted arms and legs. Silken robes drenched with blood. He choked with the gaping despair of a child made motherless.

Since the hour that he and his father had faced their loss, Judas had believed that the wounds in his soul could never be healed. Nothing in his life, he had once believed, would ever prove powerful enough to redeem him—until the gaze of her emerald eyes.

And now, years later, her gaze had found him again. He shook his head in disbelief.

How was it possible?

As he clung to the rock for support, the only thing Judas knew for certain was that he would not return to Pilate. And he prayed from his soul that the little he had told the Roman leader would cause no harm.

CHAPTER 43

Somewhere within ancient Palestine—33 A.D.

Jesus and Ruth sat on the ground eating. She had been patient while her friend struggled with the churnings in his soul. And she had other distractions. She had noticed the strange figure who followed them on a donkey drawing closer. She feared for the safety of their supporters, but most especially for Jesus.

"He is still there," she whispered, indicating the hooded figure who had dismounted and climbed high into an olive tree to watch them.

Jesus observed the man in his peripheral vision. He knew he should honor Ruth's concern but continued to stew in his apathy.

"He makes me uneasy," Ruth added.

Jesus relented. He stood with difficulty. "I will be back," he said, masking his frustration. He balanced carefully on his good leg.

"I do not think it wise for you to approach him alone," Ruth said, eyeing the shadowy figure with suspicion.

Jesus grimaced. "I need to walk," he said abruptly and left without waiting for her reply.

Ruth shook her head. "I knew you would say that," she whispered to herself.

Jesus ambled in a wide arc around the olive tree, keeping his eyes averted from its branches. He wandered from one spot to the next, picking up plants and stones, feigning interest. But in his peripheral view, he watched the man's donkey, tethered to the roots of the tree, as it grazed the dust. He also watched the man's lurking eyes glaring down between the leaves. He continued to walk, his limp more evident than ever, until he disappeared behind a bank of tall cypress trees.

When Jesus failed to emerge from the trees, the shadowy figure seemed to become curious and peered out. As time passed, his motions grew restless. Not long after, he shimmied down the tree. When he dropped the last few feet to the ground, a hand shot out and grabbed his tunic. The figure struggled to break free, as the donkey brayed and tried to avoid the skirmish. But Jesus held firm.

When the hooded man relented, Jesus demanded, "Who are you?"

The figure said nothing.

"Who are you and why do you follow me?"

The figure maintained his defiant silence.

When the man would not answer, Jesus reached for his hood and threw it back. To his astonishment, a woman stared up at him. He froze, unable to drop his gaze. It was her eyes. They shone like silver disks. Reflecting light like mirrors from within the exotic curves of her face. He released his hold and stepped back, trying to free himself of her spell. "Who are you?" he asked again. But his voice was no longer steady.

She lowered her gaze. "Do you not recognize me?" she asked in a gauzy voice.

Jesus shook his head.

"We met years ago," she said. "In Jerusalem."

Jesus blinked in disbelief.

It was she*! The one whose remembrance had sustained his lonely journey into The Narrows.*

Before he could stop it, the memory rushed upon him like a charging animal. In vivid colors, he recalled the night that he and Peter had found her, a child then, hiding behind a well. He remembered how bravely she had fought to defend the woman in plum-colored robes and then rose again to protect her mother. But more than his admiration of her courage, Jesus remembered the girl's serene gaze and the deep calm that had overtaken him in her presence. Thinking back, he then recalled her final words.

Remember me.

The woman gazed upward, into his eyes. "You remember."

Jesus nodded as if in a dream.

"I have never forgotten you," she whispered.

Jesus knew, as their surroundings dissolved, that he had never forgotten her either. *Mary*, her mother had called her. His eyes traveled from the birthmark below her right eye, to her threadbare tunic, and settled on her bare feet. Her lot had not improved since that night.

He softened his mind and let it intuit her. He was shocked at how easily he could meld his thoughts with hers. How easily she drew him into soulful connection. He gazed upon her splendid face and sensed that she was reading his thoughts with equal ease. He realized that within her gaze, within her long-cherished memory—of the night he courageously stood up in defense of her—he felt naked. And free of disguise. In her gaze, he remembered his name and all he believed. The past and present circled. The *he* met the *she*. And his mother's voice rose again in song.

Mesmerized, he held Communion within the intricate petals of her eyes. She warmed beneath his gaze, as beneath the sun.

She smiled.

After a brief hesitation, he smiled back.

CHAPTER 44

Somewhere within ancient Palestine—33 A.D.

As the afternoon sun blazed down, Mary Magdalene led her donkey northward. Jesus rode on the animal's back. His body swayed with a watery motion. Ruth had been truly grateful for the conveyance, as she feared his leg was quickly becoming too weak to carry him.

Every few minutes, Mary turned to glance up at Jesus. Having expressed her desire to stay and support their efforts, she had become an indispensable part of the group. Without any urging, she had begun to help Tabitha gather plants and herbs. She cooked meals, repaired children's tunics, and collected firewood. She made refreshing teas to cool people's throats during the heat of the day. At other times, she sat on the pallets of the ill or incapacitated. Her mere presence seemed to alleviate their pain and anguish. As Jesus wove among the people, he noticed that clouds of contentment rose from wherever she stood. And her devotion reignited his purpose.

Peter sulked at the back of the group. He had grown silent and difficult since Mary's arrival. From a distance, he scowled at the budding intimacy between Jesus and his silver-eyed admirer. He winced at how the woman blushed and toyed with his friend's affections. How she curled around his words and pressed her fingers, ever so gently, on his sleeve. He cringed at the sound of his friend's ready laughter. He had never heard him so merry. Not even when they had been shepherds!

Peter had been further infuriated when Jesus chose Mary to lead the donkey instead of *him*. He had wanted to protest, but remained silent.

How could he compete with a woman's lascivious wiles? Her empty smiles and knowing glances? Truly, she was the work of the devil!

As time wore on, Peter's love for Jesus began to brown around the edges. And he started to hate his need. His insatiable hunger for his friend's affection.

You see? This is proof! the old voices taunted. *You are weak and pathetic!*

When Peter felt Ruth's eyes upon him, he lowered his raging gaze into the folds of his tunic. And there it smoldered.

CHAPTER 45

Somewhere within ancient Palestine—33 A.D.

Judas slipped his dagger free of its sheath. He drew it repeatedly over a stone to sharpen the blade. The metal rung each time it hit the air. He thought back to the night Solomon had approached him. "What do you think of our newest shepherd?" he had asked, his gray eyes twinkling.

At first Judas did not understand why Solomon was asking. And, truly, he did not care.

Why should he be interested in a scruffy boy rejected by his father?

But then, days later, he had spotted the young shepherd squatting in the bushes some distance from camp. And he understood.

As the months wore on, Judas's admiration grew for the plucky girl who could so easily deceive a band of shepherds. In truth, she reminded him of his youngest sister. Delilah. It had been she that he and his cousin, Solomon, had been preparing to escort into The Narrows. And she who had been chosen to become an apprentice to the Sisters of The Way.

For many years the cousins, as Guardians, had faithfully conveyed young women, chosen by Solomon's mother, to the caves within The Narrows. Despite the considerable risk, all had arrived safely. Until Delilah.

Their plans had been carefully laid. And the Sisters were waiting. But unbeknownst to them, his mother Maya's beliefs and her association with The Way had been discovered. On the night before their departure, when Judas and his father had gone to pay their respects to Zahra, the murderers struck.

Since that day, Judas had woken every morning with the tang of blood in his mouth and mountainous thoughts of revenge. Of drawing knife across throat. Of ridding the earth of enemies of the Mother and false prophets who spread their misbeliefs while his sister's voice had been silenced forever.

Solomon had urged him to remember the better part of himself. And to turn the other cheek.

But Judas could not heed such wisdom.

He had thought himself irredeemable and doomed to a life of hateful thoughts. Until she arrived—the brave young shepherdess with green eyes. Whose ways had reminded him so much of his beloved childhood friend Shereen. And he had been buoyed by the idea that the shepherdess might save him. That her grace could rejoin the broken pieces of his soul.

Judas then remembered the night Solomon had revealed the young shepherd's identity: she was the only child of Shereen's sister, Yadira. And that she had been chosen by Zahra.

Solomon had then reminded Judas of his commitment as a Guardian, and asked that he help protect the shepherd until arrangements could be made for the crossing.

And in his heart, Judas had intended to fulfill his promise!

But when they had arrived in Jerusalem, his unbearable lust for the blood of those who spoke violently against women and the Mother had overtaken him. And he had left the shepherdess alone, to fend for herself.

His head dropped in shame. How far he had fallen since then. Solomon would be ashamed. As would all those he had loved. His life was no longer guided by The Way, but ruled by the god of vengeance. He had traded the grace of his spirit for the pursuit of an elusive justice. Now he was no better than the assassins who had killed his family.

Delilah.

Her neck slit from ear to ear. A bloody smile strung like a necklace across her throat.

Judas wiped the tears from his eyes and glanced back in the direction of the green-eyed healer.

This time, he vowed to the Mother, he would not fail.

CHAPTER 46

Somewhere within ancient Palestine—33 A.D.

Jesus held the elderly woman's hands while Ruth wrapped a poultice around her ankle. A dog had bitten her and the wound become infected. Mary held a bowl of warm water while Tabitha tore strips of bandaging. The woman's grandchildren nestled at her feet. They threw furtive smiles at the green-eyed man who was attending to their elder. When he winked at them, they squealed and tucked behind her. The women shared a laugh over the antics. And Mary held Jesus within her silver gaze.

A hand whipped back the camel hide door and a man stuck his head inside. The circle of women looked up. From the doorway, Peter glared at them, having grown more suspicious of their activities. He searched from one face to the next as if trying to catch them in some wicked act. The old woman and her grandchildren smiled back.

Ruth's eyes turned to Jesus. The expression on Jesus's face showed that Peter's self-centered behavior had become draining.

Peter looked to Jesus. "Look what I found!" he said and lifted a leather sling, much like the ones they had used when they were shepherds. "Come with me and let us see who is the better shot!" he challenged.

"Can it wait?" Jesus asked his friend. He glanced down at the elderly woman. "I must finish wrapping her wound."

Peter frowned. He let the sling drop to the ground. "It can wait forever, if you like," he said and turned on his heels.

Jesus watched Peter leave and knew that his feelings were hurt. This realization troubled him. After all, Peter had been his first, and only, childhood friend. And it had been Peter's mentoring that had enabled him to survive as a shepherd in the desert.

But Jesus had also come to see that he and his friend walked the world in vastly different ways, and that Peter desired something Jesus could not give. Still, the bindings of loyalty tugged on his heart. As did the knowledge that it was *his* untruth that had created the trouble between them.

It terrified Jesus to think of the danger should anyone learn of his secret.

But how else could he mend the tear in the fabric that bound him and Peter? How else but through a display of absolute trust?

But would Peter keep his secret safe?

He fought against his fear. A tangle of words clawed at his throat. He tasted the confession on his tongue.

Peter, there is something I must tell you . . .

Before Ruth could stop him, Jesus bolted outside to find his friend. But Peter was nowhere to be found.

As they drew closer to Nazareth, Jesus felt his spirits rising. Even though he knew he would not be welcomed in the village, the thought of being near his childhood home, and his mother's final resting place, urged him on.

As Mary led Jesus on the donkey, crowds ran out to greet them, lining both sides of the path. Smiling faces encircled them and bouquets of hands stretched out to touch Jesus or offer him gifts. Jesus and his sisters kindly refused.

"Your spirit is generous. But, truly, we have more than we need," Ruth told them. "When a plant is well watered, do you pour more on its head?" she asked.

The crowd laughed.

"Of course not!" Jesus said, lifting his voice above the laughter. "Or you ruin the plant. Therefore, I tell you, share your gratitude with those among you who have little. In this way, the basket of gifts never runs empty and we all share in the gain."

Following Peter's disappearance, discord among the group had faded and the usual lightness returned.

Keeping himself covered, the moon-faced magician tumbled inside the swooning crowd. He had become irritated by the steep drop in his revenues since the handsome healer's arrival, and he wanted to discover the secret of his success. He watched in awe as the scene unfolded around Jesus. It was not the healer's words that impressed him, nor his exotic looks, but rather the adoration of the onlookers. Even the magician himself, at the height of his powers, had never drawn such uninhibited trust from so many. His pulse quickened and he licked his lips. He knew well the riches that could be harvested from such trust.

Wanting to avoid detection, he lowered his face and pushed through the crowd. His path led him close to Jesus. The handsome man's legs dangled on either side of the donkey as he rode, parting his tunic. Out of the corner of his eye, the magician spotted something dark that had smeared between the donkey's back and the rider's thigh. Pushing against the toss of the crowd, he looked again to make sure he had not been seeing things. This time he was certain.

It was fresh blood.

CHAPTER 47

The city of Jerusalem—33 A.D.

The guests dining with Pilate heard the pounding of the soldier's feet long before he arrived. The soldier came to a stop before the lavish feast. "Sir!" he erupted, slapping his hand against his armored chest. "There is unrest outside the Temple's west gate."

Pilate lifted his eyes from his roast hen. He spoke calmly so as not to alarm his guests, one of whom held an amorous interest. "Are there not soldiers enough to quell the incursion?"

The soldier shook his head. "Though we are well armed, we are vastly outnumbered."

Pilate glanced across the table at Caiaphas and nodded evenly. He then tore the hen's leg from its roasted body with a wet thunk. "Tell the commander at the north gate to dispatch a third of his troops." When it was clear Pilate had issued his command in full, the soldier bowed and fled down the hall.

Pilate turned the guinea hen's leg in his greasy fingers. As Passover approached, rebellions and protests were growing in number and intensity. The rabble were angered over a variety of issues: corruption among Temple priests, unfair taxes, an emphasis on Law over spirit, the rise of one God over ancient and revered deities, and on and on went the complaints. Charged with the task of bringing stability to the Empire in Palestine, he had spent months seeking a strategy that would quell the uprisings and unite the disparate factions. But so far, he had found no way to pacify the citizens.

Pilate turned his gaze toward the woman whom one day he wished to wed. He smiled at her with a cool confidence that belied the worry itching his belly. “Soon I will make an example out of one of these unfortunate rebels,” he threatened, hoping to impress her.

CHAPTER 48

Somewhere within ancient Palestine—33 A.D.

Dawn washed slowly over the sky, soaking the horizon with the colors of ripe fruit.

Nazareth waited two days away. Ruth had woken early, stirred by anxious feelings she could not identify. She thought her anxiety strange since she felt assured that they had left the range of Temple authority. But something was amiss. A raven circled overhead. She watched the bird carve its wings into the wind. She had been dreaming frequently of birds, though she did not know why. She watched the raven level its rippling wings and cut a straight path toward the horizon. The bird vanished quickly. She imagined its sight already feasting on the contours of a distant land. Ruth reflected on the vastness of the world.

Who knew the extent of it? Or where the rivers found their end?

She closed her eyes. How humble seemed their efforts to preserve The Way in the face of such limitless life. Yet she had been pleased with their progress. Since leaving the caves, and because of Jesus's freedom in the world, the gifts of The Way had been instilled in thousands of people. And the sharing continued every day.

But how many would remember? And if she and her companions were suddenly gone, who would preserve the wisdom and mission of the Sisters? Would men and women neglect the Mother and the connection between all things? Would all be forgotten and the foremothers' wisdom pass into oblivion?

Spurred on by her restlessness and a sense that they were running out of time, Ruth returned to the others. She asked Jesus, Tabitha, and Mary to waken their supporters and gather them together.

"The time has come," she told them, "for Jesus to share the final practice of The Way."

The circle swelled like the sun, its edge ringed by hundreds of seated people linked together by holding hands. From the center of the circle rose a sound. It began near Jesus and Ruth as a low hum and slowly escalated, like the rumble of an oncoming sandstorm. Voices joined. Within minutes the tone magnified with ominous power, more felt than heard.

Children opened their eyes in wonder. And then the adults. To their surprise, the world around them burst with bouquets of brilliant color. The steady hum drew everything into alignment, connecting them like waves in a single ocean. A few were frightened by the force passing through them. Others were elated. No one had ever experienced anything like it.

Breaking from the collective intent, Mary stole a furtive glance at Jesus. Her vision swept beyond the beauty of his face and dove deeper. She did not know with what sense she was perceiving him.

Was she seeing him through her fingertips? Tasting him with her eyes?

She could not tell. She could only feel the melting of her bones as a surge of heat tunneled through her body.

Ruth, who was seated next to Mary, felt the shudder run right through her.

CHAPTER 49

Somewhere within ancient Palestine—33 A.D.

Peter hurled the oars into his boat. He left his tangled net on the shore. He had no intention of fishing. He only wanted to row as far as he could until exhaustion distracted him from the anger scraping at his insides.

"You are not fishing today?" a voice asked from the shore.

Peter started. It was the moon-faced magician. He had an unsettling way of showing up and disappearing without warning. "No," Peter muttered.

The magician nodded. He noted the young man's sallow complexion. "I thought you were hungry. And might join me in a meal." He lifted a fresh loaf of bread, a sack of goat's cheese, and a jug of wine.

Peter's stomach rumbled. He did not particularly care for the magician's company, but he *was* hungry. The magician shrugged. "Perhaps another time," he said and turned to go.

Peter stepped out of the boat. "No," he said. "I would have a meal."

The men found a shady spot under a rock outcropping. Below them, date palms bristled in the breeze. The magician introduced himself as Saul, and spoke of trivial things while his companion ate ravenously. Whenever Peter's cup ran dry, Saul filled it with wine.

Saul peppered his new guest with questions until he lured him into speaking of his days as a shepherd and his hatred of fishing. As one hour stretched into the next, Peter's words began to slur. Saul's eyes glimmered, noting the wine's desired effect. When his guest reclined and laid a hand on his stretched belly, Saul hatched his plan.

"Why have you left your friend Jesus and his sisters?"

Peter grimaced. He lifted the wine jug and poured for himself. "He does not need me anymore, it seems."

Saul nodded. "Has enough whores to do his bidding, does he?"

"I do no man's bidding!" Peter shouted.

Saul lifted a hand. "You are right, you are right. Forgive me," he confessed. "It was a *woman's* bidding you did."

Peter bit his tongue. "What did you say?" he slurred.

"Oh come now," Saul said. "You do not have to hide it from me. I am a magician, after all. I know a ruse when I see one."

Peter stared in a daze. His chest tightened and he began to wheeze.

The magician's eyebrows arched in shock. "You mean? Are you saying that you truly did not know?" He shook his head. "I thought certainly *you*, the closest confidant, would know."

"Know *what*?" Peter gasped, frustrated by the circular talk and the spinning of his head.

Saul held a shrug. "I am truly sorry to be the one to tell you, my friend. But it seems you have been deceived by a wicked, and very clever, female. For I swear to you, on my father's grave, that Jesus of Nazareth is a *woman*."

Peter said nothing. His entire body began to shake. His fingers clutched at his neck as he fought to draw air through the narrowing straw of his throat.

His mind then leapt to a time when he had punched Jesus in the chest—and thought he felt a softness there.

Remembering this, he dropped to the ground, writhing and wheezing like a desperate animal.

How could he have been so deceived?

Saul watched the poison take its effect. After some time, he lifted Peter from the dust and leaned him against a rock. He waited patiently until Peter could breathe again. Finally, Peter stumbled to his feet.

"Where are you going?" Saul asked.

"To my boat," Peter answered, weaving his way toward the water.

Saul grinned. He caught up to his new friend and swung an arm around his shoulders.

"Come now, Peter, did you not say you dislike spilling the filthy guts of fish?" Saul stopped him in his tracks. "If you will hear me out, I have a much better use for a handsome man of such obvious talents."

Peter looked up at the magician with fuzzy eyes. The man's words oozed like salve into his gaping wound.

Saul winked at him with enthusiasm. "Come, Peter," he said. "Tell me all you know of this charlatan. And I will make you a fisher of *men*."

CHAPTER 50

Somewhere within ancient Palestine—33 A.D.

The night was hushed. Families slept in circles around outlying fires.

Like shadows, a strange band of men descended on the camp and wove silently through the fires, inspecting the faces of those who slept. A young girl woke when one of the men hovered over her. She looked up at his familiar face. "Jesus?" she asked with a sleepy smile.

The flames below cast orange angles across the man's expression. His green eyes burned with rage. "Yes. It is I," Peter slurred.

The girl's eyes widened with fear.

Mary knelt by an outlying fire. In the flickering light, she tended to the blistered arm of a girl whose brother had splashed her with boiling oil for disobeying him. Looking up from her work, she saw the silhouette of a lone figure walking up a distant hillside.

When he stood atop the hill and gazed into the heavens, she knew who he was.

Jesus could not sleep. A restlessness gripped his heart. Having traveled to within a few miles of Nazareth, he felt his mother's presence all around him.

Ruth and Tabitha were already asleep when he stood and wandered into the night. He climbed to a hilltop and sat. From there, he gazed into the dome of stars. Lowering his eyes to the horizon, he faced toward Nazareth. Through the dark, he could not see the village. But he sensed the great old sycamore, waiting. He imagined her strong arms, like his mother's, bending low to lift him.

Would she recognize him? Would she be able to see through his disguise? Would anyone?

His heart ached at the thought.

Ruth woke with a start. The fire had gone out. Her body shook in the chill. She looked over and saw that Jesus was gone. She drew a deep breath and knelt to rebuild the fire.

"Greetings of the night," Mary said. She lowered herself on the hilltop next to Jesus. Even in the dim light, her eyes glittered. Even in the darkness, she blushed.

Jesus swallowed hard and made room for her.

"Can you not sleep?" she asked.

He shook his head.

She turned toward the invisible horizon. Without looking, she laid her hand on his.

His heart pounded against his ribs. He tried to speak but could not. He tried to intuit her, but could not steady himself.

Her fingers pushed gently between his.

Jesus gasped. He felt torn by joy and grief. For a moment, he considered telling her about his memories. About how they had sustained him. And healed his heart of loneliness. Then his mind shuddered with thoughts of how she would recoil from the truth.

Would he ever be truly loved?

"I remember the first night I saw you," she said.

Jesus held his breath.

"I remember how you looked right into me. Like you saw me. The *all* of me, and found it good." She smiled into the dark. "For that moment, and for the sacrifice of your life that you have made, I do now and will forever love you."

Jesus trembled with despair.

How she would hate him!

He stared between the stars and became infinity. "Mary," he whispered, his voice shaking. "There is something I . . . I am not . . . who you think."

She pressed her hand into his.

"I know who you are," she said quietly. Her tone left no room for doubt.

Jesus stared down in shock and disbelief.

Could she really know the truth—and still find him good?

He lightened at the thought. After a moment, he felt his whole body loosen and lift, ever so slightly, from the ground.

Mary turned slowly and gazed up. Their eyes met in a blaze that sustained itself without end.

Held within this light, neither of them heard the men advance from behind.

CHAPTER 51

Somewhere within ancient Palestine—33 A.D.

Mary ran and ran with a scream caught in her throat.

There had been five of them. Or more. She had not been able to see their faces.

The men had grabbed them from behind and dragged them apart.

As they struggled against their captors, another man had approached, climbing up to the hill's crest.

"Well, well, what do we have here?" he taunted.

Mary and Jesus kicked and thrashed, but neither could break free.

The man wagged his great moon face and sidled over to Jesus. He laid a hand on his shoulder. "Your charade has been impressive, my friend. You even had *me* fooled for a time." He sighed. "But, unfortunately, your days of living as a man must come to an end."

Mary shuddered at his words.

Jesus said nothing but continued to fight against his assailants.

Saul smiled and shook his head. "Do not worry, friend. I will not let your good deeds, and the ardent faith of your followers, go to waste. Oh no. I have a very good use for all you have created."

He chuckled to himself. His eyes then traveled to Mary. The men holding her tightened their grip. Without a word, Saul walked to where she stood. He ran a fingertip slowly down her cheek. She flinched at his touch. He grinned.

Jesus gasped. "Do what you want to me. But let her go!" he cried. "She is innocent and knows nothing."

Saul's eyes darkened. "Silence!" he roared. "I have had enough of you and your false piety!" He turned to his men. "Do as you wish with this freak. Make the body disappear. Then bring the woman to me."

When Saul sauntered down the hill, the men began to cackle.

Those holding Mary released her and gathered with the others. Together, they circled their prey. In a flash, one of them lunged forward and grabbed Jesus by his tunic. They tore at the fabric until Anna stood naked and shivering before them.

Seeing her exposed, the others growled with delight. Hurling epithets, they jabbed knives into her buttocks. They spat on her face. Her breasts.

"If you are truly a great healer, then heal yourself of *this*!" one man shouted as he slashed a blade across her belly.

"Why does your Great Mother not come to save you now?" another taunted then kicked Anna's legs out from under her.

Terrified, Mary screamed and rushed in, grappling to pull them off. "No! Leave her alone! She has done nothing to harm you!" she cried, but the men battered her back.

One of the assailants lifted Anna's tunic from the ground. "And what shall we do with this?" he asked. "Should we gamble for it? The robe of a great healer must be worth something, eh?" he chided. One of his cohorts snatched away the tunic and threw it into the air. Laughing, the others stabbed at it with blades until it was ripped to shreds.

While the men were distracted, Anna sought out Mary. When their eyes locked, she struggled to her feet and lunged forward. Straining, she reached for Mary's hand and pressed a palm into hers.

Enraged by the women's defiance, the men rushed forward and yanked them apart. One knocked Mary to the ground. In a flash, she scrambled back onto her feet and began searching for a stone to throw, only to discover that she was clutching Anna's medallion in her hand.

"Leave me! Save yourself!" Anna cried out as the men closed around her.

Mary lunged again, unwilling to surrender. One of the men rammed a fist into her belly. Fighting for breath, she tried to call for help but could only gasp. Frantic, she whirled and stumbled down the hill, praying that she could find Ruth and the others in time. But when she bolted through a small cluster of trees close to their camp, a man dashed from the shadows and grabbed her. She screamed and fought her captor like a demon.

A calloused hand covered her mouth and held firm. The man knew well how to restrain animals that did not wish to be caught. "Quiet," he hissed. "I am a friend."

Mary kicked his shins and scratched at his eyes.

"I tried," he said. "I tried to stop them! Please listen to me—"

Mary continued to fight until the man released his hold. When she bolted from his arms, he fell to his knees. He was bleeding from gashes on his face and chest. He began to weep.

Mary turned back and stared in disbelief. She wanted to run, but something stopped her.

"Please believe me," he cried. "I tried to save her—" His voice cracked with sorrow. "But I could not . . . there were . . . too many . . ."

Mary watched as the man's face split into shards of grief. "Who are you?" she asked him.

Judas wiped the tears from his eyes. "There is little time," he whispered, weakened from loss of blood. "In the name of the Mother, take me to Ruth."

When Jesus's followers awoke the next day, they found him gone. And his two sisters missing. No one had seen them depart. Volunteers banded into groups to search the area, but none uncovered anything to explain where their friends had gone.

Two days later, a local villager arrived with a rumor. Jesus had reappeared, he told them. He had been seen riding a donkey on the road to Jerusalem. And was dazzling his followers with miracles—restoring sight, casting out demons, making the crippled walk.

Confused as to why Jesus would have abandoned them, his supporters quickly gathered their belongings and set out to find him.

As Peter made his way to Jerusalem, word of his astonishing miracles spread to outlying villages, attracting the despairing and less fortunate in droves. Hungry for hope and desperate to believe in something more powerful than themselves, the ragged villagers soon swarmed around the handsome healer of whom they had heard.

"Behold Jesus! The Son of God!" Saul shouted to the multitudes as he led Peter's donkey forward.

The crowd cheered and raised their arms toward the sky.

Peter's eyes drifted across the swelling ocean of people. He grew drunk on their adoring gazes and bitterly regretted that his father was not alive to see.

By the time Peter arrived in Bethany, a small group of Jesus's heartier supporters had caught up to him. Uncertain as to what was happening, they lingered at the back of the crowd. From there, they stared in confusion at the strange scene—Jesus, astride his donkey, was donning a richly dyed indigo robe, and being led by a grinning, moon-faced man, while a disorderly, almost frantic mob clamored about him.

Stranger still, his beloved sisters were nowhere to be seen. Had he abandoned them, too?

As the crowd spilled into the village, a young woman rushed out of a crooked dwelling. Pushing her way through the throng of people, she threw herself in front of the healer's donkey.

"Please, please, great Master!" she wailed. "My brother has died, yet he is all I have. You must save him! Please! You must!"

The original followers standing at the back of the crowd remembered how Jesus had responded to the child with the dead sparrow. Holding still, they waited to hear him speak again of how death was an intrinsic part of life, and not to be thwarted, or "cured."

Lifting himself tall on his mount, Peter stared down at the young woman and asked, "Tell me, daughter, how long has your brother been dead?"

Smearing tears from her cheeks, the young woman answered, "He has been dead four days."

Those in the crowd dropped their heads. There was no hope. Her brother's body would already be decomposing.

While the onlookers whispered among themselves, Peter and Saul exchanged a look. Peter then took a long, deep breath. "Daughter, do not weep!" he called aloud so that all could hear. "Your brother is not dead, but sleeping. Take me to him, so that I may show you!"

An expression of shock and joy spread across the young woman's face, and without another word, she dashed back toward her village. The crowd let out an exuberant cheer and rushed to follow the moon-faced man as he hurried Peter's donkey after the woman.

Those in the back of the crowd remained behind, trading looks of astonishment. Never before had their healer suggested that death might be overcome. In truth, this message was anathema to anything he had ever told them. Baffled, they began to complain aloud.

"That is not what he teaches. That is not what he believes. Something is wrong here!" one cried.

Another, raising his hand against the sun's glare, said, "Is that truly Jesus? Could that not be his brother, Peter?"

Within seconds, two of Saul's minions approached the disgruntled supporters.

"You seem to have questions," one of them said. "Perhaps we can help. Come with us and share a meal."

Visibly upset and weary from their travels, the supporters reluctantly acquiesced and went with the men. They were not heard from again. Sometime later, Saul's men divided the followers' clothing and distributed it among the poor.

Unaware of any trouble, the young woman whose brother was dead led Peter to the mouth of a small cave. Several mourners were gathered there, weeping. The woman pushed through them and fell atop the rock rolled in front of the cave's entrance.

"Lazarus! Oh Lazarus, my brother! Please return to me!" she wailed.

Peter dismounted and strode to where she stood. He motioned for the mourners and the crowd to step back. He then said, "I am the Resurrection, and the Life: he that believeth in me, though he were dead, shall live again and never die."

The woman gaped through tears and the crowd mumbled.

"I need strong men to roll back this stone," Peter commanded. Five men leapt up and bent to the task.

As the stone began to move, the crowd drew back. Everyone pressed a palm to their face in anticipation of the stench.

When the stone was rolled back, Peter billowed his robe and drew a shallow breath, for indeed the acrid smell of death surrounded them. Turning again to the young woman, he called out, "Daughter! Have no fear! Do you believe that I am who I say I am? Do you believe in the Son of God and in the powers I command?"

The woman fell to Peter's knees, weeping. "Yes! I do! I believe you are the Chosen One! The Most Powerful! The Son of God!" she cried.

With that, Peter turned to the cave's ragged mouth and, spreading his arms wide, called out, "Lazarus! Because of your sister's belief, you have been saved. I command thee now to *come forth*!"

The crowd boiled with anticipation. All eyes fixed on the cave's entrance, everyone expecting a miracle.

A minute went by and nothing happened. Another passed. Still nothing.

Peter was about to step forward when Saul grabbed his arm and held him back. Just as he did, a shadow flickered along the cave's wall. The crowd let out a collective gasp and tumbled backward. They watched, openmouthed, as a figure wrapped in burial shrouds moved out of the darkness.

Peter, too, appeared shocked by the figure's sudden appearance. Seeing his hesitation, Saul gouged Peter's side with an elbow. Gathering himself, Peter returned to the head of the crowd and called out, "Daughter! Do you swear before us all and before the Almighty Lord that this man is your brother?"

The young woman squinted into the cave. She took a step toward the figure. Her eyes filled with tears. "Yes! Yes, I swear!" she blurted, falling to her knees.

"Behold, a miracle! A *miracle* from God!" Saul shouted. He then signaled to the band of boys lingering nearby. Fanning into the crowd, they lifted pouches and collected coins from those who had witnessed the great act.

Peter turned again to the crowd, "Know now all of you that I am the Light and the King of Kings. He who believes in me shall find eternal reward in heaven and on earth!"

Worked into a frenzy, and seeking a miracle of their own, those in need pressed up against Peter. Shouting in anger, Saul and his minions held them back. While the people were distracted, two men threw a cloak over the risen figure and spirited him away.

"Did you not hear our Master's words?!" Saul cried with indignation. "How dare you crowd so close when he is tired from his great works? Go back to where you came from and tell every soul what you have seen!"

When the crowd would not disperse, Saul and Peter quickly disappeared into the young woman's dwelling.

While they waited inside for the crowd to dissipate, the young woman brought her guests a tray of meager offerings—crusts of bread and shriveled olives. Ignoring the food, Saul handed her a small leather pouch.

"As agreed," he said.

The young woman nodded. "I would have preferred the miracle," she scoffed. Keeping her eyes fixed on Saul, she hurled the pouch to her brothers, for she had more than one, and said, "I hope it is enough to pay for the shame we have brought our brother's memory." Saying this, she returned to the fire.

While the guests sipped tea, the young woman's remaining brothers huddled in a corner of the dwelling. While one removed strips of burial wrapping from his arms, the others overturned the pouch. They gasped in amazement at the gold coins that fell clinking to the floor. The amount, they said, was more than their brother Lazarus had been worth while living!

The next day, the great lumbering walls of Jerusalem came into view as Peter and his followers moved onward. Saul lifted a hand against the sun and gazed across the city. His mouth watered at the riches he knew awaited them.

Rumors of the healer's deeds had spread like wildfire across dry land. Many were wooed by word of Jesus's miracles and his promises of salvation. Soon Jerusalem's hapless pilgrims rushed out of the walls to meet him. The forlorn and weary carpeted his path with coins and palm fronds and even the cloaks off their backs.

Peter gazed down with delight at the show of adoration.

As Saul led the green-eyed Peter toward the city, the crowd boiled in ecstasy, shouting, "Blessed is he who comes in the name of the Father!" and "Blessed is the Kingdom of the Lord!"

By this time, more of Jesus's original supporters had caught up to the crowd. They, too, were shocked by what they saw and heard. But now, finding *themselves* in the position of being far outnumbered, they were too frightened to speak out.

One elder woman among them, however, who had known Orpah when she was a child, grew angry and told the others she could not abide by the people's praising solely of the Father. Her companions tried to hold her back, but she threw them off and charged forward. When she got close to the front, she shouted up to Jesus, "Friend! Have you lost your way? Do you not say still, 'Blessed is the mother who gave you birth and nursed you'?"

Upon hearing her words, Peter grew enraged. Facing the old woman head-on, he viciously retorted, "Blessed *rather* are those who hear the word of God the Father and *obey* it!"

The crowd roared its assent and the old woman cowered. Stunned into silence, and fearing for her life, she turned and fled.

Judas stood before Pilate. Dried blood clotted his clothes.

"I thought I told you not to return until after Passover," Pilate growled, pressing his seal into a pool of hot wax. Already he felt as if security within the city was spinning out of his control.

"He is here," Judas said.

"Who is here?" Pilate asked, then blew on the wax to cool it.

"The healer. The one called Jesus."

"Here in Jerusalem?"

"Yes. He now claims to be the Son of God and means to incite a revolt. The number of his followers has grown enormously. And their efforts are well conceived."

Pilate's face shattered.

A revolt? In the city?

At first blush, the thought rattled him. But then he began to see the opportunity. He leveled a conspiratorial look at the battered assassin. "But you will help me bring him to justice?"

Judas nodded.

Pilate reached to his waist and removed a pouch full of coins. He slung it toward Judas. "Half now. Half when he is captured."

Judas took the coins and bowed.

"I will command all the men you need. Bring him *alive*," Pilate said.

Following their triumphant arrival in the city, Peter, Saul, and their men took shelter in a long tent far from the crowds. Lamps flickered on its dirt floor. Servants carried in trays of food and laid them in front of the men. A woman with glittering skin knelt before Peter rubbing his feet with perfumed oil. In the back of the tent rested several locked coffers. A set of heavy silver keys dangled at Saul's waist.

As the men leaned forward to eat, the former magician stood to address his cadre. "Friends," he began, "it has come to my ears that there are enemies in the land. Enemies who would challenge the righteousness of our one true Messiah."

Peter poured himself another goblet of wine and buried his teeth in a roasted lamb shank. The business of enemies was Saul's, not his.

Saul narrowed his eyes and said, "It is our duty, therefore, to rid the land of those who would question our Master's legitimacy."

The men grumbled in assent, eager to feel blood on their hands.

A hush fell over the tent when a rough-looking man tore down the tent's camel hide door and stepped inside.

Peter stared in disbelief. "Judas!" he blurted, his judgment dimmed by wine. "Can it be you? We thought you had met your end all those years ago in this very city!"

Alarmed, Saul and the others leapt to their feet.

Judas faced the imposter. "Yes, Jesus, it is I," he said, his voice tight with rage. With great speed, he drew Peter into an embrace and planted a kiss on his cheek.

From their positions outside, Pilate's soldiers saw the assassin's signal. Leaping from their hiding places, they swarmed the tent. Swords and armor clanked as Saul's men fought back, one losing an ear to his attacker's blade. Within minutes, the soldiers overpowered the drunken group and took their man, lashing his arms behind his back.

Peter wailed as Saul and his men slashed open the sides of the tent and escaped into the night.

CHAPTER 52

Somewhere within ancient Palestine—33 A.D.

The moonless night cast little light into the manger. A cow lumbered on the floor, chewing its cud, its stomach gurgling. Three guinea hens roosted in baskets of hay.

Outside, Mary and Tabitha stood guard. They had seen Saul's men following them and knew it would not be long before they were discovered.

Deep inside the shelter, in the shadow of a crumbling wall, Ruth guided her quill across the luminescent fabric beneath her. The dark ink soaked her fingertips. Cramps gnawed at her joints. She completed a line and then dipped her quill into the small well of ink. She squinted in the diminishing light, afraid to brighten her lamp for fear of detection. She would have to hurry.

"So that life may come of death," Judas had said when he opened the goatskin pouch on his back and handed Ruth the silk garment once worn by his beloved sister.

As the words fell under Ruth's quill, tears dropped from her eyes. Her mind turned to Anna. She knew that she was dead. That her body had been desecrated. But she knew, too, that her spirit would rise again. That new life and new hope would spring from her story and its retelling. And in this way, she would live forever.

Thinking these things, she poured all she could of The Way, and of Anna's journey, onto the sparkling silk.

Tabitha stepped into the doorway. "Hurry!" she whispered.

Ruth nodded, scratched out a few more words, then daubed her medallion into a pool of ink, pressing the image of the sycamore onto the fabric. She hoped that someday, someone would find her words, either here or in a distant land, and reopen the truth of The Way—and of Sister Anna—so that the sycamore might rise again.

Leaning down, she blew across the ink. When it had nearly dried, she rolled the silk and replaced it inside the pouch. She bowed her head and prayed that safety would accompany their separate journeys.

She then called for Mary.

CHAPTER 53

Somewhere within ancient Palestine—33 A.D.

Within minutes of the arrest, Judas journeyed outside the gates and sought out a band of Jesus's supporters. He told them of Peter and Saul's deception—and of how they had murdered the healer. He then told them to spread the word among the other supporters, and to gather them within the city. Together, he said, they would bring down the man who had dared to impersonate their beloved healer.

"But what of the teaching to show compassion to those who would harm us?" a young supporter asked.

Judas shook his head. "That time is over," he said.

The others, overcome with grief and rage, agreed.

As the rumor of treachery reached beyond Jerusalem, Jesus's original supporters flooded into the walls. Days later, a sea of anger swelled into a hostile mob that rushed Pilate's quarters demanding death for the prisoner who called himself the Son of God.

"But what harm has he done?" Pilate asked, goading the crowd beneath him.

The crowd answered with an angry roar, enraged by the murder of their healer, and the treachery of the one who dared impersonate him.

Then, knowing well the accusations that would drive Pilate to condemn his prisoner, people began to yell out, "He slanders the Lord! He disputes holy Law! He claims to possess the power of a king!"

Standing behind Pilate, the golden-haired priest, Caiaphas, grinned with pleasure, certain he would soon witness the death of the man who had once dared to challenge his authority.

Pilate looked over at Jesus, wrapped in chains, and saw fear flood his eyes. He then glanced over at his betrothed, seated next to him. Her youthful eyebrows lifted in suspense, she seemed duly impressed by Pilate's power over the crowd, and over the life of his prisoner. Wanting to prolong his performance for her benefit, Pilate turned again to the crowd.

"In honor of this holy day I will release to you one prisoner. So you must choose. First, there is the man called Jesus who claims to be the Son of God and who would see priests overthrown. Then there is Barabbas, a proven murderer and the leader of insurrection in our city. Of these two men, whom do you say I should release?"

The crowd roiled below, chanting, "We want Barabbas!"

Pilate teased further. "You wish to set a *murderer* free?" He looked askance at Jesus and saw the color drain from the condemned man's face. All of his supporters, it seemed, had fled.

"Give us Barabbas! Give us Barabbas!" the crowd shouted.

Pilate smiled. He turned toward Jesus. "What, then, should I do with *this* man?" he asked the crowd.

Furious, the people roared, "Crucify him! Crucify him!"

Unable to stand the crowd's rising violence, Pilate's betrothed lifted a kerchief to her face and fled.

Peter struggled against his chains, his eyes wide with terror, as the soldiers prodded him with spears toward his crucifixion. Stripped of his clothes, his skull gouged with a crown of thorns, he frantically searched the crowd through stinging spatters of blood. Nowhere could he find the faces of Saul or the others. To his utter shock, he had been abandoned.

"I am not he! I am not he!" he cried out to his tormentors, stumbling beneath the weight of a wooden cross.

But his denials only brought more lashes from the soldiers and angry cries from the crowd.

The lone olive tree stood tall in a gentle field. A light breeze rustled its narrow leaves.

Judas knelt beneath the tree, weeping. Unable to endure his grief and guilt. Not only had he failed those he loved; he had betrayed the very tenets he had claimed to cherish—and had encouraged others to do the same. Images of violence flooded his mind—the violence he had wrought with his own hands, and that which had befallen his family and his friend. At the recall of such senseless loss, he felt the hope leave him.

Twisting a rope around his palm, he cut a length with his dagger. Stepping to the tree, he threw his blade to the ground. He braced a foot against the trunk and, in one quick motion, lifted himself into the branches. There, balanced along a limb, he made a loop in one end of the rope and threw the other over a branch, securing it with a knot.

He then slipped the loop over his head, looked up into the tree's green canopy, and wished ardently to be rejoined with his family. Thinking this, he leaned out, and let go. The rope snapped taut and the olive tree shook with sudden weight. After a moment, a pouch of coins dropped from the branches, landing with a clink atop the dagger's sickle-shaped handle.

In his final moments, he thought he heard the rush of footsteps.

Plodding along the road and trailing his donkey, Saul wagged his head in disappointment. With Peter captured, all his dreams of power and riches had vanished.

Only a miracle could save the healer from certain death, he thought. Though, truly, he did not care.

Then, without warning, a wondrous new thought struck him like a thunderbolt, dropping him to his knees. He would later describe the experience as a blinding vision of inspiration. For, in that pivotal moment, he recalled something the brothers of Lazarus had said and realized that Jesus might actually be worth more dead than alive.

Saul was a magician, after all!

Who knew better than he how to profit from resurrecting the dead?

With a wicked smile sprouting across his moon-shaped face, he yanked at the donkey's lead rope and sped to find his comrades.

CHAPTER 54

The edge of ancient Palestine—33 A.D.

Ruth and Tabitha arrived at the coast under cover of night. In the morning, Tabitha gasped as the sun rose behind the ocean's vast expanse.

They found Zebediah in his shop. When Ruth lifted her medallion, he whispered, "Welcome, Sisters. They sent word to expect you." Looking over their threadbare robes, he asked, "Have you no other garments? It is cold on the water at night."

When the women shook their heads, Zebediah disappeared into the back of his shop. He returned promptly with two robes of richly dyed silk. He then led them to his ship. "My men will see you safely to the far lands," he told them. "The people there are wise and will protect you. I have given you something to take to them as a gift. I am sure they will make good use of it." He pointed to the stern of the ship where there sat a newly crafted loom. He then helped the women onboard, kissing their hands in farewell.

But then, keeping his hold on Ruth, Zebediah asked, "And what of my son?" His face drew apart with trepidation. "He is well?"

Ruth shook her head. "I do not know his fate," she said. "But, in enabling our escape, Judas acted with great honor."

Zebediah nodded through a weak smile then released her hand.

As the wind caught the sails, the ship drifted into the sea. Ruth stood tall in the bow of the boat, draped in the brilliant silk robe. Remaining silent, she closed her eyes and opened her arms wide as if to embrace the entire world. Looking at her from behind, the sun shimmering along her outstretched arms, the ocean racing to meet her, Tabitha could not help but think that she looked like a great sparkling bird, spreading her wings.

CHAPTER 55

A desert at the edge of ancient Palestine—33 A.D.

Mary's breathing came in desperate gulps. Streaks of sweat snaked down her face, darkening the birthmark beneath her right eye. The mountain's sharp stones had sliced open her leather sandals. Underneath, the soles of her feet were as shredded as the leather. Blood smeared her ankles and soaked into the ground. She scanned the horizon. Her vision was blurred. Her silver eyes blinked against the sting of sweat. She could not yet see the band of men and camels, but she knew they were there. She reached behind to tighten the cord holding the goatskin pouch against her back and prayed that Ruth and Tabitha had made their way to the coast undetected.

She stumbled forward until she found a hidden gash cut into an outcropping. The entry was too small for any man. Mary slipped inside. She crouched as if in a womb, remaining quiet for hours, until the day turned into night. Trapped in darkness, she struggled to bear the loneliness in her heart. Seeking comfort, she drew up Anna's medallion and held it in her palm. She ran her fingertips lightly along its face. Closing her eyes, she thought back to their last hour together. Tears ran in streams down her cheeks.

How was it possible that the woman of infinite green eyes was gone? How could it be that her spirit no longer graced the earth? That her end could have come so soon?

Mary shook her head. It seemed impossible.

Her thoughts then turned to Saul. To his taunts. His threats. His ruthless murder of her friend. She shuddered at the vicious memories.

Before they parted ways, Ruth had told Mary of the magician's attempt to steal Anna's identity and warp her purpose for his own profit. Mary cringed to recall the lies and misconceptions he was propagating. And was no doubt continuing to spread . . .

But what could be done to stop him?

As her thoughts roiled, her anger and despair expanded. Soon the crevice in which she hid started to feel unbearably tight. For hours she suffered in silence until grief and exhaustion drew her into a restless sleep.

When the dawn's light stretched a hand into the crevice, Mary awoke. Remaining still, she listened, alert for any sign of her pursuers. When she felt certain that Saul's men and their camels had moved on, she slipped out into the open. Relieved, she stretched the ache from her limbs and glanced cautiously about. She knew it would be wise to keep moving. But she did not know where to go. Ruth had not given her any specific directions. She had only handed her the goatskin pouch and told her to safeguard it with her life. When Mary had asked what she should do, Ruth had said only, "You will know what to do when you know what you are facing."

But what had she meant?

She knew the manuscript she carried was precious.

But she could not even read it! So how could she protect it?

Her thoughts began to blur as panic rose.

From above, a raven called out. Its raucous cry broke into her chain of worry. Startled, she drew her gaze skyward. His wings sharp against the clouds, the animal circled Mary several times. As he did, his dark eyes bored into hers. Just when she thought he might land nearby, the raven turned and, with a thrust of wing, sped to the west.

Watching him disappear, a thought dropped into Mary's mind. And at that moment, she knew where she must go.

Wrapping a shawl about her face, she hurried toward the road that would follow the raven's path—and take her where Anna had longed to return.

Seeing her approach, the great sycamore seemed to kneel, like an expectant mother.

The ancient tree was just as Mary had imagined, and as majestic as Anna had described. Its roots rippled like serpents through the earth. Its muscular limbs rose to grasp the sky. Seeing the tree, she recalled her friend describing the many hours she had sought refuge there.

On the wind, she heard someone in the village call out. After a moment, a child responded. The sound of voices put Mary back on alert. She knew she could not delay. If the villagers were to see her, a woman traveling alone, they might become suspicious.

With a deep breath, she approached the sycamore's knobby trunk. Seeking a foothold on the lowest branch, she lifted herself along the tree's natural lattice. Soon she found the saddle of branches in which her friend had hidden, high above the ground.

Reclining, Mary gazed out to where the mountains gave way to desert. She marveled at the heat waves shivering above the sand. Within the waves, she spotted a band of shepherds. They moved so slowly that they seemed almost not to be moving at all.

The sun then slipped from behind a cloud and Mary found herself contained within a sphere of illuminated green. The leaves surrounding her glowed with loud, confident color. She felt almost as if she could become a part of the green itself. Suddenly the brilliance began to dive and swirl. She dizzied as the ground disappeared. Alarmed, she reached out and grasped at nearby branches.

Then she felt Anna. Everywhere.

Startled, she spun around, looking for her friend. And though she saw only the tree, she had the sense of her friend being within it. As though her spirit had been poured along the sycamore's roots and had risen to inhabit its heart-shaped leaves, its curving limbs.

The feeling blanketed Mary with a sudden calm. She released her hold on the branches and slowed her breathing. As soon as she had settled, she focused her attention on the light filtering through the leaves. When an errant breeze slipped through the tree, she heard a voice inside her say, "Remember—death is not the end, but the birth of a thousand new beginnings. There is much to be done. And little time for rest. But have no fear. I am with you. Always."

Hearing this, Mary gladdened and her tears dried as if they had never fallen.

She placed a hand on her chest and pressed the medallion along her skin.

From that day forward, she vowed, it would be her duty, and the duty of all her descendants, to guard and protect the truth of her friend Anna—and to help it rise again.

How she would accomplish this, she still did not know, but she now felt certain she would receive the knowledge she needed, just as Ruth had assured her.

Ablaze with inspiration, and cradled by a sense that her friend's spirit still lived, Mary lowered herself quickly to the ground. Turning toward the east, she lifted the shawl about her face, tightened the pouch against her back, and dashed in the direction that called her—and that led her, again, into the desert.

EPILOGUE

An unknown land—33 A.D.

The vessel limped atop the sea. Its giant sails had been torn and shredded, its salt-warped planks marred with gashes. Still, the vessel remained afloat, the tide faithfully carrying it toward shore.

Ruth and Tabitha lay draped along the bottom of the boat, their faces blackened by the sun.

When the boat approached the shallows, its hull dragged across a rock. The grating noise startled Ruth. She mumbled something incoherent in her sleep. A moment later, she began to stir. Disoriented, she forced her eyes to open. When she did, she had the sudden sense of being watched. Lifting herself onto an elbow, she peered over the bow. She was startled to find someone looking back. A young woman.

Ruth squeezed her swollen eyelids against the light, then looked again, amazed by what she had seen.

"Anna?" she asked, her voice barely a whisper. She watched as the young woman lifted a rope from the boat's hull and began to lead the vessel ashore. Her lean arms rippled with strength.

Ruth's jaw dropped in disbelief. "Anna! Oh Anna! It *is* you!" she cried, delirious with wonder. Unable to hold herself upright, she dropped back to the floor.

Lying still, she heard a bird call in the distance—a loud, husky cry she did not recognize.

Mother Susana had been right, she thought. *The sycamore* would *rise again.*

Thinking this, she fell back into unconsciousness, her heart lifting on a wave of hope.

ACKNOWLEDGMENTS

If I didn't know writing's dirty little secret before, I know it now: No author writes a book alone. Though she holds the pen, a thousand others teach and inspire her well before the first word finds the page, and long afterward.

While I cannot name them all, I am particularly grateful to my mother and father for bringing nature and her magic into my life—and for teaching me how to see and care for living things; and to my brother, for his love and unfailing support in my every endeavor; and to my grandparents and extended family, for the opportunity and effort they poured into my childhood.

This book began when I was six. In my driveway. Then simmered. Aside from personal experiences and a healthy imagination, my thinking was shaped by many better minds. These include, but are not limited to: Riane Eisler, whose book *The Chalice and the Blade* opened my eyes to a new world and unforgettable possibilities. Elaine Pagels, whose scholarship in *The Gnostic Gospels* provided startling insight and validated questions I had long harbored. Merlin Stone, whose daring work *When God Was a Woman* provided a historical framework for the story I wanted to tell. I also drew upon *The Dark Side of Christian History* by Helen Ellerbe and *In Search of the Lost Feminine* by Craig S. Barnes.

I would like to thank my community of friends for their love and encouragement. Mo and the VM, Patty and Dickie, for always believing. Patrick and Shereen at Tano for the beginning. Michael and Keith for building Folly I and Folly II. Chainsaw for surprise visits and hot coffee. Rudy and Melinda for countless reads. Alice Peck and Marlene Adelstein for their editorial prowess and generosity. Joanna for being the trusted roots beneath me. And Tina for making everything possible.

Creatures and places also contributed to this book. For his warm companionship through rain and snow, I will never forget Mick. And, for slowing me down, opening me up, and showing me The Way, I am forever indebted to Melvina.

I am equally grateful to my agent, Susan Golomb, who is as genuinely wonderful as she is intrepid, and to Terra Chalberg, who never quits.

Last, I would like to thank my editor at Crown, Suzanne O'Neill, whose brilliant instincts unearthed a far better book.

My deepest gratitude to you all, and to the mystery that brought me into being.